About

Briony was born in 1944 and her early life was spent in the Welsh valleys. In 1955, her father, a newly trained teacher, moved the family to one of the new towns surrounding London. Briony went directly to Hemel Hempstead Grammar School and from there to St Albans School of Art in 1960. In the second year, she met Peter and they married in 1965. In the early 1980s she did an Open University degree, a BA in Art History and Humanities.

She has taught art, helped run a nursery, worked in infant and junior schools and towards the end of her career became 'the designated person' for child protection at her last school.

She and Peter now live in Carmarthenshire.

She has never written before other than essays and child protection reports, but just **sat** down in lockdown and wrote this.

Passing Clouds

Briony Buck

Passing Clouds

Vanguard Press

VANGUARD PAPERBACK

© Copyright 2024
Briony Merle Buck

The right of Briony Merle Buck to be identified as author of this work has been asserted by her in accordance with the Copyright, Designs and Patents Act 1988.

All Rights Reserved

No reproduction, copy or transmission of this publication may be made without written permission.
No paragraph of this publication may be reproduced, copied or transmitted save with the written permission of the publisher, or in accordance with the provisions
of the Copyright Act 1956 (as amended).

Any person who commits any unauthorised act in relation to this publication may be liable to criminal prosecution and civil claims for damages.

A CIP catalogue record for this title is available from the British Library.

ISBN 978 1 80016 719 3

This is a work of fiction. Names, characters, businesses, places, events and incidents are either the product of the author's imagination or used in a fictitious manner. Any resemblance to actual persons, living or dead, or actual events is purely coincidental.

Vanguard Press is an imprint of
Pegasus Elliot Mackenzie Publishers Ltd.
www.pegasuspublishers.com

First Published in 2024

Vanguard Press
Sheraton House Castle Park
Cambridge England

Printed & Bound in Great Britain

For Peter

Acknowledgements

The staff and students of St Albans Art School
1960 -1965
I remember you all.

Chapter 1
'*Suo Gân*' a Welsh Lullaby

June 1944 - May 1951

The jubilation that had accompanied the news of the invasion of France, at the beginning of the month, had muted somewhat in the houses in Tan y Bryn. Olive Davies had received a telegram saying that her husband Ted was 'missing, presumed dead'.

"It says 'presumed'," Olive kept saying over and over to anyone who would listen. "It's not definite." But she knew deep down it was. This was the first war death in the street and the close community grieved with Olive and her daughter Sallie. Everyone in the street knew Olive and Sal, as everyone knew everyone else. Most of the people had lived all their lives, either in the street or the village. Doors were never locked, children were welcomed in every house, and visitors just called 'cooee', came in and were offered tea. It was a lovely happy street in the main, though sadly lacking in men now as most were away fighting.

Tan y Bryn was a long row of terraced houses halfway up the valley side, overlooking the village of Aberddu. Three blocks, each of twenty houses. Each house had a tiny front garden bordered by a low brick wall and a back garden that led out onto a dusty lane. Beyond that, an unfenced field stretched up to the mountain. The road finished at the last house and a footpath led from there, over a wooden stile to the fir tree plantation, the woods and more fields. In the spring those woods were filled first with wood anemones and later with masses of bluebells. Following the path, you would finally come out into the village near the church and the police houses. This was not a mining valley. That had disappeared long ago to be replaced by a large engineering factory known as 'The Works'. However, a walk over the mountain took you into the next valley with its one remaining coal mine.

Olive and Sallie lived halfway down the street, and Sal had been born there. Now with the war on, Olive took the short walk to the works where she just screwed little things into other little things in a building that she found was cold, and noisy with the sound of machinery and the constant jolly music. It was war work but she disliked it.

The street itself was separated from the village by the railway line, although there was a footpath across the field which led to a small tunnel and access to the station yard.

This was the way Sallie would walk home when she got off the train from school. She had insisted on carrying on with her school certificate exams, as her father had been very proud when she had passed the exam for the grammar school. Today instead of going straight home she walked down the station yard to Mr Pryce's shop on the corner.

Mr Pryce was leaning against the cigarette shelf with a large mug of tea in his hand.

"You don't look too happy Sal. I thought you finished school today?"

"That last exam was awful Mr Pryce. Physics it was. I didn't do enough revision for it." Sal sighed and sat down on the bentwood chair by the counter.

"Well Sal," he said. "All things considered, with your dad and all, you've done well. This will cheer you up."

He took a magazine from under the counter and slid it across to her, "For your Mam."

Sal smiled. A magazine was her Mam's one indulgence. She slipped it into her satchel.

They heard Mrs Pryce moving about in the backroom. If she knew Sal was there she would be out like a shot asking quite intrusive questions about Olive, who hadn't been so good since the telegram came with the news about Ted.

"Are you going back to school after the summer?"

Mr Pryce took a big swig of his tea. From the back, Sal could hear Mrs Pryce singing. They both looked towards the door.

"Depends on my exam results," she said. "In the meantime, I'll look for a little job. Help Mam out."

Mr Pryce bent down and took a postcard from underneath the counter.

"Here Sal, this came in a half hour ago. I was just going to put it in the window. Take it home and if you are not interested bring it straight back. I should think there'll be lots in the queue for this one. Mrs Kendall the housekeeper from Ty Gwyn brought it in. Your Ma knows her and she's a decent woman, is Irene. She had the baby with her. Dear little soul she is though. Irene says all the information on the card is absolutely correct. Slip it in your pocket quick."

Mrs Pryce came in from the back room and headed straight for Sal.

"I must dash," said Sal. "Thank you, Mr Pryce."

He just smiled.

"Nice girl that Sal," he said. "Clever too." Winning him a sour look from his wife.

Sal retraced her steps. Her Mam was sitting outside on the wall watching for her, as it was one of her days off. They went indoors and Olive put the kettle on.

"Well Mam, I put my name down to do Highers, but that depends on my results. We will just have to wait and see. But Mr Pryce had kept you a magazine, and he gave me this."

Sal took the postcard out of her pocket.

Wanted

Older schoolgirl or student to attend to a baby at night.

No housework.

Hours five p.m. to nine a.m. Seven nights a week.

Light supper and breakfast provided.

£3.10s a week.

Please apply in writing to

Mrs L Morgan

Ty Gwyn

Mountain Road

Olive read it twice. £3.10s!

"Mr Pryce said it is quite all right. Mrs Kendall took it into the shop. You know Mrs Kendall, don't you?" Sal asked.

"Yes," said Olive. "Irene and I were at school together."

Olive read the advertisement again slowly. Turned it over and read it once more.

"Well, you could give it a go I suppose. I bet there will be loads after it with money like that though. Get the Quink and a pen Sal, you can do a letter and we'll walk up with it later. If Rene is still there, she will tell us what's what."

"Nobody knows about the job yet Mam, and I don't know anything about babies. They will laugh at me applying."

"Well, we shall see," smiled Olive. "Give it a go eh!"

They discussed it over tea and agreed that they needed to know if the wage quoted was right. It seemed an awful lot, for an adult, never mind a teenager. When they had washed up, Sallie changed into her best blue cotton frock, and mother and daughter set off arm in arm down through the village.

It was a beautiful evening and many of the neighbours were sitting outside their houses watching the children play and passing the time of day. Progress was slow for Olive and Sal as Olive hadn't been out much lately. Many of the neighbours wanted to wish her well. Eventually, though they reached the mountain road. The house was the last of three built there. It was a very large Edwardian house, painted white. A gravel drive curved up to the front door and the hedges and flower beds on each side were full and fragrant.

Sal headed towards the front door but Olive stopped her and pointed to the back. They went through a gate in the tall laurel hedge and Olive knocked on the kitchen door. They had to wait a few moments then Irene Kendall, holding the baby, opened the door.

"Olive! How lovely to see you. Ah! And Sallie? Come in. Look sit down. I was just going to put baby to bed. I won't be long."

The baby gave them a beautiful smile as she was carried out.

Sal and her mother sat down to wait.

"That baby is a joy," said Irene as she came back into the kitchen. "You just put her down and she just drifts off. Hums to herself like."

She filled the kettle at the sink and put it over the fire.

"Tea?"

"Yes please," said Olive. "I'm parched walking all that way."

Irene turned to Sallie.

"So, I expect you have come about the job? Did you bring a letter? Good, I will take it up to Madam."

"Just a minute Rene. I need to get a few things straight first before I let Sal come here," said Olive.

Well, I'll tell you what I know, which isn't much," said Irene sitting down. "Let's see now... There was a full-time nurse employed, the same time as me. I am the housekeeper, but since the nurse left, I have had to do it all, baby night and day also. Quite honestly it is too much as I have a husband at home, who is complaining. So, I spoke to the solicitor who sorts everything out here and this is what he came up with. I think this job is just to fill in whilst a new nurse is found." She paused. "As to the arrangements here? We all moved in two months before the baby was born, and she was born here. I have the feeling, and it's only a feeling mind, that this place was chosen as it is a bit out of the way and the village is quiet too. Unremarkable if you know what I mean. The nurse left two weeks ago after a row with Madam. She called Mrs Morgan an unnatural mother and a lazy cow, and I have been looking after the baby since. I hardly see Mrs Morgan and she does nothing at all for the baby or even asks about her. She rarely leaves her room and has never used the sitting room or walked in the garden to my knowledge. She does go out in the evening though. Often, she doesn't come back for a day or so and once she was gone for a week. But that is not my business. And it won't be Sallie's if she comes here."

She gave Sal a stern look.

"The rich do not like to be gossiped about."

"I understand," said Sallie.

"Yes, and me too," said Olive. "But is there a Mr Morgan?"

Irene smiled, "Well there is a lot of money and it must come from somewhere or someone. And the money for this job is good because it is at night I suppose. It won't be difficult. The baby sleeps through all night and is a lovely little soul."

"Now has that put your mind at rest Olive? If so I'll take that letter up."

Five minutes later she was back.

"She wants to see you, Sallie. Up the stairs and second door on the left."

Sallie looked at her mother. "Go on then," said Olive.

Sallie tiptoed across the hall and up the stairs. The place was so quiet. No wonder her Mam had whispered. She knocked on the door. A voice shouted, "Come in."

Mrs Morgan was lying on the bed in what Sal thought was a satin nightie. She barely looked at Sallie.

"Are you the grammar schoolgirl?"

Sal said she was.

Mrs Morgan looked Sallie up and down.

"You look clean anyway."

"Tell Mrs Kendall you can start as soon as possible."

She waved Sallie out of the room. Sal was back in the kitchen before the tea was poured.

"Well?" said her Mam.

"I can start as soon as possible and she didn't ask me if I was good with babies or anything."

"She isn't interested," Irene said. "But don't you worry Sal, you've a good head on your shoulders. Things will be fine."

Irene was pleased the job had been taken so quickly. She would be glad to get back to her own home and her husband, even if it was only for the nights.

It was arranged that Sallie would come up early the next day so that Irene could explain her duties and for her to get to know the baby. Irene would also stay the first night just in case.

"There is just one thing more," Irene said as they were leaving. "Sallie will probably be alone here at night with the baby. But she will be very safe I promise you, Olive. There is a telephone in the hall. And with a sensible girl like Sal, there should be no problems."

"Does the baby have a name?" said Sal. Rene smiled at her,

"Arianwen," she said.

"There's lovely," smiled Olive.

Sal and her Mam walked slowly home. The light was fading but it was still warm and people were sitting outside enjoying the last rays of sunshine.

"What was Mrs Morgan like?" Olive asked.

"To tell you the truth Mam, it was all so quick. Young, pretty and very bored, I would say. Though I found it strange there was no mention of the baby. I think she was just glad someone had turned up for the job."

"There's sad," Olive said.

The first evening went well. Sallie helped bath Arianwen but put her to bed herself. Then she and Irene had supper together in the kitchen. Sallie was shown a little room next to the baby. This would be hers.

The following afternoon Sallie went to the house early. In the kitchen the baby sat in the playpen. Mrs Kendall was ironing and posting wooden spoons through the bars which the baby tried to post back. The kitchen door was open so Sal knocked and went in.

"Hallo dear," said Rene. "Just let me finish these few bits then Arianwen and I will give you a tour of the garden. She likes that. Though I haven't had much time lately to take her out."

Sallie knelt down by the playpen and Arianwen lifted up her arms.

"She wants you to pick her up. You can if you want."

Sallie lent into the playpen and lifted her out. She was surprised at how heavy she was and said so.

"Ideal weight for a seven-month-old. Best girl in the world, aren't you?" Irene blew a big kiss on the baby's cheek and she gurgled.

They went around the garden then, Irene carrying Arianwen, wrapped in a blanket, Welsh fashion.

Sallie had been shown the baby's room, beautifully decorated in pale Eau-de-Nil and white. The drawers of clothes, the powders and creams. How to change a nappy and where to put it afterwards. One of Sallie's jobs would be to empty the nappy bucket and put them in the washing machine every morning. That worried her a bit, as she had never seen a washing machine before let alone used one. Most people in the street used a tub and washboard to do their washing. And as she had never had any brothers or sisters, dirty nappies were largely unknown. But the machine was quite easy when Mrs Kendall explained it all to her. Then it was how to make up a bottle for the baby, what to give her for breakfast and a lot of other little things until she felt she had no room left in her head. So, she now had a small notebook in her pocket, of exactly what to do.

Rene smiled at her. "Just keep in mind that if she cries it is for a reason. She will either be wet, hungry or bored. If all else fails pick her up and talk or sing to her. I'll come up early and help you with breakfast."

Before she went Rene showed her where the telephone was. The list of important numbers and which doors to shut and lock every night. "Always leave the side door unbolted so madam can get in." Irene said rolling her eyes "Oh! And you will be paid every Friday, same as me. The money is left on the hall table. Now I must go home."

She kissed both Sallie and Arianwen. "Good luck girls," she said. "Be kind to each other." And walked off down the drive.

Sallie looked at the baby who gave her a big smile. "Just us two now then." The baby looked at her solemnly. "Why do they call you Baby? I won't call you that you have a lovely name. Arianwen is a bit of a mouthful for a little baby, beautiful though she may be. How about Ann? No? Nan then?" The baby still regarded her solemnly "Ari then?"

The baby smiled.

Three months later and Sallie was still there. No nurse had appeared though no reason had been given. Exam results had not been spectacular so Highers were out. Besides, the money came in very handy. They already had enough to fill the coal house twice over.

She was mostly quite happy on her own at night too. At first, she had stayed in her room, afraid to be away from the baby. But gradually, as her confidence grew she ventured to the kitchen for a drink, or a bath in one of the two luxurious bathrooms, which was just lovely. But only if she was certain Lillian Morgan was out. She never had the courage though to go into Mrs Morgan's room. She would have liked to and Mam would have been interested.

Olive too was happy with the arrangement. The evenings were not as lonely as she had thought they might be as neighbours would pop in for a chat and for news from Ty Gwyn. Always the subject of speculation. Maggie next door came often and Rene popped in occasionally to tell her how well Sal was doing.

Sal had seen Lillian Morgan only that once but she was aware though of her comings and goings. The cars that came late at night and sometimes there were scuffles and giggles on the landings and in the rooms below. Often, she was not there for days. Sallie didn't let that bother her. She told only Olive.

She loved Ari and after the first few days found she really enjoyed being with her. Ari was a joy to look after, and such a beautiful child, and mostly Sallie felt quite safe and happy in the house at night. In the last warm days of summer Sal often went up early to give Rene a break and let Ari crawl about on the lawn. And they had settled into an easy routine. Irene left her supper on a dish in the larder and came in at eight in the morning when the three of them had breakfast together.

One lovely afternoon at the end of September, Sallie cycled up to the house early. She was going to take Ari for one of their jaunts around the garden.

As she got to the kitchen door, she could hear the baby crying. She went in and found her strapped into her pram but alone. She had obviously been crying for a while. Sal lifted her out. She snuggled into Sal's neck and Sal realised how damp and smelly she was. Where was Rene? What should she do? Baby first then look for Rene.

"Right stinky girl," she said. "Let's sort you out."

She walked into the hall to go upstairs to Ari's room and saw Rene lying at the bottom of the stairs.

As she said to her Mam later, "I was quite proud of myself. I didn't flap. I just got on with it."

Back into the kitchen, she whipped the nappy off Ari and threw it under the sink. Strapped her back in the pram minus a nappy, gave her a rusk and bumped the pram back into the hall. Ari was so startled she forgot to object.

Sal knelt down beside Rene. She could see she was breathing but her face was grey and her leg and arm were twisted in a strange way. Sheets and towels were strewn across the floor. Sal picked up the phone and dialled the exchange in the village. It was Bron from the post office who answered. Sal explained that she thought Rene had fallen down the stairs.

"Right you are," said Bron. "I'll get an ambulance and contact Mr Kendall if I can."

Sallie thanked her and went back to sit by Rene. She knew better than to move her but covered her with a coat from the hallstand, held her hand and kept talking to her. Moments before the ambulance came Mr Kendall hurtled up the drive on his bike. "I knew nothing good would come of working in this place. Bloody people," he growled.

The ambulance came and whisked Mrs Kendall off to the hospital with her husband in anxious attendance, his bike abandoned in the hedge.

Sallie turned to a still not very fragrant Ari.

"Right, Sweetie Pie," she said. "A bath I think."

She bathed the baby in the kitchen sink. It was easier, then fed her and put her in her cot. Within moments, as Sal sang Suo Gân to her, she was asleep. The long dark lashes closed over her pale soft cheeks. Sal looked down at her. "You are such a love," she whispered. "I wonder what will happen to us now?"

Sal went downstairs, retrieved the nappy from where she had thrown it and put it to soak. Tidied the kitchen, washed the pram and went to pick up the linen strewn around the hall. As she did so the telephone rang. It gave her such a start as she was not at all used to the sound. It was Bron from the exchange.

"Just to let you know Sal, Mrs Kendall is fine, awake and talking. She'll be in hospital for a while as she has a badly broken ankle, broken wrist and concussion. Mr Kendall has just come in and asked me to let you know. He says she will be out of action for a while and she may not come back. Apparently, she was carrying a big pile of washing downstairs and missed a stair. He also said that Rene says you should telephone Mr Fearnley in the morning... Oh! And he will be up for his bike sometime."

"Thanks, Bron."

"Anytime," said Bron. "A bit of excitement makes this boring job a little better."

Sallie went into the kitchen to get her supper. It was now gone eight and she realised she hadn't eaten since twelve. She wondered if her Mam had heard the news and was worrying. She sat for a while wondering about this and that. She decided she would ring Mr Fearnley first thing in the morning and then when she had seen to Ari take her in the pram to Mam's.

In the morning she was woken by a furious banging. She leapt out of bed thinking it was Mrs Morgan banging on the side door, which she had locked and stupidly bolted when she went to bed.

Out in the corridor she realised the sound was coming from Ari's room. The baby had managed to stand holding on to the cot bars which she was shaking vigorously. Ari was very pleased with herself and smiled her beautiful smile when Sal appeared.

After they had had breakfast and were both washed and dressed. Sal put Ari in her pram, well wrapped up with an extra blanket, as it was a little damp and misty outside. She put the pram beside her in the hall and with some trepidation she picked up the phone. It was Bron again at the exchange and she rang the London number for Sal.

"Fearnley and Fearnley, Solicitors," said a young lady. "Miss Horwood speaking."

"May I speak to Mr Fearnley please?"

"Mr Roger Fearnley would that be?"

"I don't know," said Sal. "My name is Sallie Davies and I work for Mrs Morgan at Ty Gwyn. I was told to ring if there was a problem."

"Ah yes, you'll want Mr Roger. I'll put you through."

Roger Fearnley had been head of the firm of solicitors and a lawyer, for several years. The other Fearnley being his younger brother Robert, who was at present away in the navy. They had been dealing with the complicated affairs of Lillian Morgan for some time. Everything to do with her or the child went through them and in effect they controlled a very generous purse.

Miss Horwood put Sal through.

"Roger Fearnley speaking."

As soon as she said his name Sal launched into her tale. Gently he asked her to slow down and soon he had a very good idea of the situation.

"And where is the child now?" he asked.

"Beside me in her pram, sir."

"And you say Mrs Morgan is not there?"

"No," said Sal. "Mrs Kendall said the other day that she hadn't been at home for a week at least."

"Ah!"

"Have you thought what you might do today then Sallie?"

"I could go down to my mother, with Arianwen of course. I don't want Mam to worry. I'm all right at night but I think looking after a baby all the time might be a bit hard for me. I'm a bit young for that."

"That is a sensible idea," Roger said. "I'll make a few inquiries and then let you know the lie of the land. You could stay with your mother, or might she come up to Ty Gwyn with you? Just for the time being?"

"I'll ask her if she will. I think it might be better if she comes here. The baby's things are here."

"Well, I am extremely pleased to have spoken to you Sallie. Thank you for phoning so promptly. Don't worry now. I will telephone you at the house as soon as I have news. Until then just keep on doing the fine job that you are. Au revoir."

Sal put the phone down and looked at Ari, "Well that wasn't so bad was it? Right then off to Mam's."

Olive leapt at the chance of staying at Ty Gwyn, and it was no problem as she had holiday time owing. But they were a week at the house before they had news from Mr Fearnley. Olive used the time to carefully explore the rooms. The two bathrooms with their crystal glass bottles of oils and creams. The large soft towels. Even the toilet paper, so soft and white drew exclamations of delight. Like Sal she thought she ought not to explore Lillian Morgan's room, but she did peek in the door at the peach satin sheets, piles of pillows and fur rugs.

"My," she said to Sal, "I wonder what she did to get all this?"

Mr Fearnley didn't telephone. One afternoon at the end of the week, they were sitting in the kitchen with Ari on a rug by the fire, when they heard a car stop outside. Sal immediately thought it was Mrs Morgan and shot into the hall to see. But a tall, thin, balding man was disappearing through the gate to the kitchen door. She ran back and was just in time to hear him knock and come in.

"Well, this is nice," he said, taking in the warm cheerful room, and the smiling baby. "Hello, I'm Roger Fearnley." He held out his hand, "You must be Olive Davies?" They shook hands.

"And you, of course, are Sallie." He shook her hand too.

"And this," he said kneeling down beside the baby. "Must be Miss Arianwen Morgan. I must say, she is a picture, an absolute credit to you ladies."

He straightened up and sat at the table with Olive and Sallie who were tense with expectation.

He looked at them and smiled.

"Well ladies, strangely I have not been able to locate Mrs Morgan. Though I shall of course go on trying. I have been thinking about the best solution." He paused for a moment. "If it is acceptable to you Mrs Davies, could Arianwen move in with you and Sallie? Just for the time being. Arianwen knows Sallie, and it would be a pity to move her somewhere else and with strangers. Though I cannot think where that could be. Would you have room for her?"

"Oh yes sir," said Olive. "We have four bedrooms. Well three really and a box room."

"I have no idea where Mrs Morgan might be, so I think, with winter coming on Sallie and Arianwen would be better with you, than stuck up here. Do you agree?"

"I can't think of anything nicer," said Olive.

"So, I will make the arrangements for that then. Get her cot and everything brought down. We will close this house up for the time being. Now what else... Ah yes! Do you both have bank accounts?"

"We put our money in the post office," said Sal.

"That won't do I'm afraid. I have to put your monies into a bank account now. So, we will arrange that shall we?"

Sal and Olive nodded in unison. There was more to this than they had anticipated.

"You will, of course, be getting paid as well, Mrs Davies."

"That won't be necessary," said Olive.

"Mrs Davies," Roger smiled. "Don't look a gift horse in the mouth, or something to that effect. Now how about some tea?"

Mr Fearnley left soon after, leaving them with instructions to contact him if they needed anything. He said he would keep them informed of any news of Arianwen's mother.

As he drove off, he reflected that he was glad he had taken the time to meet the Davies'. Sallie was just as he had imagined, from Irene's description. Quiet, sensible, very fair and with big brown expressive eyes. Mrs Davies was younger than he had thought. Middle thirties, he guessed. Just as fair as Sallie but looking rather careworn. And Arianwen? He was not a great judge of babies, but he thought she might become a beauty like her mother.

Besides sorting out a bank account for both women, Roger Fearnley had a telephone put in the house at Tan y Bryn. Lots of Ari's, what Sal called 'things' were brought down and put in the little front bedroom. The only thing that caused them any trouble was the pram. It was so large that it filled the hallway and was the devil to get in and out of the house. They took to keeping it in the middle room. Sal mentioned it to Mr Fearnley during one of their now regular telephone conversations.

"I'll send you the money so you can get something smaller," he promised. "In the meantime, look out for someone in need of a big pram."

Olive knew straight away. "Mary Owens has three children under four. She could put them all in there together." So Mary was given the big pram which she proudly pushed around the village. Until it was filled with numbers four and five, then the springs broke.

Weeks went by and just before Christmas, Arianwen had her first birthday. She began to walk and talk. One of her first words was 'tout' and she would point towards the garden. Sal would wrap her in a big shawl, and summer or winter, dark or light they went out. To see the flowers, the vegetables, the trees, the stars, the moon. To feel the wind and watch the passing clouds. And to laugh at the butterflies and birds. To be curious about anything and everything they came across. Ari was to like and sometimes crave 'out' all her life.

Christmas came and went quietly, as the war was still on and there had been news of two more deaths in the street. Mary Owens' brother and Cyril Morris who had lived in the end house.

Ari had touched the hearts of the families in the street. Except for Mrs Pryce of course, who said no good would come of it. What the 'it' was she didn't say. There was still no real news of her mother, but Mr Fearnley said it was rumoured she was in Canada. How she had managed to get there, with whom and why he knew not.

However, it was Roger Fearnley's job to find her. He employed two of his retired solicitor friends and they searched everywhere they could think of. Civilian passenger lists for planes and boats drew a blank, and they had no leads from gossip columns, newspapers, hospitals or casualty lists. No stone, as they say, was left unturned. It seemed an impossible task considering the amount of troops and sundry personnel moving around the world. The three men met once a week at Roger's home. Over a single malt, they pooled their information or non-information to be more accurate. Eventually, they came to the conclusion that the rumour that Lillian Morgan was in Canada was a red herring. More likely she was holed up somewhere in Britain.

Roger wrote his report after several months of fruitless searching and sent it to the relevant person. Adding his belief in the suitability of Mrs and Miss Davies to look after Arianwen if they would. He knew it was either them or an orphanage. There was no one else able to care for the child. His initial brief had been to see that Miss Morgan and her child were well provided for. Now he was part of an intrigue.

He was not at all concerned that Arianwen was still with the Davies. He admired the way they were bringing up the little girl. They loved her, and the money, though well received, did not really enter into the equation. He found that if he was in their vicinity, he would find time to visit. Also, there were regular weekly phone calls. If Sal and Olive wondered why the interest in Ari, by a solicitor, continued, they came up with only one answer. Someone somewhere was paying the bills.

It would be easy to say that life was comfortable for Sal and Olive. But the war still rumbled on. Olive gave up the job she hated and stayed at home with the baby. Sal found a little job in the grocers in the village. She was still only sixteen and was quite happy weighing sugar and cheese all day. Her Mam was often seen in the village pushing the pram, with Arianwen smiling at the world. She had grown out of all her Ty Gwyn clothes and now wore cardigans, jumpers and hats knitted for her by Olive. Most people on the street pulled together and shared if they could. Many a new mother was grateful for a pile of Ari's outgrown clothes. The little girl was indistinguishable from all the other children in the street. Although Mr Fearnley had been right. She was not classically beautiful but her face had a certain something that made you want to look again. Ari had what Sal called 'dark conker brown hair'. It had the very slightest curl and sort of rippled over her shoulders when loose. However, her hair was usually plaited in some way. Sal didn't want her catching nits. Straight dark eyebrows drew attention to her beautiful eyes. The baby blue had gone to be replaced by a soft misty grey. They could look quite stormy if Ari was cross or upset.

The bigger girls in the street regularly knocked to ask if they could take Ari out. There were several babies in the area and their mothers most pleased to let the girls take them off their hands for an hour or so. Sal was a bit nervous about letting Ari go at first. After all, she wasn't her baby. But eventually, she let Maggie, next door's daughter, Queenie, take her. The girls took the babies to the park where they sat with them on their laps gently swinging. Or if the day was warm, they sat in the long grass in the field behind the houses where they made buttercup garlands and daisy chains with which to crown the babies. Ari thrived on it all.

The war came to an end and the whole street celebrated VE day with a big party. Husbands, sons and daughters returned and took over the jobs the women had been doing. It was one of the happiest times of her life for Sal. Ari was three now and talking non-stop. She went out to play with the other children, watched by Olive from the doorstep. Though the big girls watched her carefully too. Their mothers had told them Ari's story, and they thought it so romantic. Queenie even thought Ari might be a princess. She was wrong but it was a lovely idea.

During the summer, the children played out, every evening and all day at weekends. They would be gone into the woods and fields with just some jam sandwiches and a bottle of water. Olive was often heard shouting, "Areee, Areee, Tea! Tea!"

Some child would say, "Your Nan's calling." So Ari began to call Olive 'Nan', and therefore Sal was Mam, even though she was only fifteen years older than Arianwen. Sometimes Olive and Ari would walk down to meet Sal from work. Often after tea, if the weather was nice, it was time for out, and Olive came with them as they strolled along the lanes near the house or went over the stile to the plantation. Sal bought a Brownie camera and took photographs of them all but mostly of Ari. This was in case Lillian Morgan returned. She would have a good record of Ari's first few years.

People began to look forward and be optimistic about the future. The scars of war were still visible in many places, but Tan y Bryn had come through relatively unscathed. Olive still wondered about her husband. If he was buried and where, both she and Sal missed his presence around the house. He had been a good man.

In December 1948, Ari was five and due to go to school after Christmas. Queenie bought her two unlined exercise books and some coloured pencils for her birthday. From then on drawing and later painting became an important, well-loved and necessary part of Ari's life. She would sit at the kitchen table and just draw. Sometimes imaginary castles and animals, but she also tried to draw Nan and Mam. Although her drawings were, of course still very child-like, there was something about them that lifted them above the ordinary. She did a drawing from memory of Mr Fearnley. The slightly worried expression on his face, his crumpled suit and his very upright stance were all there. It brought a lump to Sal's throat. She had it framed and Ari carefully wrote her name, Arianwen Morgan and the date on the bottom. Sal sent it to him as a Christmas present. He was overcome with delight when he saw it and many years later still had it on his office wall and could boast he had an original Arianwen Morgan.

When Sal had taken Ari to live with her and Olive, she was able to meet up again with her friends. They were all pleased she was back in the street, even if she had only been away for a little while and then only at night. They included her when they went to the church youth club, the cinema and dances in the evenings. Olive was very happy to stay in with Ari. Sal also regretted giving up on her education so easily and enrolled in evening classes. History and English literature at first.

Coming out of the school where the classes took place, one evening, Sal bumped into Fred, Maggie next door's eldest son, and they walked home together. Fred was just finishing his apprenticeship in carpentry at a joiners in the next valley. He was doing bookkeeping in evening class, as one day he wanted a business of his own.

Walking home together became a regular thing and one evening Fred asked if they could go steady. Sal was over the moon. She had always liked Fred, although hadn't had much to do with him before as he was a few years older than her. Olive and Maggie were both delighted of course.

When Sal started going out with Fred, they would go on long walks up the mountain and more often than not would take Ari. In the spring there were wild daffodils or milkmaids in the boggy patches, to take back for Nan. In the summer, some of the older boys would dam a stream and make a deep pool. Ari would paddle or sit in the cold water as Sal and Fred talked, made plans and watched her. In the autumn they would go up the mountain carrying big bowls to be filled with whinberries. Nan would make jam if she could get the sugar, or best of all whinberry tart for Sunday dinner. Ari was often told off for stirring her Carnation milk into the fruit and turning the whole lot purple. But the best thing was going out into the field behind the houses and lying in the long grass and watching the clouds.

The Christmas of 1950 was a good one. Rationing had eased and there were supplies in the shops so that Christmas puddings and cakes could be made early and left to mature, with the assistance of the occasional application of sherry.

That year they had been asked, by Maggie, to come for Christmas dinner. Olive, Sallie and Ari were looking forward to it. Altogether there would be ten of them for dinner. Sal and Fred, Maggie and her husband George, Olive and Ari, Queenie, Mary and little George who at eighteen was not so little, and Cyril's widow Violet, from the end house. Olive bought an enormous turkey, from the butcher, which she took round the day before. And Sal made a trifle.

Maggie had decorated the middle room with garlands and tissue paper bells. The kitchen table had been brought in and added to the end of the dining room table. She had covered the lot in a big bed sheet and put table cloths on top. There were crackers, candles and lots of tinsel. It was a very merry meal. After they had eaten their turkey, roast potatoes and vegetables. George called for a slight rest before tackling the pudding. Queenie gathered up all the used paper serviettes and the snapped crackers, and Fred went out to help his mother. There was a cry of 'Put the lights out' and Fred came in carrying the pudding which was covered in blue flames. From his lips hung a little box wrapped in silver paper and tied with a silver ribbon. As he passed Sal he dropped it into her bowl.

"Found this in the kitchen.," he said. "Sorry I forgot to give it to you before." Sal looked up into his solemn face. She took the box and began to open it. Nobody moved at the table. The flames on the pudding went out but no one noticed. Inside was the most perfect ring, with one diamond cut like a star. Fred took it from her and kneeling beside her chair said, "Sallie Davies will you marry me?"

Sal leant towards him and kissed him gently on the lips. "Yes please Fred," she said. Fred slipped the ring on her finger and as he did so Arianwen stood on her chair and started clapping. Everyone joined in, clapping and shouting their good wishes.

Everyone around the table let out a collective sigh. What a lovely Christmas surprise. Fred went back into the kitchen and came back with a bottle of champagne "I've had this hidden in the coal house for ages," he said.

Later, when everything was cleared away, Sal and Fred walked Violet home. She was a little unsteady on her feet but desperate to meet someone to whom she could tell the news. She went to tell Mrs Pryce when Sallie and Fred had gone.

Olive and Ari stayed a while longer then went back to their quiet home. "Come and have a cwtch Ari," said Olive, and Ari snuggled up against her.

"Hasn't it been a lovely day, Nan?" she said. When Sal came in an hour later, they were both fast asleep on the couch. She stood watching them for a moment. How she loved them both.

Fred came to Boxing Day tea. He laughed at Sal who did everything in a way so that her ring caught the light. After tea and when Ari had gone to bed, the three of them began to discuss the future. The wedding first.

There was no real decision to make about the bridesmaids, Ari, Mary and Queenie. Fred wanted his brother, Little George as his best man. Sallie wondered aloud who might give her away, as there seemed no obvious candidate. Maggie and Olive would organise the reception, in the Coop Hall, if it was free that day.

When Fred had gone, Olive turned to Sal.

"Is something bothering you cariad?"

"Well, yes. A little, Mam. I think we should tell Mr Fearnley what's happened. And also, there's all the money. I have to tell Fred soon that you and I are quite well off. There's hundreds in the bank. I couldn't keep that a secret from him. It wouldn't be right."

"Well, I don't expect Mr Fearnley is there now. We will have to wait for the New Year. And yes, you must tell Fred. Ask him to tea soon and we'll do it together."

So Fred was duly asked to tea and Arianwen went to Maggie's for an afternoon with Mary and Queenie.

After tea, Sal told Fred that they, she indicated Olive, needed to tell him something important.

"This is a little worrying." He frowned.

Sallie smiled, "It's sort of about Ari, Fred."

"Well don't worry about that. I know she isn't yours Sal."

Sal looked at him in astonishment.

"Why do some people think that?"

"Only old gossips like Mair Pryce. Mam told her quite definitely that you had never been out of sight of the street." He paused, "So then she tried sticking it on your Mam." He looked at Olive, who laughed.

"Fat chance," she said.

"Anyway Fred," Sal said. "We thought we ought to tell you what the arrangements are about Ari. Seeing she is such a large and much-loved part of us."

She stopped for a moment and looked at Olive. Olive nodded at her to go on. Sal took a deep breath.

"We have always been paid to have Ari, Fred, and very generously too. Although we don't know and have never known where the money comes from. Everything is arranged through Mr Fearnley, the solicitor. But there must be someone somewhere."

She turned to Olive, "And Mr Fearnley has become a good friend over the years, hasn't he Mam?"

"Yes, he has," Olive said.

Sal continued, "We did ask a few years back if we could adopt her, but we were told no. No one seems to know where her mother is and she would have had to be consulted and sign the papers. Anyway, we thought we ought to tell you that both Mam and I have hundreds of pounds in the bank."

Sal stopped. Fred looked at her in astonishment. "Hundreds of pounds?" he said. Shaking his head. "Never mind Sal. I'll still let you marry me."

Sal gave a nervous laugh then realised he was teasing her.

"Well, that's a turn-up for the books. Why ever didn't you spend some?"

Olive answered this time.

"There was never much to spend it on after the war, Fred. Besides which, we love living here and didn't want the neighbours thinking we were uppity."

"Uppity! You two? Never in a million years."

He put his arm around Sal.

"Thanks for telling me. It will go no further." He kissed Sal then got up and kissed Olive too.

Fred knew and that was a relief all round. But before Fred went they decided on a wedding date, the last Saturday in March.

In the meantime, preparations went ahead. The girls and Sallie went to Miss Charles the dressmaker in the village to be fitted for their dresses, although Sallie went on her own. Her dress was a secret even from Olive. Maggie and Olive set about the invitations. Quite a lot of both relatives and friends on Fred's side. All friends and neighbours on Sal's side as they had no family. There were endless discussions too about the menu for the wedding breakfast.

It had been decided that Fred and Sal would move in with Olive, so there was a general swap around of rooms. Ari long moved out of the little box room, had the bedroom above the kitchen. She loved it there; it was her own special place. The door had two glass panels in it to give light to the landing and there was a small step down into the room. Fred redecorated it for her and made a desk and shelves near the window. All of Ari's books, art materials and sketchbooks were carefully fitted on them. Olive moved into the middle bedroom so that Sal and Fred could have the big front room. Then Fred changed the boxroom into a bathroom, much to everyone's delight. No more midnight trips to the outside lav.

Sallie had telephoned Mr Fearnley and he said they had his blessing and he could foresee no problems regarding Arianwen.

Later Sal said she didn't know what made her do it but she asked Mr Fearnley if he would give her away, as she had no father, brother or uncle to do so.

She said there was silence for a moment and she thought he was making up some excuse or other. But then he said he would be most honoured and there was a slight catch in his voice. He said he was coming their way in a week or so and would call in, "to finalise matters" and he ended the conversation with "Thank you so much, Sallie."

Their wedding day dawned grey and misty, though no rain was forecast. Roger Fearnley had checked into the small guest house in the village the day before so had been there for the wedding rehearsal in the evening. Now he was sitting very quietly in Olive's front room whilst young ladies in pale lemon taffeta swirled around him. As soon as the bridesmaids were dressed, they were sent to join him, with strict instructions from Olive not to fiddle with their hair or dresses. He hadn't encountered bridesmaids before; now the three girls sat solemnly on the sofa hardly moving. All three looked absolutely splendid, in his opinion. Their dresses were long and full-skirted and they had lemon and white ribbons and tiny white silk flowers woven in their hair. Queenie and Mary carried round bouquets of primroses and snowdrops, whilst Arianwen had a little basket of the flowers. Upstairs Olive was trying hard not to cry in front of Miss Charles who had come to help Sal dress.

There was a cry from downstairs, "The cars are here!"

Olive came downstairs, dressed in a blue dress and coat the exact colour of delphiniums. She wore a little white feathered hat on her fair hair.

The bridesmaids and Olive went off to the church.

Roger still sat quietly waiting. He heard the rustle of silk and looked up to see Sal in the doorway. He could not see her face as it was hidden by her veil. He felt a big lump rise in his throat. She looked perfect, quite ethereal. White from head to toe, with a small pearl band to hold her veil and a bouquet of white carnations tied with long white ribbons in her hand.

He stood up "You look quite beautiful Sallie," he said. "Your Fred will be bowled over."

"Ready then?"

The sun appeared just as they left the house, and all the neighbours were out to wish her luck. It was the most marvellous wedding. A really funny best-man speech from Little George. Maggie looked magnificent in dark-red satin. The food was great and there was lots of it. Some of the neighbours got a bit tiddly but no one cared. Edie and Stan, who lived on the other side of Maggie, and had been married for thirty years, decided to walk home through the plantation in the dark. Edie fell over in the dry brown bracken, with Stan on top. They did something then that they had not done for several years. The next day Stan had a twinkle in his eye and a spring in his step. Edie, a secret smile.

Mr and Mrs Kendall came and gave Sal and Fred the most beautiful Waterford crystal vase. Irene had not seen Olive or Sal for a while as her ankle had healed badly and she often found it hard to get around and now walked with a stick. She was amazed at how much Arianwen had grown and what a beautiful child she had become. It was lovely to talk to Olive too. She said that she had had quite a generous sum of money, delivered by Mr Fearnley of course, as compensation for her accident. She had refused at first stressing it was indeed just an accident, but the money was deposited in her bank account anyway.

The wedding was really lovely and talked about for days and weeks after. Roger Fearnley had brought his camera. So, besides the official photographs, he took some of his own. Mainly of Sallie, Fred and Arianwen. These he had developed and sent to his employer.

Sal and Fred came home from their honeymoon in Bournemouth, and life fell into an amiable and quiet routine. Now and then Fred and Sal would talk about dreams for the future. Fred still wanted his own business. Arianwen worked hard at school as she was determined to go to the grammar school, like Sal, Queenie and Mary. She particularly wanted to wear the bottle green gymslip with the green and yellow woven sash. Her painting and drawing were constant in her life and the shelves in her bedroom were filling up with her sketchbooks. Now that the weather was improving Fred took Sal, Ari and sometimes Olive, out to watch the clouds. Lying in the backfield, surrounded by buttercups and clover, Arianwen, young as she was felt a great sense of peace and happiness.

Chapter 2
Cherry Pink and Apple Blossom White
Eddie Calvert

May 1951-June 1960

Just before Whitsun in 1951, Roger Fearnley left London in the early morning. Everywhere was already busy, with the increase of visitors to the Festival of Britain. But he was driving west, and very soon the traffic eased. The evening before he had received a very surprising phone call, and he needed to see Olive and Sallie urgently. He had not told them he was coming and hoped that only Olive would be at home when he got there.

He had become very fond of the Davies, although Sal was now Mrs Rowlands. At one time he had thought he had feelings for Olive and seriously considered proposing. However, the wedding changed his mind. He had seen how close-knit and even insular the people of the village were. They were deeply interested in who married who, where they lived, what they did, to the exclusion of all else. Olive and most of her contemporaries had grown up in the village, as had her parents and grandparents. They had married people they had known from childhood. Even Sal had only looked next door. But they were happy and comfortable in their lives. He doubted very much that Olive could have adapted to a mansion house flat in Maida Vale. He certainly could not have lived in her street. He was used to concerts, cinemas, opera and restaurants. So, he said nothing.

It was a long drive and it was nearing ten-thirty when he stopped outside the house. He knocked at the door; he could hear a wireless playing inside. He knocked again. Maggie saw him and went through to the back garden. Olive was hanging washing on the line.

"Olive, visitor at your door," she called. "That solicitor chap I think."

Olive felt an immediate surge of alarm and rushed to open the door. She was usually pleased to see Roger; he had always been so cheerful and helpful. Now he looked worn and worried.

"Is it just you at home Olive?" he said as he sat down at the kitchen table.

"Yes," she said. "But Sal and Ari will be home for their dinner at twelve."

"Good," he said. "I think it best to tell you this news first. You will know how to tell the others."

Olive could hardly breathe. "Spit it out," she cried.

"I had a telephone call late last night from Lillian Morgan."

"No, oh no, no," Olive whispered. "Does she want Ari?"

"Nothing like that Olive. Arianwen is to go to school."

"She goes to school."

"This will be a boarding school. A very good one I am told. Arianwen would go into the lower school first then into the upper school when she is twelve."

"Will she not change her mind? Is there nothing we can do?"

"From what I deduce, she is getting married and going to live in America very soon. She has demanded that Arianwen be sent to school. Why, I cannot think and she wouldn't explain when I asked. However, Arianwen will still live with you in the holidays."

He paused for a moment. "The thing is Olive, there is only one name on Arianwen's birth certificate. Lillian Morgan. There is no father's name, so Lillian is the only one with any legal right to decide Ari's future."

"Sal will be so upset. How do we tell Ari she is to go away?"

"Perhaps I shouldn't say this," he said, reaching for Olive's hand. "I truly believe that this is just a gesture on Lillian's part. Once she is safely married, she will forget again about Arianwen. She will have caused a lot of anguish and disruption, but quite honestly, from what I know of her, she will not be troubled by that. And don't mention going away to Arianwen. She is going to a new school. It is an extremely good school, Olive, in the Home counties, north of London. A new adventure for her."

However, Roger did think that this move might be a good thing for all. Not that he believed Sal and Olive were doing a bad job. He had repeatedly expressed his admiration for them. But unlike them, he had more of an idea of the bigger picture surrounding the child. She needed to see more of the world.

Olive sat; her head bowed in despair. Roger got up and put his arm around her.

"I will do all I can to make it easy for you," he said. "You know I am only at the end of the phone. If ever or whenever you need to talk or need help..." His voice trailed off.

Olive was sobbing.

"I know," she said. "You are such a good friend to us, and I thank you. But she will be so far away."

He left her then as it was nearing noon and Sal and Ari would be home.

Ari was home first and Olive was sufficiently recovered to make her dinner. Corned beef pie and salad. Ari chatted about school. The morning's P.E. lesson and a reading test. She was just finishing when Sal came in. Sal immediately noticed her mother had been crying.

"Mam?"

Olive shook her head slightly.

"Now cariad," she said to Ari. "Are you off back to school? Would you like an apple?"

Ari picked an apple out of the bowl, gave them both a kiss and was off.

"Mam," said Sal. "What is it?"

Olive told her about Mr Fearnley's visit. Sal was just as upset as she was.

"Look Mam," she said. "I have to go back to work. We'll talk about it more this evening when Fred is here. He will have some idea how to tell Ari, and it may be better coming from him. He won't get so upset."

So that is what they did.

The following evening Fred took Ari out to watch the clouds. He told her very gently about her mother and about going to boarding school. Arianwen had been told as soon as she could understand, about her absent mother and that Olive and Sal were looking after her instead. She called Olive Nan, and Sallie, Mam, because the other children had a Nan and a Mam.

She was very quiet for a while. Then she said, "Will it be like in the books I read Fred? You know, *Malory Towers* and *The Chalet School*?"

"A bit I expect," Fred said, not really knowing to what she was referring.

"Hockey and midnight feasts," Arianwen mused. "It might be quite interesting. Do you think so Fred?"

Interesting was not the word Fred would have used. "Well, it might be," he replied. Not at all sure he was right.

But Arianwen seemed quite happy with her idea of school, at least to begin with.

Over the next few weeks, boxes were constantly being delivered to the house. Dai the post said they might need a special van soon.

The school uniform was grey with a yellow edge to the blazer and hat. But there was much more.

Six vests.

Six grey knickers with six white lining pants.

Six cream Viyella blouses.

Six pairs of long grey socks.

Six pairs of pyjamas.

Three grey pleated gymslips, with grey and yellow sashes.

Two pairs of plimsolls.

One pair of slippers.

One dressing gown.

P.E. kit.

Games skirt, for hockey and netball.

Hockey stick.

Six grey school jumpers. Six assorted jumpers for weekends. And Ari chose a dark green velvet dress, for best. Dark green was one of her favourite colours.

Three pairs of corduroy trousers, and a wash bag.

Plus shoes, boots, wellies, a grey gabardine Mac and a grey wool overcoat. And an enormous strip of Cash's name tapes to be sewn on everything. Olive set to.

Also, a very large rather beautiful wooden trunk. A suitcase and a matching vanity case.

The hallway and Ari's bedroom were full. And Ari was excited even if the rest of the household were not. Olive, Sal and Fred bought her a camera, a wooden artists' box full of pencils and crayons, several sketchbooks and a large portfolio to keep them all in. Everything was ready for what they all called 'Arianwen's new adventure'.

Then, when Arianwen had finished school for the summer holidays, in July, they all went to Bournemouth for a week in the hotel where Sal and Fred had spent their honeymoon. As Sal said to Fred on their first night, "That seems ages ago, but it is only just over a year." When they had been there before they had noticed the beach huts, so they had rented one this time. On the first Saturday in August, they all got into Fred's new van and set off.

The hotel was halfway up a hill overlooking Boscombe Pier. In the morning after breakfast, one of the adults would walk along to the beach hut with Arianwen. The other two would go up to the town and buy something for lunch. The weather was spectacular. Wonderfully warm, so that sometime during the day, everyone, even Olive went in the sea. Arianwen had made friends with a little boy in the hut next door and they ran back and forth across the promenade to the beach and the sea all day. Fred made sandcastles with them and tried to teach Ari to swim. Late afternoon they went back to their hotel and dressed for dinner. This was a slightly formal occasion but enjoyed by them all, nonetheless. Afterwards, they went for a short walk. The lights would be coming on along the promenade and on the piers. It was on one of these evening walks that Sal and Fred began to formulate a plan for their future. But not just yet.

At the beginning of September, and the day before Ari left for her new school, she went around the street to say her goodbyes. Even Mrs Pryce gave her a hug, a pound of dolly mixtures and her and Mr Pryce's good wishes. Maggie and the girls were sad to see her go but said they would look forward to seeing her at half-term.

Sal, Fred and Olive all knew that Arianwen was already getting nervous about the whole thing, so they tried to be optimistic and were rather falsely jolly.

The next morning a large car drew up outside the house, much to the interest of everyone in the street. "Wonderful Roger Fearnley again," said Sal. A chauffeur got out and helped Fred load the suitcases. The trunk had already gone by rail. It had been decided between them that Sallie would go with Ari this time and the car would bring her back, as the chauffeur lived in Cardiff.

The journey was long but very comfortable. They stopped beside a stream in a pretty Cotswold village to eat their lunch from a hamper that James the chauffeur had in the boot. Then it was back in the car for the last leg.

In the middle of the afternoon, they turned into the gates of St Ursula's. Ari had been silent for a while, the butterflies in her tummy fluttering wildly.

A long drive edged with big, dark green rhododendron bushes ended outside the main school building. This looked to be a large Georgian manor, with several extensions and large houses dotted around it. Cars of all makes lined the drive and the lawn, and the approach to the school was thronged with grey-clad girls of all ages, and their parents.

They got out of the car and stood hesitantly to one side. A small, dark woman carrying a clipboard approached.

"Good afternoon," she smiled, shaking hands with both Sal and Ari.

"I am Mrs Star one of the house mothers here. May I have your name please?"

Arianwen didn't answer, so Sal did.

"Arianwen Morgan."

"Well, isn't that just excellent," she said looking at the list. "You will be one of my girls Arianwen. I believe you missed our open day. Just let me give this list to another member of staff and then I'll show you both around."

She was back in a minute. "Come along then Arianwen, your mother is coming too. Just a little tour so she can see where you will be living."

Sal couldn't bring herself to correct Mrs Star's mistake and Ari was still silent. She held on tightly to Sal's hand. This was not how she had imagined it. Not like *Malory Towers* one bit. Sal could feel her trembling as they were shown around. *Poor little soul,* she thought. *Not yet nine and having to live away from home.* Mrs Star kept glancing at Ari. She noted the pale face and the trembling hand and was not at all perturbed.

She had seen it all many times before. Eventually, they came to the dormitories.

"This will be your room Arianwen," said Mrs Star brightly. "You will share with three other new girls."

The room was large and contained four iron beds, roughly one in each corner. Each bed had a small table with a lamp at its side. There were shelves above the bed, and a large wardrobe and two chests of drawers were placed to give a bit of privacy. Ari's trunk stood at the foot of one of the beds near the window. No one else seemed to have moved in yet.

Mrs Star turned to Sal. "I think it is probably time to say your goodbyes now. I will take you back to the car."

She turned to Arianwen, "Your mother is going now dear. Say goodbye. Then if you could start emptying your trunk?"

Sal came over and enfolded Ari in her arms.

"Be brave now cariad," she said. "Be brave. We will see you in six weeks. It's not that long." She left quickly followed by Mrs Star.

Arianwen sat down on her bed. From there she could see some houses and trees. But if she lay down, the clear blue sky. No clouds on the horizon.

Sal was glad that Arianwen's room was at the back of the house. She could hardly find the car for the tears in her eyes. James was standing beside it.

"I know," he said. "Home James and don't spare the horses."

Sallie gave him a sad smile as she got in.

Meanwhile, Mrs Star had gone back to check on Arianwen and had found her fast asleep. She crept out and came back an hour later. Ari was slowly emptying her trunk. Most of her clothes were hung up and she was putting her books and a photograph of Olive, Sal and Fred on a shelf.

"There you are dear; do you feel better now?" She sat down on the bed and patted the space beside her.

"Come and sit here a moment Arianwen."

"Do they call you Arianwen at home?"

"No, they usually call me just Ari."

"Would you prefer that?"

Arianwen gave a little smile "I think so," she said.

"Right, I'll see to that," said Mrs Star. "Now I want you to know that as your housemother you may come to me with any problems you may have. You know where my room is. If I am not there, there is a little box beside the door. Put a note in that and I will come and find you. All right?"

"Yes, thank you," said Ari.

"Good girl. Now! The two girls who would have shared with you, cousins they were, aren't joining us. Change of plan somewhere. So there will just be you and Christina in this room. She will be here soon. I believe her plane was delayed."

There was a knock on the door and in came a tall slender girl dragging a suitcase.

"Hello," she said looking at Ari. "I'm Christina. Hello Mrs Star. Sabrina has gone upstairs to her room."

"Christina, this is Arianwen. The other two girls aren't coming, so it will be just you two. You can have the room to yourselves and can use all the wardrobes if you need to. Now where did you say your sister was?"

Mrs Star bustled out of the room. Christina sat down by Ari.

"Hello again," she smiled. "Arianwen is a beautiful name. Where do you come from?"

"Wales," said Ari.

"Ah yes, a lovely accent. I come from Ghana, in Africa? My father is in the diplomatic service," she continued. "And we shall be living in London now. When we get an exeat, you can come home with me and meet everyone."

Arianwen wondered what Sal would say if she turned up with a strange African girl for the weekend. Not a lot, knowing Sal. She would just try to make her very comfortable.

"What's an exeat?" she said.

"Time out from school, you know like half-term? I only know because my sister is in the upper school and I have been visiting here forever. How old are you?" She rolled her big brown eyes.

Arianwen was finding it hard to keep up with the conversation.

"Nearly nine."

"Same as me then. My birthday is just before Christmas."

"So is mine," said Ari.

The two girls smiled at each other.

"Right! I'd best get on with emptying my trunk before supper."

"I've nearly finished mine, so I'll help you," said Ari.

"Great." Christina lifted the lid of her trunk and the most exotic, delicious, mysterious smell wafted out.

"Oh drat, I bet that jar of oil has broken."

She rummaged in the trunk, throwing clothes onto the floor.

Eventually, she surfaced with a large deep orange pottery jar in her hand. "My mother makes this for me. I have to oil my skin every day, otherwise, it dries and looks grey. It's good for my hair too."

Arianwen looked at Christina's beautiful soft mahogany skin and her black crinkly hair that was cut very short. She looked sort of polished.

"Gosh, how wonderful," said Ari. "I just have Astral for when my lips are dry?"

"My Ma makes it, especially for me. She is very clever with the things she makes. Now let's be the absolute best of friends and we will go to supper together and you can tell me all about Wales."

And that is what they did. They were to remain great friends all the time they were at school. And although they did not see so much of each other for a while, later on, they were very close.

Meanwhile, Sal had arrived home. Fred and Olive were sitting dejectedly by the kitchen fire. The house seemed very quiet.

"How did it go?" said Fred.

"OK. but it was awful leaving her." Sal paused. "I met her housemother and she seemed really nice. Ari was very quiet but she said Nan would say 'Be brave Ari, be brave.' So, she would try to be. I think she will be fine once she gets used to it all."

She plonked down on the couch.

"But we won't half miss her."

"She will be back for Halloween," said Fred. "Perhaps we could have a little party. Ducking apple and games?"

Sal smiled at him. Dear Fred, always making the best of things. She gave him a hug.

Olive stood up. She had not said a word since Sal came in. "I'll just go and put the kettle on," she said, and left the room.

"Your Mam is going to find it hard Sal. She has been home looking after Ari for a few years now. In a week or two when we can all see a bit more clearly, I think we need a going forward conference."

"That sounds important Fred."

"Well, we can't just sit around for the next, what seven or eight years waiting for Ari to come home, can we?"

Sal phoned Mrs Star at the end of the week, as she had been asked to do. Everything sounded very encouraging and Mrs Star said Ari had had a little homesickness. Which was to be expected but had made a good friend, Christina, and she was joining in and enjoying most activities. Sal and Olive were much happier now they knew that Ari was not dreadfully unhappy.

But they did find it difficult. Sal had always looked in on Ari when she went to bed. Now she would often forget and go into the bedroom and just sit on the empty bed. It was a large brass bed that they had bought for Ari when she was quite small. Arianwen slept, as Sal said, 'Like a starfish.' Arms and legs spread wide. When she had progressed from her cot to a bed, they had bought a single bed for her. But she kept falling out of it. Many were the times that one of them heard a bump in the night and had gone to find Ari asleep on the floor. Hence the large bed. Now Sal sat and smoothed the soft Welsh blankets and wondered how Ari was sleeping in the little iron bed she had seen in her room. Fred often found her just sitting, staring at nothing. "Come to bed Sal. She is fine you know." And Sal would smile sadly and follow him to bed.

Olive too found the days long. There was no Ari coming home for dinner at noon. No one to make jam tarts or Welsh cakes with on a wet Saturday. No nighties, dresses or ribbons to iron. No little girl just running in and out. She wondered who did all the washing for all those girls. Fred missed her too, as they had often gone for walks together in the warm evenings or at weekends. Up the mountain or through the plantation. Sal didn't want to come out any more to lie in the field and watch the passing clouds.

So, they were all, in their own way looking forward to Ari coming home. But just before the holiday, the school secretary rang to say they had two cases of scarlet fever in the lower school, so everyone was in quarantine.

Ari and Christina didn't mind too much. Lessons were cancelled because it was a holiday, but the art room, gym and music room were open for their use. Also, they had the grounds to explore. Ari spent a lot of time in the art room. The art teacher, Miss Perkins, known to the girls as Polly, had quickly seen her potential and encouraged her to try lots of new mediums and ideas. Christina played the piano, so liked to go and practice when she could. And of course, they could use the little lower school common room. There was a record player in there although the records were mainly classical. Some Ari liked but it was better when someone smuggled in a recent recording. Ari especially liked *Cherry Pink and Apple Blossom White* as it reminded her of Olive who wore Apple Blossom perfume on a Sunday.

The weather was cold but fine so when they had time together the two girls would wrap up and explore the grounds. Ari explained the clouds and cloud watching to Christina, and if the grass was dry they would lie and talk and giggle as Christina knew a lot more about the school than Ari. She was desperate to get to the upper school where they had more freedom and were even allowed to visit the village on their own. She told Ari that her sister had a boyfriend in the village, but that she only saw him occasionally. Ari was sworn to secrecy. Much more of interest to Christina was the girl, who had left last year, and who used to meet up with the gardener when her class were supposedly on cross-country runs. Christina's sister had seen them having sex up against a tree. Ari didn't understand so Christina enlightened her and told her a lot of words that Ari had never heard before, about sex and parts of the body. Christina said they were swear words and only to be used when no adults were around. Now Ari understood why the big girls at home would often sit in the field together talking. If a little one came by they would stop and say, "Go away, this is private. You will know about it when you are bigger." Ari decided to ask Sal when she went home.

Arianwen had settled down really well. Mrs Star rang Sallie to tell her so. And when Ari came home for Christmas, she brought with her a glowing report. Sal put it, together with a photograph of Ari in her school uniform, in the box, in case Lillian Morgan ever asked to see it.

They were all in agreement that their little girl was growing up and looked well on her term away. It was good to have her back if only for a little while.

Arianwen however was finding it a little difficult. It was lovely at home, but she had expected to go out to play with her friends in the street. She did go out and most were friendly and included her in their games. But there were some who called her posh and stuck up and made faces at her. Sal knew this was probably jealousy on their part but it upset Ari.

Christmas was lovely and Ari had a bicycle. Fred spent several days running up and down the street hanging on to the back of the saddle until Ari found her balance. Then she was off up and down the road all day. But she was very generous to the other children and often let them have a go. But not those that were unkind. She would not be bullied into giving in either.

Going back to school dawned and Sal and Olive started packing her uniform. One evening when Sal and Ari were in her bedroom sorting out underwear, Ari asked Sal if she would tell her about how you made babies.

Sal was rather startled by her request. Sal had learned it from other girls at school and never a word from her mother other than 'be careful'. She rather admired Ari's straightforward question. She stood before her looking earnestly into Sal's eyes. She was growing into a beautiful young girl. Her hair was long now and she wore it in one dark brown glossy plait down her back. She was becoming long-legged and willowy. *Someday,* Sal thought. *Someone will really fall for her. I'd best tell her all she is asking.*

So, they sat on the bed together and Sal told her all about the changes she might expect in her body in the next few years. About love, togetherness, honesty, faithfulness and respect. About falling in love and how it made you feel. And what you might then want to do.

Ari, wide-eyed took it all in. "Christina says you have to try to be the best you can so that someone will want to marry you," she said.

Sal smiled "You just be yourself Arianwen Morgan," she laughed. "I'm sure you will have no trouble there."

Later that evening Sal told Olive about the conversation.

"I only answered what she asked Mam. I didn't go into how exactly babies were made."

"Time enough for that Sal," smiled Olive. "My only worry might have been that she turned out like her mother. But I truly believe now that she will not. She is a lovely child and will be a lovely woman. Thing is Sal, we never knew her mother. We don't know what caused her to abandon Ari. I suppose we should not judge."

"That is very charitable of you Mam," said Sal tartly. "But I am not going to be persuaded. She should never have left that child." Olive smiled; Sal was always so fierce.

"Still our gain," Olive said. "And I don't mean money." And she went to get her clothes ready for the morning, as she was the one going with Ari this time.

The next morning everyone was up early. It was a bright, cold day and Olive thought the drive would be interesting. She hadn't been out of the village since they had all been to Boscombe. Fred was outside watching out for the car.

"Jesus!" he exclaimed when a large Rolls Royce stopped outside the house. He went to help the chauffeur load the cases, but really just to look at the car. It was not James who got out but Roger Fearnley.

"James has flu," he said. "So, I thought I'd come in the run about."

Fred stared at him.

"Only joking Fred. I borrowed it from my brother. Tell you what when I bring Sallie back you can have a go."

"It's Olive's turn this time," said Fred relishing the idea of getting his hands on the car.

He ran his hands gently over the bonnet so missed Roger's 'Ah, good,' at the news.

They were all pleased to see Roger. Olive opted to sit in the front 'So she didn't get car sick'. Not that she ever had, and Arianwen snuggled down on the back seat.

It was too cold to stop for a picnic so they had a quiet lunch in a hotel near Oxford. Then it was on to school. Olive was most impressed by the house and grounds and liked Mrs Star immediately. When Arianwen had left them she and Roger had a little walk around, Roger trying to remember all the salient points to put in his next report. Luckily, he remembered to bring his camera.

They had a very companionable drive home. Sal asked Roger if he would like to stay as it was late evening when they returned. But he had booked a room in the guest house in the village. As he left, he called over his shoulder,

"See you in the morning, Fred."

In the morning Fred did indeed drive the car right up the valley and back. He was beaming from ear to ear when they returned, and all the neighbours came out to look. Roger was asked to dinner, and they all shared the roast beef and Yorkshire pudding, followed by plum tart and custard, around the kitchen table. Over a cup of tea afterwards, Fred asked Roger's advice. Fred was now a master carpenter and he was getting bored making kitchen doors in the factory in town. He wanted something else, something better for him and Sal, and they had come to the slow realisation that it would not be found in the South Wales valleys. What they wanted was a business they could do together and include Olive. Somewhere where there would be a home for Arianwen. "Also," Fred whispered to Roger. "We would like children of our own one day."

Roger knew that they were not averse to hard work and that both Olive and Sallie, though quiet and gentle people were good with other folk.

He said he would put his mind to it, and knowing him so well by now, they knew he would.

Back at school the girls were all admiring Christina's pierced ears. She wore small gold hoops in them. Arianwen was very envious. "I shall ask if I can get my ears done," she said, knowing full well that Olive considered young girls with pierced ears, common. But Christina wasn't, she knew that. It was the first time Ari had to consider whether Olive might be wrong.

She felt very happy at school now. Ellie, and her best friend Milly, had joined her and Christina, and the four of them formed a tight little group. Lessons were good and she was doing very well. With only ten or twelve girls in each class, they all had lots of attention. But it was her time in the art room that gave her the most pleasure and it was about this time that Ari attempted her first portrait. It was of Christina. Head and shoulders against a deep orange background, her mahogany skin shone. She had the direct and slightly defiant gaze of an Amazon. But also the slight uncertainty of a young girl. She also did a painting of Ellie and Milly, reading together on the sofa in the common room. Miss Perkins admitted in a staff meeting that she had never had such a focused and talented young girl in her class. "Her observation is remarkable for one so young. She did a portrait of Christina last week. She got the textures of her hair and skin, spot on. I mean you could tell it was by a youngish person, but even so."

"When she gets to upper school, you might point her in the way of art school if she is still interested. Trouble is some quite talented girls, music or art, go off the boil when boys come along," the headmistress said sadly. But Ari didn't.

True to his word Roger Fearnley had put the word out about a business for a client. Not that Fred was one, he was a friend. He had got some interesting and some plain bizarre ideas floated past him. There were a lot of pubs that needed landlords, but he knew Olive would not like that. A laundry in the East End of London, two fish and chip shops, several equestrian establishments, grocery shops, post offices, and three or four hotels. One especially caught his eye. It was a large hotel on the cliff top above Boscombe. The owner had died in the war and his widow soon after. There were no heirs to the estate, so the building was to be sold. Roger moved quickly. He, Fred, Sal and Olive went to see it two days later. The Welsh party travelling down by train. The estate agent that showed them around kept telling them that there was a lot of interest in the building. But Roger knew there was not. There was a lot of work to do, but the owners living quarters in the attics of the house were large, airy and in surprisingly good condition. Fred thought that with a good architect and builders it was all doable, and there was a lot of call also for his carpentry skills. After a long evening of talk, they decided to put in an offer. It was as Roger said, "A cheeky one," but no one else was interested. They bought it for a song. There and then they decided to call it 'Arian Court'. After all, it was Arianwen who in a way had provided the money.

Of course, when they got back home there was the usual 'Have we done the right thing'? conversation. But they knew they had.

Sal was a little concerned as to how Ari would react, so she phoned Mrs Star to arrange a telephone call with Ari, who was delighted with the news and to be moving to Boscombe of all things. She had loved it before and now she would be by the sea always. Her enthusiasm was catching so Sal had to remind her that for a while when she came home it would be like a building site.

Fred and Sal sat down with the architect who was another acquaintance of Roger's. The hotel had a basement with half windows to the back. This they thought could house the laundry, wine cellar, store cupboards and perhaps some large freezers. The ground floor was accessed by a flight of wide stone steps up to the front door. Inside was the lobby with a reception desk and a small office behind. On the left-hand side and looking out over the sea was a large lounge connected by double doors to the dining room. A substantial kitchen ran along the back of the building. The two floors above had a corridor running east to west with eight bedrooms on each side. There were two small bathrooms near the top of each flight of stairs. The front bedrooms had a fine view of the sea, the back ones looked over the overgrown garden. Their architect suggested that each row of eight rooms be reconfigured into five bedrooms each with a small bathroom. Fred was rather dubious about this. Fewer bedrooms meant fewer guests. But the architect knew his stuff.

"Would you rather share a bathroom with twelve or so people or have one to yourself?" he asked Fred. Of course, the answer was obvious. When it came to the actual design, each room had its own little bathroom. They were one of the first hotels in the area to offer this, and it was very popular.

Fred, Olive and Sallie moved into the attic flat in January 1953. They took Ari to school first then went back to Wales and packed up. Arianwen knew she was not going to go back to Tan y Bryn, but she seemed happy with the arrangement and was really quite excited. As long as she had a home and family, she was content.

It took them nearly a year to get it how they wanted it, which was very different from the usual heavily patterned carpeted, dull-painted hotels they had stayed in. Downstairs all the floors were polished wood. The furniture too throughout the hotel was pale and modern. There were big, sumptuous sofas and chairs in the lounge. Fred made the most beautiful, curved beech reception desk. He also built in all the bathroom plumbing, made bathroom cabinets and rearranged the kitchen. All walls were the palest green and all curtains white with a large green flowery pattern. The bed linen, table linen and towels were also either white or pale green. Olive grumbled a bit. She thought all the light furnishings would soon be marked and spoilt, but time showed they were not.

A small patio had been laid outside the lounge which had views over the sea and several benches and big pots of white hydrangeas stood around. It would be a lovely place to sit on a summer evening. It was clean, stylish, comfortable and luxurious. The guests when they came were entranced.

When they had holidayed there before Ari went to school, they had made good use of their rented beach hut. Now they inquired and were able to buy two from the council. Both were on the promenade at the end of the path opposite the hotel, which led down through some gardens, to the beach. One could be hired by their guests, the other further away, was just for themselves. Finally, they had the whole place painted white and a large sign made that said.

'Arian Court'

Bed, Breakfast and Evening Meal.

All bedrooms en suite.

They advertised first in the Western Mail offering discounts to Valley folk.

By the Easter of 1954, they were ready. Arianwen was home from school and she helped with the final touches. Shopping in Bournemouth one day with Mam, she had spotted a large copper jug in an antique shop. She had her own pocket money now, so the next day she went off on her own and bought it. She also bought fifty white daffodils on the way home. After a bit of arranging in the kitchen, she carried the whole lot through and put them carefully on the reception desk. When Sal saw them it quite took her breath away. "Absolutely perfect," she smiled. "Arianwen, bless her."

They were full for the opening and it continued like that for many years.

Life settled down for them all. They had been expecting hard work and for the first two years, it was. They closed from late November to just before Easter and during that time Fred did most of the repairs and any decorating. Maggie and George came for their first Christmas and were extremely impressed and proud of their Fred. Arianwen loved to come in the holidays and as she got older was a great help to her Mam and Nan. Roger Fearnley often visited too and insisted on booking and paying for a room. He spent a lot of time talking to Olive and they began to go for walks together, a visit to the Winter Gardens, or an evening meal in Bournemouth. He had always been fond of Olive. Her ideas were not so fixed and old-fashioned as he had found after Sal and Fred's wedding. He was revising his opinion of her and his feelings grew stronger.

Arianwen, Christina and their friends graduated to the upper school in September 1955, just before they were twelve. Life was a little different there.

As senior girls, they had a few responsibilities looking after the juniors. But that wasn't too irksome. What was however was the new head teacher's insistence on physical activity. Mrs Claybourne believed that to keep young ladies healthy and more to the point pure, daily outdoor pursuits were essential. Thus, all the senior girls had to run the perimeter of the grounds every morning. Then it was a lukewarm shower and breakfast. In the depths of winter when mornings were dark, they went to the gym instead, for what Christina called 'gym elastics'. Running round the grounds one morning, Christina said she could well sympathise with that girl, a few years back, who stopped off for a dalliance with the gardener. This made Arianwen laugh, not least because of the use of 'dalliance', a word she had not heard before. They both decided they would have a 'dalliance' when they were older. Much better than the love affair Christina's sister, Sabrina, was having, which often made her miserable. They spent the rest of their run deciding who to have a dalliance with. Christina settled on Harry Belafonte and Ari on Buddy Holly because she liked his glasses. But they did vow to let each other know when there had been 'a first time'.

Miss Perkins continued to encourage Ari with her artwork. And Ari spent a lot of her spare time either in the art room or sketching around the grounds or, her favourite, the girls in the common room. Many a girl was asked to sit still as Ari finished a drawing. Some were extremely good and Miss Perkins saw a depth of insight in those drawings she had never encountered before. But then she had also seen that Arianwen noticed a lot. She would sit quietly and just observe what was going on. She noticed relationships developing, and quarrels bubbling up, but she didn't say a word. The only time she had been very fierce and vocal was when Christina had been bullied by two South African girls because of the colour of her skin. Arianwen had threatened to 'flatten' them.

Miss Perkins had gone to art school towards the end of the war and then had done a teaching course. She wondered if it would be possible to take the girl to the art school she had attended. It was only a bus ride away into the city. She decided to look into this.

So life was mostly good for all. But there was one thing Arianwen hated. Now that they all lived on the south coast it was easier for Arianwen to go into London on the train with the other girls when travelling home. James had moved on to other things and the wonderful journeys in the Rolls Royce were firmly in the past.

The train took the girls, accompanied by a member of staff, into Kings Cross. Most girls were met by a family member and Ari would watch them all be greeted and kissed by aunties, mothers, fathers and grandparents. Much as she loved Sal and Olive, they were not her own and she silently longed for that. So Ari was escorted from the station by Mr Fearnley's secretary, Miss Horwood, who would take her to Waterloo and put her on the Bournemouth train. Fred would meet her at the other end. But Miss Horwood was a dreadful timekeeper. Many a time Arianwen was left alone at the station in the care of the station master, the staff member from school having left to catch their own train. On one occasion it was nearly two hours and the porter had brought her an apple, a bun and a cup of tea. While she was waiting, she made sketches of her surroundings. They came into their own several years later.

At the end of the school year when she was thirteen, Arianwen was again abandoned on the station platform. She was beginning to feel sick with worry. The same porter had brought her a sandwich and tea. She was just thinking that she would try to get to Waterloo by herself when she heard running footsteps and a young man skidded to a halt in front of her.

"Arianwen?" he gasped.

"Yes" she answered.

"We are so sorry. Miss Horwood forgot it was pick up today." He paused for breath.

"I'm Toby Fearnley, Roger's nephew, and I've come to rescue you."

He did look very much like a young Mr Fearnley, so Ari was quite reassured. She got up and began gathering her stuff.

Toby took most.

"Come on," he said. "This way."

They didn't go down to the underground but out to the street. There at the curb was a shiny red MGA.

"Get in," Toby said as he put her things in the boot. "I quite fancy a spin to Bournemouth. You up for it?"

Arianwen didn't have time to reply as they shot off down the road.

It was a little difficult to have a conversation as they roared along, but Ari gathered that Toby was reading law at Cambridge and was doing a summer job at his father's and uncle's practice. He had jumped at the chance of collecting Arianwen as it meant a day away from the boredom of filing.

They stopped near Winchester at a little roadhouse and had fish and chips, then it was off again. Arianwen was in love. Buddy Holly had gone out of the window and Toby Fearnley was firmly in his place. They arrived with a squeal of brakes outside the hotel by late afternoon. Sal had been looking out for them as Roger had phoned to tell them of the change of plan.

Toby stayed for a little while but then went 'to look for a willing woman in Bournemouth' as he put it. This remark quite shocked Sal.

She had noticed however that Arianwen thought he was wonderful. Her little face went rosy-pink when he spoke to her. *Bless her,* she thought. *Let's hope she has better taste next time.* She hadn't liked Roger's nephew one bit, 'too flash' and hoped not to see much more of him. Thankfully, her wish was granted, though Ari thought of him for a while.

A year before the girls were due to take their 'O' levels, Miss Perkins arranged to take Ari to visit the art school. She had spoken to her old tutor, Julius Winter and he had said he would be happy to show them around. Thus, one Wednesday morning at the beginning of May, Ari and Miss Perkins boarded the bus for the city. Miss Perkins in her best and Ari, greatly disappointed, in her school uniform. Yellow gingham dress, white ankle socks, Mary Janes and the hated Panama hat. Her hair in two long plaits. It was good though to be away from school just for the day. Miss Perkins explained that they would be meeting her old tutor, Mr Winter. He had been at the art school for some time, she said, as he had started there during the war, having been invalided out of the Air force.

Ari just smiled and continued to look out of the bus window. Miss Perkins must have continued her thoughts though, as after a while she said, "He has a slight limp so uses a stick. Some of which are very beautiful, Arianwen. I remember one which had a silver dragon, like the Welsh one, as a handle." She lapsed into thought again, a smile on her lips.

Ari had been to the outskirts of the city previously, on a history trip to see the Roman remains, but this time they got off the bus in the middle of town. The street was long, wide and tree lined. Market stalls were set up along the roadway, and around the Town Hall. Ari could hear cows mooing, and Miss Perkins explained it was also livestock market day, and pointed out where that was. They walked the length of the street and then turned into the road where the art school was situated. It was a tall red brick Victorian building with high windows and a terracotta frieze of artists' heads above the ground floor windows.

They went into the large hallway. It was break time and groups of students were standing around talking and smoking, leaning over the bannisters and sitting on the stairs. Julius Winter appeared almost immediately. He had been watching out for them. He was a tall man, quite old Ari thought, although he was only in his mid-forties. He had longish greying hair and a beard. He gave Miss Perkins a hug.

"Lovely to see you Pauline," he said. "And who is this?"

"This is Arianwen sir."

"Welsh, are you?"

"Possibly," said Ari.

He gave her a sideways smile.

"Right," he said. "Let's have a bit of a tour."

They saw the sculpture rooms and the pottery studio. Ari didn't like that. It was cold and damp. The library, the print room and the common room. But Arianwen really came alive when they entered the painting studios and the life drawing class. Julius noticed this.

He turned to Miss Perkins,

"Might your little girl like to try her hand at life drawing?"

Little girl, Arianwen thought. *Cheek.*

Before Miss Perkins could answer she said, "Yes she would."

Julius Winter laughed to himself. *Interesting one here,* he thought.

Miss Perkins was not persuaded to try herself. She said she would leave Ari in Mr Winter's capable hands and go off to do some shopping. She would be back by lunchtime. Julius took Arianwen into the studio to ask the tutor, Jon Curtis if she could join them. Jon asked her if she had done life drawing before.

"Only clothed," she said.

"You all right with it then?"

"Yes sir, I think so and thank you." She smiled at him.

She saw a forest of easels with quite grown-up students behind them. They were going to draw a new pose after their break, so there was a general shuffle around as a space was found for her, with an easel and a drawing board. Then Jon cast around for spare pencils.

"Don't worry I always carry my own," said Ari and took her box out of her big leather bag.

"Right is everyone ready?"

The model, Mr Riley, a tall, very thin black man came out of the little curtained-off area in the corner of the room and stood on the dais.

"Are you all right with drawing a naked man?" said Sean, a second-year student, standing next to Ari. He was slightly annoyed at having to move to make room for a schoolgirl.

Ari turned to look at him, "Head, legs, arms. We are all the same really, aren't we? Give or take a few wobbly bits. And I wouldn't know about them at my age, would I?" She stopped and glanced at the model, his 'wobbly bits' firmly contained in a posing pouch. She turned back to Sean and raised her eyebrows.

"And I will probably have to wait a few years yet."

Sean let out a shout of laughter. *Bloody good kid,* he thought. Mr Riley had heard the conversation and was trying desperately to keep in pose and not to laugh also.

Jon saw Mr Riley fighting not to laugh and looking up caught Sean's eye.

"Is there a problem over there?"

Sean just indicated Ari, "No sir," he laughed. "Just this one." And Jon smiled.

As Jon walked around, giving help and suggestions to his students, he stopped behind Arianwen. She was totally absorbed in what she was doing. There was no measuring or adjusting. She just drew with a heavy black pencil. And her drawing was wonderful. She had caught the pose and Mr Riley exactly. She stopped and stepped back to evaluate her work and bumped into Jon. She turned "Sorry," she said, and smiled.

Meanwhile, Julius had persuaded Miss Perkins to stay for a coffee. They were sitting in the staff room on creaky basket chairs.

"So, tell me," he said. "About this little girl of yours. Good, is she?"

"I'll only tell you if you promise on your honour not to spread it about the staff room. Do you promise?"

Pauline had been one of Julius' 'girls' when she had been a student, and they had had quite a long affair. It had begun soon after Julius had started teaching at the art school when she was eighteen. She had been fascinated by this big man who had limped into the life drawing room. He had used his stick to point out things, move a model's foot if it was in the wrong place, or reposition draperies. He had not been one wit put out if the model was slightly affronted. She fell in love with him. Their affair continued until she left to do a teacher training course. She knew him well and what an old gossip he was.

Julius promised and he never broke that promise.

"Her artwork is glorious Julius. If she comes here, you will love it, and her. She is very insightful. She did a painting last term which brought tears to my eyes. But there is rather a mystery around her. There seems to be no father on the scene and her mother abandoned her as a baby. She has been brought up by a mother and daughter quite unrelated to her. Anything to do with her goes through a solicitor first. But she is a splendid girl. Extremely bright, beautiful as you can see. Independent to the point of feisty, sometimes. Funny and very loyal to her friends. She is also very honest, so you often do not get the answer you expect. She has one fault though. She does not let many people see what she is feeling. I think that she unconsciously dreads being abandoned again. She has to be very sure of you to let you near."

Julius looked forward to seeing the child again. He asked again for her name. "Arianwen Morgan," said Miss Perkins. She got up, kissed Julius and went off to Marks and Spencer's, where she bought some new underwear. Now she was back in Julius' orbit, he might get in touch. She hoped.

At the end of the morning, the students packed up their kit and left. There were only Jon and Ari left in the life drawing room.

"May I wait here for Miss Perkins?" she asked him.

"Of course," he said. Then pointing to her bag, he said, "And what do you keep in there."

"Just my sketchbook, pencils and crayons and stuff," she said.

"May I look at your sketchbook?"

She jumped up to sit on the cupboard beside him and handed him the book. When Julius and Miss Perkins came in about ten minutes later Jon and Ari were both engrossed in talking about her drawings and didn't notice them for a while.

A few weeks later, Julius asked Jon and his girlfriend, Sarah, to dinner. Poll would be there as she increasingly was these days. After dinner when they were having coffee in the living room, Poll said "Do you remember that child I brought who joined your life drawing class Jon?"

"Yes," he said. "And she was amazingly good."

Poll laughed, "I have known her since she was eight, and she has always been such a good child. But she had her first detention last week and she was boiling as she thought it most unfair."

Julius laughed, "Go on then, Poll, tell them. And I wouldn't mind hearing it again either."

So, Poll did.

"Our new head," she said. "Wants pure girls in her school, hence the early morning runs and showers. Her latest thing is good sex education, so her girls can face the world properly. Anyway, we were tasked with ringing up the parents to see if they objected and I got Arianwen's," she paused. "I don't know what to call her but Ari calls her Mam."

"Why don't you know?" asked Sarah.

"Sorry Sarah," said Poll. "I can only say she is not Ari's mother."

"Anyway, her name is Sallie. She told me that Ari had been quite direct and had asked a while ago and she had told her a lot, mostly about love and respect, but nothing of the mechanics."

She looked around. Julius was already chuckling as he knew what was coming.

"The school nurse, Mrs Jefferies came to talk to the girls," continued Poll. "I don't think she does sex herself, and she hardly ever smiles. However, she was quite good at explaining it to them. A bit clinical, but all the right words. She even explained about orgasms. A lot of the girls looked pink and embarrassed and some were even shuddering and going 'Yuk.' Ari and her friend Christina just listened, taking it all in. In the end, Mrs Jefferies asked if there were any questions. There was silence as the girls were reluctant to ask anything." Julius interrupted with a laugh.

"So, she picked out Arianwen and asked her what she thought. Now I told Julius early on that Ari will answer as she thinks. And she said, 'Well it all sounds quite nice actually. And are you allowed to do it outside?'"

Both Jon and Julius burst out laughing.

"She got a detention for being cheeky, poor lamb, which was unfair really."

"Poll says she is going to put her name forward for interview with us. That should be fun."

On the way home, Sarah complained that they had talked art and students again. "And who is that girl they keep talking about?"

Jon explained that she was a pupil at Poll's school and was extremely good. And rather lovely, though he didn't say that.

Jon asked her often why she didn't join in with the conversation. After all, she had been an art student too, and they had met at college. But she never did. She didn't paint much either and resented the time Jon spent on his paintings. He was beginning to feel exasperated with her. Not much made her happy. What his mother called 'glass half empty', though she was no example of happiness.

The following March, Ari came, accompanied by Sal for her interview at art school. Sal and Fred had driven up the day before and picked Ari up from school the next morning. This time she was not wearing her dreaded school uniform but a tobacco-coloured tweed suit. Her hair was plaited in one long loose plait down her back. Fred went to park the car and have a look around the abbey, whilst Sal went with Ari.

It was quiet in the hallway, there were no students around. The secretary came out and directed them to a row of chairs to one side, where they sat. A middle-aged lady came down the stairs wearing a tricorn hat and a big swirling cape. She went out of the front door. Sal was certain she wore nothing beneath the cape. She looked at Ari, her eyes wide with shock. But before she could say anything, the secretary reappeared and took Ari upstairs to the Principal's room. Ari carried her portfolio and her ever-present leather bag.

There were three people in the room. The Principal, Miss Dorothy Watkins, Julius Winter and the pottery teacher Archie Fellowes.

Archie took Arianwen's portfolio to a side table to look at and evaluate the contents.

The first thing he saw was the portrait of Christina. Beneath that were several drawings, landscapes, and charcoal studies of people. He stood back and took a deep breath. "Miss Watkins," he said. "Might you come and look at these?" She spent a while looking through the portfolio and then went back to her seat.

"Right young lady," she said, frowning at Ari. "Are these honestly your own work?"

Arianwen stood up, flushed with indignation. Before she could reply Julius spoke up. "This is the young lady who did life drawing with us last year," he said.

"Ah! Yes," said Miss Watkins. "I remember the discussion afterwards. Jon was most impressed, was he not? Now I am going to ask you a question. It is not a trick question. I just want an honest answer."

Ari looked steadily at her. "Do you use a sketchbook?"

Ari burrowed into her bag and pulled out the latest. It had 2/60 written on the spine.

"This is my current one," she said, offering it to Miss Watkins, who looked through it slowly.

"And what are these numbers on the spine?"

"Second book this year."

"But it is only the beginning of March," Miss Watkins exclaimed.

"Yes, Well I do a lot of drawing."

Miss Watkins glanced at Julius who was enjoying the exchange enormously. Archie was amused too. It was time for him to ask his stock question. One to which he nearly always got the same answer.

"If I were to give you five bob, young lady, what would you buy?"

Ninety-nine percent of interviewees said some form of art materials.

"I saw a Joe Lyons down the road," said Ari. "So, a knickerbocker glory. I haven't had one in ages."

"No pencils or brushes?" said Archie.

"I have all those," she said. "I don't need more."

Miss Watkins looked at the two men who were trying to suppress smiles and raised her eyebrows in question. They both nodded. She turned back to Ari.

"Well young lady, we would normally have a discussion and then inform you by letter if you had a place. But I think we are all agreed that we can say yes to you now. We will see you in September."

"Thank you so much." Smiled Ari.

Moments later she was hurtling down the stairs to Sal. "I'm in, I'm in," she laughed, giving Sal a big hug. Jon Curtis coming down the stairs caught Sal's eye. "Someone is very happy," he said. Ari turned around and smiled at him. "Yes," she said. "I'll be here next year." Then she stopped and her eyes searched his face and a look of utter bewilderment passed across hers. Sal tapped her on the shoulder and they went on their way. Jon smiled and went to his next class. What was that child's name?

Chapter 3
The First Time Ever I Saw Your Face
Ewan MacColl

June 1960-July 1964

The end of the school year came. Milly and Ellie were coming back for the sixth form as they hoped to go to university. Ari was going to Mam and Nan in Boscombe and Christina was going back to Ghana, with her mother, for a long visit.

But before any of that happened Ari was going to stay with Christina for two weeks. She had been for a few weekends, and Christina had been to Bournemouth, but this time Christina's mother, Belinda was going to take them shopping, with a capital S.

When the girls got off the train in London, Ari was surprised to see Miss Horwood on the platform. She said she was sorry she had often been late picking Ari up in the past and had bought her a little gift to say she would miss her. It was a rather beautiful art nouveau silver bracelet. Arianwen was delighted with it and said so which pleased Miss Horwood no end. Then it was off to the big house in Hampstead.

They did not just shop. Belinda believed wholeheartedly in women making the most of themselves. She regarded the two girls as women now. So, she took them to a beauty parlour, where they had their hair styled, nails polished, and their bodies massaged and pampered. Then they went shopping. Ari had never been 'shopping' like it before. Mam or Nan just bought what they needed. They had gone to Howells in Cardiff for special outfits. Now they went to Bond Street, Fenwick's, Harrods and Liberty's and lots of little expensive boutiques Belinda knew of. This sort of shopping, Ari found was serious.

Belinda had always promised to make Ari a personal scent. Now with a bit more time to talk to Arianwen and find out what she liked and what suited her, she went into her preparation room and came out a few days later with Arianwen's special skin cream. It was a thick emulsion to be massaged into the skin, daily. The effect would be subtle, just right for a young woman. It had a gentle smell of spice and peaches. Arianwen loved it. Even so, they tried different perfumes on the cosmetic counters. Belinda decided that Mitsouko was a good fit for the skin cream and ideal for special occasions.

She also insisted on buying the girls beautiful underwear. No more cotton or regulation, grey school knickers. Lace and silk, and mostly white. Bright colours, for underwear, she opined, were common. They also went to the opera, the ballet and to see 'Oliver', which they enjoyed far more than the opera. Ari would have liked to have visited the Tate and The British Museum, but these were not on Belinda's list, and probably she soon realised, never would be.

The girls would stagger home after a hard day, smelling and looking beautiful. Ari loved most of it but was rather uncomfortable with how she now looked, but she said nothing as Christina's family had been so kind and welcoming. She was grateful too for some of the things she had learnt about dressing well, about perfumes and keeping her skin, nails and hair beautiful. Things that Mam and Nan were not terribly interested in. Clean, tidy and paid for were their maxims. The lessons she learned during those two weeks in London stayed with her all her life.

The whole family came to see her off on the train to Bournemouth, with promises to see each other soon. Christina gave her a big hug. Neither girl realised that they would not see each other for nearly five years. Christina was there though when at that time Ari needed a friend.

Fred and Sal met her off the train. They were rather startled to see her as she looked ten years older. Her hair was backcombed to within an inch of its life and fixed with a big pleat at the back. It wobbled gently as she walked down the platform towards them. Sal was incensed, "Whatever have they done to you." She hissed.

Ari said, "No problem, Mam, I dislike it as much as you." When they got home, she went immediately to have a bath and wash her hair. This took some doing as it was stiff with lacquer. But eventually, the real Ari emerged, but she kept on the silk bra and knickers. Though Olive, when she saw them, said that they would have to be washed by hand. Much better cotton which could be boil-washed.

Meanwhile, Roger Fearnley had set off one of his many searches. This time it was somewhere for Ari to live while she was at art school and it had been decided that Olive would move with her. He found a pair of 'front doors together' semi-detached cottages down the hill from the art school and quite near the station. Ideal he thought, and he bought them in Arianwen's name. They were tidied up and one was put up for rent. A young man, Lem Sewell, who had been an art student a few years previously, and now taught art at a local secondary school, took it immediately.

There were seven weeks left until the beginning of the term at art school. It was decided that Olive and Ari would move in two weeks before to get the feel of the place. Olive had never been there and knew no one so she was giving up a lot to be with Ari. Sal told Ari that she should regard the next few weeks as a holiday. No helping around the hotel. She was to do what she liked. "Within reason," said Sal. "And you know what I mean." Ari did but she only wanted to have time to herself to sketch, perhaps do a proper oil painting and watch the passing clouds and dream. She felt it was so long since she had done this and she missed it.

The weather continued to be good. Ari was often down at the beach before any other people as the seagulls' screeching woke her early. Their beach hut was to the right of the pier, and she would walk down the path opposite the hotel to the promenade and then along beside the sea. The hut was in a row of others just elevated from the roadway. Ari would open the doors, get a deckchair out and make herself some coffee. Then she would sit and people watch, her sketchbook ready on her knee. The first people were usually the deckchair attendants. Young men wearing only a pair of shorts and barefoot, they would set the deckchairs out along the promenade and beach, at breakneck speed. It fascinated Ari that they seemed to be able to throw a deckchair down and it immediately assumed its correct shape. She watched them as they ran up and down and she sketched them. One always called, "G'day," when he saw her. Within a few days, he was stopping to talk to her. His name was Jason; he was Australian and had been going around the world for the past year before university. This job was until the end of October, and then he would be going home. He came and sat beside her on the beach hut step, and she told him about going to art school soon and where she now lived. He thought her name was 'beaut' which made Ari laugh. He was rather taken with her and called by whenever he went past. Sometimes Ari was concentrating on a sketch or watercolour, but she would stop as she liked him too. One day he kissed her on the mouth as he left. Just a gentle kiss and Ari kissed him back the next time.

A day off was looming so he asked Ari if she would like to go out with him for the day. Ari said yes immediately and they agreed to meet by the pier early in the morning. When she told Sal what was planned Sal was not at all enthusiastic. Ari didn't know him. Where were they going? You know what those young men are like. Well, Ari didn't but she hoped to find out.

That night Jason made a transfer charge call home. It was morning there and he got his dad, which was what he wanted. His mother was in the shower. After the usual "You all right Son?" And "Do you need any money?" Jay didn't.

"I have a new girlfriend Dad, absolutely beautiful and real good fun. Trouble is she is off to art school at the end of August. We haven't much time together."

"Doesn't matter how long Jay, years, weeks, months or indeed minutes, treat her good and with respect. You will be fine son and so will she. Name?"

"Arianwen."

"Must come from a Welsh family then."

They talked for a while about Jay coming home and then he rang off. Jay always liked talking to his dad, he made things simple.

Meanwhile, Ari had talked Sal round and the next morning she dressed carefully in her grey linen shorts and a white cotton top. She put her bikini on underneath in lieu of underwear. She had a rucksack with a small picnic: sandwiches, fruit and chocolate that Henri their chef had made for her, plus some lemonade and a towel in case they went swimming. She was so excited and filled with anticipation that she ran the whole way down to the pier. He was waiting for her on his Lambretta and Ari nearly melted when she saw him. His hair and the tips of his eyelashes were bleached by the sun and he was very brown. His arms and legs were covered in fine blond hairs and Ari longed to stroke them. She climbed on behind him and held him round the waist as he instructed. Then they were off.

They went through Poole and across to Sandbanks where they got the ferry to Shell Bay. There they parked the scooter and wandered along the sands. Hand in hand they walked along by the edge of the sea, Jason kissing her with increasing passion, and Arianwen kissing him back. It was still early and there was hardly anyone around, just the odd dog walker. They found their way to a quiet dip in the sand dunes, and they lay side by side on their backs looking at the sky.

Ari knew what was going to happen. She had thought about it for quite some time. It was something only for her and she would keep it close to herself, though she had promised to tell Christina.

"I do this a lot," said Ari

"What? Go out with strange men?"

"No silly. Watch the clouds. Have done since I was a little girl."

Jason lent over and kissed her.

"Arianwen?" he said. "You know what I would like to do don't you?"

She turned and looked at him. Her eyes were luminous.

"I think I might like the same thing Jay," she whispered.

He eased down her shorts and bikini bottoms and took his own shorts off. Later Ari would remember the cool sand on her back, the sound of the sea and the smell and feel of Jason. He slid his hands under her bottom and lifted her slightly, and then he pushed hard and entered her. He heard her hiss with the sting of pain. He moved his hands to find her breasts and stirred inside her. She climaxed immediately and he followed. She sat up a little and kissed him. She looked a little dazed. "What happens now?" she said.

"We wait a while," said Jason with a smile.

"What for?"

"To do it again of course, that one was a bit quick."

They went for a swim later and ate the picnic. Jay had brought some lager and they drank that. Ari also shared a cigarette with him. Another first she thought, and they made love one more time before they headed back. She was rather sore when she got home and she hoped that Sal hadn't noticed any change in her. But it seemed as if Sal hadn't. She sent the promised note to Christina. 'Done it three times. Bloody lovely A'. She got a note back several weeks later, 'Done it. Twice. Not special C'.

The weather for the next few weeks was good, although there were a few gloomy days. Sal was now resigned to Ari having a boyfriend; she knew her dear girl had been brought up properly and wouldn't do anything she ought not. But Ari was so pleased that she had done one thing she had always wanted to do. She liked it.

Jason worked shifts plus he was often asked to fill in somewhere. A friend might run past with a note from him, or a note was left wrapped around the beach hut padlock. But they managed to meet up a lot. Warm days when Jay was off work, they went to Lulworth, Kimmeridge and Durdle Door. They liked each other and talked about everything under the sun and made love a lot. Both realised that the day was coming when Ari would be leaving.

The evening before she left, they met in an old disused hut and made love for the last time. Jason gave her a small, narrow silver ring for her left-hand little finger. "It is so you will remember me as your first," he said. She cried a little then. He kissed her and wiped away her tears.

"Goodbye princess," he said. "Have a good life." Then he kissed her once more, "You have been the most special and fun girl I have ever met, a joy to be with. I shall miss you. And the best fuck ever." And with that, he was gone.

She walked home slowly and slipped the ring into her pocket. It would be no good if Mam saw it. There would be who? And why? and Arianwen did not want to talk about that yet. She would put it back on her little finger when they got to their new home. Nan would never notice.

The next morning Roger came for them in his brother's Rolls. Olive sat in the front and Ari had the back seat with the cases that could not fit in the boot. They made good progress and were in their new home by lunchtime. The three of them walked up to the town, past the now-silent art school and had some lunch. Then Roger set off back to London. The house was lovely and just as Ari had wanted it. When she had visited London with Christina, they had gone to Liberty's and Ari had seen lots of things she liked. Now with Fred and Sal's help, she had two dark green velvet sofas from Heals, plus a beautiful black, lacquered Chinese cabinet, from Liberty's. Otherwise, the house was much like 'Arian Court'. The colours soft and gentle, the furnishings very modern and in places unusual.

If Olive noticed that Ari was a bit quiet over the next few days, she put it down to nerves about going to art school. But Ari was missing Jay. Her big brass bed that she had had as a child had been brought up to the new house for her. She lay in it at night and longed for his warm, hard body. She had come across the word 'wanton' in a book and wondered if that was what she was. She looked it up in her dictionary. 'Sexually unrestrained' it said, and she knew she was not that. She had just liked doing it with Jay. Just as she liked linen sheets, silk underwear, perfume, big soft towels. She also loved the smell of turps, linseed oil and paint. The feel of pencil on paper and the texture and smell of charcoal. Even as a very small child, she had liked to smell and taste and feel anything new. She had loved the smell of the coal house. These things were part of her and made her what she was. She wondered where they had come from. Her mother? Her father? But she had not learnt them from Mam or Nan that she knew. Before she fell asleep, she wondered if there would be anyone else, ever.

The two weeks went by quickly. Olive and Ari settled down together and they explored the town, the shops, the Abbey and the park. Olive met a neighbour who was a widow like herself and much the same age. Mary invited her for a cup of tea and they were soon popping back and forth across the road. They went to the cinema together and Mary took Olive to her church's coffee morning. Ari was glad of this as Olive would have been alone most of the day when she was at art school. They also met Lem who lived next door. 'A very nice young man' was Olive's verdict.

At the weekend, she and Nan went shopping, up the town and around the market where Ari discovered the second-hand clothes stall. She frequented it all through her art school years. Nan also enjoyed going to the Sunday morning service at the Abbey. Sometimes Ari went too as she liked the calm quietness punctuated by soft footfalls, the smell of flowers and incense and snatches of prayer and song.

Wednesday, the 14th of September came all too quickly. Ari had had a letter about start times, and registration at the school. The night before she got her big leather bag with her art materials ready and laid out her clothes. It promised to be another warm day, so she chose a shift dress she had bought in London.

In the morning, she washed and dressed carefully and was ready by nine o'clock. Registration was from nine-thirty to ten, so she kissed Olive goodbye and set off up the hill. Olive stood at the end of the path to watch her go.

"Have a good day cariad," she called.

Registration was over quickly and she was directed to the library. All the students from all four years were gathering there. Arianwen slipped in and sat quietly at the back.

The staff, who were in that day, were standing down the front waiting for Miss Watkins to appear and start the meeting. Julius Winter and Jon Curtis were leaning on the bookshelves, legs crossed, catching up on their holiday news. Julius had just told Jon that Miss Perkins, or Poll to him, had continued to spend many an evening with him during the holidays, and had stayed quite often. He was thinking of a more permanent arrangement if she was willing. Jon smiled at this. He was a good chap, Julius, but he had an eye for the ladies as he readily admitted and had had several affairs with his students over the years. Perhaps now he would stop ogling the female students. He had been a good mentor to Jon in the two years he had been teaching and had given him lots of pointers in dealing with the students and organising his classes. But Jon thought that fraternising and often sleeping with the students was not a sensible idea.

Now Julius turned to Jon.

"Enjoy France, did you?"

"Yes, it was good," said Jon. "I got a lot of work done."

"Sarah enjoy it?"

"She didn't come. She hated it last year. The long journey and the heat. She didn't like the people, the food, and the smell. Absolutely hated the toilets and the insects."

"Was there anything she did like?" smiled Julius.

"The wine possibly. But my mother is not the easiest person to get on with and though Sarah tried, she didn't get anywhere. I had told her not to bother but she felt as a visitor she ought to try. But my mother has always enjoyed being unkind. As a family, we have learnt never to answer back. Sarah couldn't do that. But mostly, and we have this at home also, she resents me being engrossed in my painting. She needs someone with a nine-to-five job, Julius, who will sit and hold her hand all evening and watch television. I'm not that one. She was there when I got back but wouldn't talk about what she had done when I was away. I think she will not be around for much longer."

Julius said how sorry he was to hear that but he could see that Jon was not particularly put out. To change the subject he said, "I haven't seen our little girl yet, have you?"

Jon knew exactly who he meant.

"She's not your little girl," said Jon laughing. "And certainly not mine. And no, I haven't seen her."

Miss Watkins came in then and there was a general settling down as the meeting started.

"Welcome all," she said. "Students old and new, and staff. We have no new staff this term. You older students will know that we have just a few rules, so I will just remind you all what they are. We start at ten on the dot. If you are late and you are in a life drawing class, please do not enter if the door is shut. You will just have to wait until the pose is finished or it is break time.

And lastly, no alcohol on the premises please."

There she paused.

"Now will second-year intermediate go to the office for their timetables. NDD can wait outside and collect theirs too. But no rushing."

Most of the students left leaving about twenty or so in the room.

"For you new students, the rest of this week I would like you to go wherever you wish. Just get the feel of the place. Join any class, stay as long as you like. There will be two groups and you will meet up with your tutor at the end of each day this week and weekly thereafter. Talk about anything you may wish. Your tutor will give you a timetable for next week. There are two tutors, Mr Cooper and Mr Winter.

"Right, I will read out the names of the first group. Please come up to the front and meet your tutor, Mr Cooper."

She read out a few names. "Sheila Fry, Grace King, Tom Lawrence, Carol Mason, Arianwen Morgan, James Percival, Janet Philips, Stuart Potter, Marco Reynolds, and Nell Thomas."

Both Julius and Jon pricked up their ears.

A young woman detached herself from the remaining students and walked across the room. She was very brown and her dark hair was plaited and woven in a crown around her head. She wore a plain, sleeveless deep-purple linen shift which ended just above her bare brown knees. Silver earrings and bracelet and the ever-present leather bag on her shoulder.

"Jesus wept," breathed Julius. "Just look at that?"

As she walked past, she smiled at Julius and Jon. The faintest scent of spice and peaches lingered in the air.

The remaining students were introduced to their tutor, Julius, and left the room.

Mr Ian Cooper was head of painting and he had been at the art school even longer than Julius. The only thing he said was that he would meet them in the print room at three-thirty.

Arianwen spent most of the morning wandering in and out of various studios. She went into the pottery studio where a girl, who she thought was called Grace, was throwing a very professional pot on the wheel. Ari stopped to watch her. When Grace had removed the pot from the wheel, she turned to Ari.

"Hello," she said. "I'm Grace."

She held out a very grubby hand. Arianwen shook it.

"I'm Arianwen, but please call me Ari."

"I think you live next door to me," said Grace. "I rent a room from Lem, but I only moved in yesterday."

"Oh great," said Ari. "See you later and we can walk home together if you want?"

Lunchtime came and Ari was just coming down the stairs when Tom Lawrence and a few of the others from the group came past.

"Coming to the pub?" he called.

Ari smiled. "Thanks, but not today. I need a bit of fresh air."

She went out and around the corner to a delicatessen where she bought two large soft rolls, some mortadella, a banana and a bottle of Perrier. Then she walked down the hill to a little garden of remembrance she and Nan had found on their explorations. It was very quiet there and Ari settled on a bench. She was just about to open the bag of rolls when she saw another of the group sitting opposite. She went across and said hello. It was Marco, and he had forgotten his lunch. So, she ripped one of the rolls open, stuffed it with the meat and handed it to him.

"I hope you like mortadella?" she said.

"Oh yes," said Marco. "My mother is Italian, so we have a lot of it. And thanks for this."

Ari ate the other roll, and then they shared the banana and the water.

They walked back together and separated at the door. Marco to explore the upstairs painting studio and Ari to check out the books in the library.

Jon went into the library, a little later, and saw Arianwen, her head bent over a book. He could see the little bones at the base of her neck and a few strands of hair that had escaped from her plait. He went over to her.

"Arianwen? Jon Curtis. You joined one of my life drawing classes some time ago?"

She jumped and looked up, startled. He was transfixed by her beautiful eyes.

"Jesus!" she exclaimed. "Don't do that sir. I was far away."

She looked at him. He was tall and what Olive would call bony. High cheekbones, a strong nose, deep blue eyes and dark hair that flopped over his forehead.

She smiled up at him. "It's wonderful to be here legitimately."

He laughed at that.

"Did you have a good holiday?"

"Oh yes. I went to Bournemouth. We have an hotel there on the cliff overlooking Boscombe pier. It was lovely."

She could feel herself blushing so put her head down.

He noticed her twirl the little ring on her slim brown finger. His own hand was near hers, leaning on the table. With a small movement of his finger, he could touch her. He stood up. "Well, I must get on." Though he thought he could sit there all day and look into her eyes. He was getting as bad as Julius. He was cross with himself. *Christ she was only a kid.*

Ari loved the walk up the hill to the art school. First in the summer sunshine, changing every morning to a soft autumn haze. She just loved being an art student. Every day was packed with pottery, sculpture, life drawing, portraiture and composition. They even had a gentle class in collage and how to make a sketchbook. Also canvas preparation and how to grind oil paints. She loved the building too. The tiled hallway, the wide staircase, and the splintery wooden floors. The people too were great, eccentric, accepting, thoughtful and funny.

The term gathered speed. The older students were working towards their exams. The two groups of new students met and mingled in their timetabled lessons. Given a choice some like Grace spent a free period in the pottery studio, Tom gravitated towards sculpture and Ari and Marco, painting and drawing. But there were some periods when the group came together for a specific purpose. Ian Cooper reported on the dynamics of the group in a staff meeting at the end of the first term.

"Tom is the self-crowned king of the group," he said. "And Stuart, James, Janet and Sheila his acolytes. Janet is always to be found as near Tom as she can get. Sheila is flexible." He smiled in an embarrassed way, "If you see what I mean? I do not like the makeup of that group. What Tom says or wants is law and catered for. They are all even beginning to draw like Tom and paint like him. He is very dominant."

"Arianwen, Marco and Grace support each other well and the other two girls Nell and Carol are usually together. Although Arianwen does try to include them in planning and such. I have noticed that Arianwen is a little wary of Tom. I don't know why but Marco is very protective of her."

"Are they a couple then?" someone asked.

Ian shook his head, "Marco is not that way inclined I think."

Julius looked at Jon.

"Have you noticed any problem?" he asked.

Jon had not, although he had spent some time talking to Tom about books and films and music.

They went on then to talk about other things, the timetable for next term, exam arrangements and any students they felt were falling behind.

Jon and Julius went for a drink afterwards. Julius couldn't stay long as Poll was cooking a special supper. They discussed the meeting and the problem with Ari, who Julius still called 'our little girl', much to Jon's annoyance. In the end, they decided that Tom was probably jealous of Ari and her much greater drawing skills. Things they agreed would settle down.

And they did on the whole. But Jon didn't see much of Ari. She was not in many of his classes, as he mainly taught the older students. He saw her only around the school or for life drawing.

On the last day of the summer term, Jon overtook Ari coming down the stairs.

"First year over Arianwen, has it been good?"

"Yes sir, mostly."

He thought she looked a little unhappy when she answered. *End of term,* he thought.

"You going to your family's hotel?"

"Yes, sir."

"I'm going to be down that way end of August. My friend Richard is taking up a place as a painting tutor at the art school in Bournemouth, and I shall help him move. Near Branksome Chine, I believe. I'll keep an eye out for you."

He smiled and was off out of the front door.

Ari stood for a moment; she was trembling slightly. She had wanted him to touch her, and she knew she loved him. *Bugger,* she thought.

At the beginning of January 1962, Mr Cooper asked each of the group to choose and copy a painting of their choice. Some like Tom and Stuart had resented having to copy a painting, but Ian Cooper had stressed it was an exercise in discipline as well as learning about an artist.

The task didn't go well as the weather was dreadful and for two weeks there was never a full complement of students or staff at school. One particularly cold day Ari and Grace struggled up the hill accompanied by Marco who had stayed with Ari, there being no buses running. Stuart had managed to get in as had Nell. Ian Cooper had troubles with his car with no prospect of a mechanic in the foreseeable future, and Jon had stayed with Julius and Poll. Ian rang to ask if either Jon or Julius could get to school and take his class. Jon volunteered.

It was very quiet in the studio, with only the five students. There didn't seem to be a tutor, so they just got on with their work. All five were quite busy when Jon came in, apologised for his lateness and explained that Mr Cooper was stuck at home. Marco standing near Ari heard her gasp; she had not been expecting him. And he noticed also that Mr Curtis looked for her first. Jon did a quick look around to see what everyone was doing then went to the other side of the room to talk to Stuart about his painting. From there he could see Arianwen who, after the shock of seeing him, had recovered and was now totally engrossed in her work. Her hair was up in a ponytail on top of her head and tied with a dull-pink ribbon. She wore little black boots, black tights, a short, dark grey box pleated skirt and a short black jumper. Jon moved on to speak to Nell.

Break time came and Stuart was just bemoaning having to cross to the main building to get some coffee when Ari produced a large flask from her bag. "Cocoa anyone?" she said with a big smile. "My Nan made it, in case." and Marco found some old cups on a shelf. She also produced a bag of jam doughnuts. "Miracle of miracles, the bakers on the hill were open and we stopped and got these," she said, as she handed the bag around. They all sat on the floor, even Jon. It was warm and companionable in the studio. Marco bit into his doughnut.

"I knew someone who had a holiday job in a baker's," he said smiling. "And he had to inject the doughnuts with jam, incredibly boring he said. Every so often he would put triple the quantity in one. He liked to imagine someone biting into it and being covered in an explosion of jam. Grace said that she had an aunt who always cut a doughnut in half and ate the jam with a spoon. Ari laughed.

"Perhaps she had come across one of Marco's friends' doughnuts, she said. "Once bitten!"

Marco put his arm around her and laughed. Then he said, "What the hell have you got on today, Ari? Something else you bought on the market?" She laughed.

"My school hockey shorts," she said and did a star jump. "See, culottes for nice, genteel young ladies."

"And what is that writing on the back?" Stuart asked.

"My name," said Ari lifting her jumper to show her name embroidered in big yellow letters on the waistband. Jon was fascinated and couldn't look away.

"Whatever for?" Stuart mused.

"Well, if you were doing something despicable down the field the games teacher would know instantly who you were." Ari laughed. Jon wanted to ask if she had ever done anything despicable but knew he could not.

Nell said everyone was very jolly today, and Jon thought he heard Marco say, "Well Tom's not here." But then Jon noticed Ari licking her fingers and he had to look away.

After break, Jon couldn't put it off any longer. It was Ari's turn. She had known it would be so has moved away from her painting to sit on a cupboard, but Jon went and sat beside her. Dear God, he loved the smell of her. She had chosen a Matisse painting, titled *Standing model, Nude study in blue.* Jon asked her why she had chosen it.

"Well, I don't really like Matisse, a bit too colourful sometimes for me, but I do like this one. I like the colours, the blues and greens, and I find the way she is standing rather intriguing," she said.

"And why is that?" Jon asked.

"She looks very demure and modest and young doesn't she, looking down like that, and where her hands are placed? I think most models in those days were either prostitutes, actresses or ballet dancers, weren't they? Look at Degas or Toulouse Lautrec. Their models were forever washing, standing in a bath, combing their hair or just sitting around in their knickers." Jon laughed out loud.

"And?" he said.

"She looks as if she doesn't want to be there. And have you noticed; her feet are very big?"

Jon now slightly recovered asked, "And why do you think she has no face?"

"I've been thinking about that," Ari said. "He painted several other nudes about the same time with no faces. But the way this is painted is quite sketchy while most of his other nude paintings are a bit less tentative. Some are a bit chunky really." Ari stopped and thought a moment but didn't look at him. "I think you have to decide whether there was a reason he didn't paint the face, or whether he just hadn't got around to it. Also, if it was a model, a prostitute perhaps, her face would be the least important part of her, wouldn't it? I can't decide."

Jon had no idea whether her theories were right or not, but they were very interesting, and at least she had thought about what she was painting. And he loved to listen to her, her answers were so unexpected sometimes and he could watch her all day. He looked forward to seeing this sweet-smelling, clean, soft girl and knew he should not. As for Ari, she was just glad she hadn't blushed when he had spoken to her and had managed to sound at least halfway intelligent.

The students were now into their NDD course and had gained greater skills, deeper insight and more knowledge. Ian Cooper suggested Ari limit her palette and he gave her only, white, terre vert, yellow ochre, cadmium red, Prussian blue and burnt sienna to work with. She struggled for a while but the intensity and deeply insightful subjects of her paintings responded to being less colourful. Jon noticed that her paintings were often about or based around family, and he wondered why. She did a rather startling painting of a young schoolgirl seemingly abandoned on a station platform, surrounded by empty teacups and dried sandwich crusts. It was very poignant and Jon thought it might be her. The child had plaits and wore a yellow gingham dress.

But although most worked hard there was a lot to do in the city. There was a jazz club and a dance in or around the area nearly every night. James loved dancing and he very often asked Ari to go with him. She was very happy to do so as James was good company. It made them laugh though when the beatniks and art students started their 'stomping' dance and the more regular and conventional dancers objected. James spent a lot of time with his arm around Ari and they had the occasional kiss, which was quite pleasant Ari thought. But it never went further. James was always wary of Tom as the boys in the group knew Tom fancied Arianwen, and Ari dreamt of someone quite other.

There were folk clubs also and Ari often went with Lem and Grace and some of the others from their group. One Friday evening they went to one at the pub on the corner at the top of the hill. The room was on the first floor, up a narrow flight of stairs and was hot, steamy, smoky and very crowded, as a well-known local singer was going to perform.

People sat around at tables or if there was no room, on the floor. The beer was warm and plentiful. Ari, Lem and Grace had been joined by Stuart, his girlfriend Amy and James, and were sitting on the floor in a corner, on a pile of their coats. James had his arm around Ari and he whispered in her ear. "Mr Curtis has just come in with a woman." Ari looked up. The woman was tall and blonde and had her arm through his. Ari looked away. Jon saw Archie and his wife so started across the room to them, then saw the group on the floor and said hello.

The singer was very good and after he had finished and left, the floor was thrown open to anyone who might like to sing. Grace, normally so quiet, often did and she stood up and sang *Where have all the flowers gone*, and then *Barbara Allan*. Ari liked that the best. Grace had the most beautiful contralto voice and there was loud enthusiastic clapping and cheering when she finished. A few other people sang, then as Grace and Marco knew that Ari had sung in the school choir, they persuaded her to have a go. She knew she would not be able to sing a note if Mr Curtis was watching her, so she sat on the stool facing away from his group. She sat, her long dark hair glowing in the light and sang *Myfanwy*, explaining first it should really be sung by a man and was a song of unrequited love. She was so cross with herself. Why ever had she chosen that? But it was quite lovely and when she had finished someone in the crowd shouted, "Beautiful my darling. Sing another Welsh one." So, she sang the lullaby. *Suo Gân*. Her voice was gentle but true and there was a deep hush in the room as she sang. It was such a beautiful song.

Jon and his girlfriend had been about to leave. Sarah had complained that it was all students again. This was untrue, as there were a lot of people of all ages there and they were sitting with Archie and his wife. Jon was very moved and aware of Arianwen perched on the stool, her long legs wound around the struts. But Jon wouldn't and when Ari started to sing, couldn't leave. At the end of the song there was absolute silence in the room, then Archie's wife Sonia gave a loud sob and carried on crying. Ari turned and seeing who it was slid off the stool. It was difficult getting to Mrs Fellowes as the room was so crowded, and everyone began clapping and wanted to congratulate her, but eventually, she squeezed between the chairs and knelt down beside her. "I am so sorry," she said. "Was that the wrong song for me to sing?"

Sonia saw the genuine concern in those lovely eyes. "Sweetheart," she said. "It was beautiful and my mother used to sing it when I was a child. It brought back some lovely memories. Not at all sad, just me being silly. So, thank you." And she leaned forward and kissed Arianwen.

Jon had been sitting next to Sonia. The end of Ari's plait was across his knee. He touched it with his finger.

At the end, they all herded down the stairs, James once again with his arm around Arianwen. The group stopped on the pavement to say their goodbyes and James kissed Ari before she turned with Grace and Lem to walk home. Jon, saying goodbye to Archie and Sonia, saw the kiss and he felt the most dreadful surge of jealousy and longing. For several minutes he could not speak such was his confusion.

On the way home Sonia said to Archie, "That girl is lovely isn't she, is she one of yours?"

"Who, Arianwen? No," Archie said. "One of Ian's and very good too."

"Ah," said Sonia. "Was she Julius' Polly's pupil?"

"Yes, she went to St Ursula's, I think. You would never know though; she has no airs and graces at all. Sam thinks she's the bee's knees."

"Does Jon like her?"

"Not especially. Why?"

"He never took his eyes off her the whole time she was singing."

"Well, she was good, wasn't she? Jon wouldn't go down Julius' route, he is far too serious for that."

"Yes," said Sonia, but she knew she was right.

When Jon saw Ari on the following Monday, he said how lovely her and Grace's singing had been.

"I didn't realise you could speak Welsh Ari."

"Just a bit sir, you know hello and sit down and stuff," said Ari. "But my Nan sang *Suo Gân* to me nearly every night. So, I know it off by heart. We also had things in Wales called *Noson Lawen*. They were a bit like concerts, but very informal. Nan often used to sing in the one in the church hall and when I was old enough I did too until I was sent to school of course. Was Mrs Fellowes all right afterwards then, sir?"

Jon said she had been fine and that the song was very beautiful.

And nearly added 'just like you' but stopped just in time.

Sarah had come with him. He had been on his way out of the door to go to the folk club and to meet Archie and Sonia when she had turned up. She either came with him he said or went away. Afterwards, she said she had come to ask if she could come back. But she was entirely unsurprised when Jon said no. She, like Sonia, had seen his reaction to Arianwen.

Lem and Grace were a couple now and very good together. There were loads of pubs in the city and Ari would often meet up with Marco, or Grace and Lem for a drink. And very often with some of the others, for the students of all four years met and mingled after class and at weekends. Marco was a bit of a lost soul. His parents ignored any attempt by him to explain his sexuality. They did not want to know and hoped he would grow out of it. Ari was often his sounding board, for as well as that, he too had trouble with Tom. He would come to supper at the weekend and Olive would make a fuss of him. Ari had told her the true situation when Olive had mistakenly thought they were a couple. But Olive liked Marco's gentle nature. He was a good friend to Ari.

Olive too had settled well. Besides her friend Mary, and their outings, Roger visited often. They went for walks together, to the theatre and recitals in the Abbey. Roger asked her to marry him one day when they were walking around the park. They were both of a similar age, early fifties and Roger felt there was plenty of time for them to enjoy life before they grew old together. Not that he put it quite like that but Olive knew what he meant. She said yes, but not until Arianwen could live on her own. They decided after talking to Arianwen, Fred and Sal that Easter of next year, 1963 would be a reasonable date. Arianwen would be nineteen and well able to look after herself. Roger and Olive would only be a thirty-minute train ride away, Mary was across the road and Lem and Grace next door.

The wedding was lovely. Very quiet with just close family and in a registry office. Roger remembered Sal's wedding and thought her mother looked just as beautiful as she had. Then they went on honeymoon to Spain and when they came back Olive moved into Roger's flat. She embraced his life wholeheartedly and he was very proud of her. When he thought about it, she had had many upheavals in her life which she had managed well. He felt a bit awful that those years before he had thought her insular and provincial.

After the wedding, Arianwen went back to an empty house. The first thing she did was to light and smoke a cigarette in her kitchen though she did open the window. Now she sat just loving the peace and quiet. Since Jay had shared one with her, she had bought her own, hiding them in her big bag from Mam and Nan. One day she had gone with Marco to the tobacconist on the corner, near the art school. Marco stuck with his usual Nelson but Ari spotted a pink packet on the shelf behind the counter. She asked the shopkeeper what they were. The woman turned and took a packet down for her, "Passing Clouds," she said. "They are oval in shape. Hang on a mo and I'll take one out to show you."

Jon came in behind them for his usual Gauloises. Arianwen thought the cigarettes were beautiful and bought three packets straight away. She was hopping with delight. Marco turned and rolled his eyes at Jon. "It was meant to be, sir," he said. "She spends a lot of time gazing at the clouds and stars."

Arianwen was so wrapped up in her purchase that she barely noticed him. The shopkeeper turned to Jon when they had left.

"Lovely that one, isn't she?" she said. "You know I caught my fingers in the till a few weeks ago. Really sore they were. She came in with a bunch of violets for me, bless her." Jon just smiled and went on his way. He knew how lovely she was.

Jon had struggled but now felt he had succeeded in suppressing any feelings he had for Arianwen. He was her tutor and believed that he should remain just that. Pupil, teacher relationships were not for him. But deep, deep down he still called her his 'darling girl' and the day was not the same if he hadn't seen her. However, a few things were to happen, in quick succession during the next few months which threw him off balance.

The group were now well into their third year. Intermediate exams were behind them and forgotten by most and they had decided on their specialities. One late afternoon at the beginning of March, Archie came into the staffroom accompanied by Sam, his pottery technician. Jon was seated in a corner reading *The Artist* magazine. Julius was next to him with his eyes closed, just resting. Sam and Archie were laughing together. "What's up?" said Julius instantly alert.

"You remember that beautiful child Arianwen's interview, Julius?"

Julius laughed, "How could I forget? She tied Dorothy up in knots and then said she was going to buy ice cream with your five bob. Classic it was."

Julius saw Jon shift in his chair, but his eyes never left his magazine.

"Well!" continued Archie. "She was in the pottery room talking to Grace and I asked her why she had never considered pottery as her speciality."

"Brilliant this," laughed Sam

"She said," continued Archie. "You know in that lovely voice of hers with that slight accent. 'I couldn't possibly have done that sir, it's too damp and cold in here. And anyway, I don't like the clay beneath my fingernails.'"

"So, I said she could have cut them," said Sam.

Archie laughed loudly, "You would have thought we had suggested she did her pottery naked, the look she gave us."

"Well, that would be a wonderful thing to see," mused Sam and Archie slapped him on the arm.

Ron Fleming, the sculpture tutor who was usually quite taciturn said, "I wouldn't half mind covering that one in plaster." Everyone laughed.

Jon got up and left the room. "What's up with him?" Archie said. "A lot on his mind I think," said Julius and he knew what it was.

The students had a small exhibition of their work to prepare for at the end of the Spring term.

One warm afternoon just after half-term, Jon walked past the prep room and saw Nell, Carol, Marco and Grace convulsed with laughter in the doorway. He asked what was going on as they were making quite a noise. Marco answered though he could hardly speak. "It's Ari sir," he said. "She is trying to cut framing for her paintings." He paused for breath. "She is on her fourth or fifth go now and she can't get the mitres right, and she won't accept any help. She is just brilliant when she is really cross. The language can be terrible." He started to laugh again.

"Couldn't you have insisted on helping her?"

"She might bite us," laughed Carol

82

Jon signalled for them to go and distinctly heard someone say, "Old spoilsport."

"Oh fuck," said Ari as she cut yet another bit of wood at the wrong angle. She kicked the bench then took one more piece of wood. Jon went over to her.

"Whoa! Arianwen," he said. "Stop, stop. You have the wood upside down."

"What?" she cried and spun around, the saw in her hand. He had forgotten she was left-handed and the saw nearly grazed his chin. He clasped her wrist and took it from her. Tears of frustration blurred her eyes. They stood for a moment looking at each other until Jon realised he was still holding her arm. He let her go.

"I'll get the technician to help you," he said.

"Thanks, but no thanks," she said. "I'll take the stupid things to the man on the market. He will make a bloody better job of them than I ever can."

"Look!" she said indicating the pile of wood. "It looks like the big bad wolf's been round." With which she scooped the pieces into her bag. "Kindling for the fire."

She picked up her bag and rummaged for her purse,

"Now I had better go and pay for the stupid bloody wood I've spoiled. Sorry about nearly taking your head off." She smiled at him and there was a splash of mischief in her eyes. And then she left. Jon's heart lurched. However was he going to deal with this?

The next day both groups gathered in the large painting studio, they were going to start a seven-day life painting of Miss Morris. Everyone was there, the sculptors, potters and painters. Arianwen was quite excited and got there early. Her easel and painting table were in position well before the start. Marco as usual was next to her and Nell on her other side. Their tutor for the whole seven days was to be Mr Curtis. Arianwen could still feel his hand clasping her arm.

Things started well; Miss Morris was an excellent model, she barely moved. Jon spent some time talking to Tom and Stuart about music and books, and Tom huffed and puffed a bit as he didn't really like painting. But the first two days were good as everyone tried to get the proportions and the pose right on their canvases. Then towards the end of the week,

Tom got bored and started to tease Ari again. Thursday evening, he turned up at her house and as she wouldn't open the door posted an extremely erotic poem, he had written about her, through her letterbox. The next morning, she found it difficult as he kept asking her had she read his poem and did she want to do some of the things he had written about, with him. At lunchtime, Marco, James and Ari went to the pub for a pie and a shandy.

"I'm not going back this afternoon," Ari said "I've just had enough... I think I'll go to the cinema to see *Gone with the Wind*."

"I'll come with you," James said, but Marco wanted to get back to his painting. That afternoon, Jon noticed almost immediately that Arianwen was missing and James was also. He asked Marco where they were, but he just shrugged his shoulders and said he didn't know, but Jon knew that he did and also why.

By half past four, the school was mostly empty as students and staff rushed off to begin the weekend. Jon was just putting up a new timetable on the notice board when Ari and James came in the front door.

"Where have you two been?" he asked rather sharply.

"The cinema," James said.

Jon looked at them both, Arianwen was looking at the floor.

"You shouldn't really have done that," Jon said.

Ari looked up, "It was my idea," she said. "And James thought I shouldn't go on my own."

Jon turned away to finish the notices and James went off to get his bag and go home.

Arianwen just stood there. This was so very hard, a whole week with Mr Curtis in the room all day and then Tom and his bloody poem. She had just had enough of everything and everyone and now Mr Curtis was disappointed in her. Ari just wanted to sink to the floor and have Mr Curtis lift her up, but she knew that was impossible. Jon realised she hadn't left with James and was still standing in the middle of the hall. She was wearing black harem pants, the waistband embroidered with silver thread, and a tiny sleeveless black top that barely met the top of the trousers. It was warm out and tendrils of her plait which was wound around her head had stuck to her neck. She looked like someone from

The Arabian Nights. Some might have thought she looked strange, as if she wore fancy dress, but she did not. He just ached to touch her. He couldn't just stand there watching her so he went down the short corridor to the office and to the stock cupboard beyond and took a while looking for some cartridge paper. Then he went back fully expecting her to have gone, but Ari hadn't moved. He said her name quietly and as she turned towards him, he saw a large teardrop trembling on her eyelashes. He took a step towards her but she moved then and ran up the stairs to the girl's cloakroom and went in. He couldn't think of what he had said that had upset her so. He hung about in the hall for a while and then Grace came through from the pottery studio where she had stayed to finish glazing some pots. She went into the cloakroom and in a while came out with Ari. They walked home together.

At the beginning of the summer term, something else happened that was upsetting. Jon was supervising a class in lino printing as the teacher was ill. The group had been doing it for well over two years now so were quite proficient with the sharp tools. All the students were seated round the big table, working and talking quietly. Arianwen as usual was seated near Marco and was just finishing her last and most precise tile. She got up suddenly and walked out of the room, holding her arm. Jon noticed her go and looked at Marco. Marco shrugged his shoulders, as he was want to do and glanced at the space where Ari had been working. There was a discarded lino tool and blood on the bench. "Uh! Oh! Stabbed herself with the lino tool," he said as he got up. But Jon was out of the door before him. There were blobs of blood across the floor leading towards the office. Mrs Parker, the secretary came rushing out.

"She's fainted, silly girl," she said.

Arianwen was lying on the office floor. There was a deep gash in her right arm and she had banged her head on the desk as she fell. She was as white as a sheet.

"Crikey," Marco said. "Shall we lift her up sir?"

"Help me get her up, and then we'll take her to the staff room." They lifted her and Jon carried her across the hall. Marco went ahead to open the door. The room was empty as Jon knew it would be. Arianwen's head lolled on his shoulder and he could feel her breath on his cheek and smell that lovely perfume. He stroked her hair and lowered her gently into a chair.

"Wake up darling girl," he whispered as he touched her face. He had never been so close to her before and saw the fine freckles on her nose and the deep curve of her top lip. Marco who was standing near the door heard what he said. He thought Mr Curtis was going to kiss her, so he coughed. Jon sat back on his heels and stood up.

He had not realised what he had said or what Marco had seen and heard as he was so intent on Ari. But she soon came round. She was a little dazed as she opened her eyes "Hello, sir," she said, and she sighed.

Mrs Parker bustled in with water, lint and bandages and began to clean Ari's wounds. With a backward glance, Jon went back to his class and saw that Marco was already there cleaning the blood off the table. Everyone wanted to know what had happened. So, Jon just told them Ari had cut herself with the lino tool, fainted but was now fine. Sheila and Janet sniggered at that. "Bet she just did it for attention," they said. "Silly bitch." A very pale and well-bandaged Ari came back into the room sometime later. She quietly carried on with her work, watched surreptitiously by Jon. She looked very pale but would wait and walk home with Grace. Janet was furious when Tom went over to her to ask how she was. Tom was hers, and he had no business showing concern for another girl. Least of all Miss Perfect, bloody Arianwen Morgan.

That night Arianwen dreamed she was with Jon, in a forest and he was kissing her. Her mother was there, or at least someone she thought was her mother, and she said she would be abandoned again. Ari was running through the trees searching for them both. The dream stayed with her all day. She had always been extremely aware of Jon Curtis, but now that feeling seemed more intense. But never in a million years could she tell him how she felt. Daydreams were all she would have.

Their first NDD year flew by and the end of term was approaching. After that, there would be just one more year. Work ratcheted up but Ari having plenty of time to herself was well on with her dissertation. Mr Cooper had approved it and she was going to do 'The Portrayal of the Family in Art'. Given her lifelong interest in family dynamics, Ari felt she could do some interesting work.

Jon, who taught the group much more often now, set them one last painting task for the year. They were to do a self-portrait of themselves emphasising family characteristics. They would have three weeks in which to finish and their work must be covered if they were not working on it. He wanted the paintings to be genuinely individual and the criticism, on the last day, pertinent, helpful and specific. A general criticism at the end of any task was the norm, but he wanted to see now how his students had progressed. They set up in the room above the sculpture studio.

Ari liked that room the best of all the studios, and it was the one Jon used most exclusively. It was smaller than some and not as light and reached up a flight of old dusty wooden stairs. She always felt sort of safe there. She had great difficulty though in working out how to approach the subject, as she had no idea what characteristics or traits she had inherited from a parent or grandparents or indeed any ancestor. The only people who knew her circumstances were Marco, Grace and Lem.

Those three friends were worried about her. Her accident with the lino tool had caused her absolutely no problems, but now she was very quiet and looked pale and distracted. At first, Grace asked her if she was missing her Nan but the answer was 'no, not really'. Some evenings they had an extra life drawing class and Ari stopped going to Lyons with everyone before they started. Jon sometimes went and would sit talking to Tom. They only had a half hour so it was usually a rush back. Ari would appear when they were about to start and often Marco or Grace would stay with her. She had eventually told them of her problem with Tom. They had suspected something, though nothing quite so intrusive and ugly. Grace had told Lem and he had offered to 'sort him out', but Ari didn't want to go down that route. She hadn't said anything about Mr Curtis though, she kept that only for herself. Jon and Julius had also noticed the change in her. *Probably some boy,* Julius thought, but Jon was not so sure. It was, but not in the way Julius meant.

When the students had left for the day, Jon would return to the painting studio and uncover their work. Most were well-composed and painted but were boring in content. Grandma's big brown eyes or Dad's penchant for rugby represented the limit of some peoples' imagination. Tom had painted himself against a Tudor background. His stance rather like that in Holbein's portrait of Henry the Eighth. Jon smiled at that. Either he had delusions of grandeur or his family had researched their history. Janet's was just a self-portrait with strangely enlarged eyes. Marco's and Ari's were both very intriguing and would be the most challenging for the students to decipher. He felt that his students ought to be able to give a fair criticism of work by now, but they would have to dig deep for Marco. Even though he didn't understand Arianwen's painting it was extremely beautiful. He decided they would take Tom's work first and lastly Marco followed by Arianwen.

On the Thursday of the penultimate week of term, all ten students gathered in the studio. They were all weary and it was hot. Jon asked Tom to bring his painting out first. He did so with a flourish and set it on the easel. Jon was disappointed. Most students, who offered criticism, just flattered Tom. Such was Tom's position in the group he should have expected this. No one pointed out that in places the perspective was skewed, the painting rather slapdash. Or even that he hadn't really answered the brief. There was no indication of why or any connection with family. Jon asked him the obvious question, "What was the significance of the stance and the belligerent kingly gaze?"

Janet answered that one, with an adoring glance at Tom she said, "Bit obvious that one sir." Did she mean Tom was kingly or had inherited kingly characteristics? Janet couldn't answer and just shrugged.

They struggled on through the mediocre, and the just plain awful. James had painted a parody of Grant Wood's American Gothic, with his grandfather as the man and himself in the woman's place. Jon thought it showed a modicum of intelligence and instigated rather more pertinent criticism than Tom's effort.

And then it was Marco's turn. He placed his painting on the easel and stepped back, standing next to Ari. He had painted himself very near the front of the canvas in minute detail, and he was holding his dog. Far away in the background were two very indistinct figures.

Before he could begin an explanation of his work Tom shouted out from the back, "Hey, you've forgotten to paint any pansies mate." Several people sniggered. Grace who was leaning on a cupboard opposite Ari saw her stiffen. Marco blushed but gamely carried on. He had tried to depict the gulf between himself and his parents he said. He might look vaguely like his mother but had no other characteristics in common with either of them. He had more empathy with his dog. Thus, its inclusion.

Jon asked if anyone had any perspective on this. No one seemed to have an opinion. Ari didn't want to say anything as she knew Mr Curtis would be looking at her when she did. However, her fondness for Marco made her step forward.

"I think I understand what Marco is saying. We are who and what we are and our parents should support us whatever. I know Marco's don't. By putting himself at a distance from them he is also rejecting certain characteristics or ideas of theirs. Like prejudice, ignorance and a closed mind." She turned to Marco. "I'm not being too unkind there am I?" Ari asked him. Marco shook his head, so Ari continued. "Marco loves his dog and the dog loves him, unconditionally. It also has the same colouring." She turned to Marco again and smiled. "Not that I am saying you are remotely related you understand. But you do share other characteristics. A dog is faithful, honest, loving, trustworthy and intelligent. All traits that I for one have seen in Marco. Although I don't necessarily believe Marco knew that was what he was painting. If you see what I mean? But" she continued. "Didn't Mark Twain say, 'The more I learn about people, the more I like my dog'. That sort of fits." She smiled at him again as she sat down.

Marco gave her a hug. "Thanks, Ari," he said. *That was better,* Jon thought. *At least someone had a bit more insight and was generous.* She was a bright girl too, to have reasoned all that out in a short space of time. And he did love to listen to her. Well, he loved her really.

Ari was last. She had painted herself, cross-legged, sitting on the floor but not in the colours one would expect. Her dark hair swirled about her head. Beside her was an open box made of dark wood with ivory decoration, and like Pandora's box, things were flying out. But they were not the troubles of the world, but eyes of all shapes and colours, noses, ears, mouths, feet, hands and legs. A mouth had landed beneath her nose but it was the wrong shape, she had one grey eye and was just picking a brown one to go in the other empty socket. It was sort of Arianwen but very much not. There was a long pause as everyone took in this very disconcerting painting.

She started with her explanation, "I have found this very difficult as I have absolutely no idea of any traits or characteristics I have inherited from my parents." She stopped and looked at Grace, who gave her a nod of encouragement.

"I know nothing of my parents as I was abandoned as a baby."

"Left you in a basket on some nunnery doorstep, did they? Frigid like them, are you?" shouted Tom.

Ari stopped and stood icily still. There was absolute silence in the room which seemed to go on rather too long. Jon was just about to say something when Ari stepped towards Tom, head up and her fists clenched.

"Oh, Christ!" Jon heard Marco say.

Jon stepped forward to stop Ari, but Marco put a hand out.

"Let her be, sir," he said.

Ari walked right up to Tom, pushing Janet out of the way. Tom backed away, he could see by Arianwen's face what was coming, and his little group seemed to melt away to the edges of the room.

"Oh! For fuck's sake Tom Lawrence," she said. "You are an absolute bloody shit. I know exactly why you painted yourself like Henry the fucking Eighth. He was a spiteful bully and so are you. Every time we had Mr Crisp as a model you thought it extremely funny to tell Marco his 'friend' was here. I am sure even your so-called friends are weary of that one by now. You have just insulted him again and now you start on me. You have no fucking idea about my circumstances and I do not want to hear your inane comments. You have been unkind to me for a long time."

Marco looked at Jon, "Don't blame her, sir," he whispered. "This has been building for ages. He has made her life a misery and especially lately."

Ari had forgotten everything but the need to tell Tom how she felt. He was not going to tease or bully her or Marco anymore.

"I know why you do it Tom and the answer as always is no. No amount of hair-pulling, midnight phone calls, rude messages or stupid bloody poems will make me change my mind. If you ever touch me or pull the pins out of my hair again so it all falls down, I will personally remove the last one and stab it through your fucking black heart."

She stopped then and turned to Jon, "I'm sorry, sir, but," her voice trembled. "Enough is enough." She picked up her bag and left.

No one said a word; the silence was heavy. Tom had gone very red and Marco, glancing at him, thought that he might be on the verge of tears.

"Right," Jon said, struggling to make sense of it all. "It's early I know but I think we will leave it there. Would you all go now please? ... Tom, I'd like a word."

Everyone left. He heard them clatter down the stairs talking about what had happened. Janet stayed with Tom hanging on to his arm.

"Off you go Janet," Jon said. She did reluctantly but waited outside the door listening, and very soon wished she hadn't.

Tom was looking very shamefaced.

"Why were you so unpleasant to Marco and Arianwen? I presume what Arianwen said was true Tom?"

Tom took a while to answer and then Jon remembered that at a staff meeting some time ago Ian Cooper had said that Arianwen was very wary of Tom, and they must keep an eye on it.

"Yes sir," mumbled Tom. "And more."

"But why?"

Jon could see Tom struggling to reply.

Eventually, he blurted it out.

"I love her sir and I can't stop thinking about her. I can't help it. I just want to touch her. She is so beautiful, clean and fresh and smells lovely. I ache for her all the time and I can't concentrate properly if she is around. I have asked her and asked her and she won't sleep with me. She'd rather go round with Marco."

Jon took a long moment to consider his reply.

"And why would she prefer to be with Marco, Tom? You know the answer to that, don't you? He is a really nice chap and doesn't give her any hassle. So, you make her life a misery instead. Tom, whatever were you thinking?"

Jon sighed and looked at Tom's flushed and sulky face.

"No one has the right to touch anyone if they say no Tom, and from what she says she has said that often."

Tom put his head in his hands.

"She's so bloody lovely, sir," he mumbled. "I just want her as mine. I ring her up at night sometimes, just to hear her voice."

"Good God! Arianwen must have been frightened Tom. Did you not think of that? And what of Janet?"

"She doesn't come anywhere near. She is just available, a stopgap. Ari is like a peach and smells like one too. Don't you think so sir?"

Jon thought he should stop this conversation now; he had pictures in his head that ought not to be there. The poor girl, he thought. No wonder the spark seemed to have gone from her. And he hadn't seen any of it.

"Tom," he said. "I shall have to speak to Arianwen about this and depending on what she says and what she wants done about it, I may also have to tell Mr Cooper. It is quite serious Tom, there is no getting away from that. However, an apology wouldn't go amiss. But you really need to think long and hard about it. No bunch of flowers and a muttered 'sorry'. That won't do."

"Yes, I know," said Tom. "And thanks, sir."

Poor bugger, Jon thought. Tom was very young and the feelings he had for Arianwen were very intense and had overwhelmed him. He had not known how to, or indeed thought he needed to control his actions, whilst he…

Tom left and Jon went in search of Grace or Marco. He found them both in the common room.

"Any idea where Arianwen is?" They had searched for her themselves they said and she was nowhere in the school.

"Only place I can think of, sir, is down by the lake or the Abbey, she won't have gone home. We were going to go in a minute. She likes both places when she is upset. Quiet or watching the clouds."

"Did you two know about all this?"

"Yes," admitted Grace. "Eventually she told us. But if you talk to her, you will find that is not the half of it."

"And you never thought to tell me or Mr Cooper?"

Marco looked squarely at him.

"Nope. Everyone thinks you are a friend of Tom's. You spend a lot of time talking."

He realised that Marco was right. He had let Arianwen down.

"I'll go and see if I can find her," Jon said.

Marco remembered Mr Curtis calling Ari his darling girl. *Ah well,* he thought. *Que sera, sera.*

Jon gathered up his things and then walked through the town looking for Arianwen. There was no market and it was quite quiet. He crossed the road opposite Lyons and went down the alley beside the Abbey. He went in through a side door and walked around looking in all the small side chapels, but there was no one in any of them. The organist was practising Bach's *Toccata and Fugue* and the soaring notes thundered through the nave as he walked towards the west door. A young woman in a long black cassock stopped him. "You are a tutor from the art school, aren't you?" she said.

Jon nodded.

"Ah, I thought I recognised you. If you are looking for that young girl, she is over there. I have tried to talk to her but she won't speak to me." She pointed in the direction of the font, and Jon saw the flash of Arianwen's red dress.

"Thank you," he said. "I know what the problem is. I'll go and talk to her."

Ari was curled up on a pew. Jon went over and stood beside her. "Arianwen," he said. She turned towards him and he saw that she had been crying. He just wanted to gather her up in his arms and say he would make it all right for her. But of course, he could not.

"I'm really sorry for upsetting your lesson, sir," she said, as he sat down beside her. Her answer was typical of her. *She always considered the other person first,* he thought. She had come out fighting for Marco, to begin with.

The organist started from the beginning again.

"Arianwen," Jon said. "Can we go outside? I need you to talk to me, and I can't hear myself think in here."

She moved and he held out his hand to help her. He felt the brush of her fingers, then they were gone and she was walking towards the door. There were lots of people outside, tourists, families, and schoolchildren, going down towards the lake or sitting on the grass. Jon walked over to a quiet spot under the trees.

"No need to be sorry for anything Arianwen," he said as they sat down, "From what I hear, you were justified in saying what you did. Are you able to tell me what's been going on?"

She sat unmoving beside him for quite some time. Then she straightened up and wiped her eyes with the sleeve of her cheesecloth dress, which made him smile. He watched her and could see she was struggling with whether to tell him or not. Her dear face was streaked with tears and her mouth trembled.

Her hair had come down and she wound it into a rope and put it on the top of her head. With one hand she reached into her pocket and took out four pins.

"*Kanzashi,*" she said holding one out to him. The others she fixed in her hair.

Jon took the pin from her. It was silver and beautifully engraved. He looked questioningly at Ari.

"Japanese Geisha pins," she said. "The ideal weapon?" She took a deep shuddering breath.

"Tom has always been unkind to Marco, and it is so unfair," she carried on, taking the pin from him. "He is so horrid to anyone a little different. That pretty girl with the calliper, in the first year, he always limps when he sees her, and of course, Janet laughs which makes him worse. And he has made my life difficult for a long time." She sighed deeply.

"How did it start, Arianwen, and when?"

"Our very first term, I think. You brought us down here sketching. I was sitting on the bank and watching a family feeding the ducks and you were talking to Tom about different colours in things. You know, leaves are not just green, different colours in shadows, that sort of thing. You said to look at my hair as it was not just dark brown but, in the sunlight, had lots of other colours in it, and you said it was quite beautiful. All the way back to school then, he kept flicking my plait and saying, 'Who's got beautiful hair then?'"

She stopped and for the first time, Jon could really remember looked straight at him.

"It was never your fault, sir. Never think that," she said. "And it has just gone on from there. Not so much at first, but it slowly got more insistent. He was always pulling my hair, taking the pins out or coming up behind me and putting his arms around my waist and just, well, touching me, and I didn't want him to and I told him so. I did tell my Nan when it first started but she said he was just a silly boy and it would stop if I ignored it. But it didn't, and lately, it has got more troubling. He has written some very rude remarks on my drawings, so I have had to throw them away and he constantly asks me to sleep with him."

She stopped for a moment and he could see her considering something. Finally, she said, "Actually, sir, and if you don't mind me saying it, he never says that, it's always, "I want to fuck you." There is no thought for me in there at all. Somehow, he has got to know that my Nan has moved out. He phones me at night or puts notes through the door, which worries me and I have to make sure the doors are locked."

She sighed but carried on. "He wrote me an erotic poem, so he said. I always think 'erotic' has a bit of beauty about it, like a fading or dying rose. But this wasn't erotic; it was pornographic and very ugly. That's why I went to the cinema that time. He had kept on all morning about it. I'm sorry we disappointed you, sir, but I had just had enough. I needed to get away from it all for a while, leave it all behind, and, well James wouldn't let me go on my own. He is fine when Tom is not around, as is Stuart."

"Arianwen," Jon said. "Please don't apologise for that. I just wish I had known."

She continued after a moment and wiped her eyes again. "Last week, I was coming back from lunch and he was outside school, leaning on the wall. He shouted across the road. 'Arianwen Morgan, I want to fuck you.' I was mortified. The whole bus queue turned and looked at me. It has all got a bit much."

She stopped. She had noticed a family down the field. They were there most Thursdays and she had drawn them often. She reached for her sketchbook and wrote some notes in it. Then put it away in her bag. He thought *I would do that. It was what Sarah had complained about. Ideas had to be recorded whatever else was going on.*

"Sorry, sir, that was a bit rude of me," she said. "But I just had to catch it."

She turned and looked at him.

"Do you know I am forever saying sorry to you," she said. She gave a shuddering sigh. "Do you remember when I fainted?"

How could he not, he thought.

"Well," she continued. "Tom came up to me afterwards. I think everyone assumed he was just being nice and asking how I was. What he actually said was 'If I had seen you in a faint, I'd have had you then and there.' There are lots of other things but that was typical, and it has become very unpleasant and upsetting."

"He hasn't tried to do anything more serious, has he Arianwen?" Jon said, praying she would say no.

"No sir, but once or twice lately he has tried to touch me where he should not." She stopped and gave a great sob. "There I've said it all." And she bent her head and cried.

Jon knew that what he was hearing was true and raged within himself that he had not known and had not been able to help her, his darling girl. He did so want to comfort her.

"Did you never feel you could tell me or Mr Cooper, Arianwen?"

"Mr Cooper might have wanted to take it further and I couldn't have spoiled Tom's prospects. I thought he would just get bored eventually."

She answered the rest as the others had. He was Tom's friend. "He called you Jon, unlike the rest of us, and you never spoke to any of us about books and stuff. Tom was spot on with his King Henry painting I thought. All commanding and spiteful when crossed and wanting to be the important one. It might surprise you to know that both Marco and I had had a good stab at *Finnegan's Wake* long before you mentioned it to Tom. Marco had to tell me what it was about, some dream or other. He thought it was brilliant. He is very intelligent, Marco. I didn't like it much and thought the middle was superfluous. It was the same at both ends."

He laughed at that.

"And," she said. "We've read *Lady Chatterley*. Though I'm not sure Marco liked it or saw the point really."

She gave him a sidelong glance and he saw mischief in her eyes once again. He had missed out on a lot with his students. Then he had to ask her, "What do you want to do about it all?"

"Nothing at present, sir. I have told Tom how I feel so hopefully he will stop. If not, I absolutely promise I will tell you."

She was twisting her bracelet on her arm.

"That is very beautiful Arianwen," Jon said.

She smiled. "Yes," she said. "I love it. It was given to me by my solicitor's secretary as a 'sorry'. She was supposed to collect me from the school train at the end of every term and take me across London to Waterloo and put me on the train to Bournemouth." Ari laughed. "But she was the most dreadful timekeeper and I often sat on that platform for at least an hour. The porters were kind though and brought me apples and sandwiches and things." Jon could see she was reliving all that.

"Once," Ari continued. "She forgot about me completely and Toby Fearnley, my solicitor's nephew came. He was doing summer work at their office and was a law student. He came in his sports car and drove me all the way to Bournemouth. I was in love by the end. But I have never seen him again." She sighed. "Happy days."

Jon glanced at his watch. It was gone six and they had been there for nearly two hours, though he could have sat with her forever. There were still lots of people around as it promised to be a warm evening, but most of the families had gone.

"Well," she said standing up. "I'd better get on home. Grace and Lem will be wondering about me."

"Do they live near?"

"Next door, down near the station."

"I'm going to get my train so I'll walk with you if I may?"

"Of course," she said and smiled to herself.

As they walked through the town, he asked her about her plans for the holidays. She said she was going to the family hotel in Boscombe and hoped to finish her dissertation whilst there.

She asked him what he might be doing. He was going to his parents' summer house in France. Just family, his parents and his sister Jenny with her husband and children. He told her how lovely it was and how the garden was wild and covered in flowers. He went there every year so that he could do some of his own work.

"When I was little," she said wistfully. "And we lived in Wales, there was a field behind our house that sounds like that. Fred taught me the names of all the flowers, the trees and the birds. We would go and lie in amongst the buttercups and the long grass and watch the passing clouds. I loved that, still do. I find it very soothing."

They came to the turning into her road, "Bye then sir," she said. "And thank you for listening to me. I feel a lot better now."

"Can I ask you one more question, Arianwen?"

She nodded.

"Where did you learn to swear like that?"

"Ah! Well sorry. I'm afraid I do that when I am angry. Probably a reaction to being at a girl's boarding school. You know, all quiet, pure and gentle. They eliminated my Welsh accent, but my friend Christina taught me lots of swear words. And you haven't heard the half of it," she laughed, turned and ran indoors.

No, he thought. *When you get upset your lovely lilting accent becomes more pronounced and your eyes go a dark stormy grey.*

He had a lot to think about that evening, and in the end, he rang Julius and told him all. Julius thought Jon had dealt with it well and agreed that Tom had overstepped the mark and really ought to have realised it. But he might just learn a good lesson now. Jon did however inform Ian Cooper as Tom's behaviour had been rather excessive. They put a note in his file which they agreed, would be removed after six months if there were no further incidents.

Julius decided to keep an eye on both Tom and Jon. Arianwen, bless her heart had no idea what she did to men, and he knew Jon was struggling with his feelings for her. However much he denied it to himself.

Arianwen went indoors. She was pleased with herself even though it had been a difficult day and she was glad really that it was now all out in the open. Nan had always said, "Be brave Ari, be brave." And she had been. She had also managed a near-normal conversation with sir, even though his blue eyes and the way his dark hair fell over his forehead had distracted her now and then. She thought of Christina and Belinda. They would tell her to make the absolute best of herself and 'knock 'em dead' when she went to school tomorrow. 'Battle dress' they called it. She made herself some cheese on toast and went upstairs to sort out her clothes for the morning. As she was doing this there was a knock on the backdoor, and Grace called her. She had just come to see if Ari was all right she said but could see that she looked much better.

"Did Mr Curtis find you?" asked Grace. "He was very concerned about you."

"He did and we had quite a good talk about everything."

"Good," said Grace. "What are you doing now? Do you want to come for a drink?"

"Not now if you don't mind. I'm just getting things ready for tomorrow, then a nice bath and bed, I think. It's been a bit of a day."

"You can say that again. Night then Ari and remember Lem and I are just next door." She gave Ari a hug and went home.

The next morning, Ari was up early. She felt quite apprehensive about the day but was determined to face anything full-on. She dressed slowly. Her best pale-cream lace and satin bra and knickers. On top one of her linen shifts, dark green this time. Her hair she put in a ponytail on top of her head, with a piece of dark-green linen tied at the top. Tiny copper earrings and a copper bracelet completed it all. She went to the tobacconist first and bought some Passing Clouds, then to the deli for something for lunch. She came through the school doors at a quarter to ten. Tom was waiting at the bottom of the stairs. It was unusually quiet. There seemed to be no one else about. Truth was that the row between them was now common knowledge and having seen Tom waiting in the hall for the last half hour, everyone was keeping out of the way. Only Julius stood far back on the top landing and watched.

Arianwen came in and stopped when she saw Tom and backed towards the door. But she seemed to gather herself up and walked over to him.

"Arianwen I am so very sorry," he said. "I was out of order."

He put out his hand to touch her but Ari stepped away.

"Thank you, Tom," she said. "I accept your apology. My Nan used to say that sorry means 'I won't do it again'. So, I hope you mean it?"

Tom stood looking at her. He was at a loss for words.

"Tom," Ari sighed. "I think you and I should have a talk to resolve all this, and here is not the right place. Too public." She looked about her.

"Where is everyone?"

Tom shrugged.

"How about we go out for supper tomorrow?" She was not going to invite him to her house, ever. "We can sort things out then. Can you do that?"

She saw Tom's face brighten.

"It is not a date, Tom, please never expect that."

Tom had in fact been going out with Janet, just to the pub, but he could put that off easily.

"Yes," he said. "Good idea."

"Meet you by the town hall then, about half six tomorrow. I'll book somewhere."

And she went on her way. Tom watched her go; she was so gorgeous. Lust was still in his heart, but he felt grief also, knowing he had no chance with her ever now. He looked forward with a modicum of uncertainty to their meeting tomorrow.

Julius had heard most of the conversation and had seen just a little of their meeting through the bannisters. She was some brave and generous girl, he thought. He decided not to tell Jon about the meeting. Jon's feelings were in turmoil, he knew, as regards to Arianwen. So least said was Julius' motto. But Julius was a great people watcher, and he knew how the land really lay.

The next day, being Saturday, Arianwen cleaned the house, changed the bed and went up to the market for fruit and vegetables. She met Marco for a coffee and told him about the coming evening. Marco made a booking for her at his uncle's restaurant near the clock tower.

"Vittorio will be there," he said. "So have no fears."

The evening was warm and Tom was waiting when Ari crossed the road towards him.

She was wearing a long dress of some deep orange floaty material, with a dark brown shawl over her arm. No jewellery except for her little silver ring and the silver bracelet Miss Horwood had given her. Regret flooded through him. He held out his arm but she would not take it.

It was early so the restaurant was only half-full.

Vittorio greeted them, "Ari, Bella *ragazza*? Come sit down."

"Who is that?" said Tom when they were seated.

"Marco's cousin."

Vittorio came to take their order, but as Tom was unfamiliar with Italian food, she ordered her favourite carbonara for them both. Plus, a bottle of red wine, and some bread and olives to start.

Tom seemed to enjoy his pasta and then had some tiramisu.

Vittorio came to clear the plates and brought some dark bitter coffee.

"I enjoyed that," Tom said. "What did you say it was?"

"Carbonara," she said and smiled.

He leaned across the table and tried to take her hand. She moved them quickly into her lap.

"I love you," he said.

"No, you don't Tom. What you feel is something else."

"But I do Ari, I do," he repeated, his voice rising.

Vittorio, at the other end of the restaurant, looked up in concern.

Ari shook her head at him and he smiled. He was on watch.

"Tom," Ari said. "If you loved me, you would never have done all those mean, spiteful things. You didn't think of me at all, did you? And the misery you caused me? If you love someone you think of them first. So no, you don't love me." She paused and looked at his sulky face.

"We can't choose who we fall in love with Tom, or who will love us. Why one person and not another? Or what starts it in the first place, it just sort of happens doesn't it? Something physical often, a glance, the way their hair grows, who knows? If we could control these things, we might be happier. But if they come right, well that's wonderful."

She took a deep breath and regarded Tom. He said nothing just looked at her. With a big sigh, she went on.

"Look Tom," she said. "I do understand honestly. I have loved someone for some time now. He doesn't know and I could never tell him. I would never hurt or embarrass him for a start. For all I know he may be happy with whoever he has, and he has never ever made a move in my direction. But when I see him, it brightens my day and seeing him makes my knees go weak." She stopped for a moment; Tom was listening intently. "So, we are in the same boat you and I aren't we really? Only difference is I keep it to myself just because I love him."

Her eyes had filled with tears, but she wiped them away with a napkin.

"Sadly, for both of us we have settled on the wrong person."

He saw she was twirling the ring on her left little finger.

"You always wear that," he said. "Why? Is it special?"

She looked him straight in the eye.

"Yes, it is Tom. I was given it by the first man I ever slept with. He took my virginity in such a kind, gentle and caring way and it was glorious and I loved him. I will never settle for less and never sleep with someone I do not love." She didn't say 'and neither should you,' but he knew that was what she meant.

"Tom," she continued. "You haven't said much."

"I was just thinking about my dad. He always told me to take what I wanted, when I wanted it, and especially with girls. 'Might be gone if you hesitate, son,' he used to say. And I never had any problem until I met you. I couldn't understand what I was doing wrong and why you kept saying no. So, it all sort of escalated. I'm truly sorry Ari."

"And I'm sorry that I said all those things and embarrassed you in front of Mr Curtis and everyone," she said. "Would you like another coffee?"

She took out her cigarettes and offered him one. He looked askance at the pink paper.

"Bit girly them," he said and got out his Marlboro.

She laughed. He thought he was so macho. She waved to Vittorio and few moments later he brought the coffee.

"Before we go Tom, can you tell me why you are so unkind to some people? Marco for one and that girl in the first year? They have never been unkind to you, have they? You could be such a nice person if you tried. It isn't that hard. My Nan always said, 'if you can't say something nice, don't say anything at all.'"

He couldn't answer but he looked at her sitting opposite him, and he suddenly realised that the good, kind, beautiful girls, the ones he really wanted, wouldn't come anywhere near him if he continued as he was. He had a great deal to think about.

Arianwen paid for it all. She had asked him so that was only fair. And just before they left, they agreed to draw a line under everything.

"I'll never be your lover Tom," she said. "But we could be friends?"

He nodded. He was rather overwhelmed by her generosity. Not just for the supper but for her ease of forgiveness. And she had touched a nerve in him when she said he had made her very miserable and had been unkind to others.

He realised he had been very wrong and vowed to do better.

Tom headed straight for the staffroom on Monday morning and asked for Jon. He told him all that had happened over the weekend and practically all Arianwen had said. Everything was now fine. Jon was rather perturbed that Ari had put herself in the way of more hassle from Tom and told her so when he saw her.

"Oh, it was fine sir... Vittorio, Marco's cousin is a waiter there. He carries a stiletto in his sock." She rolled her eyes.

Jon looked shaken.

Arianwen laughed. "Only joking. And sir, thank you again for listening to all that."

He could have kissed her.

He asked her then if she felt like continuing with discussing her painting, as he had to assess it. He would understand if she didn't want to. She looked rather dubious but said yes. Thus, the next afternoon, the last session with Mr Curtis that term, she did.

She started by apologising to them all for her previous behaviour and said that she and Tom had had a good talk about it all and had agreed not to mention it anymore. And that she hoped everyone else would abide by that also. And if after discussing her painting, anyone wanted to ask her a question about her circumstances she would try to answer.

Then she explained why she had painted herself so strangely. She said that she had been trying to show that she had no point of reference as to what or where her family characteristics were, having been abandoned as a baby. She told them how that had come about and about Sal and Olive taking her in.

"I love them dearly and they me," she said. "But they are not mine. Sal met my mother just the once, for about five minutes, and she told me she had dark hair. That is all I know."

She told them also about the search for her mother and how she had popped up demanding she be sent to boarding school when she was eight. Nell put her hand up. "Why did, um, er, Sal let you go?"

"They have no legal right over me, Nell. Apparently, they did try to adopt me but my mother could not be found to sign me away." Jon noticed her falter when she said, 'sign me away', but she continued. "Hers is the only name on my birth certificate, so what she says goes," she paused for a moment. "I have never met her and never once heard a father mentioned. My mother just surfaced the once as I said. We have never had any other contact with her. Everything to do with me is done through a solicitor."

Then James asked her something that was nearly her undoing.

"What would you wish for Ari, money or family?"

"I am very fortunate James, as I have money. Where or who it comes from I don't know. I would dearly like to meet my father. Sal and Olive have been wonderful to me but I am not theirs. I would just like to know where I come from. Most of all I want a family of my own. You know, with children that look like me, or their father, of course."

Grace could see she was getting upset. She glanced at Jon and shook her head slightly. He took the hint.

"I think we will stop there. Just to remind you all, Arianwen has been quite open about her circumstances. Please don't gossip about them. Have a good summer everyone and see you all in September."

They all jostled down the stairs with shouts of 'Bye sir, have a good holiday'. In a moment he was alone. He missed her already. He had had no idea that her life had been so fractured and remembered Poll telling Sarah she couldn't discuss Ari's parentage. He understood a little now why she was so interested in families.

Ari had a lovely summer. The weather was great and she was able to help Mam rather more than previously. Sal missed Olive, but Olive was going to come for a week before Ari went back. When they were all together, as even Roger managed to get away from work, they had a big barbeque on the beach one evening. The deck chair boys ran past stacking the chairs in great piles around the lampposts. Ari looked at the pink clouds drifting across the sky and thought of Jay. She tried desperately not to think of Mr Curtis.

Jon meanwhile was having not too good a time of it in France. The weather was hot and the house and grounds were great, but his father was having constant headaches and spent many hours lying on his bed with the shutters closed. Added to that his brother had turned up unexpectedly with a girl in tow. His mother was not best pleased. She was a nice girl but noisy. She liked the radio on constantly and she shrieked when she went in the pool, if she saw an insect or often for other reasons no one could fathom.

For all that, Jon did some good work and he was pleased. One afternoon he was sitting near his mother, in the shade. His father was asleep and, James and his girlfriend had gone into town. It was warm, and quiet and the air was drowsy with the scent of flowers and the ripening peaches that grew on the trees in the garden. Afterwards, he did not know if he had been dozing, but he had the most vivid picture of himself stroking Arianwen's bottom. He had to go down to the end of the garden to recover himself. Nine or ten more months, he thought, and we will be going our separate ways. This torment would end, and then he felt the most terrible sadness that he might never see her again.

September came and everyone had returned ready for their final year.

Ari was glad to be back in her little house and to see Marco, Grace and Lem. Nothing much had changed, though Marco quietly told her that he had a boyfriend called Philippe, who was an architect, and older than him. Ari was so pleased for him.

There was a new intake of students and a meeting in the library for everyone. Julius and Jon were in their usual place, leaning on the bookcases.

Arianwen came in arm in arm with Marco. They were so engrossed in whatever they were talking about that they did not notice Jon or Julius. Jon's heart lurched. She was so bloody lovely. Her hair was still long and in one loose plait down her back, but now she had a fringe down to her eyes. Those glorious grey eyes were edged in black, which made them more luminous than ever. She reminded him of an Egyptian princess. She and Marco joined the rest of their group and there was much kissing and back-slapping. He noticed her reach up and kiss Tom on the cheek. Everything was all right there then. But Julius was watching also and saw that Janet, although she had greeted Ari with a smile, gave her the most baleful look when she turned her back.

The students 'set to' finish their dissertations or portfolios. Ari had gone through her portfolio with both Mr Cooper and Jon and they had identified a few gaps, mostly still-life drawings, which she was now in the process of rectifying. Mr Cooper had read Ari's dissertation and apart from a few corrections, it was ready to be typed up. Ari did those then took it down the road to the lady who would type it and bind it for her.

That autumn was wet and cold and Ari bought the largest size man's jumper she could get from Marks. This she wore with a very short skirt, black tights and her newest discovery, Dr Marten boots. Quite soon several of the other girls in her year and younger were doing the same.

One evening after a long-life drawing class, where the room was very warm, the model kept falling asleep and the students took to coughing to wake her, Ari met Jon going out of the street door. "You going home?" he asked. She nodded.

"Mind if I walk down with you?" After that Jon had to try very hard not to engineer a meeting at the door. If he could, he would have walked her home every day. And Ari found that if she could anticipate being with him, she could manage things and hold a reasonable conversation. It was the unprepared for questions and looks that threw her.

The second Saturday in November was Roger's birthday. Olive had invited Ari for the weekend. They were going to the ballet in the evening and then out to supper with friends. A nice quiet Sunday morning and then Ari would catch the train home.

That same weekend Jon was going to an informal reunion of some friends from the RCA. He hadn't been to the last one so was looking forward to catching up on how people were doing. Richard was going and bringing his partner, Rachel.

Jon caught the early train. He planned a day in London before going along to Ed's flat near the Imperial War Museum. They always met up there as it was large and quite central for everyone.

The train was not at all full. As they stopped at the station near Ari's house, he saw her standing on the platform. God, she looked wonderful. Her hair was up in a plaited knot and she wore a dark green tweed jacket, with a dark green knitted scarf, a long, soft, black wool skirt and Chelsea boots, and she had a brown leather holdall with her. She looked around but didn't see him and Jon saw Marco run along the platform. They got into the train a carriage ahead of him but in a moment came through the doors and sat together about five seats in front. They hadn't noticed him and Jon spent the whole journey just watching the back of his 'darling girl's' head. He hung back as they left the train. Marco went off to the underground; he was going to meet Philippe and Ari went to the taxi rank. She was going to the National Portrait Gallery before she went to Roger and Olive's home.

Jon, used to London, walked to 'Laurence Corner' and had a good look around. He bought an ex-navy greatcoat. Ideal for the winter he thought if it was going to be anything like the last one. He walked to Hamleys and bought some Christmas presents for his two nephews. He would post them to Ireland the following week. He then went to the National Gallery and putting all his packages in the cloakroom, spent a few hours there. He walked around to Leicester Square, had something to eat, bought a bottle of Scotch for Ed and gin for his wife Susie, and then caught a bus to Kennington.

The evening at Ed's was good. Nine people came and they did what they had always done. They had a drink, talked, had another drink, had supper, talked, drank some more, and talked. Drank even more and then found somewhere to sleep.

Alice was there, a girl he had gone out with for several months in his first year at the RCA. He remembered sleeping with her under a grand piano at some party.

She came across to talk to him, he was still as beddable as ever, she thought. She hadn't seen him for a while as he hadn't been here last time and she hadn't been invited to the Lake District last Christmas. She had been heartbroken when he had moved on to Viola and she knew she had never really got over him.

"You're looking good Jon," she said.

"Thanks,' he replied bending to kiss her cheek. "And how are you doing Alice?"

She was rather put out that he hadn't said she looked good because she knew she did.

But she told him she lived in Cornwall now with her partner Nathan and they had a smallholding with her pottery at the side. He hadn't come with her as someone had to be there to watch the goats and chickens. They worked hard and did a lot of surfing.

She was tanned and toned as one would say, her hair still bleached by the sun, but Jon hadn't really noticed.

"On your own Jon?" she continued. Last time she had seen him he had been with Sarah.

"Yes," he answered.

"No Sarah?"

"No," Jon said. "She is long gone."

"Mutual?"

"Yes," he said. "We didn't want the same things."

"I can keep you company tonight if you like?" Alice said. She would give anything for another night with him. Nathan would never know. Rule was if you had a girl with you, you got a bed. Though there were only three spare. Otherwise, you just slept wherever you could.

"Sorry Alice," he said and smiled at her. "But my heart is rather elsewhere at the moment."

She sighed but wished him all the best and went to try her luck with Will. She wasn't going to let him see how disappointed she was. Will accepted her offer straight away.

Rachel who was sitting next to Jon turned to him, she had heard what he had said. She liked Jon and knew him well as he was a good friend to Richard.

"Someone special Jon?" she asked.

"Yes," he sighed. "Very special, but I can't tell her."

"Why?"

"She is my student." He wished he hadn't said that then. Too much wine.

But Rachel just smiled at him.

"What year?" she asked.

"Last," he said.

"Hmm," she said. "So, you know her quite well then. Not long to go now, Jon. Easy to keep under wraps for a short time. Just ask her out. She can only say yes or no."

He spent an uncomfortable night in an old shabby armchair and he went to find his new coat after a while as he was cold. But most of the night he was thinking of Arianwen leaving and Rachel saying, 'not long to go now'. He woke up with a headache.

The next morning, they all had an enormous breakfast together and with promises to keep in touch and see you next year they set off to their own parts of the country.

Roger and Olive were standing on the platform saying goodbye to Ari when Jon walked past and got on the train. It was the smell of a Gauloises that made Ari raise her head but she didn't see him amongst the throng.

Jon found a seat in the corner by the door. He watched the people on the other platform for a while then closed his eyes. He still had a bit of a headache, and Rachel's words 'not long to go now' kept intruding into his thoughts. He heard the guard blow his whistle. With more goodbye kisses from Nan, Ari hopped onto the train. She was looking for Marco as he was supposed to catch it with her. Probably, she thought, he was staying longer with Philippe. She struggled through the door to find a seat and the train gave a big lurch, which made her bang her elbow on the door frame.

"Oh! Aww," she said. "Bugger!"

Jon glanced up, he had recognised her voice and was surprised to see her standing beside him.

Ari too was quite startled and felt herself blush.

Oh! God, Jon thought. *She looked so good, her face all rosy pink.*

"Sorry, sir," she managed to say. "Me swearing again, but I didn't half give my elbow a crack on that door... I like your coat." She continued. *Stupid thing to say,* she then thought. *But it was nice.*

He laughed. "Laurence Corner," he said. indicating the seat next to him. He took her bag and put it with his on the rack above. She sat down and he immediately smelled that soft and subtle perfume.

"I have a coat from there," Ari said. "Brilliant place, isn't it? I went in the summer with Marco. He was very taken with the sailor's trousers but I told him I thought the art school and the town weren't quite ready for that yet." Jon had to suppress a smile; he could just see her saying that to Marco.

"I just love all the metal tins and cups and things," she continued. "And all the Swedish stuff. I could spend hours there."

Jon sighed.

"Are you all right, sir?" Ari said.

"Yes," he smiled. "Bit of a headache that's all. I had too much to drink last night, I expect."

He told her that he had been to the National Gallery in the morning and to visit friends later on.

"I was just around the corner," she said. "At the Portrait Gallery."

Then she told him about the ballet '*The Nutcracker* and how lovely it had been. Then about going out to supper for Roger's birthday. "I don't like going out with their friends much," she said. "They are all my Nan's age and someone always brings a grandson, a younger brother or nephew for me. I mean as if! And someone will always ask what school I went to and when I say St Ursula's you can see the pound signs in their eyes. The supper was lovely but I can't stand talking to some spotty boy about cars or cricket. Mention art and they go pale." She stopped.

"Sorry, sir," she said. "I didn't mean to gabble on like that."

He smiled to himself. She had spoken to him for some time and had looked at him twice. Improvement.

He watched her on the platform when she got off the train and she waved. An old lady sitting opposite looked at him, smiled and raised her eyebrows.

"You're a lucky one," she said and went back to her crossword. Jon couldn't work out what she meant.

At the beginning of December, the weather turned very cold. Not as cold as the previous winter which had been dire, but a heavy frost most mornings and a raw and biting wind.

On the Friday of the second week, Julius was unwell. He rang Jon in the evening to ask if he could take his Saturday extra mural class. "They are mostly ladies, Jon, all retired, I think. It will be their last class before Christmas and they look forward to it. Don't expect to do much work. Last year it was sherry and mince pies from the word go. Tell them I'm sorry and to have a good Christmas, will you?"

"Hang on," said Jon laughing. "I haven't said yes yet."

"Give you practice old son, for when you are ancient like me."

"Oh! all right then," Jon said. "But you owe me one."

The morning was just as Julius had said it would be. Various ladies emptied large bags containing bottles of sherry, glasses, serviettes, Christmas cake and mince pies. It was warm in the studio and they all, including the model in his dressing gown, sat around gossiping and eating. No work was done at all. There was a large carrier bag full of presents for 'Dear Mr Winter'. Jon smiled at that. Julius had not lost his touch. He promised the ladies he would take them when he could. When everyone had gone, he decided that as he had nothing better to do, and there was no one to get home for, he would walk to Julius' and deliver the presents. Julius lived in a little village about a half hour's walk away, so Jon set off. Being a Saturday, he knew Poll would be home also and might feed him.

Poll opened the door to him. "Thank goodness you've come," she said. "He has a sniffly nose but you would think it was the plague. Have you eaten?" she added taking Jon's coat. He said no. Within moments he was in their warm kitchen with a bowl of soup and some big chunks of bread in front of him. Julius was sitting by the Aga.

"Went the day well?" he croaked.

Jon described the morning and gave Julius the bag of presents.

Polly returned to get something from a cupboard.

"How is Arianwen?" she asked.

"Better than she was I think," said Jon.

She went back into the other room.

"She's decorating the tree," Julius said.

"So, what's new then Jon? How's our little girl after all that upset?"

Jon had long ago stopped responding to 'our little girl'.

"I haven't spoken to her much this term," he said. "Ian says her dissertation is the best he has ever read." He didn't mention walking to the station with her.

"That's not what I meant Jon. You still ignoring your feelings for her?"

"Julius, stop it, please. I have no feelings for her. Christ! I am her tutor and nearly ten years older than her."

"Oh, come on, those are just excuses. Why I'm nearly fourteen years older than the new Mrs Winter."

Jon said nothing just looked at his feet. What could he say? Yes, I love her and want her and think of her constantly. What good would that do?

Julius went on, he was going to tell Jon this whether he liked it or not.

"Well, you know me, and you know I like to watch people, and I have watched you both. You always look for her directly when you enter a room. She on the other hand will watch the door and when you come in, look away. She constantly checks where you are and if you are getting near. She always used to sit on a donkey to draw. Now it is always an easel, so she can move away easily if she needs to. You can see her prepare herself to speak to you. Then she will close her eyes when you move away as if to settle herself. She loves you Jon but she won't let you see it." He stopped and got up.

"Poll," he called. "Come and tell Jon what you told me about Arianwen."

Poll came in from the other room.

"Are you sure Julius?" she said laying a box of candles on the table.

"He needs to be told Poll," Julius said.

Poll looked hesitantly at Jon and took a deep breath. She sat down beside him on the sofa.

"Well Jon," she said. "You know I'm very fond of Arianwen, she spent a lot of time with me when she was at school. I have always met up with her for the odd coffee but more so lately since her Nan got married. Knowing her as I do, I would say something is making her very unhappy."

She paused but she knew she had Jon's attention. "I thought perhaps it was being on her own or that nasty business with that boy last term. But she said no when I asked, but I did worry about her. So, I took her out to tea again last week. She seemed fine, full of her dissertation and her painting, as beautiful and fragrant as she ever is, but just not the Arianwen I have known for nearly twelve years. I asked her outright what was troubling her. She tried to pass it off, lots of work, worry about the exams… But I know her so well, Jon, I knew that wasn't it, so I just kept asking." She paused, took a deep breath and looked at Julius.

"Go on Poll," he said, so she continued. "She realised I wasn't going to let it go so she told me. Bless her she just sort of crumpled."

Poll stopped again. There were tears in her eyes.

"It's so sad Jon. I can hardly say it." Poll paused again and Julius put his arm around her. Jon was very apprehensive as to what she might say next. Was Arianwen ill? Had Tom upset her again or hurt her or worse? Poll could see Jon thinking of all and any scenarios.

She took another deep breath and wiped her eyes.

"Ari studied *Jane Eyre* for her English literature exam and she just loved it. Drew and painted bits of it all the time and she knew passages off by heart. She said to me, 'Do you remember when Mr Rochester tells Jane he has 'a string somewhere under his left ribs, tightly and inextricably tied and knotted to one on her'? Well, I have one of those Mrs Winter,' she said. 'I've had it a long time and it doesn't fray or stretch or go away.'" Poll wiped her eyes again. "Then she touched her heart 'It's here, constantly with me but I am well able to manage it now unless I am caught off guard.' She looked so very sad Jon."

Julius got up. "I think we all need a drink," he said and went to pour three large brandies.

Poll continued, "I said is it a fellow student Ari and can you not tell him? And she said it wasn't and she couldn't because he might be appalled and embarrassed, and she thought he might have someone special of his own. Then, bless her, she said 'Please don't worry Mrs Winter. I would rather have it as it is now than not at all.' She looked so despairing that I leant across the table and gave her a hug. I shouldn't have as she cried then, well sobbed really, and I had to take her outside, for quite a while. She just needed someone's arms around her for comfort. Then we sat down again and she wiped her eyes on her sleeve, as she has always done, gave me a watery smile and said 'Sorry.' And then I just knew. Call it women's intuition or whatever, but I just knew who it was." She stopped then and looked Jon directly in the eye. "It's you, Jon."

Poll sighed, "I have gone over and over all the conversations I have had with her lately and she will talk about everyone and everything else but never ever mentions you. Or if I do, answers with a yes or a no, and will look away. I have thought about it and thought about it and I know I'm right."

Jon sat quietly for a while and Julius and Poll said not a word.

Jon thought about their walks down to the station. Julius was right, she talked to him but hardly ever looked at him directly. Or if she did, she was gone in a flash so he could not read her face. And he remembered what Tom had said about her being in love with someone for ages. Not him surely? Never him?

He got up to leave and Poll gave him a hug. Julius came to the door with him.

"Don't leave it too long Jon," Julius said. "You might just regret it."

He left them then and began the walk back to town. One of the morning ladies had said that the lake had frozen, so he decided to go back to town by way of the park and see. The park looked lovely in the fading light and there were still lots of people around. There had been a heavy frost overnight and it still clung to the trees and the grass. The boating lake had frozen but not all of the lake itself and the island in the middle with its weeping willows looked white and forlorn. He took some photographs of it. It might make a good painting. But Jon wasn't really interested. He was thinking about what Julius and Poll had said. Julius, he knew was usually right about these things and if he was honest with himself, he did love and want Arianwen. But what of her? Was Poll right? He walked round and round the lake trying to decide what to do until it was dark and most people had gone. He was so cold his head felt disconnected from his body and he was shivering. He would go home and mull on it over the weekend.

He walked up the path from the lake, past the pub which looked warm and inviting, past the trees where he had talked to Ari after the Tom argument and up the alley into town. As he came out onto the street, he saw her across the road by the clock tower. She was saying goodbye to Marco and another man who was holding Marco's arm. They walked off down the hill, and Arianwen turned back towards the market. She was wearing a big coat of a dull green, much like an army great coat, he thought. Her 'Laurence Corner' coat? On her head she had a Fair Isle tam pulled right down to her eyes, and a matching scarf was wound around her neck. As she walked up through the market several stallholders called greetings to her. She stopped and bought some bread and the man came out and kissed her cheek. She walked by the picture framer's stall and he came out too and gave her a hug. Jon smiled to himself when he remembered her cutting the framing and swearing. She stopped at the 'Vintage' clothes stall and the lady there handed her a small parcel.

The town looked splendid. There was an enormous Christmas tree, covered in white lights, and with a great shining star on top, near the town hall and all the trees that lined the street had more white lights wound in their branches. Every market stall was also decorated with coloured lights or lanterns. The smell of roasting chestnuts, tangerines and cinnamon filled the air. Ari stopped to listen to the Salvation Army singing *God rest ye merry Gentlemen* and to watch the ladies who were banging and twirling their tambourines. Jon was just behind her and was about to say hello when a young man who looked very much like Marco came up and swung her off her feet. 'Bella ragazza,' he said. It was Vittorio, on his way to work. He kissed Ari on both cheeks, put her down and went on his way. Ari laughing turned and saw Jon.

"Hello Arianwen," he said. "One of your admirers?"

"No, sir, just Vittorio, Marco's cousin. He always swings me around like that. No idea why."

Then she said, "Are you all right, sir, you look half-frozen? Are you off home now?"

"Yes," he said. "I'll walk down with you if you're going that way. Give me your bag, it looks heavy."

She handed it to him, "Only some tea cakes, bread and stuff," she said.

When they got to the end of her road they stopped and he handed her the bag. He wanted to say something but for the life of him couldn't think what.

Arianwen heard Nan say, 'Be brave Ari, be brave.'

"Would you like to come in for a cup of tea, sir?" she asked. "Thaw you out a bit before you get your train?"

He hesitated only a moment.

The house was beautifully warm and smelled subtly of Arianwen. She took his coat and gave him a pair of fisherman's socks from a large, black lacquered, Chinese cabinet beside the door. "My Nan knits them; your feet will soon warm up."

She sat on the stairs to take her boots off, and when she removed her hat, her hair was unplaited and fell over her shoulders. She took a piece of string from a bowl on top of the cabinet and tied it back, then took him through to the living room. It was beautiful. A log burner was built into the fireplace on the party wall and two large green velvet sofas were at right angles to it. A large flokati rug filled the space between with a beautiful wooden trunk on top. Arianwen threw a couple of logs from a wicker basket onto the fire. "Sit down," she said. "And get warm. I'll just go and make the tea."

But Jon couldn't stop looking. There was a large bookcase on the far wall stacked with books. All sorts, art books, novels, poetry, travel, history, and biographies. He saw *Finnegan's Wake*, *Lady Chatterley* and a leather-bound copy of *Jane Eyre*, and *Sylvia Plath's Colossus*. To the side were all her numbered sketchbooks, a big bottle of shards of sea glass and a photograph of a dark-haired little girl with two fair ladies, standing on the mantelpiece. *Definitely Ari in the middle with her Nan and Mam*, he thought. On the wall opposite the fire, was a wonderful portrait of a young black girl. Ari came back with a large tray. Teapot, cups, sugar, milk, toasted tea cakes, butter and jam. She put them on the wooden trunk and went back to the kitchen for plates and knives.

"You'll have to sit down now," she said. "You are not allowed to wander about eating. Or so my Nan says."

He laughed and sat down, and it didn't take long to leave a clean plate. She hadn't said much so he told her about Julius' ladies and their sherry and mince pies and about walking to Mr Winter's with a bag of presents and then back to town.

"You should have worn your big coat," she said. "Then you wouldn't have got so cold."

She was right, he thought.

Then he asked her about the wooden trunk. "It was my school trunk," she said. "See on this side is my name."

He looked and saw 'Arianwen Morgan' branded into the wood. He felt strangely sad about it. He asked her about the portrait.

"That's my friend Christina from school. She's the one who taught me to swear," she said.

"And you painted it?" he asked.

"Oh! Please" she said. "I had all that 'did you paint this dear?' stuff from Miss Watkins at my interview. You ask Mrs Winter she was there when I did it. I was twelve or so I think."

"Sorry," he said. "I didn't mean it quite like it came out. I should have added 'when'." But he was very impressed. He helped her stack the tray and carried it out to the kitchen for her.

"Go back to the fire," she said. "I'll be there in a minute." He left her and sat on the sofa watching the flames. In a minute he was asleep.

Arianwen stood leaning on the draining board trying to calm herself. She gazed out of the window at the moon and the scudding clouds and felt a little less agitated. He would be gone soon then she could breathe properly.

She went back and saw he was asleep and so quietly got her sketchbook and started to draw him. Twenty minutes or so went by, and she had almost finished. She wrote at the bottom of her drawing, 'Mr Curtis asleep in my house'. 14/12/63 and underneath. 'Dear God, I love him'.

A log shifted in the fire and woke him. For a moment he wondered where he was, then saw Ari. She looked up from her drawing and their eyes met. She looked away immediately and got up. But he moved quickly and caught her and held her shoulders, just as she reached the kitchen door. "Arianwen," he said. "Look at me." But she shook her head and fought to get away.

"No," she cried "No please don't. Let me go." She held on to the handle of the door behind her. Panic filled her. She had dreamt often about something happening between them, made up lots of different scenarios, but had never ever thought it would. She was totally unprepared and felt unsure as to what to do.

Jon let her go. He had remembered her problem with Tom.

"Arianwen," he said. "I won't hurt you. You know me well enough now to know that."

Jon had never before been alone with her like this. All his resolutions disappeared. She had filled his thoughts for months and he knew he loved her beyond reason.

"Arianwen please look at me?"

She lifted her head a little and he saw the deep uncertainty in her eyes. "Please, sir," she said. "Don't do this unless you mean it. Not here today and gone tomorrow. I don't do that."

"Arianwen," he said. gently, "Come and sit down. There is something I really need to say to you, something I think you should know. But you must look at me when I say it. And when I do there is no going back for me. Do you understand?"

A great feeling of dread washed over her. Whatever had he thought she meant by 'here today and gone tomorrow'? He was going to tell her not to be so silly, he had a wife or a girlfriend at home. She nodded but didn't close her eyes.

She sat on the sofa. Jon perched on the edge of the wooden trunk. They were knee to knee.

Jon looked at her lovely face and her beautiful mouth that he just ached to kiss.

"I love you Arianwen, and I will stay with you forever if you would have me."

She looked at him in disbelief.

"Me?" she whispered. "What me?"

Jon nodded.

She looked at him for a long minute and he could see her thinking what to do, and then her eyes filled with tears. She didn't move and was silent, but her eyes were still fixed on his, and a tear rolled down her cheek. More minutes seemed to go by, and then she reached for the sketchbook that she had discarded on the sofa.

Whatever was she doing? he thought.

She found the page she was looking for, stood and handed him the book.

He saw the wonderful drawing of him asleep and read what she had written beneath.

And then he stood too and had her in his arms and was kissing her as if his life depended on it.

He took her hands and laced her fingers in his. They felt small and soft, and she held his hand tight against her. He could feel her heart beating fast, and then she cried. Great tears fell down her cheeks. "I never thought," she sobbed. "I never ever thought." And she sobbed again. He held her until she stopped.

After a moment she put her head on his shoulder. Her hair was against his cheek. Jon sat down on the sofa and pulled her onto his lap. He wiped a tear from her cheek with his thumb.

"What did you never think, my darling girl?" he said.

"That you might want me," she whispered. "I love you so much, and it's been so very hard."

"Oh! dear God, I am truly sorry Ari," he murmured. "It has taken me forever to do anything about you and I have loved you for such a long time." He kissed her lovely face. Eyes, nose and mouth again and again. She was so soft and warm and fragrant. He undid the string and her hair flowed down her back like water, and he wound his fingers in it. He was here with her and she loved him, after all this time wanting her, she loved him, she loved him.

"No need to say sorry," she said. "You are here now and I'm so very glad."

She lifted her head and looked directly into his eyes and put her arms around his neck. "I love you, I love you, I love you," she said and kissed him every time she said it. "I am so, so happy. Do you know it was my birthday last week? You are the best present I could ever have hoped for." And she kissed him again.

He couldn't stop himself. He slid his hands beneath her jumper and encountered just a little silk vest and then her soft skin. He moved his hands further and found her breasts and caught the nipples between his finger and thumb. Ari closed her eyes and sighed.

She felt something hard move against her thigh, and she shifted slightly.

"Don't do that Ari, please," Jon said.

She cupped his face in her hands and kissed him, her long soft fingers stroking his ears. It was strangely erotic.

"Come on," she said, though her heart was beating fast with fright. "I think we had better do something about that." And taking his hand, led him to her bed. She drew the curtains and put on a light beside the bed. In silence and with concentration, Jon undressed her. She stood before him and she was as beautiful as he had imagined. Then she undressed him, slowly, glancing often into his eyes and smiling. She had a little trouble with his belt but soon they were both naked and in each other's arms. They lay down on the bed and just looked at each other. Ari stroked his beloved face, kissed his eyes, his ears, his chin. Then she opened her legs, just slightly and he entered her. He felt her whole body tremble with delight and she arched her back so that he could thrust harder into her. He looked at her face and she was deeply absorbed in what was happening. In a while he saw and felt she was nearing orgasm and he pushed just once more and twined his hands in her hair, drawing her tight against him. He saw her climax and the sight made him follow directly after. She collapsed against him and opening her eyes said. "At last."

"Are you all right Ari?" Jon said

"Yes sir. Thank you," she said.

Jon began to laugh. "For Christ's sake Ari, you will have to stop calling me sir. I feel like the lord of the manor and you the parlour maid."

She sat up, her legs crossed, her hair spread all around. He marvelled at how unselfconscious she was. She had no idea of the effect she had on him. He took her in his arms.

"Do I call you Mr Curtis then?" she said laughing and kissing his collarbones. There was no answer as she slowly moved to his chest, his stomach and his navel.

"Ari," he managed to say. "What are you doing?"

"Just checking everything is in order." She paused and kissed his mouth," She moved down his body. "Hmm," she said. "I think I'll kiss you all over." And she did. "You are just wonderful my darling girl," he said, and they couldn't but do it again.

"Shall I call you Jon now then?" Ari said. "Now I know you better." The gleam of mischief was in her eyes.

"God, I love you Arianwen," he said. "I never knew how much until now." He had not really known how funny and mischievous she could be.

She lay in his arms and he watched as her eyes closed in sleep.

She slept with one arm across him and one leg between his. He could feel her breath on his chest. She was so young and so very beautiful.

We fit together well, he thought. Toe to toe he was just over half a head taller. He looked at his watch, it was just seven o'clock. A little over two hours ago he had seen her in the town. He had spent months and months trying to suppress his feelings for her that now this seemed like a miracle. He didn't care anymore that she was his student or that she was younger than him. They could sort that out, and it seemed not to bother her at all. At the moment she filled his thoughts and feelings and he knew he would never have enough of her. He moved slightly and twined his fingers in her hair. He looked down at her. One grey, laughing eye looked back. "I'm starving," she said and sat up.

"I must go home at some time Ari," he said. "But I could come back tomorrow?"

"No," she said. "I want you to stay with me. I can drive you home to get anything you need, and then we can find somewhere to eat. We'd best not go up the town. That OK with you? I wasn't expecting company, and especially not you. I've got loads in the freezer but not much in the fridge. But you are coming back here, aren't you?"

"Yes, my darling girl, of course I will." Then he added, "You have a car, and more to the point a licence?"

"Yup, passed my test a year ago. First time I'll have you know, and I've been back and forth to Boscombe quite a few times now. The car is in the garage at the back. Fred calls me Mrs Fangio, whoever she might be."

So, they washed and dressed and went quietly down the garden to the garage. Lem and Grace, next door, heard the car start up.

"Wonder where she's off to?" said Grace.

"I thought I heard a man's voice just now," said Lem. "And I did see her walking down the road with some bloke when I was coming home."

"Lem! Ari wouldn't be with 'Some Bloke'. What did he look like?"

"Tall, longish dark hair, Reefer jacket, I think and cords."

"Mr Curtis," said Grace. "Well, I never. She hasn't said a word."

Ari hurtled through the lanes to the village where Jon lived. He had to hold on tight when going round corners, but the day had been so extraordinary that he found he was enjoying the thrill of it all.

They picked up his 'stuff', as Ari called it and drove to a transport cafe that Jon knew of and which was famous locally for their steaks and burgers.

The cafe was almost full, but they found a table towards the back. It was warm and steamy and smelt deliciously of chips. Most of the customers were lorry drivers and several of them stopped eating to watch Jon and Ari when they came in arm in arm. A large man, his shirt sleeves rolled up and with a reasonably clean apron around his ample middle, came to take their order.

"May I have a small burger and chips please?" said Ari.

Jon ordered a large steak and chips. Plus, two large coffees.

"Been working hard, have you?" said the man, looking at Jon and with a lascivious nod towards Ari.

"No," Ari interrupted. "He has no need to. It comes naturally, he is my most lovely man."

The man laughed, "Well said little lady."

Ari was seated with her back to the room so didn't see the men watching them. She fed Jon chips and stood up once to kiss him on the mouth. When she looked in the direction of the counter and indicated more ketchup, three men appeared each with a bottle. She thanked each one individually. *Probably made their day.* Jon thought. But Ari seemed not to notice.

Later when Jon went to pay, the man said, "You are a lucky sod mate with a lovely one like that. Keep her close if I were you. Don't want to misplace her, do you?"

On the way back, Jon said, "Do you know Ari; I feel I've known you forever?"

"Since I was fifteen and I came to your life drawing class. Do you remember Sean, teasing me?"

"And I remember," he said. "On your first day and you were in the library reading some book."

"*Schiele*," she interrupted. "All thin and emaciated. And you came to say hello and your hand was near mine on the table. And I wanted to touch you. Your lovely square nails and the dark hairs on the back of your hand."

"Oh, Arianwen," he said. "And me you. But I did try hard to resist you. Didn't work though, did it? We have wasted so much time."

"You might have been doing time," she laughed. "I was only sixteen." He smiled and lent over to kiss her neck. This made Ari drive over the grass verge. Just a little. They went back to Ari's then and to bed.

It was the most marvellous sex he had ever had. He had been with a few girls, Sarah, and even a prostitute when he had been doing his national service in Cyprus but this... Afterwards, he thought it was like lighting a blue touch paper. He pulled her into his arms and she was off, and everything she did was for him and he knew it. At the end great wild waves of absolute pleasure rippled through his body, they went on and on. He had never experienced anything like it. He heard Ari sigh, "Yes, Oh Yes," and he wound his hand tighter in her hair and kissed her. When he was more himself, he lay back against the pillows.

"Bloody hell, Arianwen," he said. "That was something else." She looked up at him and smiled. "Chips," she laughed. "It's the chips." Jon laughed too and kissed her.

"Jon." She then said, "I can't move. You are holding my hair so tightly." He released her and she rolled off him with a groan. "I hate that bit," she said. "Now I shall make us some tea and then I need to ask you something."

She brought the tea and got back into bed. She turned to Jon and he saw her eyes looked troubled.

"How did you know, about me I mean?"

"Julius, Mr Winter has known for a while how I feel about you. Then I think you talked to Poll? She said she knew it was me as you never ever mentioned me."

"Bugger," Ari said. "I thought I was doing so well. I couldn't ever let you know as I thought you had someone of your own."

"No, darling girl, I haven't. Why did you think that?"

"I saw you sometime back at the folk club, with someone."

"That was Sarah," he said. "I knew her from art school and we met up again just as I finished at the RCA. We lived together for about two years. But I was not what she wanted and she was not what I wanted, so she left. When you saw her, she had come to ask if we could try again. I said no. We were not good together." He stopped for a moment; he didn't want to talk about Sarah.

"So, tell me about your birthday then," he said. "I didn't see any cards."

"I do housework on a Saturday morning so they are all tidied away. We went to Marco's uncle's place, last Friday evening. Everyone in our group except Janet. She said she was doing something else. Tom came with Nell, Grace with Lem, of course, and Stuart with his girlfriend Amy. Even Carol and Sheila came. James was late as he had to see his gran, but he had pudding, and Marco was amazingly brave and brought Philippe. It was great. Tom was a bit 'whoa' about Philippe, well you know what Tom's like, but Philippe is full of Gallic charm and soon talked him round. He even got Tom smoking a Gauloises. So, it was a lovely night."

"Who is Philippe?"

"Marco's boyfriend. He is French and very Parisian, so Marco tells me." Ari laughed rolling her eyes. "Marco met him in the Reading Room at the British museum, you know when we had to go on Fridays. He lives in Paris, and he was doing research for something, and it progressed from there. Marco has a small flat now, down by the dairy. He really couldn't have lived at home any longer, and he goes to Paris often, mostly during the holidays. Anything else you want to know Mr Curtis, any other bits of gossip or can I go to sleep now?"

He pulled her to him, "Sleep sweetheart," he said and kissed her once more. He lay there for a while marvelling at all that had happened. She loved him. He smiled and went to sleep also.

In the morning, after she had bathed, Ari sat naked on the side of the bed and reaching into the bedside cupboard brought out a large blue pottery jar which she opened. Jon still lying in bed was immediately assailed by the perfume that was essentially Arianwen. "What is that Ari?" he asked.

"It's for my skin," she said, scooping a little of the thick cream inside onto her fingers. She began to rub it onto her legs. "Christina's mother makes it for me and I do this every morning. But I have a perfume called Mitsouko as well for special occasions, it smells very similar." She moved on to her arms.

"Can I do that Ari?" Jon said and she smiled a yes and held out her arm. "Not that bit." Jon laughed. It took him ages and one thing led to another so they were quite late getting up.

Jon had brought some work to do in his 'stuff,' so after they had had breakfast, Ari cleared the table for him to use. There was a whole staff meeting, late Tuesday afternoon about the intermediate students, and he had to prepare. The house was quiet and warm. Ari had taken some chicken out of the freezer and made a casserole for supper and then went upstairs to change the bed sheets and clean the bathroom. Jon thought that if Sarah had still been with him, she would have kept asking him how long until he finished, and what was he doing. Ari just left him alone. He could hear her singing upstairs. That beautiful song she had sung at the folk club. It was such a restful house. Ari came in and made some coffee. She placed a cup near him on the table and kissed the back of his neck. "I missed that bit yesterday," she laughed and then went off into the living room. He could hear her rummaging about so, taking his coffee went to see. She was kneeling before the fire, cleaning the glass. Behind her was a pile of kindling and some newspaper. He sat on the sofa to watch. She turned to him, "I like doing this. I like the smell. When I was little, I used to watch Nan, though we had an open fire then. I loved it when she held a sheet of newspaper up to get the fire to draw and it would sometimes catch alight. Absolute panic."

She got up and went outside, coming back with the log basket stacked full of logs. He got up to help." No, no," she said. "I'm used to it, but thanks." She went to him and wrapped her arms about him and kissed him. "I can't believe you are actually here with me," she said. Jon marvelled at how natural everything was between them. There was no coyness or artifice about her. She loved him and trusted him and that was it. This time yesterday he had been sitting with a group of ladies discussing when to put the turkey in the oven and puff pastry or short crust for mince pies. He thought about her soft voice saying, "Would you like a cup of tea, sir?" He smiled to himself. Arianwen Morgan was the most wonderful thing that had ever happened to him. They had just seemed to fit together straight away.

When they had come back last night, he had told her she was the most beautiful girl he had ever seen and she had said, "No, don't be silly.

Fred always says Mam is beautiful and she is small and fair. Not like me at all. And anyway, Fred always calls me 'funny face'." He realised then that she had no idea of her effect on him or on anyone else.

After a while Jon went back to his paperwork. He called her and asked her to sit with him a minute.

"Ari," he said. "What do you know of Flora Brown?"

"Not too much," she said. "She often comes in looking tired and sometimes dirty. I have seen her washing in the girl's cloakroom, and she is often bruised. But she doesn't say a lot. Elias is the one she is close to. They sit together in the common room and I think she talks to him, and people tell Marco a lot. He might know."

"Thanks," he said. "I must bring that up in the meeting on Tuesday. Her work has dropped off alarmingly lately." He knew Ari would not say one word to anyone.

When he had put his things away, he went into the living room. Ari was sitting by the fire writing notes in her sketchbook. The phone rang and she went to answer it. It was Mam for their usual Sunday chat. They talked for a while about arrangements for Christmas. Maggie and George were coming, plus Roger and Olive and perhaps Queenie and her husband. Ari wished with all her heart that she could take Jon and show him off but she knew he was going to Dorset as his father was still unwell. Mam rang off with, "See you very soon sweetheart," and Ari went to make them a cheese omelette for lunch. After they had eaten, she made Jon another cup of coffee and as she placed it beside him, she gently bit his ear. Then disappeared. Jon felt such a rush of desire that he went to look for her. She wasn't upstairs where he thought she might be, but he found her sitting outside, wrapped in a blanket, on the bench beneath the kitchen window.

"Ari," he said. "What are you doing? It's freezing out here."

She wrapped a bit of the blanket around him.

"Just saying thank you," she said.

"Who to?"

"Oh, the passing clouds, the sky, the trees and stuff."

Jon smiled. There was an awful lot of 'stuff' in Ari's world.

"Why?" he asked

She turned and looked at him and her beautiful eyes were alight with love.

"Well," she said seriously. "If you have wanted something for a very long time, something you thought you would never ever have and then you get it, and it is so, so wonderful, you need to say thank you, don't you? I just cast it to the wind, bit like an invisible prayer flag, I suppose."

He didn't know what to say, but he was deeply affected by the thought of her thanks blowing about amongst the clouds.

"Come on," she laughed. "I need to bite your ear again."

He knew then that she wanted him just as much as he did her. Poll had been right, and it was just marvellous.

Afterwards he said to her, "What's all this biting my ear then?"

She sat up and looked at him and smiled that mischievous smile.

"When we had a life drawing class, I always used to like sitting on the donkey. I liked the lower angle it gave me. But when you came round to see what we were doing and suggest a correction or something, you always forgot I was left-handed and knelt down on my right side. Then you would have to lean across to borrow my pencil. Why you never had your own I don't know? Your ear was always very near. You will never know the number of times I had to stop myself from touching it. That's why I moved to an easel."

Jon pulled her to him, "I never forgot Ari, I just liked getting near and the smell of you."

They lay for a little while talking, then Ari said, "Jon?"

"Yes"

"You know you said I was not to call you sir?"

"Yes."

"Shall I call you Jon, tomorrow then? That should cause a stir."

"I think you will have to revert to sir."

"I might forget."

He saw that she was lauglaughing.,However am I going to manage being near you tomorrow," he said. "We have a life drawing class, don't we?"

She rolled over and looked at him. "A whole day without touching you will be very, very difficult. I had best put some in store." And she proceeded to kiss him all over again and he did the same to her.

Halfway through she leapt out of bed. "I forgot to put the fucking casserole in," she said, and ran naked, downstairs. When she got back, she was cold so he had to warm her up. They lay in bed for a while afterwards.

"I think I might find it difficult tomorrow," Jon admitted. "I've only had you for a night and a day."

Ari smiled at him. "Well just think of tomorrow evening," she said. "And how lovely that will be. And remember that wherever I am I will be thinking of you because I love you, Jon Curtis." He pulled her into his arms and held her tight. His beautiful Arianwen.

Jon left early the next morning. "No sneaking about," Ari said. "Just go out of the front door." She had found him a navy blue knitted hat and scarf in the Chinese chest.

"My Nan knitted them for Marco last winter when it was so cold, but he didn't think the colour suited him and I don't want you blue with cold again."

Jon said he felt rather in disguise and kissed her. Then again and she had to practically push him out of the door.

Jon walked slowly up the hill to the school. He smiled to himself all the way, and the people he passed smiled back. What a weekend, and what a wonderful, wonderful girl. That she felt the same for him was a miracle and he couldn't quite believe it. The world was a whole different place and he just loved it.

Julius was feeling better and was already in the staffroom drinking a mug of coffee. "You're early old son," he said. "Couldn't sleep?"

Then he noticed Jon's face.

"You bugger you," he laughed. "Jesus! That was fast work. Got it together at last, haven't you? Well bless my soul."

He shook Jon's hand and Jon realised that he had not stopped smiling since he had left Ari.

"And how did that come about?" Julius asked.

"I met her in the town, after I left you and she asked me in for a cup of tea as I looked cold."

"There," Julius laughed. "Easy, wasn't it?"

"I can't quite believe it Julius," Jon said. "You and Poll were quite right. She feels the same for me as I do for her. I don't think I have ever met a more beautiful and generous girl. I think I laughed or smiled the whole weekend."

"And where did you spend that," Julius asked raising an eyebrow.

"Well, I'll leave you to guess that," Jon laughed. "Suffice to say we got there pretty quick."

"Going to be a little difficult today, is it?"

"I think we'll manage," said Jon. "She's a sensible girl."

"Well, you've made my day," said Julius. "Just wait till I tell Poll."

And what of Ari? When Jon had left, she had gone into the garden and looking at the sky said another heart felt thank you. She walked up to school with Grace, who if she suspected that Mr Curtis had stayed all weekend didn't say a word. But she noticed that Ari looked extremely happy.

By nine thirty Jon was missing her. Julius had helped him set up the life room, an old couch on the dais for the model and several electric fires put in position and turned on. They would normally have gone back down to the staff room, leaving there only just before lessons started, but Jon went out onto the top landing to see if Ari was in yet, so Julius went with him. They lent on the banister rail smoking. About ten minutes later Ari came up the stairs with Grace. She wore what Jon thought of as her army great coat, and Grace was wrapped up in a duffel coat as it was very cold out. They got to the half landing and went into the cloakroom. Julius could see Jon shaking. In a while the girls came out and walked up the stairs to the life drawing room, their drawing boards under their arms, and Grace went in. Ari was wearing her black wool skirt and the little dark-red velvet jacket that the 'Vintage' lady had kept for her. It had a row of tiny buttons down the front and a small peplum. Her hair was loose but tied back a little from her face with a piece of black lace. She looked wonderful. As Ari walked past, she said, "Good morning, Mr Winter, good morning, Mr Curtis. Did you have a good weekend?"

"Thank you, Yes," said Julius. "And you Miss Morgan?"

"The best ever," she said and she did not look at Jon once.

Julius gave a great guffaw of laughter but Jon just couldn't speak. Dear God, he wanted her. For all her quiet and gentle nature, she could be a naughty one that Arianwen. Christina had taught her a lot.

When Julius went home that evening, he told Poll.

"I thought he was going to collapse," he laughed.

"Oh! Bless him," Poll smiled.

The life drawing class was not quite as easy as they had hoped. Jon had to talk to each student if he could, and it would have been noticeable if he had left Ari out. He had posed the model, a large middle-aged lady as Manet's 'Olympia' on the old slightly tatty couch. Mrs May was a regular model and Ari loved to draw her as she was all lumps and bumps and massive thighs. She was the lady Sal had seen at Ari's interview. The pose made her smile though and she just knew Jon had done it on purpose. When she saw him heading her way she went and sat on the heating pipes. He sat beside her and just brushed her fingers with his whilst discussing her drawing. That evening Ari made him laugh.

"I nearly asked Mrs May to move off that couch," she said. "And then please could Mr Curtis and Miss Morgan borrow it for a while?"

At lunchtime Jon went up to the common room to get Marco. The noise was horrendous as someone had brought in a record of *Do You Love Me* and every student seemed to be dancing to it. He caught Ari's eye and indicated Marco.

Ari shouted in his ear, "Sir wants you."

Marco looked bemused, "What's he want me for?"

"No idea," said Ari.

But Jon wanted any information on Flora that Marco had. The only thing he could tell him was that Flora had left home and was sleeping wherever she could, but that Elias would know the true story.

Marco went to fetch Elias. Elias was so relieved that someone had noticed and was interested that he told Jon everything. Flora's mother had a new boyfriend who thought Flora was part of the deal. When Flora objected, he hit her. So, she had left. Sometimes she slept at his house but she had spent one or two nights on the streets.

"Thanks Elias," Jon said. "I'll tell Miss Watkins later and we will see what we can do. Don't worry now; I'll let you know how things go. If you see Arianwen, could you ask her to come and see me please?"

Elias gave Ari the message. "What's going on?" she said, knowing full well.

Jon was waiting for her in the studio. He shut the door behind her.

"My darling girl," he said and winding his hands in her hair pulling her gently towards him. "I couldn't wait a moment longer."

"You like doing that, don't you?" she smiled.

"What?"

"Holding my hair."

"Amongst many other things," he laughed.

"Jon," she said. "Please kiss me."

After a while he said, "I'll see you this evening?" To which she nodded. "I will come as soon as I can, and then I think we must have a serious talk about when I stay and Christmas. It would be good to get away together. Now you had best go." And he kissed her long and lovingly again.

Jon was exhausted when he arrived at Ari's, what with all the Flora stuff and being so conscious that Ari was around, but he felt better after supper and they sat down in the living room. Ari snuggled up to him on the sofa. He kissed the top of her head. "Now," he said. "Staying nights and Christmas."

They agreed that he would stay Friday night to Sunday night and go to his home on Monday. After all he did have his own work to do and he needed time for that. Ari was fine with the arrangement. All artists needed their own space at some time, and he could stay any time he wanted really. But there were to be days in the middle of the week when they hadn't been together for a night or so, that were very hard. Jon saw Ari coming down the stairs at school one morning and he very nearly pulled her into his arms and kissed her. She just widened her eyes at him as she went past, she knew and wanted him also.

Then they decided that as Ari would be in Bournemouth and Jon at his parent's house in Dorset, over Christmas, Jon would look for an hotel for them somewhere between. Just for a few days.

The following evening Jon went back to his own home. He was working on a half-finished painting when the phone rang. It was Poll.

"Jon," she said. "I'll come straight to the point. Julius has told me about you and Ari. Please take care with her."

Poll paused for a moment to gather her thoughts.

"She always carries the thought of being abandoned with her. You know her mother surfaced when she was eight, and demanded she be sent to school? Yet not another word has ever been heard from her, or her father. Lovely though she is, underneath she is very insecure. She told me once she always felt she stood alone in the world. She obviously trusts you, Jon, so look after her."

"I will Poll," he said. "She is the best thing that has ever happened to me and I'll not let her go."

"Good," Poll said. "See you don't." There was a pause, "And Jon I'm really pleased for you both."

Moments later the phone rang again. John picked it up.

"Hello, Mr Curtis, it's Arianwen... Oh! Fuck," she said.

Jon laughed.

"Sweetheart." He smiled. "Try again."

"Hello Jon, it's Ari."

"Yes, I know, I recognise your voice."

"Jon! I need to ask you something. I know it's early days yet but I would like to tell Marco and Grace about us. They were wonderfully supportive with all that Tom malarkey and they both told me straight away when they had someone special. So, I would like to do the same. What do you feel about that?"

"Fine by me," Jon said. "I think we can trust them not to say anything."

"Oh! absolutely" Ari said. "Then I shall ask them to supper tomorrow and the next time Philippe is over we can all get together."

She asked then about the meeting, and he told her it had been hard but that they had eventually made a plan to help Flora.

"There were those," he said. "Who said wait and see." But he had been adamant that they should not. "Ian," he had said. "Had noticed Arianwen was wary of Tom quite early on but they had not kept an eye on it and she had had all sorts of problems." In the end Ian Cooper had said that they must help Flora. He had an unused bedsit at the top of his house where she could stay, as long as his wife agreed of course. Then after the holiday they could involve social services if necessary. It was agreed by all that it was a good plan, and Ian had phoned his wife, and came back with a yes. Miss Watkins said they would talk to Elias in the morning to see what he thought before they approached Flora. Archie Fellowes was her tutor and he would be there also.

"Has she got clothes and stuff," said Ari. "If not, I've got loads. I'll sort some out tomorrow."

So, Ari sorted out some things for Flora. Unbeknown to Jon she went to M&S at lunchtime and bought several sets of underwear. Flora looked about her size. Then she went to the bank and withdrew £100, which she put in an envelope and buried amongst the clothes. She gave the lot to Julius and said, "Not a word please sir." Flora was moved to tears again when she saw what was in the bag. She knew where it all came from. The clothes were unmistakeably Arianwen Morgan.

After she had spoken to Jon, Ari rang Marco and then Grace.

Marco was more than happy to come for supper and Ari said he could stay if he wanted. Grace had already told him about Lem seeing Ari with Mr Curtis, so he wondered if this was what the unexpected supper was about. And as Lem was at his evening class on a Wednesday Grace was happy to come also.

Ian Cooper took Elias and Flora to see the bedsit that lunchtime, and to meet his wife. A very relieved but tearful Flora moved in after school that day.

Marco, Ari and Grace walked down to Ari's after a late life drawing class, on Wednesday evening. Jon saw them go and when they had got some way, set off himself to the station. Ari made macaroni cheese and with that, two bottles of wine and some big chunks of fruit cake, she sat with her dear friends and told them all. Marco of course was not the least bit surprised but both he and Grace were so very happy for her.

Thursday was very quiet for Ari as Jon had gone with the sculpture tutor, Ron Fleming, to supervise the second-year intermediate students on a visit to the Tate.

Ari was home by four-thirty. She tidied up and got everything ready as Jon would be staying Friday night. She made a big pan of cawl for tomorrow's supper, which she left to simmer gently on the stove. Then she had a long bath, painted her toenails and washed her hair. It could dry naturally. She put on a pair of old winceyette pyjamas that Nan had given her ages ago and settled down in front of the fire to read her book. But she didn't do much reading. She just thought about Jon and how wonderful it all was. She was just thinking of making something to eat when there was a knock at the front door. Her stomach turned over.

Tom? She crept into the hall and looked through the side window. It was Jon.

She opened the door and he practically fell in.

He looked at her face; it was white. "Ari?" he said.

"I thought it was Tom," she breathed.

"Oh! I am so sorry sweetheart," he said. "I didn't think. I was coming past and saw your lights on. No Ari for a few days and I come over all..."

"Impatient?" Ari laughed. "To be polite?"

He pulled her into his arms.

"Jeez! You are freezing again," she said, his lips were cold on hers and his nose against her cheek.

You smell wonderful," he said. "And are you a little damp?"

"Yes," she said kissing him again. "I've not long had a bath."

"If only I'd got here earlier," he laughed.

"Dear God, Arianwen," he continued, his nose in her hair. "I have really missed you. Two days without you is two days too many."

She put her arms around his neck, "I miss you too you know," she said and kissed him.

They went through to the kitchen.

"Have you eaten?" Ari said. "I was just going to have something. There's loads."

"That will be great," Jon said and Ari got the pan of cawl from the stove. She would find something else for tomorrow.

"This is good," Jon said. "What is it?"

"Cawl," Ari explained. "Welsh lamb stew."

Jon had two bowlsful then some crackers and cheese and a cup of coffee.

"I can't move now," he laughed.

He told her he had been late back from the trip as Andrew and Josef, two of the students, had decided to walk up to Westminster to see *The Burghers of Calais* on the green by the Houses of Parliament and hadn't told anyone. So, there had been a long-protracted search for them. The coach driver agreed to wait a half hour but then would have to leave as he was taking an office party to Caesar's Palace in Luton that evening. Jon said he would wait for the boys and Ron went off with the other students in the coach. The planned for detour down Regent's Street to see the Christmas lights was abandoned. Much to the disappointment of everyone.

Jon sat on the steps of the Tate for nearly half an hour until the two boys wandered back. They were most apologetic, having misread the time. So, they set off to the underground to get to Kings Cross and a train home.

Jon looked tired.

"Have you a lot to do at home?" Ari asked.

"No, nothing. But I have to get clean clothes for tomorrow. London always makes me feel grubby. I'll stay a while as you look very fetching in those pyjamas, but I'll get the last train."

Ari excused herself and went upstairs. She came down with a large carrier bag which she gave to Jon.

Inside, socks, pants, two blue shirts, a navy Guernsey jumper, a wash bag with shaving things, soap and deodorant, and a toothbrush.

"Emergency supplies?" she said. "I went to Green's at lunchtime."

God, he loved this dear girl. He kissed her deeply. "Thank you, my darling," he said. She was so thoughtful. Why ever had that not occurred to him?

"Just in case you couldn't get home or anything," she said. "You can stay now if you would like to, and there's lots of hot water for a bath."

Ari washed up whilst Jon ironed one of his new shirts for the next day, then went and had a bath.

After a while Ari wandered into the bathroom. Naked, and winding her hair on top of her head.

"Is there room for another in there?" she asked.

"I thought you had already had a bath" Jon said.

"Well," she said very seriously. "I need to clean your ears if I am to bite them later."

Jon laughed. He had never thought she would be as much fun as this. It was just wonderful.

So she climbed into the bath and sat on Jon's lap facing him. She found the flannel, after fishing about a while between his legs and then just as her Nan used to do, put it over her finger and twirled it about in his ear. There was a lot of muttering about potatoes. Jon couldn't speak for laughing. But after a while he started to kiss her and things progressed quickly thereafter. By the time they were ready to get out of the bath, the water was nearly cold and the floor was awash but it had been such fun, and Ari had bitten his nice clean ears.

Lying in bed later Jon asked her how it had gone with Marco and Grace. "Great," she said. "Marco had his suspicions anyway. Something you said when I fainted, and Grace was just so pleased. She said her situation had been similar. She had known Lem for years as he had been a friend of her brother. And she had loved him for a while. When she knew he was looking for a lodger she had gone to see him immediately and everything had thankfully fallen into place. They won't say anything Jon so don't worry."

Then she said, "I was a bit worried after I had bought that stuff for you that you might think me a bit presumptuous. I just didn't want you going home late in the dark and cold just for some clean socks. I love you Jon, but it's not all about sex, is it? Though that is quite marvellous. It's being together and trusting each other, and I want to look after you. To find you a woolly hat or a scarf so you don't get cold, and to ask why you aren't wearing your new warm coat? She stopped and looked up at him. "I have never had anyone to look after before." And her eyes filled with tears.

He pulled her tight against him. "And I have never had anyone to look after me," he murmured. "My mother was very much not into nurturing. I love you Arianwen Morgan and as I said, just a few days ago, I intend to stay with you forever, so we can look after each other. I cannot believe that this time last week I had no idea I would be here with you." She smiled up at him.

"Life can be just wonderful sometimes, can't it?" Ari said and wiped her eyes on the sheet.

"Right," he said. "Sleep now and I'll make love to you again in the morning. That should see us both through the day."

Ari laughed. "That sounds like a bowl of porridge," she said and kissed him. She did so love him.

He spent some time watching her sleep. She really was very beautiful. Funny, generous and thoughtful too. He had known her for just over three years and had wanted her for almost as long. Once or twice perhaps, he had seen a flash of mischief in her eyes, but not often, she had been very guarded. Now that she was his, trusted him and loved him, he experienced the full force of Arianwen Morgan. She was marvellous in bed, quite uninhibited at times. Sometimes serious, sometimes playful, and it was always great fun. He thought again of her cleaning his ears in the bath and how he had laughed so much his face had ached. He was the most fortunate and happy person alive. When they were in the bath, she had asked him if they could 'do it' in the sea one day. He remembered Poll telling them about her getting detention for asking if you could 'do it' outside. As far as he was concerned it was all so wondrous that they could make love whenever and wherever she wanted. She was so very special and she was his. And even though they had been together less than a week he could not imagine life without her now.

Friday was another quiet day and Ari had no lessons with Jon as everyone finished at lunchtime for the Christmas break. There was a dance that evening for the students, just down the road at the Coop Hall but Ari wasn't going. James had asked her but she said she had to get ready to go to Bournemouth. Lem and Grace were off straight away to Scotland and Marco never went to dances anyway. The first one Ari had been to at the end of their first term had been awful. The local band was good, brilliant even, but both Janet and Sheila got dreadfully drunk and had been sick everywhere. It had not been a nice evening. Now though Jon would be coming as soon as he had sorted out everything he needed to. She went to the deli and bought a ready-made lasagne for supper, then went home, lit the fire and waited.

He came just before three o'clock and flopped full length on the sofa and in just a while was asleep. He slept for an hour then Ari made a cup of tea, and she lay on the sofa in his arms and they talked. About their childhoods, their schools, and their families. Jon asked if Ari would tell her Nan and Mam about him.

"Nan yes," she said. "If I can find a good time, but Mam can be very prickly and I will have to judge that one carefully. She never wanted me to go to art school so will be shocked ridged if I say I'm with you. And if she even suspects I am sleeping with you there will be a terrible atmosphere. So, on reflection, and as they have visitors, probably not. I wouldn't want to ruin Christmas, though I would just love to take you with me and show you off."

For a while, Jon was silent. "What are you thinking about?" Ari asked quietly. She thought he was possibly thinking over what she had just said. She saw he was gazing into the distance, far away in his thoughts.

"I know," she said before he could answer. "Are you thinking of your painting, what to do and such?" He turned to her but didn't speak. He saw her dear face crease with concern and doubt, and he smiled at her.

"How did you know?" he said.

Ari laughed. "Because I do it all the time. It's like having one of those unwanted tunes going round and round in your head, isn't it? What do I want to say? Why do I want to say it? How shall I say it? And then how can I get it out of my head and onto the canvas? Fred always said, 'She's away with the fairies again,' when I did that. They didn't understand at all." She paused for a moment.

"Fred used to make me think I was odd to do that, but I had a friend at school who wrote a lot. Stories and stuff. She did it also, so I asked her about it and she said she was getting her sentences in the right order. Same thing really, I suppose."

He pulled her to him, "I have never met anyone who knew about that or talked about it or understood it before," he said. "You are a marvel, my love. There are bits of you I never ever thought of."

"Are you a little stuck with your painting then?" she asked.

"A little," he admitted.

"Shall we go to your flat tomorrow and take a look together? I'm not really qualified to make suggestions but you might get a different perspective if I am there?" Then she added, "And have you got a sofa big enough for us both?"

He just smiled at her, his darling Arianwen.

She drove them to his flat the next morning. It was one of four in an old Victorian school, and Jon lived top right. Ari loved the place now she saw it in daylight. The enormous, tall windows had been kept, the playground with its netball markings was the car park, and the entrance to Jon's side of the building was through an old, heavy, wooden door above which was a stone lintel with 'Boys' carved on it. Inside, up wide stone stairs was a long, light, high-ceilinged living room with a huge bookcase at one end, stacked with books plus piles on the floor. A large record player with two big speakers, and four wooden crates full of records beside it. A big sofa, four armchairs and three side tables with big pottery lamps with deep orange shades. The floor was herringbone parquet and uncovered. The room was sparsely furnished for its size, but quite beautiful. At the far end there was a door to the kitchen and another to a corridor which housed the bathroom and two big bedrooms.

Ari turned to Jon. "I like it here," she said. "Can we stay all day?"

The last bedroom was where Jon painted and his large canvas was up on two easels turned to the light. He went off to make some coffee leaving Ari to contemplate his painting. Ari looked at it for quite some time. It was of a frozen waterfall Jon had seen in the Lake District last winter. He had gone to spend Christmas and New Year at a rented cottage with his college friend Richard and several others. They had been snowed in for two weeks.

He came back with the coffee which he set down on his painting table and put his arm around Ari. "Well?" he said, and he lifted the edge of her jumper and slipped a finger under the waistband of her skirt. Her skin was so soft.

She leant against him. "I love you," she said. "And I haven't told you today." It was nearly his undoing when she said things like that, unexpected and very honest. He kissed her.

He just knew that Ari had seen his difficulty straight away but she was very reluctant to give an opinion. "I can't," she said when he asked her. "Who am I to tell you what to do?" He loved her so much.

"All right then," he said. "If it wasn't my painting, what would you say, sweetheart." She turned and smiled at him and kissed him.

"I would say there is too much foreground," she said glancing up at him. "For that waterfall, you need a really big drop to have impact. It needs to fill the canvas. It isn't about where it is, is it? But about what it is. All those lovely cold colours and strange frozen shapes." And she was right. It was easily rectified.

They had lunch sitting in the kitchen, just sandwiches and coffee. Jon tidied up and when he went through to the living room saw that Ari was fast asleep on the sofa. He sat and watched her for a while, his beautiful darling girl. Then went to look at his painting and work out how to rectify it. Throughout the afternoon he went to check on her but she remained asleep. He got his book *The Spy Who Came in From the Cold*, pulled up a chair near her and read for a while. Dozed a bit and then read some more. He had worn her out he thought, wanting her constantly, and felt quite guilty. She woke around six after five hours of sleep and looked quite dazed and bewildered. She looked very young. He saw her bottom lip tremble.

"Ari," he said. "What is it?"

"Tell me honestly Jon. Has this been a good week for you?" she whispered.

"What do you mean?" he asked and he came and sat beside her.

"Well," she said a little hesitantly. "I dreamt you were tired of me... I did disturbing things that annoyed you intensely and a week was long enough for you."

"Never," he said. He turned her so that he could look into her eyes. "And what things might you mean?"

"Well," she sighed. "I cry a lot, don't I? I talk a lot and I kiss you all the time. You might not like it."

He smiled. "Yes, you do cry, Ari, but it has been a very emotional week for both of us hasn't it? I would have been worried if you had been stony-faced throughout. And we talk a lot but always to each other, my love. Which is as it should be."

He paused for a moment. She was listening to him intently.

"As to the kissing," he said. "My mother never ever kissed me and when I was growing up fathers didn't kiss their sons either. A pat on the back was sufficient. I kissed girls later on, to get them in the right mood, if you know what I mean. But I never ever had anyone who kissed me just because I was there with them and they loved me. Which is what you do Ari, and it is marvellous. Don't ever stop that. As many times as you like and whenever you like, and I will learn from you. It is quite different to making love and very, very special."

"Listen to me sweetheart," he continued. "You disturbed me the moment I saw you at that registration meeting, but not in the way you mean. You were beautiful, clean, fresh and fragrant and I wanted to touch you. But you were so young Ari, that I thought my feelings for you were inappropriate. I tried and tried to suppress them but you always intruded somehow, fainting, nearly injuring me with that saw, and you were of course in my classes and always around school. I gave in in the end and admitted to myself that I loved you. I knew you were special, kind, thoughtful and honest, but I didn't really know you, Ari, you wouldn't let me... You disturbed me all the time then and now I know you, you disturb me even more, my love," he said. "I was settled with you the moment I kissed you. I had worried I was too old for you and your teacher. But all that just melted away. I would never want to go back to before; you have made my life..." He searched for a word. "Sparkle," he laughed.

"We are together now Arianwen forever if you are happy with that?" And she smiled her answer.

"God," Ari said, happy now. "I was so in awe of you. I nearly fainted that first time. I had dreamt often of kissing you but never anything else. I was in bed with Mr Curtis, for God's sake! It was wonderfully terrifying..."

"Well, that is just as it should be," Jon teased and kissed his warm, soft, fragrant girl again.

"I love you Jon Curtis," she said

"Are you all right now?" Jon asked

"Fine now after that sleep," she smiled. "But nought to thirty or so in a week is a bit full on." And she laughed and sat up and kissed him again.

"Have you been counting then?" Jon smiled.

"No," she said. "Just an educated guess."

"Are we going to get fish and chips now?" she continued and got up. Her hair had come out of its plait.

She searched on the sofa and found the bit of lace that had tied it, beneath a cushion. Then she went off to the bedroom. She came back carrying the little wooden stool he had made in carpentry lessons at school and used for sitting on to contemplate his paintings. In her other hand her hairbrush. She placed the stool on the floor between Jon's knees and sat on it handing him the brush.

"Would you mind plaiting my hair please Jon?" she said.

He took the brush from her and began to slowly brush her hair. His hand trembled when he did so. Her hair was so beautiful, he really just wanted to gather it up in his hands and bury his face in it. It took him a while to get it smooth and he had to concentrate hard on the plaiting but when he had finished, she turned and kissed him.

"Thank you," she said. "Will you do it again tomorrow? That was just lovely."

Jon put his arms around her.

"Arianwen," he murmured. "Oh! Arianwen, Arianwen."

How had she known he had been longing to do that? She was so perceptive.

"Come on Mr Curtis," she said. "My Mr Curtis."

She pulled him to his feet and standing on the stool looked into his eyes. Soft grey looked into deep blue.

"If we don't go and get our supper soon it will be number thirty-one. Or have you already started? I think I'm going to need some chips by the look in your eye."

Jon smiled his lovely wide smile and kissed her.

They walked round the corner to the fish shop then back to eat their supper. Then they made love on Jon's squashy sofa, and as it was their weekiversary, or so Ari said, started all over again in Jon's big bed.

He remembered later thinking about Ari's dream and what Poll had told him about how insecure she could be. He would keep her close.

In the morning Ari absolutely refused to get up. She held on tightly to the slats of the bed head.

"I want to stay here with you Jon," she cried. "I'll ring Sal and say I have chicken pox or something."

Jon laughed. "I have to go to see my father Ari," he said. "It's only a few days sweetheart." And in his own inimitable way, he persuaded her to let go of the bed.

He came down with her to the car. "Just remember, my love," he said as he breathed in her scent. "Wherever I am I will be thinking of you."

"And I will be thinking of you," Ari said. He pulled her to him and kissed her deeply. If Mrs Martin in the bottom flat was watching, so be it. Then his darling girl got in her car and drove home. She was a little tearful but she had to pack for going to Boscombe the next morning. Jon sighed and went indoors. He would stay at home to work on his painting until Tuesday afternoon. He went into the room to start painting and kicked off his shoes on the way. When he had first moved in Mrs Martin had complained that it sounded as if there were a troupe of Irish dancers above her, as Jon did move around a lot when painting. So now he painted barefoot and peace had been restored.

He would leave it as late as possible to drive down to his parents' home. His mother was not one to enjoy a happy Christmas. He just knew Christmas would be Scrooge-like. A small artificial tree on top of the television perhaps. It was a duty and he would be glad when he could leave, but he loved his father and knew he had been unwell of late. He wanted to see him.

Jon, as the eldest, had tried to protect his siblings from their mother's lack of empathy for her children and indeed for his father, and her dreadful cutting remarks. She had been extremely impatient and critical of them as soon as they could walk and talk and all three children had turned to their father for love and support. Jen, his sister had escaped by marrying young and would spend Christmas with her in-laws, her husband and her two small boys. They lived in Ireland but her husband, Eric had a new job near Cambridge and they would be moving there soon.

James, the youngest, had learnt early on to keep out of his mother's sight. Any request to his mother "Can I?" was always met with a 'No.' From a very young age, he had gone his own way. Where he was at the moment no one knew.

Jon got there late Tuesday evening. His parents lived just north of Wareham. The house was large and beautiful but cold and comfortless, so after having a sandwich and a whisky with his dad, Johnny, he went to bed.

It was cold in his room, the flock mattress on his old bed, lumpy and the room looked dusty and uncared for. He longed for Arianwen's warm body beside him and wondered if she was asleep and where.

The next morning his mother put the radio on and sat listening to it until lunchtime. Jon and his father put a small turkey in the oven and later made lunch. Afterwards, Gwen, Jon's mother went back into the living room to watch some television. She had barely said a word. Johnny went to sleep in his little study and Jon walked down the lane to visit Mavis and Hector who had a farm nearby. Jon and his siblings had spent a lot of time with them. They had always welcomed the Curtis children and Jon was very fond of them. Hector still came up to the house regularly for a chat with Johnny and the two men often had a day out together. The farmhouse was warm and their kitchen smelled of mince pies. Jon could have moved right in, but eventually, he set off back home with a dozen mince pies in a paper bag.

He made tea, but his mother just grunted when he set it beside her, so he went back to his father and over tea told him all about his beloved Arianwen. Johnny was delighted for his son, but said, "She is not going to be one of those girls who changes character once they are married, is she Jon?" Jon was happy to tell him no, not his Arianwen, but he was sad at that glimpse into his parent's marriage. How they had ever had three children was a mystery.

The next morning, he was up early. One more day, one more night and he would be on his way to his precious girl. He heard movement in his father's study and looked in. Johnny was making up the fire.

"Breakfast Dad?" Johnny smiled up at his son. "That would be good. In here?" And Jon went off to the kitchen to make it. Egg and bacon for his dad plus toast, marmalade and coffee for them both. There was no sign of Gwen, but the kitchen sink was full of cooking apples bobbing slightly in the water. He had nearly finished when his mother came into the room.

"I hear you have a new mistress, Jon," she said.

"I doubt my father would have used that expression," he replied.

"Doesn't matter what expression he used. We all know what she is. Young too by all accounts. The whores start early these days, don't they?"

Jon had read about a red mist forming before your eyes, and now one did. He sat down with a bump.

"Touched a raw nerve there, did I?" his mother laughed and began to viciously peel the apples. Jon picked up the tray and left the room.

After they had eaten Jon said, "Dad, I'm afraid I can't stay. I nearly hit Ma just now. She was so very unkind about Ari."

Johnny looked sad. "I just don't understand her, son. I thought she would be happy for you," he sighed.

"Dad," Jon said. "I'll ring the hotel, see if they can do me an extra night, and I'll speak to Hector and see if he can arrange a day out with you next week. I don't care where but I will bring Arianwen to meet you."

"I would like that dear boy," Johnny said. "But before you do that there is something I want to ask you." He reached forward and held his son's hands in his own. "I have been in the medical profession, Jon, long enough to know what these headaches I have might mean. I may have weeks, months or years, who knows? But I worry about your mother if and when I die. She has no friends now; she has alienated practically the whole village with her nasty remarks, and I have never understood why she does it. I might have depended on Mavis and Hector once, but not now." He stopped for a moment and looked at his dear boy of whom he was so proud.

"You know how helpful Hector and Mavis have always been, Jon? Hector did little jobs around the house for us often, and Mavis came for years to help with the cooking, cleaning and ironing. Last winter when we were snowed in, they both struggled up the lane. Neither of them are spring chickens, are they? The snow was often waist-deep, and Hector had to dig a path in some places. They had two big baskets with them. A chicken, eggs, butter, bread and milk. A very large cabbage, two dozen mince pies and the thing I will always remember a steak and kidney pie that Mavis had made. They came into the kitchen, very wet and their cheeks red with cold and I went to get them a drink. Your mother came in. 'Ah! My floor scrubber,' she said looking at Mavis, and laughed. Never a 'Thank you'. Hector and Mavis carefully emptied the baskets and left. Mavis said later she felt belittled and has never set foot in this house since. So, I would ask you Jon to just keep an eye on your mother when I am gone. I know it will be difficult but help her if she asks. No need to visit but a phone call now and then. I shall ask James and Jennifer to do the same."

Jon promised that he would though he didn't relish the prospect.

After lunch, Jon left. The hotel had been very accommodating. He stopped at Hector's farm and explained and Hector was more than happy to arrange an outing.

As he drove along, Jon thought about the last two days. He didn't know if he loved his mother, but he knew he didn't like her one bit. He loved his father a lot and was sad to see him so frail and uncared for. Soon though he saw the sign for Lyndhurst and his heart lifted. She would be with him tomorrow.

Christmas was lovely with Fred, Mam, Nan, and Roger. Queenie and her husband, Gwyn managed the journey with their longed-for, newborn son Owain, and George and Maggie. Sal was a bit wistful when she saw the baby as she and Fred had always wanted children but none had come along.

Ari was unable to find a suitable time to talk to Nan and Sal was so preoccupied with everything that Ari knew her news would not be well received. So, she left it for another time.

Ari explained that she couldn't stay until New Year as she had a lot of work to do for exams. They all waved her off from the hotel steps on the day after Boxing Day. As she changed gear and sped down the hill she was overcome with a feeling of great happiness. Jon would be waiting for her.

The hotel he had chosen was on the edge of the New Forest. When Ari got there, she saw that his car was already in the car park. Registration was no problem and she said she would carry her own case as it was not heavy. She knocked on their room door and went in. Jon was lying on the bed in just his shirt.

"It's me," she said.

"I should bloody well hope so," he said. laughing. "I heard the clash of gears and the squeal of brakes and knew it was you. So, I got ready."

She threw off her clothes, jumped on the bed and lay full length on top of him.

"Hello, sir," she said.

"My! Miss Morgan," Jon laughed. "I do believe you have put on weight over Christmas. I feel quite squashed."

"I might just withdraw my favours if I get insulted," she replied.

"Never," he teased and of course he was right.

They made love slowly and gently. When they climaxed together, she let out a great sigh. "I do so love you," she said. "You won't just leave me one day, will you?"

And he said he had no intention of ever doing so.

Jon told her all about his bleak Christmas, and it was arranged that on the following Tuesday, New Year's Eve, they would meet Johnny, Hector and possibly Mavis in Sherborne. There was a small model railway exhibition there together with an antique fair. Jon booked a table for lunch at a nearby hotel.

They had a lovely few days. The weather was dry, cold and sometimes overcast, but they took long walks, ate in old pubs, came back and made love and slept. And of course, talked and talked. Jon told her that his father was still far from well. He still had dreadful headaches and was now looking frail and old. His mother, never the most sympathetic and caring of people was trying hard to ignore it all. His father had an appointment at the hospital for tests in a week or so, and then they might get some answers. Otherwise, Christmas had been quiet, uncomfortable and sparse and he had missed her. Arianwen, for her part, told him about their neighbours from Wales coming. And Sal's sadness when she held the baby. "She has always wanted children, but has only me, and I am not part of either of them."

Jon had been told by Julius about the things Ari had given Flora and he was proud of her generosity but a little worried about the money. She was annoyed with Julius for having told him but said the money was no problem.

"Jon," she said. "I have a lot of money, I'm sorry but I just do. When I was a baby, Nan and Mam were paid to look after me. Not that they didn't love me or want me. But for me it was that or an orphanage, I believe. Anything they needed for me was supplied and willingly. The money they saved helped buy them the hotel. Roger, who is now married to my Nan must know where the money comes from, but he has never revealed by even a smidge who it is. Even my Nan doesn't know. The house I live in was bought for me, and the car. I have £200 put in my bank every month. That's a lot, Jon. I don't need that and if I can, I will share it. I do save some as I have no way of knowing when it might stop. But the sad part is that there is no one to thank. Sometimes I write my thanks on paper and then burn it and let the ashes blow away, or I just say them to the sky and the clouds. Perhaps someone somewhere knows that. I often wonder if it is my father or even grandparents that provide it all but of course, I know nothing about them."

She began to cry. "All I want is you and perhaps to meet my father one day." She stopped and wiped her eyes on the sheet. "Explanation over. Can we talk about something else now?"

"Come here, darling girl. I have a better idea.," he said, and he lifted her on top of him.

On Tuesday morning, they set off early for Sherborne. Ari was excited to be meeting another Mr Curtis. Once again, the weather was cold but bright. They parked near the castle; the car park was nearly empty, so they sat in the car for a while watching for Johnny's Rover. Jon leant over to kiss Ari.

"Crikey Jon," she laughed. "Your nose is freezing again." She considered him for a moment. "I'll ask Nan to knit a little bag thing for your nose with bits to hook over your ears. That should keep it warm and have the added advantage of catching the drip that forms on the end."

For just a fraction of a second, he looked at her in disbelief. Then he saw the mischief in her eyes.

"Arianwen," he laughed. "I'll..."

"You'll have to catch me first." She grinned and she was out of the car and running off down the car park. He could hear her laughing. She ran fast; she had been a wonder in the hockey team. At the bottom, the road divided. To her right a large cul-de-sac with more parking spaces; a big oak tree at the end, with a seat at the bottom. In front of her, empty flower beds and box hedges and to the left the car park exit. But she had hesitated too long and heard Jon steaming up behind her, struggling into his big coat. She laughed and held her arms out straight from her sides and he caught her and swung her around; her legs straight out and the toes of her boots pointing to the sky. He set her down in front of him and kissed her. And then he felt all the little bits of love that he had hidden away and had got tamped down beneath his mother's cruel words and indifference, break free and like champagne bubbles course around his body. He knew it was a physical experience and he pulled Ari closer and kissed her harder. There was the crunch of tyres on gravel, laughter, murmured voices, and the caw of rooks quarrelling in the trees. But for a while, they heard none of it. A middle-aged lady and her husband walked past. They smiled at each other. "Love," she said. "Isn't that just beautiful?" A car door slammed and Jon and Ari were back in the car park at Sherborne.

"Right! Sweetheart," Jon said. "Let's find my father."

"What are we looking for?" Ari asked.

"A cherry-red coat," Jon said.

"What!" Ari exclaimed. "Your father wears a cherry-red coat? That's very avant-garde of him."

"No Ari," Jon laughed. "Mavis will be wearing the coat. She told me she had it for Christmas. It will be easy to spot. And my father could never be described as avant-garde. He was a consultant paediatric surgeon. At least until he retired two years ago."

"I see them" Ari said. "Sitting on that bench under the tree." And Jon put his arm around his darling girl and they walked to meet, Mavis, Hector and Johnny Curtis. Johnny saw only a pair of beautiful soft-grey eyes fringed with long black lashes, a dusting of freckles across her nose and a rose-pink mouth that smiled at him. All the rest was hidden beneath a raspberry pink Fairisle tam and the new dark brown tweed coat that Sal had bought for Ari for Christmas. She had thought the green one made her dear girl look like a refugee.

"Hello, Mr Curtis," Ari said and gave him a big hug. Introductions over they walked into town to find the exhibition. The three men in front; Mavis with her arm through Arianwen's. They got to the hall which was cold inside. All the stallholders wore numerous scarves, shawls, hats and fingerless gloves. The men disappeared into the railway room and Mavis and Ari walked around the stalls. Ari bought a little grey velvet, silver embroidered purse with a loop to hang on a belt, whilst Mavis told her everything she could remember about Jon's childhood, which Ari was quite happy to hear. Jon didn't last long looking at the trains. "I couldn't stand it Ari," he said later. "All those model trees in nice straight rows, I wanted to bunch them up and make forests. And the people on the platforms, evenly spaced in a row. People don't stand like that! My fingers were itching to move them." Not a word about the trains.

Johnny came out then looking a little tired and Jon took him over to the improvised cafe for a coffee. Mavis went to find Hector and Ari continued looking at the stalls.

"What was all that running in the car park?" Johnny asked his son. When Jon told him, Johnny laughed so much he had to wipe his eyes.

"You have a lovely girl there Jon," he said. "Treasure her."

"I already do Dad," Jon smiled. He looked across the hall and saw his beloved girl wandering around the stalls. He still could not quite believe that she was with him.

They all got back together then and Jon with his arm around his Arianwen led the way to the hotel for lunch.

Johnny's heart lurched with love for his son when Ari took her hat and coat off and he saw her long, glossy, loosely woven plait, and just how very beautiful she was. He was so happy that Jon had this and that it was very obvious that Arianwen loved him. She held his hand, touched him, or kissed him whenever she could.

After a long lunch, the sun was beginning to set so they walked back to the car park. Johnny and Mavis had come in Hector's battered Land Rover. Jon thought he shouldn't have been looking for the Rover; Hector would never have let his dear friend drive. And Ari gave them each a little present. A silk scarf printed with cherries that Mavis had admired on one of the stalls. A large green silk handkerchief with his initials embroidered on it for Hector and a small silver Vesta case for Johnny. Hector, who had hardly taken his eyes off her was visibly overcome. "I'm sorry they are not properly wrapped," she said.

Johnny pulled her close. "Look after my boy, dear girl," he said. She looked into his eyes so like Jon's but a little faded now and with a shadow of pain. "I have already started," she smiled, and Johnny was content. It had been a lovely day and Jon promised his father there would be others. Jon and Ari stood and waved them off.

"Come on," Ari smiled at her lovely man. "Let's go back and you can take me to bed." It would take them near an hour to get back to the hotel. Ari snuggled up against Jon, her head on his shoulder and within moments was asleep. *What did she call it?* Jon wondered. It came to him *A cwtch*. He kissed the top of her head. Her eyelashes fluttered and she smiled then went back to sleep. And Jon felt a great sense of wonderment and peace. Yes, he was worried about his father, but Johnny had met Ari and if all went well would many times more. Jon marvelled that this girl who had been with him for only a few weeks could bring him such happiness. His life had been turned upside down and he loved it. He smiled to himself and drove on into the gathering night.

All too soon they had to go back. Jon went to his home and Ari, hers, as they both really did have work to do. Some of the staff and students at the art school noticed that Jon was much happier. Also, Ari's close friends knew why she was much improved. Julius knew why also and Ian Cooper suspected that Jon and Arianwen had some sort of relationship but as it was very discreet, he did not feel the need to inquire into it.

The next two terms were pretty hectic, getting all their work ready for assessment. The students would also have a life drawing to complete plus three weeks to work on their specialities. Grace had nearly finished throwing a thirty-piece dinner service and Marco and Ari had their painting ideas mapped out. Ari went to see Mr Cooper as she wanted to do a triptych for the painting exam. He said that had never been done but could see no reason why she should not, though it would be a lot of work. The subject had been in Ari's head for some time and she was looking forward to expressing it. Some students though were panicking as dissertations were not complete and sketchbooks rather meagre. Jon had a lot to do to make them focus and complete everything. Ian Cooper was having particular difficulty with Janet who was rude, surly and incredibly slapdash. He asked Julius to try talking to her, but if there was a problem, she was not going to tell him either or Jon when he tried.

But there were also some good times. In the middle of January, Philippe came over from France for a long weekend and everyone came for supper at Ari's house to meet him. He was the most lovely gentleman. Whenever he came back, they would meet up, either at Ari's or Grace and Lem's. Jon got on particularly well with Lem, and when his serious side disappeared, he was excellent company. He and Lem both played the guitar, so they often had a good singsong. And Grace and Philippe would sing sometimes solo, other times together. They were lovely happy evenings and often they laughed so much at Jon's reminiscences, about college and his national service that they thought the neighbours might complain.

Jon had often been invited to Julius', in the past with Sarah, and more recently on his own and really, they were pleased to see him whenever he was passing. Both Julius and Poll were very fond of him and now Julius asked him if he would like to bring Arianwen for supper one evening. Ari was a little apprehensive as Poll had been her teacher, and here she was sleeping with Jon. But she needn't have worried. Poll and Julius were very broadminded and Jon reminded her that they had had the same sort of relationship themselves.

Ari dressed with care as this would be the first time she and Jon had been invited out together and she wanted to be a credit to him. She wore black, low slung hipster trousers, with a silver belt, the little purse attached, and a soft grey angora jumper, the same colour as her eyes. Underneath just a white silk vest. Her hair she drew back off her face and fixed on top with a silver clasp. The rest hung down to near waist level, and she had curled the ends a little. Silver earrings and her silver bracelet completed everything. Jon was so overwhelmed by her beauty that they had to have a 'quickie' before they left as he would not have lasted the evening otherwise. Or so he said.

Julius didn't know her as well as Poll, as he was not her main tutor, but he had taken a few classes, canvas preparation, life drawing and one or two anatomy sessions with Ari's group, and of course he always called her "our little girl." However, within a few minutes of her coming in with Jon, Julius was enchanted with her.

Poll asked her if she would call them Poll and Julius now and Ari said, "Well I'll try. I have enough trouble with sir, Mr Curtis and Jon, at the moment so it might take me a while. But thank you." So, Julius, ever inquisitive, asked her what she normally called Jon. Very seriously she said, "Oh! He absolutely insists on Sir." And Julius caught the flash of love in the glance between them. And she was so enthusiastic about Poll's cooking. Poll had made an enormous chicken, ham and leek pie. "I haven't had such a lovely meal since Nan got married," she said. Poll asked if she cooked for herself. "I didn't when it was just me, just went to the deli, but when Jon comes, I do. My Nan taught me quite a lot, but we didn't do cookery at school, did we? It was expected that someone would do it for us. And well when I go to Boscombe we have a chef at the hotel. Wonderful food but sometimes you just long for a bag of chips."

Jon was just eating a piece of potato and he nearly choked. Poll had to pat him on the back. When he had recovered, he narrowed his eyes at

Arianwen and she gave him the sweetest of smiles. He laughed. They went back to the subject of cookery and he asked what they had learnt instead as he could remember his sister, Jen coming home from school with tins of rock cakes. Ari laughed and rolled her eyes. "Etiquette," she said. "I'll be a real asset to you if the bishop comes to tea, Jon."

The evening was lovely and very relaxed. Poll thought of the evenings when a morose and silent Sarah had dampened their spirits somewhat. After they had had coffee and were sitting in the living room, Ari stood up and held her hand out to Julius. "Come on sir," she said. "Let's do the washing up." Julius was there like a shot, much to Poll's amusement. When they got back Ari was immediately enclosed by Jon's arm, and Poll and Ari got on to the subject of school uniform. The head at Poll's school wanted to change it and there was a lot of objection from parents. Jon was reminded of Ari wearing her hockey shorts and asked what he had wanted to ask before.

"What despicable things did the girls do down the field?" Ari turned to him and she was laughing already.

"We used to practice kissing," she said. Jon's face was a picture.

"What, with each other?" Julius and Poll could see Ari's eyes alight with mischief. She looked seriously at Jon.

"How do you think I got so good at it?" Jon was at a loss for words, so Ari relented. "No not really," she laughed. "We did this." And she gave her arm a big kiss. Jon put his arms around her and turned to Julius and Poll.

"See what I have to put up with?" he said and kissed her lovingly.

"Well," said Poll. "Now I know what those bruises were on some girls' arms. You live and learn."

"They are not called bruises, Mrs Winter" Ari said. "They are love bites."

"Well good gracious." Julius laughed, "Whatever will the young think of next?"

Later when Jon and Ari had left and Poll and Julius were getting ready for bed, Poll said, "Bless him, Jon looks as though he has been hit by a bus, sort of dazed. He can't quite believe it can he, and he never takes his eyes off her? When you were out doing the washing up, he watched the door the whole time. He said he had always known she was special but had never thought things would be quite so wonderful. What did she say when she was with you?"

"She wanted to know really if things were all right at school for Jon, now she was with him. No difficulties or anything. I assured her things were fine. I think no one has noticed." He stopped and got into bed.

"Then she said she loved every little bit of him. I am so glad we told him Poll."

"Did you see his face when she said about practicing kissing? And what was that about chips? She knows just how to tease him doesn't she?" Poll laughed. "I think he couldn't wait to get her home. He had a finger under the edge of her jumper most of the evening."

And with that Julius put his arms around his new wife and kissed her.

Jon and Ari only just made it home. Before the front door had properly closed Jon was kissing her and had her trousers and knickers off and then his own trousers. They made love on the hall carpet, and even though Ari had had no chips, just the thought of them seemed to work magic. Afterwards, they lay out of breath and semi-naked side by side on the floor.

Ari started to giggle. "That was like doing a few rounds with Jackie Pallo," she said. "Honestly, what if someone had looked in the window? But I do love you so much Jon Curtis."

"Come and lie on top of me Ari," Jon said

He began to stroke her bottom. "I had a dream about doing this a long time ago," he murmured.

"And did you dream about what comes after," Ari said kissing him. "You do know Jon that men are supposed to need an interval to recuperate between fucks?"

"Well, no one told me," Jon laughed. "And they haven't got you, have they? Where do you want it, here or in bed?"

"I can't get up, so it will have to be here. Please."

The next day Jon appeared at Julius' just after lunch with a dozen Welsh cakes which Ari had made as a thank you. Julius came to the door. "God, you look tired old son," he said. Jon just smiled.

The cakes were much appreciated.

Jon and Ari had planned to go away at Easter. Ari had everything ready for her exam. Paints, brushes and three ready primed canvases. Two tall and thin, one wide. She still used the restricted palette Mr Cooper had suggested when she had first started, but now she had added two more colours, black and rose madder. There was nothing else to do but get it all out of her head.

They were going to Cornwall for a week and Jon rang Hector to see if another meeting could be arranged on their way down. His father had said all his tests had proved negative, but there was a suggestion of a compression of the vertebra in his neck, which might be causing the headaches. Jon was a little cheered by that but wanted to see him. Hector said he had tried ringing Johnny several times over the past week but always got Gwen. Johnny was asleep or out. No other explanation. In fact, Johnny was in hospital and died two days before they were due to go away. He had had a tumour at the base of his brain but had told no one. Once diagnosed he seemed to lose heart and the end came very quickly. Gwen kept the news of his death from everyone for a few days, and Jon was so very angry that she hadn't let them know. He really couldn't understand why. Gwen raged against the doctors, against being on her own, and the fact that none of her children had been there when their father died, which was extremely unfair, and Jon, furious, told her so.

Jon went down to Dorset. Nothing had been done about a funeral and when Jen came, they had a very difficult few days with their mother. They managed to contact James who said he would help but wouldn't come down until the funeral. Jon came back for a few days then had to go back again. Of course, Ari wanted to go with him. She had met Johnny Curtis just once but had loved him on sight. Jon had to be quite direct and tell her 'No'. This was not a good time for a first meeting with his mother. He and his siblings just knew that she would be extremely difficult and hence nasty. He did not want Ari to experience any of that. So sadly, but understanding Jon's reasons, Ari stayed at home.

The funeral was bleak. Jen, her husband Eric, and Jon stayed at the house over night, but no preparations had been made for them. The beds were unmade, cold and damp. Jon, Jen and Eric suggested a meal at the pub, but Gwen said no, so they went without her.

Their brother James was waiting for them at the crematorium the next day. He never entered the house if he could help it. The only time now he saw his mother was if he came to the house in France, and even there he gave her a wide berth.

Jon offered his mother his arm to follow the coffin in, but she refused it and stalked in on her own. She had said not a word to any of the large crowd of mourners. People from the hospital, the village, the pub, the bowls club and the cricket club. Johnny had been well-liked.

His children had bought a large wreath for the top of the coffin, Daffodils, tulips and narcissi, all yellow. Yellow had been Johnny's favourite colour and he had been well known for his yellow scarves and ties and a yellow flower in his buttonhole. There was nothing from his wife, and she hardly moved during the service. She didn't join in at all with the prayers and sat silently when they sang *Immortal, Invisible*. Jon could hear Mavis sobbing behind him and Hector blew his nose a fair few times. Outside, afterwards, Gwen stood with the vicar and her children to say thank you. Many of Johnny's friends held out a hand but she didn't take it. She stood silently with what could only be described as a slight sneer on her lips.

Jon, James and Jen walked around talking to their father's friends and looked at the flowers. Amongst all the elaborate wreaths was a bunch of white lilac, tied with a dark blue ribbon. Jon picked it up. The card just said, 'To Mr Curtis with love, from Arianwen'. Jon had not been expecting that and his eyes filled with tears. His dear, dear girl. He just knew she would have cried in the florist's and that there would be a good reason she had chosen what she did.

Then Gwen just left. No 'Goodbye' or 'Thank you for coming'. Jon had booked a room at the pub on the Quay and everyone was invited there, but they now had no car other than James' old Ford Pop. As they walked towards it a woman approached Jon.

"Excuse me, I think you may be Jon Curtis?" she said and held out her hand. "Louise Turner."

Jon said he was indeed Jon Curtis, but he had no idea who this woman could be. He had seen her at the service but was sure he had never seen her before.

"I need to talk to you urgently," she said. "About your father's will."

Jon was intrigued. She was a pleasant looking woman with curly brown hair now liberally streaked with grey, soft-blue eyes and glasses. A little black hat with a feather and a fitted black coat. About his mother's age he thought.

"It won't take long," she said. "But your father made me promise I would talk to you, and only you he said."

She stopped and waited for Jon's response.

"Do you have a car here?" he asked. She did.

"Then may I come with you? We were going to the pub, but Jen and James can manage for a little while."

He went ahead and told his siblings what he was doing. They looked a little quizzically at him but got in the car and lurched off.

Jon got into Louise's car and as other cars left the car park and new mourners for the next funeral arrived, Louise told him what she had promised Johnny.

She had had a phone call the previous week from Johnny's solicitors about the reading of his will. She was mentioned in it, she had been told, but had decided for reasons of propriety not to attend. She had been his father's mistress for nearly twenty years. They had worked together at the hospital where she had been Johnny's theatre nurse and they had got together one evening after a long and complicated operation on a three-year-old who had been mauled by a terrier. Johnny had a little flat behind the hospital, used when he was on call and for late nights such as this. He had asked her up for a drink. Things progress quite quickly after that. She was married and her husband had MS so needed her help and support and although they did not have a close marriage any more, she had wanted to stay and help him. Johnny of course needed love and comfort, and he would never have left his children. So, they had settled into a relationship that made neither of them feel guilty. They met whenever they could, had managed a few holidays together, a few weekends, that sort of thing. And her husband, Frank had been quite happy with the arrangement. "And of course," she said with a smile. "Johnny and I loved each other."

"Did my mother know about you?" Jon asked. It might go some way to explaining Gwen's behaviour if she had, he thought.

"No Jon," Louise said. "Never." She paused for a moment and smiled at Jon. "The only people who knew about us were Johnny's dear friends Hector and Mavis. We met up many times at their farm."

She took Jon's hand in hers. "My husband died three years ago," she said. "And Johnny and I were beginning to talk about moving somewhere new together. Then your father started getting his headaches.

I just wanted to say Jon, that your father was loved for many years by me. He loved you children dearly and was very proud of all three of you and I know the highlight of his last few months was meeting your beautiful Arianwen."

Jon smiled.

"So, Jon Curtis, who looks very much like his father, be prepared for me being mentioned tomorrow."

She leant over and kissed Jon. "Thank you for listening," she said. "I promised Johnny I would talk to you." And Jon with tears in his eyes hugged her. He asked for her address and gave her his. He was so pleased to have met her, he said and perhaps they could talk some more about his father at another time.

Then she drove him to the pub but wouldn't come in. After a double whisky, Jon found James, Jen and Eric, and in a quiet corner told them all. Like him they were so pleased that Johnny's life had had love and comfort in it. They raised their glasses in a silent toast to Louise. Then they thanked everyone for coming to wish their father farewell and went back to the house, picked up their things, said goodbye to Gwen, who hardly acknowledged their presence, and drove off. The will reading could go on without them. Their mother never ever mentioned it, though Jon learnt later that his father had left Louise a sizable amount of money and his flat.

Jon drove back to his darling girl. She had a rich beef casserole in the oven, hot water ready for a bath and later in her clean warm soft bed, her warm soft, fragrant and generous body.

When Jon had parked outside her house, Stuart had been passing by on the other side of the road. He was returning from visiting his girlfriend, Amy. He saw Mr Curtis take a holdall out of his car and then go and knock on Arianwen's door. He just saw a glimpse of Ari as Mr Curtis bent and kissed her. He decided not to say a word to anyone. Tom, he knew still fancied Arianwen. He wouldn't want to disturb the fragile peace just before exams.

A few weeks later Jon went to Hatton Garden with the money his father had left him and bought the best diamond ring he could get. He planned to ask Ari to marry him, at the end of the school year. His mother was making increasing demands on them all as she was lonely. But he broached the subject of bringing Ari with him to France in the summer. His mother was not keen. "No," she said. "She will be noisy. The young always are. After that girl your brother brought last year, I need some peace." Jon left it but was determined to get her approval. The house had originally been left to Johnny by his parents and was now Gwen's and she was enjoying saying who could and could not visit. It had all been much more carefree and relaxed when his father had been around. Jon had moments when he thought he ought not to subject Ari to his mother. But he could just see his beloved Arianwen lying in the garden of wildflowers and watching the passing clouds. His body shivered with longing. He wanted to take her there.

The exams seemed to be going well. Grace finished her dinner service and it was utterly beautiful. Marco and Ari did well in the life drawing and now had their painting compositions to tackle. The weather was warm for May, but all the painting students were in the large studio at the back of the building which was a little cooler.

Ari set up her canvases on three easels, so she could work on all three together. A narrow one on the left, the wide one in the middle and lastly a narrow one. Her concentration was extraordinary. Several times Marco or another student spoke to her but she did not answer. Break times she would sit and study what she had done. It was difficult to get her to come for lunch or a coffee in Lyons. But she was happy with what she was doing. What was in her head was slowly coming to life on the canvas. Everyone stopped at four and after cleaning their brushes and tidying their work areas the students left and the room was locked. Jon therefore had no real opportunity to see what Ari was painting. If it was his evening to be with her, he would often find her asleep on the sofa when he got in. He would make the supper and then take her to bed. She was never too tired for that. He didn't mention France as his mother was still being awkward.

The relief at the end of the exams was immense. They finished at lunchtime and everyone, all twenty students went to the pub. That was it now. Tomorrow the examiners were expected.

All the students were in the next day and were sitting in the common room or outside on the fire escapes, ready if the examiners needed them to discuss their work. Three examiners came to assess the painting. One woman and two men. They were in the studio for some time. Jon was going down the stairs when the woman came out and stood on the top landing. She had tears in her eyes. The men then came out, "I have never seen anything so beautiful, so poignant and so well painted," she said. "And extremely thought-provoking." And she blew her nose on her handkerchief. One of the men went to get Ian Cooper, and then all four went back into the room. Jon was intrigued. What could that be about?

It was Arianwen's triptych that was causing all the fuss. The first panel showed a young child, a girl of about three or four, possibly in a bare room as the edges were not clearly defined. She was standing all alone clutching an enormous bunch of bluebells. "Victorian language of flowers," the woman examiner said. "Bluebells for constancy?" But the floor was littered with dead and dying flowers, and the bunch in the little hand was wilting. The child was half turned and looking at the next painting.

This larger painting was based in part on Manet's 'Les Dejeuner sur L'herbe'. A family were having a picnic in a sunlit wildflower meadow. The woman still in the water in the Manet painting was now a grandma leading a young child. The men were obviously father and son. And the naked woman staring so boldly out of Manet's canvas was now a young modestly dressed mother with a baby sleeping at her feet. Two older children were playing in the distance. The colours were beautiful, warm and golden, and there was an air of contentment and happiness surrounding the people.

The last canvas showed an old lady dressed in black, sitting on a bench. In the background the Abbey. She was holding what looked like a funeral order of service. But she was turned away from the middle painting, as if she was waiting for and could see someone in the distance. What you could see of her face was alight with expectation and love.

They sent for Arianwen. She nearly died of fright when the message came. Ari thought it was because she had done a triptych and they were going to disqualify her. She was sitting on the fire escape having a cigarette with Tom and Marco. "Fucking hell," said Tom. "What have you done?"

As she walked up the stairs one examiner said to Ian, "If this is her, she is just like her painting. Beautiful."

But they just wanted to shake Ari's hand and say hers was the best painting they had seen anywhere that year. Would she explain it? "It's very simple" Ari said. "The child wants constancy, but will she get it or keep it. The family have it, and the old lady, did she have it or not?"

"Brilliant," they all said. She went back a little bemused, but very relieved. When Jon saw it later in the day, he remembered her stopping to record something in her sketchbook. The middle painting was the same family that had been near the abbey when he had been talking to Ari about Tom. It was a stunning painting.

The next day they all had to empty their lockers and sort out any work they needed to take home. Ari went to get her car and transported Grace with her dinner service plus her own paintings. They had to do two runs. And then that was it. They were officially out in the world, apart from the leavers' party the next evening. All students from first year to fourth were invited plus staff and partners. In the past they had had a fancy-dress theme, this time it was evening dress. Ari had a new silver dress with thin shoestring straps, and a skirt like an upturned tulip with silver petals. It was short, ending halfway up her thigh and it had a narrow silver belt on which she hung her velvet purse. Her hair she wound up on top of her head with her silver pins. Jon had gone home to collect his things as he was going to stay with Ari overnight before taking his mother to France. His car was outside Ari's all packed and ready for his early start in the morning.

Gwen had not relented in allowing Ari to go, but Jon would not stay with her long, just take her and come back as he was very annoyed about it. As soon as his sister came that would be it. Then Jon and Ari were going away somewhere warm and very, very, private.

The large studio had been cleaned and decorated for the party, with tables around the room. Jon, Julius and Poll were already there sitting around a table when Marco and Ari came in together, arm in arm. They had been such good friends from the very first day, when Ari had given Marco half her lunch. She didn't want him to come alone as Philippe was in France working. So, she told Jon she was going with Marco. "Anyway," she said. "Can you imagine the tongues wagging if we walk in together?"

Jon was to regret not saying, "It doesn't matter now. I just want you with me." And walking in with Ari on his arm.

Marco looked superb, in a purple velvet suit with a pink bow tie and Ari was pleased to be going with him. They came in and said hello to everyone, then went across to Julius and Jon, and Marco was introduced to Poll. Lem and Grace came in then and joined them all. Julius asked Ari to dance and then she danced with Elias, James and Stuart.

Then it was a slow dance and Jon claimed her and held her very close. He slipped a finger through the strap of her dress and stroked her back. Ari lifted her head and smiled at him. "I want to kiss you Mr Curtis," she said.

"I want to do more than kiss you, Miss Morgan." Jon laughed. "Ari," he continued, "I have something to ask you. If I go to the small studio, will you follow?"

No one saw that Janet was watching them. She had hated Arianwen ever since she had taken Tom away from her. With Tom she had been someone, albeit a 'stopgap' as Tom had described her to Jon. Tom had taken note of what Ari had said and was now with Nell, and they had a much better relationship. Janet was out in the cold. She had watched Ari for a while and had noticed that the little silver ring she always wore had moved to her right hand, just before Christmas. There must be a new man on the scene she thought, remembering what Tom had told her about it. She was determined to find out who it was, and so watched Arianwen with obsession. She was jealous of Ari for her ability, her money, her generosity and her beauty, and now she had someone new. Tom still thought she was wonderful and look at all that bloody fuss about her exam painting. It wasn't fair. She hated, hated her. Arianwen, in Janet's eyes, had everything and she didn't deserve it.

Janet thought she knew now who that person was and had been sitting at a table near Jon and Ari and had listened to their conversation with Mr and Mrs Winter. She was furious that everyone at that table seemed to know about and be pleased about their relationship. Everyone fucking knew! Except her.

Janet was sharing a table with James, Stuart and his girlfriend Amy, Carol and her boyfriend and a few third-year students. Tom and Nell weren't there. They had left directly the day before, as they had a job running an art workshop at a children's summer camp near Hastings.

Janet leant across to Stuart. "Did you know he was fucking her?" she growled, indicating Jon. Stuart was very laid back.

"Why are you always so bloody angry about everything Janet?" he said. "But yes, I think so. Anyway, he spends a lot of time at her house. I've seen his car there several times, and I saw him go in and kiss her once."

"Since when?" Janet hissed.

"Not sure" Stuart said. He was enjoying this. Janet was such a truculent person, and possibly the worst fuck he had ever had and spiteful with it. He couldn't care less about her now.

"Last Christmas possibly?" he said. "We saw her car outside his flat when Amy and I went to her auntie's. Anyway, what's it to do with you?"

"How do you know it was his flat?" Janet said.

Stuart looked at Amy and could read her thoughts. If only Tom was here. Janet behaved then in the hopes that Tom would have her back. "Some hopes," Tom had said.

Janet glared at him, but Stuart carried on.

"Well," he said. "Tom and I went there once. Mr Curtis was getting rid of some old LPs and Tom wanted them. Really cool place he had, in an old school."

"And it was definitely her car there?"

"Oh! put a sock in it, Jan," Carol said. "It's like a Gestapo interrogation. You are always going on about Ari."

"Yes," Stuart sighed. "Her dark green Mini. We went past about lunchtime didn't we Ames and it was there when we went back around ten that night?"

"Just leave it Jan," James said. "They probably got together when he went looking for her after all that Tom stuff. Ari never did anything to you, just leave them alone. You may never see either of them again after tonight."

But Janet couldn't leave it. She felt a great flame of jealousy and rage grow in her chest. How had she missed that? She watched Jon and Ari on the dance floor. Their relationship was very obvious. A lot of things fell into place. She knew where they met. Jon left the room and Janet followed. She suspected that Ari would follow soon after. He went outside and up the stairs to the small studio. It was beginning to get dark and it was gloomy in the room. Jon heard the door open. "Ari, my darling girl," he said. "Come here."

Before he realised it was not Ari, Janet had pinned his arms behind him and was kissing him. She was a big girl, strong and determined and he struggled to free himself. Her lips were attached to him like a limpet. In the half-light they could have been making love. He heard the door open, then Arianwen's gasp "No oh! No." followed by a groan. Then he heard her run down the stairs. Janet lifted her knee and gave him a hard vicious jab between his legs. He fell to the floor, his whole body it seemed engulfed in white hot pain.

Janet caught up with Arianwen just as she reached the street door and grabbed her by the arm.

"You stupid, fucking, stuck up cow," she spat. "Thought you could have it all didn't you? Well, he's mine now. We didn't know how to tell you, so we showed you." Janet's face was red with rage. "All your fucking fancy clothes and perfumes couldn't keep him. And your stupid bloody name."

"No, no," Ari said. "I don't believe you. You're lying."

"Me, lying?" Janet screamed into her face. "After all that stuff you said about Tom, you've got a bloody nerve."

She stopped and slapped Ari's face so hard that Ari's head rebounded on the door frame. Ari struggled to free herself, but Janet wouldn't let her go, her grip was like steel.

"You took Tom from me you fucking slut. So, I'm taking your bloke. Or your 'lovely man' as you so soppily call him."

Ari wrenched the street door open but Janet hit her again and again. She fell onto the pavement, grazing her knees and losing her shoes and Janet kicked her, once, twice, three times. Ari struggled to her feet but Janet knocked her down again. She seemed to have lost all control. She couldn't stop hitting and punching Arianwen. A man, queuing for a bus across the road came over to help Ari, but Janet hit him too. Blood poured from his nose. Ari managed to stand and then ran. Down the hill, across roads, past the pub with the people sitting outside and home, where she fell inside and locked and bolted the door. Only then did she begin to cry. "No, oh! No no no."

Meanwhile Janet had crossed the street and pushing to the front of the queue boarded the bus that had just stopped.

Flora had been coming down the stairs and had seen Janet attack Ari. She ran back to find help. The first person she met was Julius and when she explained what she had seen he rushed down to help. There was no sign of Ari. Julius went outside. A man in the bus queue, holding a bloody hanky to his nose shouted across, "The one in the silver dress ran off down there, mate, the other hopped on that bus. Fucking lunatic, she is." He waved his hand in the direction of a bus disappearing round the corner. Julius looked around but there was no sign of Jon. He went back inside and that was when he saw a very white-faced Jon leaning on the stairs. "That Janet girl assaulted me," he gasped. "Where's Ari?"

"Ran off home we think, Janet laid into her too."

Ari went around the house and locked and bolted all the doors and windows. Janet might come after her and would bring Tom. She was very frightened. She struggled up the stairs. Her whole body hurt. Her feet were filthy and bleeding, her knees too, and her face and ribs hurt. She took off her silver dress and hung it up carefully and put the little velvet purse with her keys in a drawer. Then she found an old cotton nightie and put that on. Over the back of a chair was the navy jumper she had bought Jon, which he had left behind, she put that on too. It smelled of him. Turps, oil paint, and Gauloises. She lay on the bed and slept.

A little while later she woke up and wondered where Jon was. He was supposed to be staying with her. She wandered round the house for a while. She caught sight of her swollen and cut face in the hall mirror and remembered with a dreadful gush of fear and dread what had happened. Why had Janet said those things if they were not true? How did she know what she called Jon? She had never done anything to hurt her so she must be right. She, Ari, had lost Jon and he was with Janet. That's why he wanted to talk to her and why he wasn't here now. The whole thing, the words, the slaps, the kicks she lived over and over in her head, until she fell asleep crying in desperation. She had lost Jon, of that, she was sure.

The phone rang. She thought it might be Jon, but for some reason she didn't want to speak to him, so she went back to sleep. The phone rang again. She went down and picked it up. It was Jon again. "No, No, No," she shouted down the phone, then replaced the receiver. She took the phone off the hook and went back to bed.

Jon was outside with Julius who had driven him down as he had been in no fit state to walk. He had a key but Ari had bolted the doors. "She's in shock I think Jon. Let her be tonight and she will be better in the morning. You can come and stay with us." But Jon wanted to stay close. He would sleep in his car, but Grace said he could have their spare bed so he took that. In the middle of the night Grace woke him. "She's out in the garden, lying on the lawn," she whispered.

Ari had woken feeling thirsty, so she went downstairs for some water. She opened the back door. It was warm outside but the grass was soft and cool on her sore feet. She lay on the lawn watching a near full moon dance amongst the clouds. She could smell the lilies she had planted near the log store and the lavender at the edge of the path. She slept.

Jon looked out of the window. Ari was curled up in a foetal position on the grass. He watched for a while and then quietly opened the window. But she had heard the faint creak and got up and went indoors. The door slammed and he heard the bolts being shot.

Next day all of them, Jon, Julius, Grace, Lem, Poll and Marco tried to talk to her. But they got nowhere. They could hear her pacing around and sometimes there was heart-breaking crying. Then Grace said she was out in the garden again. Jon asked Lem to give him a lift and he climbed over the garden gate and undid the two bolts at the bottom. Ari wouldn't notice and they could get in easily, if necessary.

Ari was sitting on the bench under the kitchen window. She was stabbing holes in the wood with one of her Japanese hairpins. She wore only a dirty cotton nightie as it was warm. Jon's heart turned over with love and sorrow when he saw her. She was filthy, her hair matted, her feet and knees blood-caked, her beautiful face white with a livid bruise on her cheek. She did not notice him at first so absorbed was she in stabbing the bench. He called her name softly. At once she looked up and screamed, "Go away Jon, Go away." And she was off into the house and the door locked and bolted. But she had left her silver pin on the bench. Jon picked it up and put it in his pocket along with the ring he had so hoped would be on her finger by now. He sat there for some time but she did not appear again.

Julius came back and Jon told him all that had happened. "What did that girl say to her?" Julius wondered aloud. "I wonder if Flora knows?" And of course, Flora did, she had heard it all.

"Wicked, wicked girl," said Poll.

Jon was beside himself with grief for himself and Ari, and rage at Janet. He had rung his mother to say he would be a day late and she was absolutely furious. But he had to leave as he had promised to take her to France, and this was the first thing she had asked of him in years. He rang his sister but she couldn't do it as the children were still in school, and he couldn't find James. He consulted Julius. "Take your mother Jon," Julius said. "Three days maximum and you will have fulfilled your promise to your father. Arianwen will be all right in a few days. She has had a bad shock but is young and will be herself in no time. Lem and Grace have said they will keep an eye on her, and Poll and I will check often. And you know Arianwen will understand when you get back." So, Jon went, sure that very soon he would get his darling girl back. He would phone them every day. But it was with a very heavy heart that he set off.

But Ari did not get better. The next night she spent the whole of it outside, alternately pacing the garden and lying prone on the grass. To Lem and Grace's knowledge she hadn't eaten or washed for three days. Grace crept in through the garden gate the next morning. Ari was sitting on the bench again. Grace said not a word but sat quietly beside her, and after a while Ari seemed to accept her. Grace had brought two pieces of shortbread with her which she knew Ari liked. "Thank you," Ari said politely and lined them up on the arm of the bench and kept rearranging them. They sat in silence for a while, Ari humming to herself.

Grace said, "Would you like something to eat Ari?"

"No thank you," she said. "I'll wait for Jon. He will be hungry when he comes home." Then Ari resumed her wandering. Upstairs, then back down again, down the garden and back indoors. Grace, in her gentle way asked what she was doing. "Looking for Jon," came the reply. "But I can't find him."

Then Grace seeing the state of Ari's feet, all cut and bruised said, "Would you like a bath Ari?"

Ari turned and smiled at her. "I'll wait for Jon," she said. "We often have a bath together." And then Ari seemed to remember where she was and began to sob and Grace put her arms around her. "I hurt, Grace," Ari said. "My body hurts, my heart hurts and I am frightened. Why Grace? Why?" But Grace had no words to tell her.

In the evening when Ari was asleep Lem came round and he and Grace stood by the garden gate. "She needs her family Lem, not us," Grace said. "We can't make decisions for her. She doesn't know where she is most of the time and she is constantly looking for Jon." Lem rang directory enquiries and got the number for 'Arian Court'.

Sal sent Fred to get Ari the next morning. Grace and Lem told Fred all that had happened. He had not known about Jon. Ari hadn't mentioned him. And they couldn't get in touch with Jon to tell him what had happened anyway. On getting to France his mother had had a small stroke. She was in hospital and Jon was just waiting for one of his siblings to take over.

Chapter 4
Dream, Dream, Dream
The Everly Brothers

July 1964 - March 1968

Fred had just lifted Ari up and laid her on the back seat of the car covered with a warm blanket. Grace had gone into the house and packed a small bag for her; she remembered also Ari's big bag and slipped a new sketchbook in it. You never knew if she might want it.

Sal was practically hysterical when she saw Ari. "Look at her Fred. Look at her. Whatever have they done to her?" Fred carried Ari upstairs and Sal ran a deep bath and undressed her like a child. Ari said not a word as Sal washed her and cleaned her poor feet and knees and washed the blood from her hair. There were deep purple finger bruises on her arms where Janet had held her and Sal suspected broken ribs. Her face looked bad too with a deep cut on her cheekbone and bruising around her eyes. She dressed her in a clean nightie, but Arianwen went over to the dirty clothes on the bathroom floor and found Jon's jumper, which she put on. Then Sal put her to bed. She slept for about an hour then she was up looking for Jon again. Sal sent for the doctor, who said Ari had some broken ribs, which he strapped. She was also suffering from shock, so he gave her a sedative, and she slept on and off for several days. The doctor came again and said not to worry, she would heal in due course and she did. Olive came to see her and Ari began to tell them what had happened. Neither Olive nor Sal had known of Jon before now.

One bright day about four weeks after the assault, Ari and Nan, who had come down from London again, to see how she was, were sitting outside in the sunshine watching the waves. Both were sitting on the bench, eyes closed enjoying the sun on their faces. It was quiet with only the distant hum of the crowds down at the beach. Sal had gone indoors to make some tea. Olive turned to Ari and saw that silent tears coursed down her cheeks. She gathered Ari into her arms.

"Please cariad," she said. "Don't get so distressed."

"How can I not Nan?" Ari sobbed. "How can I not? I love him and I thought he loved me. He said he would stay with me forever, but he hasn't, has he? Nothing. I go over and over it all the time. Is he with Janet? Did he hate the sight of me when I was ill? Nothing from him at all Nan."

Olive wiped her tears away.

Sal came back with the tea then.

"Where did Jon go Mam?" Ari asked.

"Grace said he went to France Ari," she said sadly. Ari said not a word but went indoors and lay on her bed. She loved him with every bit of her being and thought he had loved her but he had abandoned her. Gone away when she needed him most. Perhaps having seen her at her worst he had had second thoughts. She was very sad and perplexed by it all, and she never asked for Jon again. Some days it was as if a great grey cloud enclosed her and she could not find a way out, but as the days passed, the clouds passed and she began to see a little more clearly.

They were all worried that Jon would come looking for her and set her recovery back, as she was still very fragile. One day she said to Olive,

"I don't want to go back to my little house. Janet and Tom might know I'm back there and come for me. And how can I live there when I know Jon will be walking up from the station every day? Or if I go shopping, I might meet him. What if he crosses the road so as not to speak to me? I couldn't bear that Nan." Her voice ended in a wail of pure despair.

Olive looked at her dear beautiful girl all bruised and pale and thin. Sal was beyond furious with everything and everyone at the art school, and she knew that she too would find it difficult to forgive Jon Curtis for leaving their beloved child in this condition.

"Stop now Ari," she said. "You are getting yourself all upset."

When Ari had calmed a little Olive continued.

"We as your family have talked about all this, sweetheart, when you were ill and we had to make some decisions for you. You don't need that house now as you are not at art school, so you need not go back there. It won't be good for you here, too crowded and noisy and Sal is very busy. Similarly, we think London might be a bit too much for you at the moment. You need somewhere quiet and peaceful where you can get well and sort out all the thoughts in your dear head. Then when you feel really well, we can decide what to do next. Roger is looking already. He will be here later and I believe he has some photographs of a house to show you. And Christina will be here tomorrow. Just be my brave Arianwen, cariad. We are all here to help you."

Roger had indeed found somewhere for her to go. Wherever it was she would need someone with her for some time. Olive made one last suggestion to Sal, that they try to get in touch with this Jon Curtis, through the art school, and see if there was a possibility of sorting it all out. Ari heard the proposal and she was adamant it was no, never. He had left her; she wasn't going to beg anyone to love her, so no.

Help came in the form of Christina. She had been married for two years, but her husband was a cruel controlling bully so bravely she had left him. Could she come to them for a while to hide until her divorce proceedings started? Of course, she could and Sal explained to her about Ari. Then she booked them both into a grand luxury hotel with a spa for two weeks as they both needed a bit of pampering.

When Ari and Christina were away, Sal, Fred and his brother Little George, who was staying with them, to help out for a few weeks, went to Ari's house and brought away all her personal possessions. Ari was most concerned for her pot of skin cream. Sal found it easily and also a large box of Durex. This really shocked her. "What had Ari been doing?" She practically screamed at Fred. "That man had a lot to answer for, if she ever met him." Sal was convinced that Jon Curtis had seduced Ari. Fred went off to pack Arianwen's painting things and Sal sat on the end of the big brass bed. There were no soft Welsh blankets to smooth now, just the bare mattress. She felt terribly sad. She and Fred had courted for a long while. There had been lots of kisses and cuddles and sometimes Fred wanted to go further, but Sal wouldn't let him. She had been very proud that she was a virgin on her wedding day. She was disappointed for Ari.

George drove Ari's mini back to Bournemouth. He was glad he was on his own. Sal looked absolutely furious when she got in the car with Fred. His brother was not going to have a pleasant journey home.

Then they arranged for the removers to put the furniture in storage. A week later they came. They carefully packed all the linen, crockery, books and paintings and wrapped all the furniture. They cleared all the free papers and flyers that had accumulated in the hall and left only the curtains, carpets and white goods. The house looked clean and tidy and Sal and Fred on a last inspection were pleased. Ari now had to decide what to do with it.

Roger knew that Ari owned a house, part of her trust fund, of which she was unaware, in North Wales. It needed some work, as not only was there a big farmhouse, which hadn't been lived in for some time, but a large stone-built barn also. This he suggested could be made into an excellent studio for Ari. He showed Ari some old photographs of it and Ari loved it immediately, and Christina said she would stay with her for perhaps two months. So, Roger set about finding some rented accommodation for the girls that was within walking distance of the house. Roger was slightly anxious about what he had done. Might he have made things worse? Ari was where he thought she should be. He had interfered enough and the rest must be left to fate.

Arianwen was much better. She and Christina had had a good time, although she was still very frail. The owners of the hotel had been told that Ari had been ill and needed a bit of pampering, so kept an eye on her. The girls had been massaged with beautiful oils, had their hair and nails done, dabbled, in Ari's case very cautiously, in the pool, gone for long walks and eaten scrumptious food. Christina was the ideal companion for her and had even got her laughing several times but she did see the terrible sadness Ari carried with her and she noticed something else, a sort of stillness too about her friend, but was unsure what it was. Now it was back to the hotel for a day or so and then up to North Wales.

When Ari and Christina came back from the spa and before they went to North Wales, Roger took them to visit Grace and Lem. Ari had also asked if Marco could be there. One warm, gentle evening towards the end of August, the large black car stopped outside Grace and Lem's house. All three were upset to see Arianwen. When she stepped out of the car, she looked white and frail. Later Lem said she looked like a ghost. She walked with a slight stoop and when they went to hug her, she smiled at them and said, "No, please. My ribs have not yet healed." Only then did they realise the full extent of the beating she had had from Janet. They didn't stay long but Ari had brought something for each of them as they had been such good friends to her. To Lem and Grace, she gave the deeds to their house. "You never knew it was mine, did you? Well, it is yours now." And to Marco the deeds and the keys of her house next door. "I have no need of all these houses," she smiled. "Better you have them." Roger had sorted it all out and was there to witness their signatures and do all the legal bits. Ari told them then where she was going and gave them the address, adding that they were honour bound not to give it to anyone. She didn't mention Jon at all but they knew what she meant and then she was gone. All three sat in silence for a while thinking of the unexpected generosity of their dear friend. Then Lem got up and got them a drink.

"To Arianwen," he said raising his glass. "Let her find happiness again." And Grace and Marco agreed most wholeheartedly.

Jon had had the most awful time in France. The journey down had been easy, even if his mother had barely spoken. He had said he would leave her at the house as she would be fine until Jen came in a day or so. But the pump which supplied all their water had seized up and he spent the next day repairing it and repriming it. He went to the village to get some groceries for his mother and when he came back, she was sitting at a very odd angle in full blazing sunlight, down the garden. She had had a small stroke. The ambulance came and took Gwen to hospital. His sister came a few days later as promised but no sooner was she there and ready to take over, than their mother had another stroke. Much more severe this time. She had died three weeks later in hospital and Jon had to organise the shipping of her body home and then the funeral. He had tried, whenever he had a moment to ring Grace or Marco but had had no luck. He even phoned 'Arian Court' but Sal put the phone down on him. So eventually he wrote Ari a long letter, telling her all that had happened. It did get delivered to her house, but unfortunately the removal man clearing the hall only gave the pile of papers a cursory glance. Everything went in the dustbin, including Jon's letter.

He was frantic for news of Arianwen, so as soon as he arrived on English soil he drove straight to her home. He knocked and knocked and then went next door. There was no reply there either. Mary, opposite came out. "Lem and Grace are on holiday," she said. "And Arianwen went to her family." She didn't say that the house was now empty.

"Thank you," said Jon. *At least she was safe,* he thought. He took his things home. He hadn't been there since the leaver's party, and that seemed so long ago, and in two weeks' time, a new term would start. He had thought things would have been so very different.

The next morning, he set off for Bournemouth. As he drove down Sea Road he tried to remember where the hotel was. Ari had said only on the cliffs overlooking Boscombe pier. He parked the car near the pier and set off up the hill. He went the wrong way at first but retracing his steps went into a little cafe and asked for directions. The owner was most helpful and came outside to show him the right road. "Big white place up there." He pointed. "Lovely inside it is." Jon thanked him and set off again. He found it immediately. 'Arian Court', his heart leapt. He walked up the drive, a little apprehensively, and up the steps into the open front doors. A huge copper pot of white gladioli sat on the reception desk and Sal was seated behind it. As soon as she saw him, she knew who he was. She recognised him as the man who had come down the stairs after Ari's interview. Longish dark hair, bright blue eyes and an air of quiet intensity. He came up to the desk and read her name badge. He was surprised that she was so young. But then remembered that Ari had said she had been only fifteen when she had looked after her. Only five or six years older than him then?

"Mrs Rowlands?" he said. "I'm..."

"I know very well who you are," Sal snapped. "You are Ari's Jon." She paused and opened a door marked 'office'. "Fred, can you take over? Jon Curtis is here." Fred, looking extremely concerned, took over. Sal took Jon into the empty dining room and asked a passing waitress to get them some coffee.

"Well," she said. "I suppose you are looking for Arianwen? She isn't here. She has gone away with her friend Christina. Whatever did you do to her, poor little love?"

Before he could reply the waitress brought the coffee and Sal carried on.

"Lem phoned us, you know, as they were very concerned about her. She hadn't slept or eaten, they thought, for three or four days and most nights she spent either lying in the garden or wandering around the house. She did let Grace in but when Grace tried to stop her sleeping in the garden, she fought her. Grace did stay with her though and slept on the sofa. She asked Ari what she was doing when she was wandering around, and Ari said, 'Looking for Jon, he is not in bed.'"

She looked at Jon with real anger in her eyes. Jon flinched.

"They were afraid to leave her so phoned us and Fred went to get her. To say we were upset when we saw her is putting it mildly. She was filthy. Her hair all matted with dried blood, and she was very pale and fragile looking. Fred carried her upstairs and I ran a bath for her. It was like bathing a child again." Sal stopped; she was quite overcome by the memory. After a moment she carried on, tears in her eyes.

"She was so quiet, she said nothing, and she was bruised all over. Feet, hands, knees, face. I put her in a clean nightie and led her to bed but she went back to the bathroom for that dirty jumper of yours, then got into bed and went to sleep. But she was awake again within the hour and looking for you. She was so, so disturbed. We had to get the doctor then and he gave her a sedative. The poor child slept for three or four days. But he found she had three broken ribs and said she was in deep shock. That girl must have been wicked to do that to her, Jon, and why? I'd prosecute her if I could find her." Sal paused for breath.

Jon told Sal then that they had all been sure Ari would be all right so he had set off for France.

"Well, I'm sorry to say this but I think she thinks you left her, abandoned her. Do you know what she said to her Nan?" Sal paused. "Arianwen said she was glad she had been a baby when she was abandoned the first time as she had known nothing about it. Then she said she couldn't have borne it twice." Sal stopped, she was near to tears herself, and saw the look of horror on Jon's face.

"Never in a million years," he said. "My mother…"

Sal stood up suddenly. Her hands flat on the table.

"I don't want any excuses and I don't want to know about your mother, Jon. I am concerned only for my girl. Ari should have come first with you and she didn't. You didn't keep her safe. Well, I won't tell you where she is now or where she will be moving to. She needs to be left alone to heal and get on with her life." Sal moved away. "I can't help you anymore," she said and visibly upset, left him.

Fred came then. "You had best go.," he said. "Sorry, but we are all very concerned for Ari at the moment." They went to the door together and said goodbye. Jon walked back to his car.

On the way home, driving through the New Forest, he passed the turning to the hotel where they had had that wonderful time after Christmas. Only eight or nine months ago. He pulled into a layby up the road, put his head down on the steering wheel and sobbed and sobbed. When he had recovered, he got out of the car and lit a cigarette leaning on the bonnet. He understood Sal's antagonism but he was determined not to give up on his darling girl. He looked up at the clouds drifting above the trees. Was she doing the same he wondered? How had it all gone so wrong? Where was his beloved Arianwen?

After a very bad sleepless night at home, Jon went to see Julius. Poll answered the door. "Come through Jon," she said. "We are in the garden." Julius was sitting in a deckchair, in the shade, reading a newspaper. As soon as he saw Jon, he knew there was a problem.

"Coffee Poll!" he called and gave Jon a seat.

"She's gone Julius," Jon said. "I went to their hotel yesterday and got a very bad reception. Ari has been very ill and is still not good. There was no way they were going to tell me where she is."

"I went round several times," said Julius. "First time to tell Ari about your mother. The woman across the road came out and said they had all gone away. I had just missed them. Lem and Grace up north, Marco, she thought with a friend to France and Ari to her family. I went again when you had even worse news of your mother but there was still no one there. I knocked across the road but no answer there either."

Poll brought the coffee and sat down with them.

"So, what of Arianwen?" she asked.

"I spoke to Sallie," Jon said. "And she was very hostile. Apparently, they had to come and get Ari as she was so ill. Broken ribs, bruised all over, and from the description Sallie gave, very shocked and ill. She blames me for not keeping her safe and they are moving her away somewhere, so I can't see her or be with her. They don't want me anywhere near her."

Poll put her hand on his arm, "Then we will just have to find her Jon."

Which time would tell was easier said than done.

They did not know that Mary was still friendly with Olive and after Julius' first visit, had been going to meet her for a day in London. She told Olive of the visit and Olive asked her not to speak to him again. She had hidden the next time Julius came knocking. No one at 'Arian Court' told Arianwen that Jon had come looking for her.

The rented house Roger had found was fine. It was clean and functional but rather old-fashioned, with a huge open fire in the living room and extremely noisy plumbing. Its advantage was that it was only twenty minutes' walk from Ari's new home. Fred drove them up there in Ari's car, stayed the night, and then got the train home. The girls spent the rest of the day sorting their clothes out and putting away the food shopping that Sal had bought for them. The next morning, they went to see Ari's house. The sun was shining, it was warm and for the first time in ages, Ari noticed the clouds drifting across the sky. They walked along the high-banked lanes and saw the first signs of autumn.

The house was reached by a steep drive down from the lane. Standing in the lane you could look down upon it, but it was screened somewhat by a copse of trees with several rowans near the gate. The house was called Ty Griafolen and was built at right angles to the lane. Parallel to it, across a wide muddy courtyard was a big stone-built barn. The builders were working on the house first. All work stopped when they arrived. Christina had grown her hair and it was now a slightly wild Afro. She had also taken to wearing black clothes and lots of dull gold jewellery. With her beautiful golden skin, she looked like a princess. The two girls had made quite an impression on the locals. The beautiful, tall black girl, accompanied by an equally beautiful but frail-looking friend, striding around the lanes. The foreman stepped forward. "Hello,"

Arianwen said. "I'm Arianwen Morgan and you are doing this house for me." Christina had gone to sit on a pile of bricks and was lighting a cigarette, watched by all the other men.

The foreman, named Huw, shook Ari's hand. "Yes Miss Morgan," he said. "And we will try to get it done by Christmas for you." He had been told by Roger Fearnley when engaged to do the work that Ari had been ill and he could see she still looked rather pale. Ari and Christina then had a quick look round before walking back.

Their visits to the house were the highlights of the next two months. They would often appear mid-morning with buns they had bought in the village, and everyone would sit around smoking and talking until Huw said, "Right lads, we'd best get on." One brave plumber asked Christina out. She went several times and told Ari it was most enjoyable and enlightening. Which made Ari laugh.

"What would you put on your postcard now then?" she asked her friend.

"Utter heaven," said Christina. Their relationship had resumed exactly how it was at school. They were able to tell each other anything and everything. In the evenings they sat beside the log fire with a glass of red wine each and talked about their troubles. Christina about her cruel and controlling husband, who had been very attentive and kind before they had married. Everyone thought it to be an extremely good marriage. Ari talked about Jon and what had happened at and after the party. Christina said that Jon didn't seem the type to just leave her, but then you could never tell with men, they could deceive you no end.

Then it was time for Christina to go back. Her divorce was well underway and she would stay with Belinda in London until the decree absolute. Olive came to replace her and was pleased to see Arianwen looking better. They went to look at the house and Olive was most impressed by the work that was being done. But there was something about Arianwen that concerned Olive, the same thing Christina had noticed. Something she had seen before in other women. A certain look about the eyes. She thought to bide her time until the right moment, and that came sooner than expected.

Ari was reaching up to get something from a cupboard and Olive saw the definite curve of her stomach. "Ari," she said. "Come and sit with me a moment." Olive leant forward and held Ari's hands.

"Cariad," she said gently. "When did you have your last period?"

Ari looked at her in astonishment. "Not for ages," she said. She stopped and thought about it. "Before the party perhaps? I thought because I was ill, they had stopped." She sighed. "Why Nan? Do you think I might be pregnant then?"

"I think you may well be," said Olive. "We'll have to visit the doctor but looking at you I would say yes."

The look of absolute delight on Ari's face was to stay with Olive for the rest of her life.

"Oh! God, Nan, how wonderful," laughed Ari. "How bloody marvellous. I'm going to have Jon's baby. I shall have something of Jon." And she collapsed against Olive sobbing with joy. "Oh! Nan, Nan," she said. "If only."

And Olive in tears said, "I know cariad, I know."

She seemed to get much better after that. Sal, when she heard the news was not best pleased and didn't have much to say that was nice about Jon Curtis. But when she saw how Arianwen was she relented somewhat. Ari went to the local doctor and although he was quite censorious as she was unmarried, she cared not a fig. They worked out that the baby was due mid-February and Huw was given instructions to decorate the baby's room. Ari chose eau de nil and white. Sal never said a word but remembered the little bedroom at Ty Gwyn.

One evening sitting by the fire Olive asked Ari if she would tell Jon.

"No Nan," she said. "I have thought about it a lot but he may be with someone else now and wouldn't want me turning up on his doorstep with a baby. And if not, I wouldn't want him to feel obliged to marry me. I'm fine as I am. I love him and miss him so much but that will always be so, and I will have the baby soon."

Huw and his men had done an amazing job on the house in such a relatively short time. The whole of the downstairs was now one enormous L-shaped room. The kitchen was up the end near the back door and the living part at the bottom had large French doors to the garden. There was a small hallway with a front door that was never used, and stairs to the three bedrooms. A beautiful white and green bathroom next to the largest bedroom, and a small one in between the other two. All of Ari's furniture which had been in storage fitted well, but she could see that she might need more. Some spaces looked rather empty. Upstairs her old brass bed was installed and a cot for the baby was in the corner. Just until it was old enough to sleep in its own room. That all sorted, Huw started on the barn and the paving of the courtyard. They had also installed a tall fence with a large gate at the end of the drive and this joined the house to the barn and kept the courtyard secure. Ari and the child would be very safe.

When Christina and Ari had been visiting the house, they had often met an older lady walking her dogs in the lane. A bit older than Mam, Ari thought. She had always said "Bore da" and asked how the work was going. Her name she said was Shona and she lived at the top of the lane at a house called Cae Coch. One morning when Olive had decided to stay at home, Ari went on her own to the house to talk to Huw about bathroom fittings. She met Shona with her dogs, lurchers named Otho and Nerva and asked if she would like to see what had been done. Huw and the men all stopped what they were doing when Shona came in and touched their foreheads. Shona was very interested in all the work, as the house, she said had been empty for some time, which was a pity. She said it had once belonged to Cae Coch, and she thought it might have been the bailiff's house once upon a time. When Ari mentioned the idea of turning the barn into a studio for her, Shona was most enthusiastic. She said that she managed a large gallery in Conwy and was always on the lookout for new talent. Perhaps when Arianwen was settled she could come and see her work.

They were to become good friends and later Shona helped Ari negotiate the locals, as a single pregnant woman, moving into the area was subject to a lot of gossip. Which, Ari noticed stopped abruptly if she entered a shop, for instance. But in part, it was her name which helped. She remembered years ago it seemed, Mr Winter asking if she was Welsh. Now older people in the village would often say, "There's lovely. We haven't heard that in years." Shona asked if she had Welsh origins but Ari said she was unsure but had been born in South Wales. Shona herself said she was named for a very rich Scottish aunt in the hope of some favours, but nothing had come of it.

Ari learnt also that Shona's family had lived in the area for several hundred years and were considered by all as the local gentry. Hence the forehead touching Ari surmised. Once or twice, Shona asked her up to her house for tea, Olive too of course. But Olive preferred to stay home, as she wasn't very enamoured of the North Walian people, finding them very insular. When Ari mentioned this to Shona she laughed. "So speaks a true South Walian," she said. But Ari loved the area. She loved the peace and quiet, the clean air, and the long winding lanes with their steep banks. She loved the rivers, the waterfalls and the mountains, and she liked the people too, who in the main had accepted her. And most of all the wide, wide skies.

Shona's home was extremely large and very old. Tudor origins, Shona explained. They entered the grounds from the lane, through tall black wooden gates in which there was a wicket. This led to the stables which were a Victorian addition. "Unused now," said Shona. Then through an archway to a long, wide, stone-paved terrace in front of the house. This too was Victorian, but in fairness Shona said, they had tried to build it in keeping with the house. From there a long drive bordered by lawns, thickets of rhododendron bushes, and tall trees led to the main road. The house itself Ari thought, was beautiful. Three storeys high with a large porch, it was built of local stone with a Welsh slate roof. "It's all a bit of a mish-mash really," said Shona. "There's some Georgian bits around the back and three quite large Arts and Crafts cottages at the edge of the grounds, up near the woods."

Shona shared the house with her brother. He lived entirely on the ground floor as he had been injured in the war and used a wheelchair. He very, very rarely went out and kept mostly to his rooms. The dogs were really his, Shona explained and she took them out for him most mornings. Shona had rooms of her own upstairs but she said she always made supper for them both in the evenings as he liked her company and to hear all the news.

They walked up a great oak staircase flanked by family portraits to reach Shona's rooms. Shona pointed out who was who. "My father and mother, grandfather, and aunt Shona. Great uncle Rhodri etcetera."

Ari asked if her parents were still alive.

"They died in the Blitz," Shona said. "My father had a desk job at the War Office and my mother went down to stay with him when he had leave. They died together in a theatre that took a direct hit. The only thing that was found was my mother's silver purse. You know one of those Edwardian ones with a ring to hang it from your finger. I have it somewhere."

"And what of your brother? Is there not a portrait of him?" Ari asked.

"No," said Shona, rather sadly. "And I doubt there ever will be."

Ari felt she did not know her well enough to ask why.

In her lovely drawing room, Shona took Ari's coat and was surprised to see that she was pregnant. She asked when the baby was due and saw an expression of such sadness pass across Arianwen's face that she wished she hadn't. But Arianwen answered her quite easily. "I can't wait," she smiled. "The middle of February I think." After that, they visited each other often, but Ari never saw Shona's brother, David.

Ari was so much better that she started drawing again. The sketchbook Grace had put in her big brown bag had remained untouched. Now she took it out and used it a lot. The builders, Shona and the dogs, the garden. All were new and of interest and Ari was glad to find that her drawing had not deteriorated. She was as happy as she could be in the circumstances, but missing Jon was a continual ache.

She and Olive went back to Bournemouth for Christmas. Sal was rather anxious as she could envisage Jon turning up and seeing, a by now, rather large Ari. But he did not and Sal went back with Ari, to move her into her new home and to stay with her until the child was born.

Olive went home with Roger. She had enjoyed her time with Ari and was glad she was looking better. She was the brave girl Olive had wanted her to be. But she was sad that Ari would have to bring up the child on her own. She sat on the sofa in their stylish flat, shoes off and a gin and tonic in her hand and told Roger all that had happened. She described the house and how it was progressing and how Arianwen was settling into life in North Wales. "And," she said. "She has made another friend. A lady called Shona who lives up the lane. She has been for coffee to her house several times. Apparently, she has a brother, rather older than her, but Ari hadn't met him."

Good, Good, Roger thought to himself. *Give it time.*

He turned to Olive, "Where might you like to go for dinner this evening?" he asked.

"Hmm," said Olive. "I'll have to think on that one."

On the afternoon of Sunday the 13th of February 1965, Ari's pains started. Sal was with her and for a few hours they just walked about the house. When it began to get dark Sal thought they should head for the hospital as it was a good hours' drive away. This they did with Ari gritting her teeth with the pain. Sal was not allowed to stay. She left her little girl calling Jon Curtis all the names under the sun as she gave birth to his daughter. Gwenllian Morgan was born at eight o'clock the next morning. "Monday's child," said Olive with a smile. "And also, Valentine's Day."

When Sal saw the baby, she knew there would never ever be any doubt as to who the father was and wished with all her heart that things could have been different for Ari. Ari was just delighted with her daughter; she was the most perfect baby ever.

Sal stayed a few more weeks and then went home. It was coming up to the end of March and the hotel needed to be got ready for the new season. Ari said she would be fine, as Grace and Lem were coming for Easter and Marco might pop up for a weekend.

One beautiful afternoon, when the sun was shining and daffodils, primroses and celandines still covered the banks up the lane and the bluebells were just beginning to show themselves, Ari wrapped Gwenny up and put her in the pram. They would go for a walk; they would go out. She had just got to the top of the lane when she met Shona who asked her in for tea. They struggled a bit getting the pram through the wicket and then into the house, but Gwenny was fast asleep. "We can leave her here at the bottom of the stairs," Shona whispered. "We will hear her if she wakes." So, they went upstairs and Shona made tea, and they sat at the table talking.

Downstairs Gwenny had woken up but was not yet in full throttle. David, sitting reading in his room, heard the odd squeak and snuffling noise and went into the hall to see what it was. He had thought it was the dogs but they were asleep near him.

At the bottom of the stairs was a dark green pram and when he looked in a little face with bright-blue eyes smiled at him. He put a finger near the baby and it was grasped immediately. He was so engrossed in the child that he did not hear someone coming down the stairs.

"You have met Gwenny then?" said a woman's voice. He looked up and for a moment his heart skipped a beat. He thought it was someone else.

"Hello," she said. "You must be David, Shona's brother? I'm Arianwen Morgan and this is my daughter Gwenny." She held out her hand and shook his.

David was astounded. By not one blink of her lovely eyes had she registered his injuries or the wheelchair. It was as if they were nothing to her.

"She's awake now," Ari said. "Would you like to hold her while I sort her bottle out?"

And without waiting for a reply, she whisked the baby out of the pram and settled her against his good arm. The baby smiled at him. Shona, coming down the stairs to see where Ari had got to, was amazed. Her brother, the recluse, sitting happily with a baby in his lap!

From then on whenever Ari came up, she would knock on David's door. Sometimes if he was in pain he would not come out, but mostly he did as he loved to see Gwenny.

The barn was finished and it was just as Ari had hoped. Sturdy wooden stairs led to the top floor where the floorboards had been sanded and sealed. Long cupboards were fitted against one wall with a sink in the middle. Shelves above housed all Ari's art materials and three easels stood near them ready to be used. There were two large skylights let into the north facing roof and at the narrow western end a wide floor-length window had been installed which could be opened onto a wooden balcony with stairs down to the garden. There was a wood burning stove set on a large piece of Welsh slate with a big fire guard around it. Near this was a cot for Gwenny and a playpen. The ground floor had a little bathroom and a big storage cupboard but was otherwise empty.

Underneath the balcony Huw had built a little wooden seat, ideal for Ari to sit and watch the passing clouds. She loved it all and was very sorry when the men left to go to another job.

Ari began to paint again. In the morning, she would get up, sort out Gwenny, and then take her across to the barn. If she was sleepy, she went in her cot and Ari painted. If not, it was warm enough for a bit of playtime on the rug before the fire. They soon fell into a happy routine. Shona came one afternoon and had a tour of the barn and looked at some of Ari's work. She was very taken with the triptych that Ari had done for her exam and asked if she would exhibit at the next open exhibition at the gallery. But Ari was a bit hesitant about putting anything of hers on public display. "Perhaps in a while," she said. "When I feel more confident?" And Shona not really understanding that reply had to be content with it.

Grace and Lem drove up on Maundy Thursday. The weather had been fine at the beginning of the week but now it had turned grey and gloomy. Ari had spent the previous day getting ready for her visitors. She hadn't seen them since she had visited them with Roger, although she had spoken to them on the phone, often. They had married just after New Year and of course had asked Ari to the wedding. She had not gone using as an excuse that she still felt unable to return to the city. In reality she was enormously pregnant and did not want that bandied about the art school. Flora went as did Marco, and Tom and Nell who were still together, and Marco rang her to tell her all about it.

Lem and Grace arrived mid-afternoon. They had stopped for lunch at The Royal Oak in Betws-y-Coed but were gasping for a cup of tea. Gwenny was asleep upstairs. Tea and Welsh cakes finished they sat around in the living room just catching up with the news. Ari was well attuned to Gwenny by now and heard the first stirrings of her waking.

"Excuse me for a moment," she said and went upstairs.

Gwenny was awake and waving her hands and feet at a mobile suspended above her cot. She turned her head when she heard Ari.

"Hello sweetheart," Ari said. "Did you have a nice sleep?"

The baby smiled.

"Well, we have visitors downstairs who are going to be mightily surprised to see you," Ari said, lifting Gwenny out of the cot and blowing a raspberry on her tummy. Gwenny gurgled. "We had better get you dressed."

She laid Gwenny on the bed and after changing her nappy dressed her in navy angel top and white tights. Then she brushed the dark hair.

"Right then Miss, let's go." And carrying Gwenny on her hip went downstairs and into the living room.

Lem and Grace were still sitting on the sofa when Ari came back and for just a moment didn't register what they were seeing. Then Lem said, "Who's is that Ari?"

Grace looked at him. "Don't be obtuse Lem. I think it is Ari's baby. Am I right?" she asked looking at Ari.

Ari smiled at her, "This is my daughter Gwenllian, known as Gwenny. She is just over two months old."

Grace put her arms out for the baby who happily went to her.

"And I can see who her daddy is too. Oh! Ari why didn't you tell us?" Grace said looking up.

For the first time in ages, it was all too much for Ari who just left them and went outside. Grace handed Gwenny to Lem and followed.

Ari was sitting on the bench by the kitchen door and crying as if her heart would break. Grace put her arms around her.

"I'm so sorry Ari," she said. "I didn't mean to upset you."

Ari wiped her eyes and gave her a wobbly smile.

"I get good days and bad, Grace. Mostly I just don't understand where it all went wrong. I loved him so much and I thought he loved me. But as my Nan would say, we are where we are and I have to make the best of it. For Gwenny at least." She paused and stood up.

"Come on let's go and rescue Lem. If I give in to crying, I'll be at it all day."

But Lem didn't need rescuing. He was having a lovely time bouncing the baby on his knee. He looked up concerned when the girls came back but Grace gave him a slight shake of the head.

"We need one of these.," he said. jokingly, tickling Gwenny.

"Well," laughed Grace. "As soon as we can Lem." Lem's face was a picture of happiness.

And they all laughed, even Gwenny.

That evening after supper, when Gwenny was asleep, they sat around talking. Lem said that while they were here, they might look at some properties with a view to moving. "We love the house you gave us Ari but we wondered if you would mind if we sold it?"

"Oh, for goodness' sake," she said. "It's yours to do with as you like."

"Thing is," Lem continued. "Grace would like to have her own pottery and there is nowhere we can do that where we live now, as it would be far too expensive. Also, I wouldn't mind getting back to doing some wood carving. So, we have been looking around. If we sold our house, we could get a much bigger, more suitable place up here, maybe. Anyway, we thought we would have a look."

"I cannot think of anything nicer than having you two near," Ari smiled. "Unless of course Marco came too."

But Marco, Grace said, spent most of his time in France with Philippe as things were a bit more liberal there, or so he said. The house was rented to three students from the art school. Which Ari thought was great.

Good Friday they all went into Llandudno, though most of the shops were shut. Ari drove and then when they arrived, carried Gwenny in a sling across her chest. They walked the length of the promenade, and watched the sea for a while, then went to Forte's for some lunch. The waitress was very helpful and warmed Gwenny's bottle for Ari. Grace and Lem were impressed with the town, and on the way back Ari took a slight detour and drove through Conwy. "You could come here tomorrow," she suggested. "As the estate agents will be open, and in Llandudno too."

The next day Ari stayed home with Gwenny and Grace and Lem went off to see what was on offer. In the car they began to discuss Ari. "There is something missing in all this Lem and I can't think what it can be. They were so close, Mr Curtis and Ari, they couldn't leave each other alone. And now this. Nothing. She is so sad Lem."

"What did she say when she was upset?"

"Only it is what it is, really. But what is it? She said did I remember when we had to do that portrait thing and afterwards, she had said she wanted a family with children who looked like their father? Then she said she had forgotten to ask for the father to be with her. If he could see that baby? She is beautiful isn't she, and so like him?"

"You would never tell him Grace, would you?"

"No," she said. "I wouldn't. It is not our place to do so. We love Ari don't we, and she has been so good to us, we must never let her down Lem. And of course, that's why she didn't come to our wedding. She must have been quite large then."

"He was a really good chap," Lem said. "And I got on well with him. He told me once that he had struggled for ages with his feelings for Ari, but when they got together it was marvellous. Like you I can't think what the problem might be. Have you seen him at all?"

"No," Grace said. "But Flora said he is not himself at school and she thinks she heard him say he had moved. Let's just hope it gets sorted out for both of them. And if and when we move here Lem, we will keep a close eye on her."

They went to several estate agents that day and got the particulars for three properties that looked interesting. One in particular they liked and so drove past it on the way back. After supper they showed Ari all the details. The one they liked she knew well as it was very near where her rental home had been, just on the other side of the village. Lem said he would ring and arrange a viewing.

"Hang on a moment," said Ari. "Just let me phone Shona. She will know everything there is to know about the place."

And Shona did. She came down next morning to meet Grace and Lem and insisted on accompanying them on any viewings as she said, "I have some clout around here, and you will get a fairer description and price if I am there. Some agents think the English have pots of money. Others don't like selling to them anyway. So, if I come, they will see you as my friends, OK?"

It was fine with them all and they thanked her.

Lem arranged two viewings for the following Tuesday and they would pick Shona up from the gallery. They were hopeful that the one they really liked would be suitable.

Shona knew it straight away. It hadn't been empty too long as the owner had recently died, and no one in his family wanted the property. It was a large farmhouse, similar in build to Ari's but with several single storey outbuildings and a large plot of land. Shona said it had once belonged to her family but had been sold sometime between the wars. The agent was a little late but he was most apologetic when he saw Miss

Rhys Williams was there. There was a large kitchen and two big rooms downstairs. Upstairs, three large bedrooms and a very outdated bathroom.

"Nothing that can't be fixed," Lem said. "And we could have a great vegetable garden and perhaps chickens?" He looked at Grace who smiled her agreement. The outbuildings were also in reasonable condition and all had running water. Ideal for a pottery and just what they wanted really. The agent named a price but when Shona raised an eyebrow at it, he came down by two thousand.

"Thank you, Mr Davies," Shona said. "I shall remember your generosity." Mr Davies looked most grateful.

Shona laughed all the way home. "Silly ass," she said. "He knew I could make it difficult if I had wanted to. He does all our buying and selling. At the moment!"

Shona received a large bunch of flowers the next day as a thank you and Lem put in an offer on the property which was a little lower than that of the previous day but accepted all the same. "Hurray for Shona," they all said and Ari found a bottle of champagne under the sink left over from Christina's visit.

At the end of the week Grace and Lem went home. They put their house on the market straight away and it was sold three days later.

They planned to move up to North Wales in August, Lem having had to give in his notice at school.

The summer was not all that good, mostly dull and cloudy. But on fine days Ari would walk up in the afternoon to see David, as Shona was at the gallery. Once or twice, on a nice day, she was able to entice him outside as she said Gwenny needed the sunshine. He was quite happy sitting with the baby on his lap and Ari did quite a few sketches of them both asleep. Otherwise, they just talked. About art, the news, the garden or the weather. Gwenny was a constant amusement with her attempts to roll over and her astonishment when she did.

"She will be crawling soon," Ari said. "And then look out."

One day Shona had to go to Aberystwyth for a meeting with other Welsh gallery owners, and asked Ari if she would call in on David in the afternoon, to keep him company and to make him some supper, as she wouldn't be back until late. Ari was more than happy to do that, so after lunch she packed all Gwenny's supplies and set off. When she got there David was waiting in the hall. Ari bumped the pram up the steps and leaving Gwenny asleep went into David's rooms with him. She had never been in them before, they had always sat in the hall or outside, and she was astonished at what she saw. One wall was dominated by a large bookcase with hundreds of books on the Roman Empire.

"A very deep interest of mine," David said. The other long wall was covered in paintings. Beautiful ones too and all obviously by the same artist. She said nothing but walked around, looking and marvelling at them. David followed in his wheelchair.

"These are yours, aren't they?" she said turning to David. How she knew she didn't know, she just did.

He admitted that they were. "And do you still paint?" Ari asked.

He held up his burnt left hand.

"Tell me," Ari said and he did.

He had always painted he said and was getting quite well known before the war. Then he had been employed by the Ministry of Information, to record various aspects of war life. He had been what was known as a 'war artist'. In June 1943 he had been commissioned to record the work of some conscientious objectors who were detailed to firefight and he had gone to a large bracken fire with them. The wind had changed and the fire was swiftly out of control. He had fallen over a wall running from it, been knocked unconscious, got severe burns down his left side and had broken his back. He had been in hospital for months after. His back had healed somewhat and he could walk a little, but it was often very painful so he used a wheelchair most of the time. His burn injuries were, he said, obvious. The whole of the left side of his head and face was red and scarred and this extended down to beneath his collar, and lower. He wore a patch on his left eye as he said it had been damaged and although he could see with it the light bothered it and made it painful and watery. And he always wore a black velvet beret on his head to cover the burns there.

Ari took his burnt hand in hers and David tried to pull away.

"No," Ari said. "Let me see."

She stroked the puckered and reddened skin with her fingers.

"Do you know," she smiled. "I have just the thing for this."

She told him then about Belinda and the lotions and potions she made from herbs and flowers and other unnamed things. Christina said, insects, fungi and African spells. But she might have been joking.

"The stuff she makes is just marvellous. She made me a lotion that I used to rub into my tummy when I was pregnant. I haven't got one stretch mark. I think it might soothe your skin in the short term and I will ask Belinda to make something especially for you. Would that be all right?"

He was willing to try he said as he would love to be able to hold a paintbrush again. He had tried with his other hand but had been disappointed with the results. Ari understood, as the struggle to get down on canvas what was in your head was difficult enough without additional problems. Perhaps the skin on David's hand could be made a little more pliable?

"Life is strange isn't it," she said. "There you are going along fine, lovely life. Very happy and something comes out of the blue and turns it all around."

David was just going to say something when she continued.

"There was a girl at school with me, Jessica, whose mother, she said, said every morning, 'I might die today.' If she walked down an avenue of trees it was 'one might fall on me' or for a car ride 'the car might crash'. She thought that as these things didn't happen it was because it would have been too much of a coincidence, her having said they might. My friend said her mother was forever muttering about some accident which might befall her. It was very exhausting she said. Her mother died watching an aeroplane flying overhead that just might drop a lump of ice on her. She stepped in front of a bus." She paused for a moment. "Mind you she had nervous problems poor woman. She also thought, so Jess said, that the movement of the clouds made the wind." She stopped for a moment. "But you can't live your life like that can you? Trying to anticipate everything. You can never know what is around the corner," she added. "I don't believe in the foreseeable future. I could never have foreseen what happened to me."

David looked at her lovely face. She was biting her lip and struggling not to cry.

"Arianwen," David said gently. "Might you tell me what has made you so unhappy?"

"Perhaps one day," she said and got up quickly and went into the kitchen to make him some supper. David resolved to find out what it was.

Ari got in touch with Belinda and a week or so later David's salve arrived in the post. It was in a most beautiful gold patterned ceramic pot. They opened it together and the smell was just amazing. Flowers, herbs, sweet, sharp and an underlying something which neither of them could grasp. The instructions said it had to be massaged in once every day. So, Ari took some on her fingers and began to gently rub it in to the scarred and reddened skin. "You must do this yourself when I am not here," she said, and he promised he would. When she had finished, she stood up and kissed him on the cheek.

It was the first time anyone had kissed him for years, and it was so generous and natural that he remembered it for the rest of his life.

August came and Grace and Lem were soon to move into their new home. Huw had been employed to fit out the pottery. The kiln and wheel had been installed and lots of racks and cupboards built. There were no really major things to do in the house but Huw and his men put in a new bathroom and decorated all the rooms. Ari was very busy. Apart from her own work she had Gwenny to see to who was getting more mobile by the day. She also went to see David as he just loved Gwenny and she him. And she liked to go up at weekends when Shona was there. Also, Lem had asked, if she had time, could she keep an eye on the builders. For a little while that summer she seemed to push the pram back and forth through the village at least once a day.

Huw was always pleased to see her when she came and noticed how much better she looked. She was quite beautiful he thought and he fancied her rotten. One warm afternoon she sat with him, Gwenny on her knee, having a cigarette and chatting about Lem and Grace's immanent arrival. Huw couldn't help himself and asked her out for a drink. Ari was astonished, she never thought about going out with someone anymore. For quite some minutes she didn't say anything. Huw thought perhaps she was insulted as he was only a builder. Eventually she spoke. "Sorry," she said. "I was just trying to work out the practicalities. If I can get a babysitter, then yes. Can I let you know next time I see you?"

Huw was so pleased he nearly kissed her there and then. But then Ari added, "Just a drink mind."

On the way home, she said to Gwenny, "I wonder if your daddy has a lady he goes out with and if she makes him happy?" And then felt most dreadfully sad.

Shona babysat for Ari, but the evening was not as Ari had hoped. She dressed with care, in a new dark brown dress, and her hair up with her Japanese pins. Though she could only find three. Huw came to collect her and they went to the village pub. He was obviously proud to have her with him but there were a lot of whistles and shouts from his friends when they went in. Ari was embarrassed. It was extremely hot, crowded and noisy in the pub.

"Local rugby team are in," Huw shouted at her. They sat at a table with some of his friends and Ari recognised one or two of the builders and Christina's plumber, Evan, who asked after her. The men ogled her; the women put their arms tightly around their partners. The time passed slowly as everyone talked rugby or village gossip and Ari felt excluded. The rugby players and their friends began singing, and great jugs of beer circulated. The songs were pleasant at first and some quite funny, but very soon became more and more filthy. One of the men was openly fondling the barmaid's breasts and there was a lot of surreptitious groping going on. Also, many of the men kept giving her sidelong looks and when passing Huw would say things like, "She might need a good sorting," or even, "Give her a good one lad." In the end Ari was so astonished and then so cross she asked to go home. She had to shout in Huw's ear to get heard, which prompted more crude comments from the by now drunk rugby team. There were again a lot of shouts and whistles when Ari and Huw got up to leave. Huw stopped the car at the edge of the village and tried to kiss her.

"Come on Arianwen," he said. "Just dip your toes in the water, you might like it, and I bet you haven't been in for some time. We could go up the forest?"

Ari got out of the car. "I will walk from here, thank you," she said furiously. "I may have a child and be unmarried but I do not dip my toes in any old water as you so strangely put it. Every single person in that bloody pub thinks you are going to fuck me." She saw Huw recoil at her use of the word. "Yes," she said angrily. "Fuck! That would just be what you want. No care, no consideration and no love. Just up against a bloody tree in the forest. Then back to cheers in the pub because you'd had me. Well sorry Huw, that isn't going to happen."

She slammed the car door and set off down the lane. He followed and persuaded her into the car as it was a fair walk and pitch black. She sat in the back though. Shona heard the car stop in the lane and a door slam. Then the car drove off, fast. *He's not bringing her down then*, she thought and went to the kitchen window where she saw Ari's torch light bobbing down the drive. Then she heard the gate shut and nothing more. Shona waited a few minutes then opened the back door. Ari was sitting on the bench under the window, smoking a cigarette and gazing at the sky. "Ari, cariad?" Shona said softly and Ari fell into Shona arms.

"They thought I was easy," she sobbed. Shona had a word with Huw later in the week and he realised he had read Ari all wrong. Ari had an apology. He had been rather egged on by his friends he said, besides being a little drunk. But she would not go out with him or anyone else again. She felt very lonely.

And so, the time went on. Grace and Lem moved in and Shona, after having seen what they produced, gave them both gallery space. She also introduced them to local shops who would sell their work. Lem found a part-time teaching job at the local secondary school and was very happy as Grace became pregnant that autumn. Ari was painting well too but found it a little more difficult as Gwenny was walking and talking now and slept less. Her first word was 'Daydo' for David and then Mam. Ari had started another triptych this time called 'Abandoned'. She had had it going around in her head for some time and knew she just had to get it down on canvas. The first canvas had a very young Sal carrying a baby, Welsh fashion, in the garden. They were surrounded by a tall bed of white gladioli and the baby was just peeking out of the shawl. The middle and largest canvas caused Ari the most anguish. It was her and Jon. She was naked and lying full length on top of an equally naked Jon, who had gathered her hair in his hands and was about to kiss her. Their total absorption in each other was startling. The third canvas was Ari lying on the grass at night in her old nightie and Jon's jumper. When she had finished them, she left them where they were for some time and when Gwenny was asleep would go over to the barn and just look and remember and cry.

David's hand improved no end, and within six months he could hold a brush confidently, albeit only for an hour or so. He asked Ari if he could paint her portrait. "Yes," she smiled. "If I can do yours after? There is a gap on the wall leading upstairs that is just right."

It took David a few months to complete Arianwen's portrait, as apart from anything else it was difficult to find a time for her to sit. Gwenny was over two now, very mobile, chatty and curious so Ari was on the go with her nearly all day. Ari therefore could only really sit for David if Gwenny was occupied or asleep. They would go up to the house on a Sunday or Monday, Shona's day off, and Shona would entertain Gwenny. Or as Shona said, "She entertains me actually. I have never met a child so interested in everything." Those hours spent with Arianwen were precious to David and after a while he got her to talk about what had prompted her to move to North Wales. Not that he didn't know some of it, but he wanted to know her side of things and he was curious about this Jon.

So very hesitantly at first, she told him about liking Jon but as he was her tutor saying nothing and she had thought he had someone of his own anyway. And that Jon had liked her for a while but as he was older than her and thought student-teacher relationships were not sensible, had done nothing either. But more by luck than judgment they had met up one Christmas and their relationship had progressed rapidly from there. She said that she had and still did love him completely and couldn't understand what had gone wrong really, as she had thought he felt the same for her. "Our relationship was very special," she said. "Very loving, honest and wonderfully physical." Then she told him what had happened at the leavers' party, her beating by Janet and her illness. "Then of course I came here," she said. "I couldn't have borne seeing him every day if he didn't want me."

He asked her then what she thought of it all now.

"Well, I think all that stuff in the studio was set up by Janet and I do believe Jon had nothing to do with it or went off with her. But where was he when I was so ill? He just disappeared."

David was now resolved to find out about Jon, but there was something else more urgent that he had to tackle first. He rang his old school chum Roger.

David Rhys Williams and Roger Fearnley had met and become friends on their first day at preparatory school when they were just eight. They had stayed together right through their public school days.
i David had then gone to art school, followed by the RCA, whilst Roger went to Cambridge to study law. At the outbreak of WW2 both men were still very good friends, met often, and both were doing well in their chosen professions. David was becoming an established artist, whilst Roger had taken over the family law firm on the death of his father. In 1942, David fell in love with a girl he met at a dance in London. She was very beautiful and her name was Lillian Morgan. His friends warned him that she was 'flighty'. She was just nineteen to his thirty-four, and in the April of 1943, she told him she was pregnant with his child. Before he could do anything about it, war work intervened and in June of that year he had had his dreadful accident. When he was able to, he got in touch with Roger and asked him to find a home for Lillian and the child and to see to their every need until he could do so himself. Ample funds were then made available to Roger. Of course, no one could have predicted that Lillian would disappear and so then Roger had a quandary. The young girl who had been looking after the baby was happy, with her mother's help, to go on doing so, and so Roger left things as they were until such time as David wanted some other arrangement. However, when David eventually left hospital, it was obvious he could not care for a child and his sister had no idea of its existence. Furthermore, both men thought it unfair to ask her to do so. Arianwen was therefore left with the Davies, as they were doing an excellent job.

Now how did David tell Arianwen that he was her father?

But what of Jon? He had come back from France with a ring in his pocket for Ari and looking forward to time just with her. If Mary hadn't come out when she had seen him, he wouldn't have known where Ari was. He had had a hostile reception from Sal when he had been there, but he could understand their concern for Ari. He was bewildered though by the turn of events and very sad.

There had been a staff meeting at the beginning of term and the assault on Ari had been discussed. Only Julius knew the true facts but Ian Cooper had noted the growing closeness between Jon and Ari. As her main tutor he had phoned her family to ask after her, a week or two into the holidays.

"I spoke to her mother," he said. "She was very sharp and off-hand with me, and just said that Arianwen was extremely ill." He paused. "Then I asked her if she felt we should do something about Janet, as the assault had taken place on school premises? She said the family had thought about prosecution but realised they had enough to do looking after Arianwen without pursuing some demented girl through the courts. Then she just put the phone down."

Ian asked then if anyone had had contact with Ari. He looked around the room. Everyone shook their heads.

"Jon?"

"No, nothing," said Jon.

Julius and Poll were very good to him, and as time went on Jon did pick up a little. Julius asked everyone he knew in the art world to let him know if they came upon an Arianwen Morgan. They thought they had found her at one point but it turned out to be an Angharad Morgan in Pembrokeshire.

Jon bought a house in the village near Julius. It had a large conservatory at the back which he used as a studio. He began to paint with obsession. It was the only thing that stopped him dwelling on Ari.

His canvases were large, at least five feet by five, and he painted small parts of the landscape in huge, intricate detail. A snowy riverbank with a gnarled tree became a near-abstract design, until you were able to find one thing that would bring it all into focus. They were very clever, very beautiful and after his first exhibition in Manchester, very sought after.

Julius and Poll asked him to dinner often and rolled out a succession of presentable women for him. Jon went out with one, a young teacher from Poll's school, and even ended up in bed with her. But it was not a success and not repeated. His heart wasn't in it. She was so needy. It was all, "Is this alright Jon? Do you like that, Jon?" Ari had just been herself, no questions, enjoy it all and have fun. God! How he missed her!

Before David could come up with a solution about Ari, he found out, through an old friend that Jon Curtis was having an exhibition in London. This time he was sharing gallery space with his friend Richard, who was teaching at Bournemouth art school.

David asked Roger if he would go along and see the exhibition.

Roger had done a lot of things for David outside of his remit as his solicitor but had never been asked to go to an art exhibition before. He was very familiar with concerts, theatre and opera but not at all knowledgeable about art. However, he agreed to go.

Since Olive had been with him his style of dress and presentation had changed. He now wore made to measure suits and shirts and had his greying hair cut regularly. He was no longer the slightly crumpled person Olive had met many years ago. So, when he set off for the exhibition, he looked like a very prosperous man, which gave him some confidence. But he needn't have worried. As soon as he stepped into the gallery any uncertainty disappeared. He was bowled over by the sheer beauty of Jon's canvases. He spent a long time looking at them. They were so intriguing. Then in a corner he saw a drawing. It was Arianwen, asleep in her starfish position and covered in part by a sheet. He bought it immediately for Olive but would keep it hidden until the right moment. He then reported back to David as to his conclusions and David sent his manager, Taliesin down to London for his opinion.

David finished his portrait of Ari and they were both pleased with the result. Then it was Ari's turn. She knew he was sensitive about his burns, so she angled the light in such a way as not to focus on them. He was seated in his wheelchair, his patch over his eye and a new velvet beret on his head. He was looking directly at her, Otho at his feet and Nerva at his side.

The portrait took four weeks and Shona encouraged them both to exhibit them in the gallery's open show coming up in February. David said he would call his portrait simply 'Arianwen'. Ari's of him was titled 'David Rhys Williams' and was suitably framed and hung in the vacant space on the stairs. "Just where it should be," said Shona. Neither was sure about exhibiting them, so Shona left it.

Chapter 5
I know I'll never find another you
The Seekers

January 1968 - July 1976

At the beginning of January 1968 Jon received a letter from a gallery in North Wales asking if he might be interested in staging an exhibition of his work in the summer. If so, could he contact them and arrange a meeting to talk about the logistics. It was signed Taliesin Griffiths, for David Rhys Williams. Tally said he had seen Jon's paintings at the exhibition in London and was very interested in them. Jon showed it to Julius. "That Rhys Williams name rings a bell," he said. He thought about it for some time and then said, "Got it. He was a brilliant war artist, amongst other things. I believe he had a bad accident, and I haven't heard of him for years. Came from an extremely well-off family too. I thought he had died. Obviously not."

Jon wrote back and agreed a day and time to visit in March. Their letter had intrigued him.

Meanwhile David had contacted Roger. Could he come up sometime as there were two pressing issues he needed to discuss? "Just be a bit careful," David added. "I don't want Arianwen seeing you yet."

Roger phoned Olive who was still at 'Arian Court' to tell her he was going up north to see a client and would be away for a few days. He hired a small car which Ari would not recognise if she saw it. He was quite enjoying this cloak-and-dagger stuff. He got to Cae Coch after dark and stayed in the room that was always kept for him.

David looked very well when they met up next morning. He had long ago forgiven his friend for placing Arianwen in his proximity, as he had come to love her and Gwenny too. He wanted, somehow or other to tell her he was her father but also, he did not want Jon to think he had been offered the exhibition because of that connection. There was also Shona to consider.

The two men sat for quite some time trying to puzzle out what to do. If Ari were told she would feel honour bound to tell Jon of the connection, if ever she met him. They decided that it would be best to see how the land lay for a while. Ari didn't need to be told yet, but they thought it only fair to tell Shona. But Shona had had a suspicion anyway. Both David and Arianwen shared the same unusual eye colour. Of course, David's left eye was covered and the other was often reddened. Thus, it was not very obvious, but Shona knew. And there were other things too, both were left-handed, they had very similar ears and of course both painted. Shona would not say a word, though she was mightily pleased to be told she was Arianwen's aunt. But Roger and David did not feel it appropriate to tell her yet why Ari was in North Wales.

Two weeks later Jon went down to Bournemouth to see Richard, who wanted some advice on a changing curriculum. The meeting was first thing in the morning, so Jon was there early. The hallway at the college was busy with staff and pupils and he made his way to the reception desk. As he gave his name, he heard a gasp and turned to find he was face to face with Janet Philips. She blushed a dark red when she saw him. "Hello, sir," she managed to say. "How are you... and Arianwen?" she added.

"I have not seen Arianwen from that day to this," he said stiffly and was grateful that Richard appeared and they went into the meeting, otherwise he might have been very rude to her. Their meeting was fine and very productive and at the end Jon asked Richard about Janet. "I believe she is a pottery technician," he said. "Very cantankerous by all accounts."

It was a long meeting and when Jon came out, he was surprised to see that Janet was waiting and she asked if she could speak to him. He was calmer now so said 'yes' as he was rather intrigued as to what else she might say. They walked to the cafeteria for a coffee. She went off to get them and brought back two white coffees. Jon only drank black, but she hadn't asked.

She started by saying that she knew she had caused a lot of trouble but looking back realised that it all seemed very silly now.

"It was never silly Janet," Jon said. "Whatever your reasons for doing what you did they were vicious and calculated, and I am still suffering the consequences."

She hesitated at that.

"Arianwen took Tom away from me," she said. "And she didn't want him. So, I hated her. She had everything."

Jon tried to interrupt because he knew that Ari had not taken Tom away. But Janet didn't seem to notice.

"She had everything," she repeated. "She was clever, beautiful and she had money. It wasn't fair."

Jon tried again, "She did not take Tom away, Janet. She just told him how she saw things and it struck a chord with him. Arianwen is the most generous and forgiving person I have ever known. Look how she dealt with Tom. All that unpleasantness sorted and then never mentioned again."

Janet glared at him, "Well you would say that wouldn't you. You were another one trying to get into her knickers."

Jon stood up abruptly. "How dare you," he said. "Arianwen was kind, good and beautiful and I miss her every hour of the day. If it hadn't been for your jealousy, we would have been married by now."

Jon realised that he had raised his voice. People were looking. He sat down.

"And yes," he said. "She did have money, but she was very generous with it. I expect you know what she did for Flora. I know she wanted it kept quiet but I have heard it talked about around school."

"Tom told me she also gave Grace and Marco her houses down by the station. Lem's sister told them all at the wedding when she got a bit drunk. Those three know where she is you know. Just not telling you," Janet added spitefully. "Fucking Lady Bountiful."

Then she had a sudden disturbing thought. She had gone wild when she started art school and in her second term, she had become pregnant. Tom, Stuart, or someone else. She didn't know who as she had been to several parties over Christmas and had been drunk at all of them. She remembered now, being very distraught and sitting in the cloakroom crying and talking to Sheila about it. Her mother had found some doctor who would do a private abortion but it cost over £200, and they didn't have that sort of money. Arianwen had come in, gone into the toilet. Came out, washed her hands, combed her hair and left. Two days later Janet had found a large envelope tucked in her coat pocket with £200 in it. Nothing was ever said about the money, she had just assumed it was one of the boys. Now she was not so sure but wasn't going to mention it to Mr Curtis. He seemed to think Arianwen was some kind of fucking angel.

Jon realised he was not going to get anywhere with this conversation.

"Never think what you did was just silly," Jon said, as he stood up to leave. "It was downright bloody malicious. You have ruined my life and possibly Ari's. Ari might be forgiving, but I am not. I hope you can live with what you have done." He turned and left, leaving Janet the object of much curiosity among the staff.

Janet lit a cigarette and finished her coffee. Jon had drunk none of his, so she had that too. She was due back in the pottery studio to prepare for the next lesson but couldn't be bothered. The fucking students could wedge up their own clay. She was glad that Arianwen and Mr Curtis were apart and that he was suffering, and hopefully Arianwen too. She smiled to herself, she felt powerful. She had spent the whole of her life wanting to be special and resented those who were. The girls who were always top of the class, the spotty girl who even so, got all the boys, and got invited to all the parties. The girls with nice houses, cars, and good clothes. She had been made much of at school for her painting and drawing and had expected to be at the top at art school. But she was not. Talented but not exceptional. She had thought she had got there with Tom, until she had heard what he said to Mr Curtis.

When she had hurt Arianwen, she had felt no remorse at all. She had gone home, packed a bag, left her mother a note and decided to go to her grandmother in Abergavenny. She had hitched a lift with a lorry driver who had demanded payment. They had sex in the back of his cab and he was very rough with her, but she was so angry with everything and everyone that she gave as good as she got. He dropped her off on the outskirts of the town, very sore but relieved to be away from any repercussions from the art school. She stayed with her gran until well into the next spring and got a letter from Tom, redirected by her mother.

He told her about Arianwen being very ill and then disappearing. About Lem and Grace's wedding and what Lem's sister had told them about the houses. About Nell leaving him for James. And he told her everyone thought she was an absolute bloody bitch for hurting Arianwen. She could have screamed with the anger she felt, and was extremely rude and unkind to her gran, who had had enough of her granddaughter's sullenness and self-pity and asked her to leave. So that was that then. Janet applied for several jobs, one of which was at the art school in Bournemouth, and to her surprise got it.

She had been there ever since, though she found it hard work and boring. She got up and went to the office pleading a migraine; she couldn't face any students today. As she walked home to her little flat just off the Christchurch Road she wondered if Claude would be there. She had met him six months ago near the pier and he had moved in straight away, but was often missing for days on end, with no explanation. He barely spoke and there was not much love between them, just the occasional 'shag' as he put it. Still...

Jon felt very agitated as he got into his car and thought he might just drive out to Hengistbury Head for a walk before setting off home. The sea air might clear his head. In the past few years, he had visited Richard often but although he had looked constantly had never seen Ari. Now as he drove through Boscombe he saw the sign for the sea and on impulse drove down and then up the hill to 'Arian Court'. It looked all closed up but he walked up the steps and rang the bell anyway. Olive answered. "I am afraid we are shut at the moment," she said and then saw a man who could be no other than Gwenny's father.

"Jon?" she said. "I'm Olive, Ari's Nan."

"Hello," he said shaking her hand. "I was just passing, and you never know Ari might have been here."

"No," she smiled. "Not since the summer. We had Christmas with her this year. But come in and talk to me and I'll make you some tea. Sal and Fred are away at the moment. Little holiday before we start again at Easter. I'm just hotel sitting."

He looked very tired she thought. "Are you all right?"

"Oh," he sighed. "I've just had a nasty experience. I went to a meeting at the art school in town and walked smack bang into that girl who assaulted Ari. She had the cheek to say she saw it all as silly now. I'm afraid I was rather rude to her."

Olive smiled, "I can understand that."

"Truth is I'm weary of this. Bumping into her brought it all back, and I keep reliving it over and over. I have looked for Ari for over three years and it gets no easier." He sighed and rubbed his hand across his eyes. "I have been offered an 'artist in residence' position at a good university in New Zealand and I am seriously thinking about it. Just to give me some peace from this constant searching. I haven't got to make the decision until September though. Until then I have an exhibition to prepare for in North Wales and shall be going up there at the beginning of March. So at least I'll be busy for a while."

Olive leant forward and took his hand.

"Jon," she said. "None of this has been anyone's fault, you know. We have all made mistakes. Sal wouldn't listen to you, the first time you came, I know. In her defence, she has never been able to have children so is fiercely protective of Ari. She has always seen herself as Ari's mother, even though there is only fifteen years between them, as she was the one left with her. And Ari, poor girl was not really with us for some time. She was very poorly, Jon, physically and mentally I would say. As you know she has always been very conscious of being abandoned as a child, and she thought you had abandoned her. We told her early on that her mother had gone away, but never used the word abandoned. Ari got that from a book and always used it herself. If we hadn't someone else would have told her." She had a fleeting image of Mair Pryce.

"And we inadvertently compounded that insecurity. We were always afraid that Lillian Morgan would come back and accuse us of not looking after Arianwen properly, because we did get paid well. So, Sal took photographs constantly of everything you can imagine. Ari has a big ebony box with ivory decoration and all the photos are in there."

The box from the painting, Jon thought.

Olive carried on, "One reason Ari has such long hair is that we were afraid to really cut it. It can be construed as assault, you know."

Olive paused. "This can get sorted Jon. I can't tell you where she is, that is up to Ari, but if I get you some paper will you write down what you have told me? I promise to send it to her."

He looked at her and smiled "Thank you," he said. She was more forgiving than Sallie.

He wrote to Arianwen.

My darling girl,

Much as I want you back with me, I cannot spend the rest of my life looking for you. I am weary now and am considering a move abroad to have some peace. I have talked for a long time to Olive and hope she will plead my case with you. You know where I am and I will continue to hope that you will get in touch. I miss you every minute, of every hour, of every day.

Jon.

He left then and crossed the road to the path that ran down to the beach. It was early evening. All the lights were on around the bay and on the two piers. A near full moon shone across the water. He passed a beach hut, where a young couple were seated outside drinking something warm and spicy by the smell. He said, "Good evening."

The boy replied, "Happy New Year to you mate." *Oh, I really hope so,* thought Jon. And from somewhere the strains of Etta James singing *At Last* drifted across the sands.

Olive added a note of her own.

Sweetheart,

Jon has just been here. He was upset as he had just had a run in with that girl who assaulted you. And he explained about France too. His mother had a stroke when they got there and another, three weeks later and then died. He had to stay and arrange for her body to be brought home and then there was the funeral. He managed to get in touch with Mr Winter, but when he came to tell you, you were of course with us and the others had gone away. So, he didn't leave you Ari. He didn't abandon you and he has been searching for you all this time. You need to talk to him about it. He looks so tired and sad and he is such a lovely man. Can you not find it in your heart to give him a chance? He is coming up your way soon to arrange an exhibition at Shona's gallery. March, I think he said. Be brave Ari, be brave!

Love Nan xxxx

She put both notes in an envelope and walked down the hill to post them, that evening.

Two days later Ari got the letter. She made two phone calls. The first to Shona to ask her to pop round when she could, and the second to her Nan to thank her for the letters and to say she had thought about it and would try to contact Jon.

Over a few glasses of red wine Ari told Shona all about Jon and what had led to her coming to North Wales. True to his word David, although tempted to do so, had not told Shona what he knew. They made a plan of what Ari would like to happen next, and Shona was more than happy to help.

Jon meanwhile was resigned to the fact that Ari had got his letter but didn't want to contact him. It had been nearly six weeks since he had spoken to Olive. He was however looking forward to his visit to North Wales as he had never been there before.

He usually taught on a Thursday but the whole of the 1st year NDD were going to Cambridge, to the Fitzwilliam. Ian and Julius were supervising and said that there was no real need for him to come; the students were supposedly adults after all. Jon decided to make a day of getting to North Wales, and go to Bala, if he could, to see where Augustus John and James Dickson Innes had stayed at Nant Ddu, and where Innes had painted 'Arenig', one of Jon's favourite paintings. He set off early in the morning and drove to Shrewsbury after which he decided to go across country. He ended up at Lake Vyrnwy and then took what seemed to be a forest road, then across moorland littered with bedraggled sheep and lambs. The blackthorn was in flower and he could see the yellow of new gorse.

There was a lot of stopping to consult his map but he was enjoying just being out, and he was really glad he had had the foresight to bring his camera. The landscape was spectacular and he vowed to come back one day and do some drawing.

He wound the car window down and the cold, gorse scented air was exhilarating. Eventually he rounded a corner and the narrow road hugged the mountainside and fell very steeply to the valley floor and then continued on into the distance. He stopped the car and got out. His map said this was the Hirnant Pass. He thought you would have to be very brave to negotiate that on a dark, stormy night. There was absolute silence, and then far, far away the plaintive call of a lamb and the echoey bark of a dog. Above him a buzzard soared lazily in a sky that was clear and blue and enormous. Jon thought of Ari sending her prayers and thanks to the sky, so he did that also, then got back in the car and drove on. Strangely he felt a lightness of spirit he had not felt for a very long time. He dropped down into Bala and skirting the lake, stopped and parked in the main street. He went into a cafe and had a good lunch, and then walking back to his car saw a bookshop. The bookseller addressed him in Welsh first but with a smile, changed directly to English. He was very knowledgeable about his stock and Jon bought a really good and well-illustrated book on John's and Innes' time in North Wales. Before he left, he asked the bookseller if he had come across an Arianwen Morgan. He shook his head, "Lots of Angharads," he said with a smile. "But you don't often hear Arianwen these days. I would have remembered that." With clear directions from the bookseller, he found the view of Arenig that James Dickson Innes had painted, quite easily, and was really pleased to have taken the time to do so. He got to his hotel in Conwy by late afternoon. It had been an extremely enjoyable day but he was a little tired with all the driving. He hoped his visit to the gallery tomorrow would be as good.

Ari had had to wait a few weeks but on Friday the eighth of March she woke up with dreadful butterflies in her stomach. Today was the day.

She took especial care with dressing. She wore a large burnt orange jumper ove a short black skirt and tights. Plus, her beloved boots. On top, her brown tweed coat. Then she dabbed her perfume behind her ears and she was ready, though her legs felt very wobbly. She took Gwenny to Grace's. Grace, ever supportive, knew what was happening and was very, very, pleased. She wished her luck. Then Ari got into her car. She had replaced her mini soon after she had had Gwenny, and now had a big Land Rover. She parked near the castle and walked up the steps into town. Shona had said he was due at twelve and that Jon and her colleague, Taliesin, would have a working lunch. She expected him to be free by about one-thirty as Tally had to leave for another appointment then. Ari got to the top of the street just on one o'clock. The gallery was up a side street, so she went into Woolworths, for by standing near the window she could see the gallery's front door. She browsed the records, the magazines, the birthday cards and then did it again and once more. A man approached "Excuse me madam, I'm the manager. Do you need any help? You have been here rather a long time."

"Oh God, I am so sorry," said Ari. "Truth is I am waiting to surprise someone I haven't seen for a very long time. He will be coming out of the gallery soon, and I can see the door from here." The manager a romantic at heart, smiled.

The gallery was at the top of a side street looking down towards the main road. It was an enormous disused 'Seion' Chapel. During the war it had been used to store beds and blankets and other emergency supplies, but then there was no use for it and David bought it for a song in 1947. When the idea came to him about setting up a gallery, it seemed the ideal place. A great deal of work was done inside to create galley space. The floor was lowered, and the balconies removed, so as to create two upper floors with two very large galleries on each, and the outside steps made shallower to accommodate the lowered floor. A few pews were left in each gallery and two placed in the reception area. The floors and staircases sanded and sealed and all the walls painted a very soft green. The outside was left much as it had been but the sombre grey walls were painted white. Downstairs a small reception area with an office and two smaller galleries, plus a small shop with a meeting room behind. It was a very impressive building from the outside and when Jon went through the new wide, heavy glass doors, to be met by Shona, he just knew this was an ideal place for his paintings. It reminded him in a way of Arianwen's little house. The colours perhaps he thought. David Rhys Williams had certainly known what he was doing; the atmosphere in the building was great.

Introductions over, Jon asked Shona about the gallery connection with David. "Oh!" she had said. "He is my brother and owner of the gallery. But you won't meet him as he never leaves the house. It was Tally who saw your exhibition. We are always on the lookout for excellence which is why Tally got in touch with you. I hope you agree to exhibit here." She smiled at Jon, "We are a nice lot, you know."

Jon and Tally had had an excellent meeting; Jon agreed to exhibit and then they walked around viewing the gallery space. He explained that he had one or two really large canvases but Tally assured him they would be no problem. Shona brought them some coffee and superb ham sandwiches and they completed everything necessary for the time being. Jon would visit again in five to six weeks to check the catalogue proofs and anything else needed.

And then Jon said goodbye to Shona who was at the reception desk and went out into the street. He stopped on the steps and lit a cigarette. Ari grasped the manager's arm, "There he is," she whispered. Just the same, navy jacket, cords and a big satchel over his shoulder.

She went quietly out of the shop, only to be stopped by a mother from Gwenny's playschool. The manager and one of his assistants came out too. They stood outside the shop and watched the whole drama unfold. When Ari had rather abruptly taken her leave of Elin's mother, Jon was nowhere to be seen. But Shona, bless her, was standing on the gallery steps and pointed downhill. He was outside a small gallery on the corner of the street, looking in the window. Ari went up behind him and said "Jon?" He didn't move. He had heard her, but he had heard Ari say his name so many times and in so many places, only to find it wasn't her, that he now ignored it. He went into the shop and Ari saw the owner, Ray, take a small carving of a wren, one of Lem's, out of the window. He looked up and saw her and she indicated Jon.

"Beautiful these," Ray said to Jon, wrapping the bird in tissue paper and putting it in a little box. "We sell quite a lot of Lem Sewell's work and his wife's too."

"Yes," said Jon. "I recognised it. They used to live next door to a friend of mine."

"Arianwen's paintings too if they are small enough," laughed Ray as Jon handed him a cheque and put the package in his bag.

"How do you know Arianwen then?" continued Ray.

"I was her tutor at art school," Jon, faintly bemused, replied. "But I haven't seen her for some time. Why do you ask?"

"Sorry, I thought she was with you. She walked down the street just behind you and she's not one you could miss easily, is she?" He laughed, then continued. "I think she may be waiting for you outside." Ray smiled.

Jon turned and there she was her back to the window. For a moment he had to hold on to the counter his heart was thudding so hard. Then with a 'Thank you' to Ray he went outside. Ari heard the tinkle of the shop bell and turned.

Neither said a word just looked at each other, and Jon saw the uncertainty in her lovely eyes.

"Hello, sir," she whispered.

He put his bag down slowly on the ground, then he stepped forward and pulled her into his arms. "Oh! my darling girl." He could barely speak. Her image blurred as tears filled his eyes. "Thank God! Oh! Thank God." She was all he remembered, she smelled the same and felt the same, and when she tilted her head back so he could kiss her, she tasted the same. Tears coursed down her cheeks also. He kissed them away. His darling girl was in his arms and it was as if those three years apart had never been.

"Bit more than a tutor," Ray said to himself and carried on watching. They stood for minutes with their arms around each other. They heard nothing, saw nothing, just felt the marvellous presence of one another. A child bumped into them, and a car tooted. The manager of Woolworths and his assistant held hands, rather unexpectedly for the assistant.

Ari said, "I think we are causing a disturbance standing here." Tucking her arm through his, they walked around the corner and through a gateway between two shops and into the churchyard. They sat on a bench by the wall, and Jon said, "I'm so sorry Ari."

But she put a finger to his lips. "No," she smiled. "It doesn't matter now. Perhaps we will talk about it later, but not now." He pulled her towards him again and she kissed him long and lovingly. "Oh! Jon, I have missed you so very much," she said and kissed him again. They sat for a while just holding hands. Relieved and pleased to finally be with each other. People were walking through the churchyard from the shops but they didn't notice. Jon kept searching her lovely face. Apart from a small scar high up on her cheekbone, where Janet had hit her, she was the same. He touched the scar.

"You had a really bad time, didn't you?"

"All over now." She smiled, then looked at her watch.

"Jon," she said. "I have to be somewhere at three. Do you want to come with me and see where I live?" She raised her eyebrows at him and he saw again that brilliant flash of mischief in her eyes. He had missed that so much.

"Come in my car then and I'll bring you back if you want," she stopped. "Or you could stay, I've lots of room?"

"Can I just get some things from the hotel? Make it a lot easier?"

So, they walked back the way they had come and Jon went up to his room to get some things for overnight. Ari waited downstairs talking to Shona's friend Val who was at reception.

"Well, I can see whose daddy that is," she laughed.

"He's going to have a terrible shock in a while, but I am so, so glad he is here," Ari said.

Val leant over the counter.

"God bless you both," she said and gave Ari a big kiss on the cheek.

They walked back through the town. Ray was still watching out of his window "Lucky sod," he said to no one in particular.

Jon was looking for the mini in the car park, but Ari stopped beside a large dark-green Land Rover. She leant against the door and pulled him towards her by his coat lapels. "Do you know what?" she laughed, smiling into his eyes.

"Yes, Miss Morgan I do," he said. And they were back to how they had always been.

They got in the car and Jon asked her if she was sure she could drive it. "Oh, I'm much better than I was," she said seriously and shot off out of town. They roared over the bridge and turned right down the valley. Past rows of shops and houses then out into the open countryside. Jon saw the wide river on the right and the hills, cliffs and trees on his side, mountains in the distance. He had never been here before either and he wondered why? Another spectacular place.

"See," Ari said. "I'm much better now." They turned off the main road into narrow, winding lanes with steep banks. "That's why I got this so I could see over the hedges." But she still drove too fast really and Jon began to laugh. He didn't care. He was so incredibly happy to have found her again that she could drive any way she bloody well wanted. He could not quite believe she was sitting beside him. His darling Arianwen. He couldn't stop laughing. The world was back to rights. "What?" said Ari. "What?" And she skidded to a halt in a quiet lay-by.

"Several years ago," he said laughing still. "I started my day taking a life drawing class for retired ladies and ended up in bed with you. Now you've surprised me again." He laughed. Jon leant towards her and slid his hands under her jumper. He felt her arch towards him.

"Oh Jon," she sighed. "I'd love to, just here, just now, but Grace will be waiting with the little ones. They moved up here about a year after me. They have been such good friends and I promised to pick her up at three." She rammed the car into gear and they shot off again.

She stopped outside what looked like a church hall and got out. Grace came out almost immediately, a tiny baby in a sling on her chest and with two other small children. She came up to the car window while Ari helped the children into the back. "Hello Mr Curtis," she said. "It's really great to see you at last." Then she got in the back with the others.

"Sing along and stories," Ari explained to Jon. "Every Friday afternoon." Ten minutes later and they stopped outside a whitewashed farmhouse. Lem came out to the car and spoke to Jon whilst Grace took her children indoors. "Nearly there," Ari said, as she turned into the lane, and down a steep drive. Jon saw a large farmhouse and opposite it a big barn. They stopped by some gates and Ari got out. He followed her as she unlocked the house door.

"Go in Jon. I won't be a moment." She went back to the car and lifted a drowsy child from the back. "I'll just see to this one then I'll be back." She took the child upstairs. *Where had that child come from?* Jon wondered. He had thought it belonged to Grace. He took his coat off and saw that the fire was just embers, so put another log on. All Ari's furniture and all her books were here plus a bit more he thought. Upstairs Ari had taken off Gwenny's coat and hat and brushed her hair and told her they had a really special visitor. Jon heard Ari coming downstairs. She was carrying the child. "I'd best introduce you," she said in a slightly shaky voice. She set the child down in front of Jon.

"Jon, this is Gwenllian, but we call her Gwenny."

Then she turned to her daughter, "Gwenny, sweetheart, this is Jon."

"Hello Gwenny," said Jon.

Gwenny turned and looked at Ari, who smiled at her daughter and nodded. The child turned back to Jon.

"Hello," said Gwenny. "Are you my Daddy?"

Jon was shocked at the directness of the question. Then he looked at the child standing in front of him. Same bright-blue eyes, same dark hair falling over her forehead, same wide smile, but Ari's top lip and nose. Her little hand on his knee had his blunt fingers and square nails.

"I think I most certainly am, Gwenny," he smiled. He looked up at Ari who was fighting back tears.

She came across and kissed him, "I know this is another shock for you today, but I hope not a bad one?"

"My darling girl," he said. "She is just beautiful." And he kissed her back. Then Gwenny put her little arms around his neck and kissed him too. Jon found it difficult to hold back the tears. What a day!

They had spaghetti Bolognese for tea and Gwenny insisted on sitting as close to Jon at the table as she could. "Girls always sit next to their daddies," she said.

"You might regret that," Ari laughed, as Jon fielded a piece of flying spaghetti. Ari told him that they had gone to an Italian restaurant with Marco the previous summer and pasta was now Gwenny's favourite.

"And," said Gwenny. "I'm going to marry Marco when I am a big girl, aren't I Mammy?"

"I think she is remotely connected to a switch somewhere. On at six, off at seven, and full on in between." Ari laughed, "But we wouldn't want you any other way, would we, my precious?" And she dropped a kiss on the child's head.

Then Gwenny had a bath and Jon had to read to her as she fell asleep. He marvelled that this wonderful little person was his child. It had never crossed his mind that Ari could have been pregnant.

He went downstairs and Ari was sitting on the sofa. He moved her onto his lap as he always had. "Now tell me," he said. "Why did she ask me if I was her daddy, just like that?"

"Well," she said. "It's quite funny really. She started playschool in January and she came home one day a bit upset. She said that this boy Charlie wouldn't play with her as she didn't have a daddy. There has been a bit of that sort of thing in the village but always directed at me. Anyway, I told her that of course she had a daddy and his name was Jon and that someday he might come and find us. I wasn't going to have her be like me and be wondering all the time, who and where was her father. The next weekend the milkman came for his money and I said 'Thank you John' to him, and Gwenny immediately asked him if he was her daddy.

Now, John the Milk is seventy if he is a day. He said he was very flattered to be asked but he was sorry to say he wasn't." Jon laughed at that. "The next time wasn't so good." Ari continued, "We were in the butchers and he had a new lad, a Saturday boy, only about fourteen, who was helping wrap the meat for delivery. Gwenny heard the butcher call him John and shouted across to him 'Are you my daddy?' Well, the poor lad went the colour of the meat he was wrapping. I was so embarrassed for him. The woman behind me in the queue said something very pointed about children of unmarried mothers not knowing their fathers, which upset me a lot. So, I told Gwenny then that she was never to ask that question again, but I would tell her when she could. And I did."

"Why didn't you tell me, Ari?" Jon said.

She turned and held his face in her hands. "I was very ill, so they tell me. I don't remember much at all. Apparently, I spent a lot of time looking for you. Then Mam told me you had gone away and I didn't ask again. I thought you had left me. And it was Nan who saw I was pregnant. I think I was nearly six months. It hadn't registered with me at all. I was very muddled about a lot of things. Then of course when Gwenny was born and she looked so like you, I couldn't imagine turning up on your doorstep with her. I could never have passed her off as belonging to anyone else and what if you had someone new? It wouldn't have been fair to you."

She paused for a moment. "None of us knew about your mother Jon and I am so sorry about that. I named Gwenllian for your mother and mine. She has to know her grandparents as well as her father, and I have told her about Johnny. I only ever knew my mother's name, so I wanted Gwenny to know as much as she could. I know Gwenllian is a name in its own right, I think she was a warrior princess, a Welsh Boudicca, but I thought Gwen for your mother and the rest for my mother Lillian." She stopped then, her eyes brimming with tears and began to cry. Great shuddering sobs shook her body. He held her very tight until she stopped, and then he kissed away the tears on her cheeks.

"Have you been here all the time Ari?" Jon asked.

"Yes," she said. "With Christina at first, then Nan, and Mam was with me when I had Gwenny. They were afraid to leave me on my own I think."

"I never thought to look here," Jon sighed. "Only south Wales where I knew you had lived."

"Tell me what you have been doing," she said. So, he told her about moving and about looking for her, and how Julius and Poll had been great and very supportive. And about the two exhibitions he had had and how they had been very well received with great reviews. And that he had sold a lot of his paintings. "Talking of paintings," he said. "I had an excellent meeting today at a gallery in Conwy. An exhibition at the beginning of July."

"I know," Ari said, with a smile "Nan told me and I asked Shona who is a friend of mine. It all worked out well, didn't it?"

"Well thank God for your Nan," he said and kissed Ari long and hard. "Can I stay 'til Monday? Would that be all right, darling girl?"

"That would be so good," she said. "Gwenny and I would love that."

"Then I must ring Julius and ask him to cover my class. He owes me one so it should be OK."

Jon phoned Julius, and Poll answered.

"You still in the wilds of North Wales then?" she asked.

Julius came to the phone then and Jon said he had to stay for a day or so more so could Julius take his class on Monday.

What's delaying you then old son?" Julius asked.

Jon laughed, "Guess?" he said.

There was a long silence. Then Julius said, "Jon Curtis you have a smile in your voice I haven't heard in a long while. You've found her, haven't you? Well, how bloody marvellous. You lucky bugger you!"

Jon said he would tell him all on Tuesday and as he put the phone down, he heard Julius shout, "Good news Poll, good news."

He went back to Ari then. "I have something for you," he said, and finding his bag took her silver pin from the pocket where it had been for over three years. She exclaimed in delight when she saw it and wanted to know how he had it. Then he told her about climbing over the gate and seeing her stabbing the bench with it. "Then you saw me," he said. "And ran indoors and locked the door."

She looked at him aghast. "I don't remember that," she said. "I just remember being very frightened, but of what I didn't really know." And she looked distressed.

He gathered her into his arms. "All in the past now Ari. From now on it will all be fine. But I do have something to ask you. Something I was going to ask you that awful night. I have carried this with me for three years also." He bent and took the little box with the ring that he had bought so long ago, from his bag and knelt down in front of her.

"Arianwen, my precious, darling girl," he said. "Will you marry me?"

Ari looked into his deep-blue eyes and stroked his face. It was late in the day and he needed a shave. His chin was rough with stubble. The first time he had ever kissed her it had been like that and she loved it. She put her arms around his neck.

"Oh! Jon," she smiled. "My lovely, lovely man. Yes of course I will." She kissed him once again as he put the ring on her finger.

Jon gave a great yawn. "Come on," said Ari. "Let's go to bed. To sleep. It's been such a strange day for you, I bet you're shattered."

They went upstairs, peeping in at Gwenny, who slept like a starfish, just like her mother. And then they collapsed into bed.

Jon slept for four hours, but Ari got up after a while and putting on her warm dressing gown went downstairs and stood outside the back door. The moon and stars were very bright, it was very cold, and there was a hint of frost on the grass. It was silent and there was not a cloud in the sky. Ari looked up at the stars. "Thank you," she said. "Oh! Thank you." Then she went back upstairs and settled on the sofa at the bottom of the bed as she didn't want to disturb Jon, who was fast asleep.

But he woke up with a start, "Ari!" he said. "Where are you?"

She got up and slid into bed beside him. "Do you feel better now?" she asked. "Are you hungry?"

"No, I'm fine," he said. "But there is something I just must do." He pulled her on top of him and began to kiss her all over. She moved with him and when he entered her, she gave a deep sigh. Not for one moment did she take her eyes from his face and as she neared orgasm, she raised herself a little and kissed him deeply. They both came together and not one word had been said. They lay in each other's arms for a while and then Jon asked her to tell him about having Gwenny. Her ebony wood box was on the chest of drawers and she took a photograph from it. It was her, looking extremely tired and with hair damp with sweat, holding a just born and unwashed Gwenny. She looked triumphant. "I asked the nurse to take it," she said. "Just in case." Jon felt very humbled and proud that she had gone through all that on her own. "I got better then," she said smiling at Jon. "I had to look after Gwenny and quite honestly, she has kept me sane. She must be a tenacious little soul as I was pregnant when I was hurt. But she stayed with me."

"Was it a bad experience Ari?" Jon asked.

"Well, it wasn't fun, and the nurse had big gouges from my fingernails in her hands by the end, and apparently, I swore a lot but I had nothing to measure it against. And some of the nurses were a bit frosty to the unmarried mothers. I was glad to get back home. Mam was here and she stayed with me for a while. I've been on my own since then."

He gathered her up in his arms again, his darling girl, his Arianwen.

"Talking of children," she said. "Gwenny will be in here first thing in the morning. She likes to get into bed with me and we have a chat about the day. Do you have anything like pyjamas with you?"

Jon said, "No." He didn't wear them anymore.

"Well," she laughed. "Gwenny isn't used to men so you might be in for a full-on anatomy lesson in the morning. I can give you a nightshirt if you want, delay the inevitable a bit?"

Six o'clock in the morning and Gwenny appeared at the bedroom door. "Why is Daddy in your bed Mammy?" she asked a little worriedly.

"Daddies always sleep with Mammies," Ari said easily. "Come on, get in the middle. It's nice and warm in here."

So Gwenny climbed on the bed and walked all over Jon to her place between her parents.

"Morning kiss Mammy," she said, and kissed Ari.

"Morning kiss Daddy," she said turning to Jon. But he didn't open his eyes. Gwenny bent over him and looked closely into his face. Ari could see just the glimmer of a smile on his lips.

Gwenny tried again "It's Gwenny, Daddy!"

Jon opened one eye.

"Well so it is. I thought it was an elephant." That gave Gwenny the giggles.

Knowing Jon might visit Ari had removed the last painting of her 'Abandoned' triptych. The first canvas with Sal carrying her she retitled

'Out'. The large one of her and Jon she kept as 'Abandoned', but with a different connotation. The last one of her in the garden, she destroyed. She knew now that he had never meant to leave her.

After breakfast they went across to the barn. Jon saw the large canvas turned towards the big windows at the end of the room and walked around to see it. His heart lurched in his chest when he saw the subject. Him and Ari. It was so beautiful. Very gentle, very atmospheric and very, very sensual. It was their hotel room in the New Forest. The window was open very slightly and the curtains were just lifting in the breeze. Outside were the bare winter trees. Ari's case and boots were lying in a corner, and Jon's navy jumper hung at the end of the bed. He was utterly amazed. He would find out from Tally if it could be exhibited somewhere alongside his. But only if Ari agreed.

They went into town later and had lunch in a small restaurant near the castle and because it was fine went for a walk along the river, Jon carrying Gwenny on his shoulders. She loved that and held on tightly to his hair or ears. Then Jon went back to the hotel to pay his bill and pick up his car. He followed them home.

When Gwenny had gone to bed they lay together on the sofa to talk about what to do next. That they should all be together was taken for granted, but where? Jon had his exhibition to prepare for and his teaching, so needed to be at his own home. He would, he thought, give in his notice to finish at the end of the school year, and tell the university in New Zealand that he wouldn't be coming. He had been very impressed with the barn and with the addition of more windows downstairs it could accommodate two large studios.

They decided that Jon would go home on Monday and come back and stay for a week over Easter. Then he would have to go back to finish his paintings and to see his students through their last term. He would come back as and when he could. He knew Arianwen understood and agreed with these arrangements. She would also be able to explain to Gwenny.

On Monday morning he left. Leaving a tearful Ari and Gwenny. When he had gone Ari showed Gwenny her ring. "Do you know what this is Gwenny?" she said.

Gwenny shook her head. She was very sad and wanted her Daddy.

"Well, it means that Daddy will always come back. He has only gone to do some work then he will come and stay again. I know," she said looking at Gwenny's tear-stained face. "Shall we go and see David and Shona? She's home today. Then you can tell them all about your daddy."

They got their coats and walked up the lane.

Jon drove home in a daze. He could not quite believe that he had driven up on Thursday with absolutely no thought that he would find Ari, at long last. And have a daughter too. He smiled the whole way home. It was bloody marvellous, and it hadn't taken more than a moment for them to be as they always had been.

David and Shona were eager for news, and they were both so happy for Ari when she showed them her ring. Shona said she had liked Jon on sight. "He's a bloody intelligent chap, isn't he Ari? And quite good looking too." She smiled at Ari. "You'll be happy now cariad."

Gwenny was sitting on David's lap telling him absolutely everything daddy had said or done all weekend. "You liked him then, did you?" David asked her when he could get a word in.

"Yes," said Gwenny. "And I shall tell Charlie that my daddy is lovely and Mammy and me love him and kiss him lots."

Later that day Ari rang Sal but got Olive, who was on another quick visit to 'Arian Court'.

"Nan," she said. "Would you mind very much if Gwenny and I stayed here for Easter." She hesitated, "Jon has been here and he is coming back then." She didn't say anything about her ring. One thing at a time. Nan and most definitely Mam needed to get used to the idea that Jon was back with her and Gwenny.

She heard Olive's whoop of joy. "My brave, brave girl," she said. "And how was Gwenny?"

Ari laughed, "He absolutely loved her and she him. She sat next to him practically the whole weekend, and he was so natural with her Nan. It was just lovely to see. Will you tell Mam and Fred for me?

I am so, so happy. And thank you for putting me straight, for the letter and all, and for being happy for us. I'll tell you all the details next time I see you."

Sal was a bit stiff about it. "And she accepted him just like that. No recriminations about all she has been through on her own?"

"She wouldn't Sal, would she now? She has always been very forgiving and quite honestly there was nothing really to forgive. Just a trail of misunderstandings. She has always just wanted him back. It's sad it went on so long."

Sal looked very troubled. After a while she said, "Mam I have a confession to make. I could have stopped it earlier." She paused and sighed, "We were down at the beach hut, just Ari, Gwenny and me, last summer. End of June perhaps. Well, just before they went back home anyway. Ari took Gwenny down to the sea and I was just standing leaning on the railings, watching the world go by, when I saw Jon coming along with that friend of his who lives down here; I suppose that's who it was. I just panicked and went into the hut and stood at the back so he wouldn't see me. I could see Ari at the water's edge playing with Gwenny and prayed that she wouldn't turn around.

Jon stopped and was shading his eyes with his hand and looking at her. Her silhouette was dazzled by the sun on the sea; and her plait was tucked up under her sunhat, otherwise he might have known it was her. Then she bent to pick up Gwenny and walked into the water. He sort of shook his head and walked on. I could have shouted out, 'Yes, it is her,' or some such thing or just gone out and said hello. But we had all been so concerned for her, I just couldn't." Sal had tears in her eyes. "I feel awful about it now."

"Well," said Olive. "We didn't know then what we know now, so you did what you thought right. We can't turn back the clock Sal, and everything has turned out all right, hasn't it. You are happy about her and Jon now, aren't you?" And Sal had to admit, just a little grudgingly, that she was.

"Right," said Olive, giving her daughter a hug. "I'd best do my packing or Roger will wonder where I am. Though," she added thoughtfully. "He is probably well up with all the news. I think secretly he has enjoyed all this intrigue. He did wonder the other day, why no one has ever heard from Lillian Morgan since Ari went to school." But Roger, of course had looked into it, and the only thing he had discovered was that she had long ago been divorced from the millionaire.

Julius couldn't contain himself when he saw Jon on the Tuesday morning. There had been a lot of speculation around Arianwen being assaulted at the time, nearly four years ago. But since the summer holidays had then intervened it was just assumed, amongst the staff, that if there had been anything between them, she had gone her way and Jon, his. Flora who had seen and heard it all, and even seen Mr Curtis stagger into the hall white-faced with pain, had only ever spoken to Mr Winter and Elias. She was fiercely loyal to Arianwen. She still had Arianwen's shoes, wrapped up now in tissue paper, that she had found in the gutter that awful evening. Now and again when another leavers' party was being arranged someone would say, "Do you remember the 1964 one?" And if they didn't someone would enlighten them. But now all the students there at the time had moved on, and most hadn't known the true story anyway. Only Julius knew that. And hard though it had been he hadn't said a word. The beautiful Arianwen Morgan had however become a bit of a legend at the school, her beauty, her astonishingly thought-provoking paintings and of course the assault.

Jon, Julius and Poll went out for a drink that evening, and Jon told them all about meeting Arianwen. He gave Poll the little wren, which she was delighted with, and then explained what had happened after he had bought it. Then about going home with Ari and meeting Gwenny.

Poll shrieked when he said, "Then I met Gwenllian, my daughter. She is just three. The dearest little thing and amazingly she looks very much like me." He smiled broadly.

"Oh! Jon," she said. "What a shock for you. No one ever thought, did they, that Ari might be pregnant? Oh! Bless her. What a marvellous outcome to all that sadness. A daughter, how lovely. And Arianwen, how is she?"

Jon said she was well now and a wonderful mother to Gwenny, and that she was as much his 'darling girl' as she had ever been.

They then wanted to know what would happen next.

Jon explained that he would go up whenever he could as he did have the exhibition to prepare for. Though a visit at Easter was definite.

"Bloody hell Poll," Julius said when they got home. "He's some lucky bugger."

And Poll agreed.

Five weeks later, Jon returned. Gwenny and Ari were very excited and had decorated the house with spring flowers. The garden was awash with blossom and Ari had twisted some forsythia and winter jasmine into a garland and hung it on the back door. Lem, Grace and their children, Skye and baby Saffron were invited for Easter Sunday lunch, and Ari had bought everyone an Easter egg. Gwenny could hardly contain herself when they saw his car turn down the drive.

Jon got stiffly out of the car. The journey had been long and the traffic heavy. It seemed the whole of the Home Counties were heading for Snowdonia or the sea. Gwenny reached him first and he swung her up into the air, making her squeal with joy. He kissed her little face. "I have missed you such a lot sweetheart," he said. "Have you been a good girl for your mummy?"

"I am always a good girl," said Gwenny stoutly.

Ari came up then and still holding Gwenny he put his arm around her and pulled her close. She leant against him and he once more smelled that wonderful perfume of spice and peaches that was his darling girl.

They had waited lunch for him and after eating, Gwenny, worn out by the excitement, fell asleep on the sofa. Jon carried her upstairs and he and Ari then went and lay down on their bed. Ari settled into the crook of his arm and within moments he too was asleep. All this driving back and forth was too much for him, Ari thought, along with getting ready for his exhibition and helping his students. Still, it wasn't for too long. They should decide soon where they would live, though she thought she knew.

Gwenny woke first and came to find them. She settled herself against Jon. He opened a sleepy eye. "Hello sweetheart," he said. "Did you have a nice sleep?"

"Yes, Daddy," she said. "And now I'm thirsty." So, they got up. A little later Jon took Gwenny to his car. Ari, in the kitchen heard Gwenny's scream of delight. He had bought her a bicycle. Bright blue, with stabilisers, blue and orange streamers on the handlebars, a little basket at the front and a bell. Gwenny was on it like a shot and Jon watched as she wobbled around the yard, her face pink with happiness.

Later that evening when Gwenny had finally gone to sleep, Jon and Ari went to bed. It was lovely and warm in the house and they sat on the bed naked. Ari was seated across Jon and facing him, her legs each side. "Ari?" Jon said. "Why did you choose me. There must have been so many others?"

She took his face in her hands.

"There weren't any others Jon, once I'd seen you, and only one before you," she said. "It doesn't work like that. You chose me first. I can remember the exact moment, though then I didn't know what had happened."

She kissed him gently.

"I expect you won't remember my interview. Well, I came down the stairs after it and you were walking past. You said, 'Someone's happy,' to Mam, and I turned to look at you and had the strangest sensation. I had no idea what it was and forgot about it until I saw you next. Then I knew. I had no choice in the matter. I remember talking to Tom about it, though I never mentioned you. Because I understood to some extent, how he was feeling." She stopped. She could feel something moving beneath her.

"Jon stop it," she laughed. "I'm being serious."

"I can't stop it," he grinned. "And I'm very serious." And he reached for her breasts.

"I would choose you now," Ari said breathlessly. "Because you are so bloody... male!"

"And you, sweet thing, are so gloriously female."

He lifted her slightly and entered her.

"I suppose we are lucky that we both chose each other," Jon said. "Though I too always felt I had no choice. Do you not think people can learn to love each other then?"

"Yes of course they can, but it is better with a spark don't you think. We were so good in lots of ways right from the start, weren't we?" Ari drew in a deep breath.

"And talking of lots of ways," Jon laughed. "I have waited long enough."

Afterwards they lay quietly in each other's arms. Jon said, "Tell me about the first one then Ari?"

She laughed, "An Australian deckchair attendant in Bournemouth, a student really travelling round the world. I was going through my rebellious phase, I think. Anyway, he was very nice, a bit special really, and he asked me out. Mam didn't want me to go, and she said I had to be careful because you know what these boys are like. Well, I didn't so I thought I'd better find out... I bet you can't guess who was the first person to ask me out at art school?"

Jon couldn't.

"Sean! He was in his last year and saw me in the hall. He said I had much improved. Cheek!"

Jon laughed and kissed her.

"How about you then Mr Curtis?"

"That would take far too long Ari," Jon teased. "Let's do something else instead. Have you had chips this week by any chance?"

In the morning when Jon woke up Ari was gone and there was a note on the pillow.

Just gone into the village to get Hot Cross buns.

Love A and G xxx

He was washed and dressed by the time they got back with a baker's dozen of warm fragrant buns, some of which they had for breakfast. The three of them had a very quiet day together. Gwenny was eager to show Jon that she didn't need stabilisers on the bike any more, as she tore around the yard. They walked around the garden and Jon was shown her swing and the gate which led to a footpath beside a stream. Though Gwenny assured him that the gate was always locked. They all had an early night because tomorrow was going to be special.

The next morning, they were up early and dressed in their best. Jon, handsome in a dark-grey suit, Gwenny in a white Broderie Anglais dress with a pink cardigan and Ari, her hair plaited with silver ribbons and wound in a crown about her head, in a plain grey, empire line silk shift and her silver jewellery. They met Lem, Grace and the children outside the town hall in Llandudno. Grace handed Ari a bunch of white and purple hellebores she had picked from the garden that morning. There was a small one for Gwenny too, and one each for Jon and Lem's buttonholes. Ari and Jon were going to get married. Jon had arranged it all, and afterwards they would re-register Gwenny's birth. He had remembered the man in the transport cafe saying not to misplace Ari, and he was making sure he did not. He had not told anyone else, just asked Grace and Lem to be witnesses, for they had both been of enormous support to Ari, right from the beginning. They would have a great big family party later.

When the registrar finally said they were man and wife, Jon took Ari in his arms, "We made it, my darling girl," he said. And kissed her, and then Gwenny.

Afterwards the four adults and three children went to a nearby restaurant where the adults had champagne and enormous cream cakes and Gwenny and Skye had ice creams and the baby slept. Then they went their separate ways. Grace and Lem were coming to lunch tomorrow, Easter Sunday, anyway.

Ari and Jon went home the long way, Jon driving the Land Rover this time. Along the Nant Ffrancon valley and then down to Capel Curig, Snowdon in the distance. From there to Betws-y-Coed and then over the mountain, past the lakes to Llanrwst. Jon was struck again by the spectacular and grand beauty of the area. The sweeping landscape, the small, intricate unobserved details. The colours and textures and the brilliant light. There was everything here he needed for his paintings. He would talk to Ari about living here. And of course, she said yes.

Easter lunch was lovely and afterwards whilst Grace fed the baby, Lem and Jon sat outside with the children. Gwenny fetched her old three-wheeler bike out of the barn for Skye and soon the two little girls were riding round and round the garden. Jon and Lem sat on the bench by the kitchen door, smoking. They had always got on well, and now Lem was telling Jon all the benefits of moving up to North Wales.

On the Tuesday Jon went to meet Tally. He had persuaded Ari to exhibit some of her paintings and Tally said there was a room downstairs which would be ideal. All that was left to do was to transport Jon's paintings mid-June and hang them. In the afternoon Jon went home. The next few months would be busy so he had given Ari no definite date as to when he would be able to come back.

The first evening when Ari was on her own, she knew she would just have to ring Mam and Nan to tell them the news. She couldn't decide who to tell first so tossed a coin. Nan first.

Roger answered the phone. "Hello Ari," he said. "How is everything with you?"

"Fine thank you, but may I speak to Nan. It's quite important?" Olive came to the phone.

"Hello cariad," she said. "News, Roger says?"

"Nan," Ari said and took a deep breath. "Jon and I got married on Saturday and afterwards re-registered Gwenny."

"Oh Ari," Olive said. "That is such lovely news. You have both been through so much."

"He arranged it all Nan. He said he didn't want to misplace me again. And now Gwenny is legally his too. It is so marvellous Nan."

"Have you spoken to Sal yet?"

"No," said Ari. "I didn't know who to phone first, so I tossed a coin."

Olive laughed. "Just don't tell her that Ari. Well, cariad I am really pleased for you both and I know Roger will share that. I liked your Jon on sight, he is a good man. Just be aware you might not get the same reaction from Sal."

"So, tell me cariad," she continued. "What did you wear?"

Ari laughed, "Well it was all a bit sudden Nan, so that grey silk dress I had for your wedding. And I had some silver ribbon left over from Christmas, so I plaited that into my hair and wound the plaits round my head. I think it looked all right? Grace brought me a bouquet of white and pale purple hellebores, so that was lovely. I will send you some photos."

They said goodbye and see you soon.

Ari phoned Sal next but Sal was busy with a guest and Fred said she would phone her back.

It must have been a difficult meeting as Sal was quite sharp when she rang.

"Yes Ari, what do you want?"

"I just wanted to tell you that Jon and I got married on Saturday."

There was a very heavy silence then Sal said,

"Oh, Ari are you sure you should have done that, it is all so quick. You haven't had time to think about it properly, or to get to know each other again." Sal stopped, then said, "I always wanted you to have a white wedding Arianwen."

"I know you did Mam but one is supposed to be a virgin for that and I was hardly that was I, with Gwenny and all?"

"That place has a lot to answer for Arianwen." Sal suddenly had a vivid picture of all those contraceptives in Ari's drawer.

"It has nothing to do with the art school or Jon for that matter," Ari said crossly. "I lost my virginity before ever I went there. Please Mam, don't ever blame Jon. What we did we did together because we loved each other and could do nothing less. I wanted to as much as him."

Sal could not believe what she was hearing. She wanted to ask, when did you lose your virginity and with whom, but knew she could not.

"Anyway," Ari continued. "I only ever wanted Jon and he me, so we got married. There was nothing to think about, … But we would have liked your blessing Mam," she added.

There was silence from Sal.

Finally, Ari said, "I love him very much Mam, and have for years. There was never anyone else for either of us. I am sorry to disappoint you, but we did what we wanted to do. Jon said he didn't want to misplace me again. I'll say good night now then. Nos da."

She was just about to put the phone down when she heard Sal shout.

"Ari, Ari, don't go. I'm really sorry. I did dream of a white wedding for you, and you going down the aisle on Fred's arm, but things change…"

Ari interrupted, "Mam you must not worry. Jon and I have a lovely relationship. Gwenny loves him and is never far from his side, and he dotes on her. We thought to have a big celebration sometime around Jon's exhibition, which we will send you an invitation for anyway. So, all is well here. Although Jon has gone home now and I miss him already."

Ari also had things to do. She sorted out which paintings she wanted to exhibit and discussed adding them to the catalogue with Tally. Then she had, slightly warily spoken to Huw about putting more windows downstairs in the barn and sorting out a downstairs studio. Huw was pleased she had asked him and felt a little forgiven. He would do the best job for her he could.

One Wednesday morning, a week or so later she and Gwenny were sitting in bed.

Gwenny put her arms around Ari. "I want my Daddy," she said.

Ari looked at her for a moment. "Gwenny, shall we go to see him, and look after him for a bit. What do you think?"

The answer was a resounding, "Yes."

The next morning, they got up very early and Ari put their cases plus Gwenny's beloved bike in the back of the Land Rover. It was a fair old way but Gwenny slept a lot and they had just one stop for an early lunch. They arrived and parked the car near the cattle market, just before twelve-thirty. Ari knew that most of the staff would be in the staff room at lunchtime. She and Gwenny walked along the main street through the town. It was quiet as being a Thursday it was coming up to half day closing. Ari had loved and known this place so well. The streets and little alleyways. The shops, the pubs, the market and the Abbey. They turned into the road where the art school was and crossed the road to the tobacconist. It had been difficult to get 'Passing Clouds' in North Wales, so she took the opportunity to buy several packets. The usual lady was behind the counter and she recognised Ari. "Hello dear," she said. "Is this your little girl? She is like her father, isn't she?" Ari nodded. "Well," said the lady. "Your husband's not long been in for his Gauloises." Ari said they were just going to see him. The lady still on the same tack said, "He used to look at you as if he could eat you when you came in before, so I'm not surprised." Ari laughed. She said how well Ari looked and gave Gwenny a penny lolly.

At the art school door, still painted a deep blue, Ari hesitated. The last time she had been here she had been battered, bruised, bewildered and very frightened, but she took a deep breath and holding Gwenny tightly by the hand they went inside. Ari stood in the middle of the hall. It sounded just the same. Music from the common room, people's voices. The same smell of paint, turpentine, dusty wood and cigarettes. A student crossing the upstairs landing saw her and came down.

"May I help?" he asked, thinking this is one lovely woman. She wore a bright pink, very short dress and her dark hair was in a ponytail on top of her head. Ari smiled at him and held out her hand. "Thank you," she said, shaking his hand. "I was a student here so I'm just remembering. I'm Arianwen Curtis and I've just come to see my husband, so I'm fine."

Ari stepped forward and knocked on the staff room door. She heard someone shout, "Julius you're nearest." The door opened.

Those inside just heard Julius bellow, "Well bugger me." When a little girl dressed in blue shorts and a white T-shirt came in. She stopped for just a moment by the door. She was entirely unafraid as she scanned all the people in the room. Sam the pottery technician was just about to get up and ask her what she wanted, but Archie put a hand on his arm.

"Let's see what she does," he whispered. "She has the look of someone in here." He indicated Jon who was sitting in the far corner reading and had not seen the child come in. Gwenny spotted her father's dark head and walked across the staff room to him. She stopped beside him and tapped him on the arm. "Daddy," she said. "It's your Gwenny."

"Good God," said Jon swinging his daughter up in his arms. "Where did you come from?"

"Out there," said Gwenny pointing to the door.

"Did you come on your own?"

"No silly," said Gwenny, giving her father a kiss. "I can't drive a car. Mammy is out there kissing a big man."

Archie looked at Sam. Now for the mother?

"Is she, by God?" laughed Jon. With which Julius returned, his arm around Arianwen.

"Jon," he shouted. "Look who I found."

But Ari had detached herself from him and walked straight over to Jon.

"Hello my lovely man," she smiled. "We've come to look after you." And she kissed him.

Jon kissed her back then turned her around to meet the staff but before he could say anything, Archie said, "Well bless my soul! Arianwen Morgan."

Ari smiled at him.

"No Mr Fellowes," she said. "Mrs Curtis." and she held up her left hand.

And Jon added, "And our daughter Gwenllian."

Everyone shouted their congratulations and looked at each other in astonishment. The older staff knew who she was but a few of the new staff didn't. This was Arianwen Morgan. Where had Jon been keeping her?

Julius crossed the room and shook Jon's hand then gave him a hug. "Well done lad.," he said and he had tears in his eyes. Of all the staff he was the only one who knew what Jon had been through, and even he, who prided himself on his observation skills, hadn't noticed that Jon had been wearing a wedding ring for the past few weeks. Archie realised that his wife had been right all along. He had much to tell her this evening. And Ian Cooper was pleased that his suspicions had been proved right.

The boy, who had asked Ari if she needed help, had seen Mr Winter swing her off her feet also. Soon the news that Arianwen Morgan was in the building spread to all, and the students were on the alert to see her.

Jon's credibility took a very sharp rise when he introduced her to anyone who asked, as his wife.

Jon took Ari and Gwenny up to the small studio then to give them his house keys and a map of how to get to his house. Gwenny said goodbye to everyone in the staff room.

"*Hwyl Fawr bawb,*" she said as she left. There was a buzz of conversation as the door shut. Ari hesitated a little as they climbed the stairs to the studio. There were some students working and some just sitting talking. Jon introduced Ari and Gwenny and then asked the students to leave just for a moment. Gwenny roamed around looking at the paintings and in the cupboards. Jon pulled Ari close, his fingers in her hair.

"Darling girl," he said. "Thank you. Just one thing, I have a large canvas in the conservatory. It is covered and the blinds are down, but please don't go in there Ari. Please?"

"Of course, I won't if you ask me not to Jon." She reached up and kissed him. "Come on then Gwenny," she called. "We had better go and find Daddy's house. There must be washing to put on."

They found the house easily. It was set back behind a long front garden and not far from Poll and Julius. It was a Victorian red brick cottage with a white painted wooden porch. Inside it was a little untidy but clean and smelled of paint, turps, Gauloises and Jon.

Ari took their things out of the car. There was a side door from the kitchen to the garden, so she took Gwenny's bike out there and Gwenny was quite happy to ride around and explore the garden. She had brought a leg of Welsh lamb with her in a cool box, plus everything to make dinner. She tidied the kitchen then put the lamb in the oven and laid the table. Gwenny came in after a while and lay on the sofa. She was worn out by the excitement of the day and the very early start. Just after four o'clock Ari saw Jon's car pull in behind hers. He leapt out and rushed in, dropping his bag in the hall. He came into the kitchen. "Where's Gwenny?" he said. Ari indicated their little girl asleep on the sofa. "Good," said Jon. "Come with me." And he pulled Ari into the little scullery next to the kitchen and shut the door.

"Mrs Curtis," he said. "Don't ever turn up unannounced in a dress like that again. I have had the most uncomfortable afternoon."

"This is very romantic," laughed Ari.

"Bugger romantic," Jon said and he slid his hands under her skirt. He leant her against a cupboard and entered her. She wrapped her legs around his waist, and her arms around his neck, and he took her weight.

"Ooh," she said in delight. "Jon Curtis, how I have missed you."

In the middle of the night Ari got out of bed and walked into a cupboard. Jon heard the crash and switched on the bedside light. "Ari," he said. "What are you doing?"

"I'm looking for Jon and I can't find him."

He realised she was asleep and gently guided her back to bed. He wrapped his arms about her and in a moment she was quiet. The visit to the school must have brought back bad memories for her he thought. He pulled her tight against him and vowed to keep her safe always.

In the morning Ari said not a word about it and was her usual loving self. Jon didn't tell her what had happened but he realised that the trauma she had been through was far worse than he had thought. He understood now why her family had been and probably still were so protective of her.

Jon did not teach on a Friday now, so after breakfast he disappeared into the conservatory. Ari and Gwenny went shopping in town to restock the cupboards. Ari planned to go to the market on Saturday as that was one thing she really missed. When they got back, they tidied everything away and made lunch. Gwenny knocked on the conservatory door.

"Daddy, lunch is ready." And a smiling Jon came out.

"I thought Gwenny and I could visit Mrs Winter this afternoon as I haven't seen her for a long time. Will she be in do you think Jon?"

Jon thought she may well be as Julius was at school on a Friday. So, he told Ari where to go, and after they had cleared the table, she and Gwenny set off.

It was a lovely warm day and it took them just five minutes to walk to Poll and Julius' house. It was a large brick and flint cottage just across the green and Ari remembered it as soon as she saw it. Ari lifted Gwenny up so she could bang the knocker which was a fox's head. Gwenny giggled in delight. Poll came to the door and just stood and looked at them for a long moment.

"Arianwen," she said. "Oh, Arianwen, how wonderful, and little Gwenny too. She is so like Jon isn't she, but she has a lot of you too I think, Ari." And she shepherded them into the garden.

"Julius came home yesterday bursting with the news. Married at last. I can't tell you Arianwen how very pleased we are for you both."

"Thank you, Mrs Winter," Ari said. "It is marvellous, isn't it?"

"Ari, no Mrs Winter any more please. Poll to you now and Gwenny also."

Poll brought out some cold homemade lemonade and some shortbread then and Gwenny went to sleep in a deckchair. It was lovely sitting in the garden and Ari told Poll all that had happened, being ill, moving and having Gwenny. Then finding out that Jon was coming up to North Wales and planning how they could meet.

"And it all worked out beautifully. It is so, so good being back with Jon, I can't tell you Poll, and Gwenny loves him too."

"Well, you are kindred spirits, aren't you? Sad you both had to go through what you did though."

Ari then told her about the exhibition and asked if they would like to come, as they were going to have a big party once the private view was over.

"I think nothing in this world would stop Julius coming." Poll said, "He is very fond of Jon."

"And might you both like to come out to supper tomorrow night?" Ari asked. "It will have to be early because of Gwenny. I will book at Marco's uncle's place. Gwenny likes pasta."

She stopped and put her hand on Poll's, "It will be a very small thank you from me for looking after Jon and I have missed you a lot, Poll."

Poll smiled; Arianwen was such a dear girl.

They moved on then to talking about school and what teachers were still there, and any news of girls Ari knew. She told Poll about Christina and her divorce, and that she was now living in Canada, and how she had been such a good friend to her.

"She was a bit of a naughty one, wasn't she?" smiled Poll. "But you were always so good."

"Well, I had to be, didn't I?" said Ari. "When I was little, a lady up our street, a Mrs Pryce, told me I would be sent back if I wasn't. I never knew where back was but sort of thought it was like the mountain opening up in the *Pied Piper* and swallowing the children."

"Mind you," Ari went on. "I did rebel a bit when I was older. I always wanted my ears pierced like Christina, but Nan wasn't keen. When we left school, I went to stay with Christina, and her mother Belinda took me to have them done. It was just a small thing, but I had sort of realised that there was no one who could tell me no, only my mother. But thank goodness I soon grew out of that. I had to fight a bit about art school though. Sal saw it as some den of iniquity."

"Oh, I remember Belinda," said Poll. "And Sabrina. They liked the good things in life, didn't they?"

Ari laughed. "When I stayed with them, I went home with the silk underwear that Belinda had bought for me. I loved it and still do. My Nan was appalled. She thought all underwear should be boil washed." Poll laughed.

Gwenny woke up then, so they left Poll to go home to make dinner.

The next morning, Jon was again painting so Ari and Gwenny went to the market. Ari didn't need much, but they were late back to make lunch. Nearly every stall holder that Ari had frequented, the bread man, the picture framer, the vintage clothes lady, recognised her and wanted to know about Gwenny and where she lived and what she was doing now. It was really lovely but a bit exhausting. They went back home to Jon glad to have been but needing a rest.

That evening Jon, Ari and Gwenny picked up Poll and Julius and they went out for supper.

The restaurant was much the same but had had a coat of paint recently. They were shown to their table by a young man Ari did not know, but within moments they heard a shout "Arianwen, Bella ragazza." Vittorio, now the manager had spotted them. He came up and kissed Ari on both cheeks, then Gwenny, who went pink, then Poll and shook hands with Julius and Jon. To Jon he said, "You are one lucky man, congratulations." Then he went back to his duties as the restaurant was beginning to fill up. The food was wonderful and they sat talking over coffee. Gwenny was drooping and leaning against Jon. Suddenly she sat up, scrambled off her seat and dashed off towards the door. "Marco, Marco," she called. "Come and see my daddy."

For Marco was back for a short visit and staying with his uncle and Vittorio, who had phoned him when he saw Ari. Gwenny dragged Marco to their table. He was looking extremely well and prosperous. He was now doing art conservation at a museum in Paris and was still with Philippe. Ari got up and put her arms around him, and he her. They didn't have to say a word.

They all had more coffee and sat for a long while catching up. Gwenny went to sleep on Jon's lap and Julius was looking the worse for wear when they finally said their goodbyes. But Ari had asked Marco and Philippe to the private view and party if they could come.

Ari had said they would stay with Jon for two weeks, and he was so grateful for the extra time this gave him. He had always had the ability to concentrate for long periods and now with nothing to do but paint he got on amazingly well. He taught three days a week now, but when he was home, he would stop late afternoon to have time with Gwenny, and of course an added bonus was that he had Ari in his bed every night.

After Ari and Gwenny had done the jobs for the day, the washing, ironing, dusting, and preparing the evening meal, Gwenny would knock on the conservatory door and tell Jon lunch was ready. Then in the afternoon Ari took her out somewhere. There were lots of things to do. The swimming pool, a paddling pool in the park, the Abbey, the market, the swings and a car ride away, lovely woods and of course visiting Poll and Julius, if he was there. Then they would come back in time to make tea, and Jon would smile to himself when he heard them talking or very often singing.

In the evening, he put Gwenny to bed and read her a story. She would put her little arms around his neck and kiss him goodnight, "Nos da Daddy," she said. *"Gweld chi yn y bore,"* which Ari said meant 'See you in the morning."

Then he would go downstairs where Ari would be waiting with a glass of wine or a cold beer. He would pull her onto his lap and in no time at all they were in bed.

Jon got on so well that he took a day off towards the end of the week. The weather was good so in the afternoon they went to the park. There were lots of people about, watching the model boats on the pond and the playground was full of children. Jon pushed Gwenny on the swing for a while then swapped with Ari. He had brought his camera and wanted photos of them both to send to his sister. She had been delighted with the news when he had rung her. His brother seemed to have disappeared again.

Ari and Gwenny wandered off to get an ice cream from the van, and Jon sat on a bench checking his camera. A young woman pushing a pram stopped by him.

"Sir," she said. "Mr Curtis?"

Jon looked up. It took him a moment to realise it was Flora and the baby newborn.

He moved so she could sit beside him and asked how she was.

"Very well now, sir," she said. "And thank you for all you did for me."

Jon saw Gwenny heading his way holding a runny ice cream for him.

She went straight to Jon. "Here you are Daddy," she said. "You'd better lick it quick."

Flora laughed. "My daughter Gwenllian," he said and as Ari arrived. "And my wife."

Flora turned and there was Arianwen. She was at a loss for words.

Ari smiled at her "Hello Flora," she said. "And who is this?"

"Our daughter," she stammered. "Ariann, after you. We thought Arianwen a bit long," she smiled hesitantly. "And you did such a lot for both of us."

Ari hugged her. "Thank you, Flora and who is her daddy?"

"Tom."

"Tom! What Tom Lawrence? He didn't marry Nell then?"

"No, she went off with James. I think she and Tom didn't get on too well living together when they went to Hastings. And Tom, well, he had changed a lot and it was nice going out with him. We got married last year."

"And Elias?" asked Jon.

Flora's face clouded over. "He died in a car accident, not long after we finished at art school. Tom was a real help then."

"Oh Flora," Ari said. "How very sad."

Flora looked quite upset, so to change the subject Jon said, "Flora, Ari is with me for another week. Would you and Tom like to come round one evening? Have some supper?"

"I'll ask Tom and let you know may I and I have your shoes Ari?"

Ari looked at Jon, but he was as puzzled as her.

"My shoes?" she said.

"Yes," said Flora. "The silver ones. I found them in the gutter after… you know?"

Ari looked absolutely stricken. Jon caught Flora's eye and shook his head. He gave Flora their phone number, then Flora checked on little Ariann and went on her way.

That evening she told Tom about seeing them. "It was very strange, you know Tom. He said Ari and the little girl were with him for another week, so they must live somewhere else. Yet he introduced Ari as his wife and they both wear wedding rings. The little girl is about three I would say, so Ari must have been pregnant around the time of the leaving party and there is no disputing the fact that the child is his. I can't remember her name, something Welsh, I think. A mystery ay Tom?"

"I'll go ring Jon now," Tom said. "Perhaps we will find out what happened when we go." Tom was very much looking forward to seeing Arianwen again but he didn't say so to his wife. Poor Flora was upset though that she had brought back bad memories for Arianwen.

That evening when Gwenny was in bed Ari said, "Jon, I don't want those shoes. I don't want to even see them. Will you take them if Flora brings them? I don't want things that make me remember. I can do that on my own. I dreamt the other night that I was looking for you, but I think you found me."

Jon held her tight. "I'll take them," he said. "Now darling girl, I haven't had a proper taste of you all day." And he kissed her long and deeply.

Monday was another day Jon was not teaching. "Nearly there Ari," he said. "I'll ask Sam and Archie to help crate them up next weekend. They helped me last time."

"I'll make lunch for you all then and Jon, I think we will go back on Sunday."

Jon felt such a wave of sadness that he could not speak.

Ari came and held him tight.

"It's only for a few weeks, lovely man, and then we will be together always."

Gwenny knocked the milk over then and wailed her distress.

"What we need," Jon said to her when she had finished hiccupping and sobbing. "Is a kitten to lick that up."

Gwenny brightened.

"When I come to live with you shall we get a kitten?"

"Oh yes," said Gwenny. "And what shall we call it?"

"Well, you have a good think and let me know."

He finished wiping up the milk then Ari said she and Gwenny would go up to the village shop to get more, and perhaps some sweets for Gwenny.

They had only been gone a few minutes when the doorbell rang. Jon went to answer it and it was his sister Jenny.

"I just had to come Jon," she said giving him a hug. "I know you said you'd send me photos, but when you said they were here I just couldn't stay away."

"They have just gone to the shop," said Jon. "They won't be long."

"Jen," he continued. "I just cannot think what I did to deserve those two. Gwenny is an absolute joy and Ari..."

He stopped. "Well just you wait and see, and she is as lovely inside as out. I love her completely Jen."

"I am so pleased," Jenny said. "When you were with Sarah, I constantly worried she would become pregnant and tie you to her that way. She wasn't good for you, was she?"

"No," said Jon. "And to be fair I was not what she needed either."

They heard someone singing then.

"Shussh," Jon said. "Gwenny."

Gwenny came into the kitchen and stopped when she saw Jon with a tall lady with very short dark hair.

"My God," said Jen. "A clone." And laughed.

"Where's your Mummy?" Jon said.

"She is helping Mrs Mason with her dustbin, she couldn't get it up the path," said Gwenny, and then Arianwen came in.

"Hello," she said, knowing instantly that this was Jon's sister. "I'm Arianwen."

Jenny just looked at her, she was so beautiful. "And I'm Jenny. I just had to come and meet you both. The boys couldn't come this time as they are in school."

Jon abandoned any idea of working and they sat in the kitchen drinking coffee and eating the doughnuts Ari had bought.

So, Jenny got to know Ari and Gwenny and promised to come up to North Wales with her two boys, Will and Ben, in the holidays. It would be good for Gwenny to meet her cousins. Ari thought it marvellous. Her child was going to be part of her own family. Although she never forgot that Mam and Nan loved her as their own too.

Jenny left later in the afternoon, as she lived near Cambridge and wanted to be home before Eric, her husband saw the boys to bed. Jon went with her to the car and Jen gave him a big hug.

"You've hit the jackpot there," she said. "I think even Ma might have loved her." And with that she waved and drove off.

Wednesday came all too quickly and Ari made a large lasagne for supper plus tiramisu. She had been to the wonderful deli near the art school for the ingredients. She was slightly worried about meeting Tom but Jon would be there and watchful she knew. She thought she seemed to have spent the whole two weeks meeting people she had known previously. The cigarette shop lady, Poll, Julius, Sam, Archie Fellowes, Mr Cooper, Vittorio, Marco, Flora, and tonight, Tom. Jen was the only new one.

Jon had asked her the previous evening if she had found it difficult coming back.

"Not difficult," she had said. "Because you were here, but strange. I have always loved the town, and I loved being at the art school."

"There were some real bad bits for you though weren't there?"

"Well with Tom, yes, there were. But it was just now and then to begin with, though I must admit that it was getting more frequent and more upsetting. But it did get resolved, didn't it?"

"I think my darling girl, you were very brave and resolved that yourself," said Jon.

"You were the worst thing though. Most of the time if I was busy, or painting I could forget, but then it would hit me hard. You were always there. It was lovely sometimes but very sad others. I used to think 'I wonder if when I am a very old lady and perhaps married to someone else, whether I will still think of you' and I knew that I would. And there was never anyone I could talk to about it. I think now Nan might have understood but Mam would have been appalled. I think Marco guessed but he would never have asked me outright."

"Oh! Ari," he said. "I am so sorry. And there was me trying desperately to ignore the fact that I loved you."

"And it only took the offer of a cup of tea," Ari laughed. "Tell you what, how about you show me now how much you love me?"

They went to bed, arms around each other, and he undressed her as he had that very first time. She was still his beautiful, generous, fragrant Ari and he knew she always would be.

Supper with Tom and Flora went well at first. Tom was impressed and rather gratified that she had made Italian. She obviously remembered their 'date'. Gwenny stayed up to see them and then said goodnight. Tom couldn't get over how much like Jon she was. When Ari went out to the kitchen to make coffee he came to help.

"So, it was always him then was it Ari?" he said.

"Jon? Yes Tom, it was."

"Do you know there were a few times when I would be talking to Jon and he wouldn't really be listening. He would be watching you. It did cross my mind then but, well, I was a bit self-absorbed at the time so thought nothing of it." He leant over and tried to kiss her. "Just for old times' sake Ari," he said. But she pushed him away.

"Oh, come on," he said. "I have tried really hard to be a nice person. I deserve a reward."

She held him at arm's length.

"No, Tom, you did that because it was the right thing to do. You don't need a reward, but if you do you have Flora and Ariann."

Jon came in then.

"Need any help?" he asked.

"No thanks," Ari said. "All sorted." And she smiled at Jon. He knew exactly what she meant.

They left just before midnight with promises to visit them in North Wales if they could. Ari wondered if they would ever see them again. She would like to see Flora but wasn't too sure about Tom. The shoes were never mentioned. Neither Tom nor Flora felt they could ask why Jon and Ari lived apart; it was to remain a mystery to them for some time,

Saturday came all too soon. Ari cleaned the house and did some more cooking. Jon's freezer was now full of 'meals for one' as Ari put it. Archie and Sam came and there was lots of hammering and swearing as they crated up the paintings to be transported to North Wales. Only the really big one was left, as it was still wet in places. They would come back to do that another day.

They had a very quiet evening together. Even Gwenny was not so talkative. Ari got the calendar down from the wall and showed her when Daddy would be coming to live with them forever. It was just over three weeks away. Gwenny brightened a little at that but was sad and tearful the next morning when they left. Ari could hardly speak when she got in the car and how she got to the end of the road in one piece, with her eyes full of tears, she didn't know. The journey was easy and she began to look forward to seeing the changes to the barn and to be in her own house, but she missed Jon already.

When she turned into the lane, she felt a great surge of excitement.

The barn looked splendid.

Next day, Ari took Gwenny to playgroup and when she got back Huw and some of his men were there. He took her round the barn to see what had been done so far.

The end wall underneath the balcony had had a large stone lintel fitted and they were just waiting for a floor to ceiling window to be delivered. On the north side there was a large sliding door and the beginnings of a little stone patio being built outside. As you came into the barn there was now a wall on the left-hand side and the new door in this had two glass panels, just like the one in Ari's bedroom in Tan Y Bryn. The room was nearly empty but a wood burner stood ready to be fitted and all the cupboards, just like those upstairs, had been built. There was only the plumbing to do. Three windows had been put in the wall facing the house.

Ari was truly impressed. "You must have been working so hard Huw," she said. "I've only been gone two weeks."

Huw smiled. "You deserve it cariad," he said. "When is your husband coming?"

"Few weeks yet, and I want to move all my stuff down here so Jon can have upstairs. It's bigger and he has some enormous canvases."

Huw not really au fait with the art world just nodded, "I'll give you a hand with that then when we finish down here."

Everything was completed a few days before Jon was due. Ari was so pleased she gave each of the men a bonus, which was received with many thanks.

The next weekend Jon drove up with as much 'stuff' as he could get in his car. The specialist carriers had left early with Jon's paintings and would leave them at the gallery. He arrived very tired in the late afternoon. Ari and Gwenny were waiting.

Monday evening and Jon helped Ari put her paintings in the back of the Land Rover. She had decided on 'Out', 'Abandoned'. A large canvas of her, Sal and Fred in the backfield lying amongst the flowers, titled 'Passing Clouds', the exam triptych, and Shona had insisted on the portrait of David too. She dropped the paintings and Jon off at the gallery on Tuesday morning and then popped into the surgery.

Meanwhile David had been busy. He had contacted everyone he knew in the art and newspaper world. All had had an invitation to the private view. Many were intrigued as he had been silent for years. Some would come because of his name but many because of his recommendation.

Jon spent a lot of time at the gallery with Taliesin, during the next two weeks, deciding how and where the paintings should be hung. Shona had engaged caterers for the private view and Ari had organised the big party for the Sunday after the opening and also where everyone might stay. She had wondered if Mam and Fred could come as it was a busy time in the hotel, but they had a very capable manager now so there was no problem.

One morning when Jon had just come into the gallery, Shona stopped him.

"Jon," she said. "If you have some spare time my brother would like to see you."

"Oh," said Jon. "I am so sorry. I should have gone to see him before now."

"No," smiled Shona. "It doesn't work like that. He hates anyone dropping in unannounced," she laughed. "He has to ask you. You have seen Ari's portrait of him and he feels more disfigured than he is. He doesn't go out and he has very few visitors."

"Will he come to the opening?" Jon asked.

"I very much doubt it," Shona said sadly.

The following afternoon Jon walked up the lane to Cae Coch, where David was waiting, with his dogs beside him, in the hall.

They shook hands and Jon bent to stroke the dogs.

"Otho and Nerva," David said.

"Ah," said Jon. "Roman emperors, good choice. Better than Nero and Caligula anyway."

David laughed; he was going to like this Jon Curtis. They went into David's room and like Ari, Jon immediately noticed the paintings. He was going to ask about them but David said, "Would you like a whisky Jon? I feel you may need it when you hear what I have to say."

"Don't look so worried," he continued. "It has nothing really to do with the exhibition, but I have a tricky situation to resolve and I need your advice."

Jon was intrigued.

"Would you mind if I just told you and then you can ask questions later?"

"Last year Tally and I were discussing trying to be a bit more eclectic in our exhibitions. The trouble with Wales is that it likes its own if you see what I mean. Anyway, I saw an article in either the Times or the Telegraph on your London exhibition and sent Tally down to have a look. Hence the letter we sent to you. You with me so far Jon?"

Jon nodded though he was faintly bemused.

"Thing is, until recently I had no idea that you were Ari's Jon. We have got quite close and she has told me a lot of what happened but she always referred to you as 'Jon' or 'my Jon', which I thought rather lovely, but never Jon Curtis."

Jon took a sip of whisky; he felt he was going to need it.

"So," David continued. "You know that you are not here due to any connection with Arianwen?" A little white lie was acceptable he thought.

Jon nodded.

"Right," said David and he reached behind him into a bureau and took out a manilla envelope which he passed to Jon.

"Have a look inside," he said.

Jon pulled out a large, faded photograph of a beautiful dark haired girl.

He looked inquiringly at David.

"Lillian Morgan," David said. "Arianwen's mother."

David hesitated, and Jon felt he knew what was coming.

"I am her father," David said simply. "And although I have known her for over three years now, I have never been able to bring myself to tell her."

"She would love to know, sir," said Jon. Then he told David what Ari had said when James had asked her 'money or family'. "She said she wanted to know her father and to have a family of her own with children that looked like her or their father. She has that with me and Gwenny. You could give her the other, sir. Just tell her. You know how generous and forgiving she is. I can't do that for you, it wouldn't be fair on Ari. If I even mention it, she will be on the alert."

"I nearly told her when she was painting my portrait, but just chickened out at the last minute," David said. "And I wouldn't ask you Jon, I know it must be me." He stopped and thought for a while. Jon sipped his drink again. He felt quite shaken.

"I expect Arianwen has mentioned her solicitor Roger Fearnley... now married to her Nan? Gets complicated, doesn't it? Olive is unaware of the connection also. Well, Roger has been a good friend to me all these years, and he has looked after Ari's welfare when I was unable to do so. It was he who got her up here when she was ill, unbeknown to me. I did know it was her later, because of her name, and Roger has sent lots of photographs over the years, but I chose to ignore that as I think I was afraid to meet her. Roger thought it was high time things got sorted out. But they didn't. All my fault of course. I am afraid, I suppose, that she will blame me for just sitting back and not being a proper father to her. But how could I be Jon?" he said indicating the wheelchair.

"She won't blame you at all, sir. I know her well enough to be certain of that. Just find a good time and tell her. That is all I can say."

Jon thought for a moment.

"You know," he said. "I spent months and months trying to ignore my feelings for Ari, just because I was her tutor and thought them inappropriate. But it had to be faced in the end and it was Ari who initiated it, though not purposely. I wasted a lot of time when we could have been together... I think what I am saying is it is best done sooner rather than later."

"Yes Jon," David mused. "I think you are right. On her own or with people around do you think?"

"I would say on her own. Give her time to get used to it?"

David changed the subject then and told Jon about the first time he had seen Ari. "She had been living near for months and was here often with Shona but I had never left my room. One day when Gwenny was about six weeks I think, Shona met Ari in the lane. They managed to get the pram into the house but not upstairs to Shona's rooms, so it was left in the hall with a sleeping Gwenny. I could hear this snuffling noise so went out to see and looked into the pram. I swear Gwenny smiled at me. Anyway, Arianwen came down the stairs then and my heart turned over, I thought it was Lillian. But Ari just plucked Gwenny out of the pram and plonked her in my arms. 'Can you just hold her while I warm her bottle?' she said and she was gone. No 'do you mind, can you manage, is it all right?' She never mentioned my face and gave me a hug when she left. They have visited often since and I love them both. I have told my sister about Ari but she won't say a word until I do."

But David had to wait a while to speak to Ari as she was very busy with the exhibition, the party, Gwenny and sorting out the barn.

Huw had helped her move all her things to the ground floor studio. And Ari was very pleased with the space and the light. Also, she knew that going up and down the stairs all day would soon be beyond her. Jon was amazed at the transformation Huw and his men had achieved. There was ample room for his big canvases and the light was fantastic. He went out one day to thank Huw who was there to do a few final touches to the hallway.

"I did it for your Missis," said Huw simply. "She's a real smasher."

Jon smiled to himself. *Another of Arianwen's conquests,* he thought.

The day of the private view arrived. It was a hot day and the evening promised to be warm. Poll and Julius arrived just after lunch. They would be staying with Jon and Ari as they knew no one else. Fred and Sal, Olive and Roger were invited to Cae Coch, with Shona under strict instructions not to mention the link between David and Roger.

Marco and Philippe were staying with Lem and Grace, and apparently, the Castle hotel in town was fully booked. Jen and Eric had also made the journey and they were in a B&B in the village. Their boys Ben and Will were in Ari's house with Skye, baby Saffron and Gwenny. Val, from the hotel, as 'babysitter'.

Jon dressed with care and looked fantastic in his dark grey suit and blue tie, his dark hair a little longer now. Ari had a new dress, deep dark-red linen and slightly less fitted than usual, and with a very low back. Her hair was up in a big knot on top of her head and fixed with new, more elaborate silver pins. They stood and looked at each for a moment then Jon took her in his arms. "I love you so much Mrs Curtis," he said.

Ari smiled into his eyes. "And I will love you Mr Curtis, sir, forever," she said.

The private view was a triumph. Jon welcomed everyone and it was packed. Shona was relieved she had ordered twice the amount of champagne and canapés than usual. Within minutes there were red stickers on many of the paintings, both Ari's and Jon's. But Ari and most other people there were rendered speechless by the beauty of Jon's very large painting. It had been positioned so that when you came up the stairs it was the first thing you saw although it was two rooms away.

The whole canvas was a surge of pink, red, lemon, lavender, purple, orange, blue and grey paint. At the bottom, a very thin black streak with just the suggestion of a rooftop and a church spire. And above that in the left-hand corner, one small thin line of pure bright white. Great boiling clouds underlit by a rising sun. It was called 'Passing Clouds' and underneath 'for Arianwen and Gwenllian'. Later Jon told Ari he had seen that sunrise when going down to Dorset to finalise the sale of his parents' house. It was February 1965, just when Gwenny was born, not that he knew that then.

Jon was looking for Ari as he hadn't seen her in a while. She was standing, completely absorbed in his painting. He slipped a finger onto her back. She jumped, "Oh it's you," she said.

"Were you expecting someone else then?" he laughed.

"No, only ever you," she said and kissed his nose.

He slipped another finger along her back.

"Jon! Stop it," Ari smiled. "Not here."

Jon had a bleak moment of déjà vu. Slipping his finger under the strap of her silver dress that awful night. But Ari didn't notice she was still looking at his painting.

"You know," she said. "If you stand quite still you can imagine those clouds moving. It is quite majestic. You are so clever."

They stood for a while neither wanting to move. Ari put her head on his shoulder.

"Jon," she said. "You know it says to Ari and Gwenny by your painting?" She paused. "You could add plus one?" She looked at Jon and her eyes were luminous.

It took him just a moment to understand what she meant.

"When?" he said.

"That pink dress, in your house," she whispered in his ear. "Due early February."

And right in the middle of the melee he pulled her to him and kissed her.

Sal was overcome when she saw 'Out'. It was very expensive, she thought, but it was so wonderful that she bought it straight away. She had never bought a painting before, or even contemplated buying one, but she would hang it in pride of place in the hallway at 'Arian Court'. She even went with Tally to see the red sticker put beside it. She had never really been interested in Ari's painting; she didn't really understand it. It was something Ari had done as a child, and she hadn't wanted her to go to art school. She had wanted a good career for Ari, like a teacher or a nurse. That Ari had remembered their early visits to the garden and had recorded it so beautifully made her feel very humble. Now seeing all those paintings together, she understood and was very proud. Though she thought 'Abandoned', rather unnecessary. That went to a private buyer as did 'Constancy'. The National Portrait Gallery acquired David's portrait although Ari was reluctant to let it go, but Shona said she could do another. David deserved recognition and it would be hung with the other war artists. Ari agreed with that, but she was possessive with all her work really as they were all so personal. Julius and Poll bought Ari's 'Passing Clouds', and Marco a small pencil drawing of Ari by Jon.

Archie and his wife had come and they bought Jon's painting of the frozen waterfall. It was beautiful; all white, grey, turquoise, blue and black. Two of his other paintings, a large landscape and pebbles on a beach went to private collectors. Jon's 'Passing Clouds' was acquired for the British Art collection. Several reporters asked for interviews from both of them, separately or together. The whole thing had far exceeded any expectations David, Shona, Tally or Jon and Ari could have anticipated. They were exhausted.

That night when everyone was in bed, Jon and Ari lay side by side, Jon stroking Ari's tummy. It was very warm even with all the windows open.

"Jon," Ari said. "Shall we go out?"

"You're not too tired?" Jon said turning to look at her.

"No, come on it will be cooler."

So, they wrapped themselves each in a blanket and crept along the landing. Julius came out of the bathroom just as they got to the top of the stairs.

"Where are you two going?" he laughed as they looked like red Indians.

"Just out for a bit," said Jon. Julius raised his eyebrows and saw Ari's laughing eyes.

He said goodnight and went into his room. Poll was still awake. "What's going on?" she asked.

"Jon and Ari, sneaking down the garden."

"She is really good for him. He used to be so serious. Do you remember me telling you about Ari asking if you could do 'it' outside? I bet that's what it's all about."

Julius got into bed.

"Shall we try that when we get home Poll? I don't think we are too old, do you?"

"Never too old," she smiled. And Julius knew just the right place in their garden. Soft grass, the stars and the sweet pungent smell of privet.

If Julius had stood at the landing window, he would have seen two pale figures under the trees at the bottom of the garden. Ari dropped her blanket and Jon enclosed her in his. For several minutes they stood, breast to breast, stomach on stomach, thigh on thigh and Ari's hands on Jon's back. When he could stand it no longer, he pulled her to the ground.

"I won't hurt you will I, darling girl?" he said.

"No," laughed Ari, kissing him. "But we might have to find some different positions when I get bigger. The one we have now is just lovely."

The day of the party was very hot. Everyone had arrived by late morning and helped put the tables out under the trees. Jon filled a very large old zinc bath with water and soon Gwenny, Skye and Jen's boys were jumping in and out of it.

Endless food seemed to come out of the kitchen, and Shona had brought an enormous pork pie, sausage rolls and a gargantuan green salad. A whole ham, a cold salmon, and two roast chickens. Bread, bowls of olives, tomatoes, and sliced cucumber. A large trifle and mounds of strawberries and jugs of cream were in the fridge for pudding. Jon came out with two large pitchers of Pimm's, complete with borage flowers, also cold white wine and beer. And some squash for the children.

Just before they were to sit down Shona said, "Can we just wait a mo? I've forgotten something at home." And she shot off in her car, the tyres churning up the gravel on the drive. She was back just over fifteen minutes later with David in the front seat. He had asked her the evening before if it was manageable and it had been relatively easy to get him from his chair into the front seat, his wheelchair in the back. When Jon saw what was happening, he went to help. David looked triumphant. It was the first time in he didn't know how many years he had left the grounds of Cae Coch. Instead of his velvet cap, he wore an old Panama. Ari rushed over to him and gave him a big hug, then introduced him to everyone. Jon called everyone to the table and David was seated at the end in the place of honour.

Then Jon just said, "Find yourselves a place everyone and start." Julius ended up next to David and the two men had a very good conversation about the art world, and the injuries they had sustained during the war. Although Julius was the first to concede that his were insignificant compared to David's.

Jen had a very wet Gwenny next to her but she didn't mind and Poll was on the other side, which was lovely. Lem and Eric enjoyed talking about Scotland and Grace had a long talk with Sal. Everyone enjoyed the company of the person next to them and it was a most special meal and very relaxed. There was rest before the pudding was brought out and Shona excused herself from the table and asked Marco to come with her. They appeared a few minutes later, Marco carrying a two-tier white iced wedding cake. Shona with silver plates and little forks. Marco with a wink at Ari set it before her and Jon. From somewhere Marco produced a large knife. "Come on then, Mr and Mrs Curtis," he said. "Cut the cake."

Philippe crept round the table and gave Gwenny a box of dried rose petals. He explained in his broken English what she should do. Gwenny smiled at him, walked around the table and climbed up on Jon's chair. Jon saw her out of the corner of his eye and knew what she was going to do and that she wouldn't be able to reach, so turned quickly and swung her up to sit on his shoulders. Gwenny squealed in surprise but from there could scatter the petals over her mother. She then, to everyone's amusement tipped the rest over her father's head and asked to get down. Jon lifted her down and she gave him a big kiss, which brought tears to Sal's eyes.

There was a lot of cheering and clapping, and then Jon thanked everyone. Sal surprised herself by thinking what a lovely man he was. The rest of the afternoon everyone sat around under the trees, nibbling at this and that, drinking coffee or wine or just dozing. Gwenny and Skye went back in the water and little Saffron crawled about in the grass. Ben and Will found a football and went down to the end of the garden to play.

David sat dozing in his chair under an apple tree near the hedge, in heavy shade, and Ari went over to him.

"David," she said. "Thank you so very much for coming. It has made this day very special." They went on to talk about the exhibition then and how well it had gone. Jon already had two commissions from it. Then Ari said she would have to do a new portrait of David, to go up the stairs. They laughed about Gwenny always trying to get on David's lap when Ari had been doing the first one.

"Perhaps," said David a little hesitantly. "We should have left her in then we could have called it '*Taid*'." He looked at Ari questioningly. He had meant to tell her on her own, but it had just slipped out. She knew what *Taid* meant.

Ari stood up and fainted.

Jon who had been watching, jumped the low wall at the end of the courtyard, followed closely by Marco. He picked Ari up and took her indoors, Marco going in front to clear the way.

"We've been here before, sir," he said. and Jon smiled at the memory. "She's pregnant Marco and just had some welcome news if I'm not mistaken."

In a while Ari was fine and she and Jon went out together and announced to everyone that she had fainted because she was pregnant. Then Ari went over to David. "Hello, my lovely Pa," she smiled kissing his cheek. "You are going to be *Taid* to another soon."

"*Secondus*." David smiled.

Ari laughed. "We could call the baby that until it is born. How lovely."

"Anyway" she continued. "That's why I fainted, not because of what you told me. The heat and being pregnant. That was really wonderful news and thank you. I'll come up soon shall I and you can tell me all about it?"

When she came back all the ladies were waiting for news. "Middle of February, I think," said Ari. "Just like Gwenny."

Most of their visitors went home the next day and there were a few tearful farewells. Sal, Fred, Olive and Roger decided to stay another two days as Olive and Sal wanted to get to know David a little better. Jon popped into the gallery the next day and came upon his friend Richard with his wife Rachel. Tally was there and they got talking about future exhibitions. As well as painting Richard produced very intricate wood cuts. They didn't decide on anything definite but Tally mused on Richard having a joint exhibition the coming year with Lem, and his wonderful wood carvings. It was an idea Tally thought would fit well and he would put it to David.

When Ari went up to see David, he asked Sal and Olive if they might like to come as well. Some of his story Ari knew, like his accident, but he explained it all from the beginning for the benefit of the two ladies. All three completely understood why he could not have had Ari and he was genuinely grateful for the wonderful way Sal and Olive had cared for her. "Her mother didn't want me to have her, and she would have had to have been looked after by a nurse or some such person anyway. She was happy with you," he said.

In Lillian Morgan's eyes he was there just to provide the money and he had done that he hoped, willingly and generously. He smiled at Olive then. It was Roger who had kept him informed all these years of Arianwen's progress and anything they might want. Perhaps Olive should have a talk with her husband now, as he knew Roger hadn't liked keeping secrets from her. Like them he had never heard another word from Lillian Morgan. Olive asked him how long he had been in hospital. "Between my burns and my broken back, on and off for nearly three years," he said. "Arianwen was settled with you by then."

Then Ari asked a question she had been longing to ask for some time. "Where did my name come from, and who named me?"

David smiled at her; he did so love his daughter, and he had been waiting for her to ask.

"There was a Welsh chieftain named Brychan, in the fifth century or perhaps just in legend, who had a daughter called Arianwen. The eldest sons in our family, since the time this house was built, have always had Brychan as a middle name. I have never been able to find out why, though I have researched it constantly. Though it is thought Brychan had numerous children so it is possible we could be related in some way."

He looked at his beautiful daughter.

"I wanted you to have a name that was relevant to us." He smiled, "I absolutely insisted on naming you, and your mother did let me have my way with that. Thankfully."

He didn't tell them that quite soon after Ari's birth, Lillian had come to see him in hospital. He had told her that if he didn't have a small link to the child, perhaps choosing her name, he would not cooperate. She saw the decision as between his money and her desire to call the child 'Daisy'. His money won.

All four sat for a moment in silence when David had finished. Then Olive said, "Life is a bugger sometimes isn't it, but we just have to soldier on." They left then as Gwenny was going to stay with Mam and Fred for a few weeks and they needed to leave soon. It was a long way to Bournemouth.

Sal hung back a moment, "We did our very best for her you know?" she said to David. "Yes," he said. "You both should be proud. She is a lovely young woman and one of the most generous, good-hearted people I have ever met."

Then she asked, "Why did she have to go away to school?"

David looked very sad. "Sit down a minute Sal," he said. "And please never tell my beautiful daughter this." Sal promised she would only tell Olive.

"I think Lillian became pregnant on purpose. She knew I would do the honourable thing and marry her, and I was infatuated with her, Sal. But I disappointed Lillian by having that accident. She had seen a bright, fun and money filled future in front of her with me as her husband. Nothing to do, everything done for her, parties, travel, an easy life.

Roger of course was in contact with her the whole time she was at Ty Gwyn and must have told her of my injuries. When she saw me in hospital after Ari was born, I think she found me repulsive. She decided then to cut her losses and look elsewhere, Ari had served her purpose, and she had no interest in her. If she ever had? Arianwen was a means to an end which didn't materialise. So, she took her disappointment out in spite. Whether she knew Ari was with you and happy I don't know, Roger never ever told her? Did she want to upset you and Olive or just me, I can't fathom, but she said either I paid for Ari to go to school or she would take her to America? She didn't want her; she was just using her again. I couldn't contemplate that, so I did what Lillian asked and sent Ari to the best school I could; to St Ursula's." He stopped for a moment.

"I think we all agree now that the school was good for Ari. It was hard for you and Olive I know and I'm sorry about that. But I still do wonder why Lillian chose school, which would be advantageous for Ari? I suppose just because it would cost me money. I really can't decide why? Roger did wonder if she was just acting the 'caring mother' in front of her husband-to-be. As good an explanation as any other I suppose. Sometimes you just can't work out why people do what they do can you? I do sometimes wonder though where Lillian is now. She must be only in her early forties."

Sal never the most empathetic of people gave him a hug. He was such a kind and generous man.

On the way down the lane, Ari stopped.

"There is something I must say," she said. "Before you both leave." And they sat on the bank amongst the flowers, the Ragged Robin, oxeye daisies and honeysuckle and Ari said, "When I was little, Mair Pryce, the sweet shop lady, and I think a lady called Violet, told me I didn't belong to you." She looked at her Mam and Nan, "And that you could send me back whenever you wanted. They also said my mother hadn't loved me so had just left me. I wished then, with all my heart for a proper family of my own. Then when I was at art school Jon set us a self-portrait exercise to emphasise family characteristics. I found that incredibly difficult, as I concentrated on the physical aspect."

She stopped and looked at them both, so like each other and so different from her.

"But I realised when I was ill that I did have a proper family who loved me and they were hell-bent on protecting me simply because they did. And I did have many of their characteristics. They taught me love, respect, honesty, faithfulness and generosity. Now I have all I ever wanted. A father, a husband, a child and another on the way and the added bonus of Nan and Mam." She looked at Sal and Olive again. "I love you both dearly, and you will always have a special place in my heart. Never ever think that because I have now found my father, you move down the pecking order, so to speak. My heart is big enough for you all. Though," and she smiled. "Jon comes top.

I know I have caused you both a few heartaches along the way and I am truly sorry for that." she added, "Let's hope things go a bit more smoothly now."

Not long after they waved a very excited Gwenny off with Sal and Fred. Olive and Roger walked back to Cae Coch to say goodbye to David and collect their car. Then they were off back to London and a long, sometimes funny conversation about Roger's cloak and dagger career. When they got home Roger gave Olive Jon's drawing of Ari that he had bought at that London exhibition. She was overcome with the beauty of it and put it on the wall beside her bed straight away.

Ari would go down by train in a week or so to Bournemouth and Jon would come to collect them both when the exhibition had finished. They had nearly three weeks to themselves, and it was the first time they had been completely alone since before that awful art school party. Not that Jon reminded Ari of that. He knew she wanted all that put behind them. Ari did fret a bit about Gwenny though, as Gwenny had never been away from her before. But a phone call from Mam and a very happy Gwenny put her mind at rest.

Jon was looking forward to having Ari to himself for a while, but he was surprised at how much he missed Gwenny. She was such a funny little thing and he missed her trotting along the landing in the morning and climbing all over him into bed.

The night shirt hadn't been used for long. One morning he had forgotten about it. Ari was in the bath and he had been standing at the sink, naked, having a shave. Gwenny came in.

"Charlie's got one of those," she said.

Jon looked down at her. "What?"

"A willy," she said.

"And how do you know that?" said Jon, trying not to smile.

"He showed me, in the Wendy house," said Gwenny.

Ari had disappeared under the water, laughing.

"Did he by Jove?" laughed Jon, "And what did you say Gwenny?"

"I said it was a bit small," she said and wandered off back to her bedroom.

"Poor Charlie," Ari said, when she surfaced. "Found wanting and only just four."

Gwenny came back then, completely naked and got in the bath with Ari.

"Can we play mermaids Mammy?" she said and Ari put her head back in the water so her hair fanned out, and Gwenny did the same.

"You can't play Daddy," she said. "You have to have long hair."

Jon went off to get dressed. "Crushed," he laughed. "Me and Charlie." His daughter had inherited her mother's direct answers.

The weather continued to be hot. Jon would still wake at six. Ari had been more tired lately, so he let her sleep in. He would prop himself up on one elbow and just watch her. She was so beautiful. He remembered that cold winter afternoon, when she had offered him a cup of tea, and how marvellous all that had been. Then she would stir and opening her eyes, would smile at him and put her arms around his neck and they would make love.

Some mornings Jon went into the gallery just to see how things were and Ari went up to Cae Coch as she had started on David's portrait. She wanted to finish it before her ankles swelled and she would find it hard to sit or stand for long stretches. Then they would meet back at home for lunch and if it was warm lie out in the garden all afternoon.

Jon was still slightly worried that he would hurt her when they made love, so Ari decided to ask the doctor next time she had a check-up. It hadn't been a problem with Gwenny.

Dr Morton hadn't been very nice to her when she had had Gwenny, calling her Miss Morgan constantly, with an emphasis on the Miss. Now she had to go at the end of the week to see him and to book a home birth with the midwife if it were possible. Ari wanted Jon with her and he, having missed Gwenny's birth, wanted to be around for the next.

The doctor, Ari reported later was 'snotty'. Ari asked him about lovemaking. He was astonished. "Mrs Curtis," he said. "You must ask your husband to restrain himself." She reported back to Jon. "And when I said what about me wanting to, he had no answer. Just tut tutted."

She laughed. "Can you manage a bit of restraint then Jon?"

"Anyway" she continued. "I then saw the midwife and asked her. She said right up to the last minute, not literally of course, is all right, but don't squash baby. On the kitchen table is a good one she said. Keeps the bump out of the way." Ari could see by Jon's face how this was going. "I suppose you want to practice that, do you?" she said, and was rewarded with a big smile. So later on, they did and Jon had never laughed so much in all his life.

The next evening Ari was out at the cinema with Shona. The phone rang and it was Julius just to see how they were and to thank them again for the lovely weekend. Jon told him that Gwenny had gone for a holiday with Sal and Fred, they were missing her, but otherwise they were fine.

"You and Ari enjoying having a bit of time together then?" Julius asked.

"Yup," laughed Jon remembering the previous evening.

Julius ever inquisitive wanted to know what Jon was laughing at.

Jon hesitated. He didn't really want to tell Julius any details of his and Ari's sex life, wonderful though it was. On the other hand, it had been so funny, Julius would appreciate it.

"Julius," he said. "I will tell you if you absolutely promise to only tell Poll, and I will leave some of the more intimate details out, OK?"

"Fine by me," said Julius.

"Right then. Yesterday Ari went to the doctor. She had to go to have a check-up and to book a home delivery for the baby. Anyway, the doctor is not Ari's favourite person. I think he gave her a hard time with Gwenny because she was unmarried. The first thing he asked her this time was whether this coming child had the same father as her first. Ari was not amused. He judged her fine to have a home delivery and then asked if she had any questions, so she asked about sex during pregnancy. In Ari's words, he sucked in his mouth like a chicken's arse and said, 'your husband will have to practice restraint.' So, then she asked, 'what about if I want to?' The doctor she said, looked at her in amazement and just tut tutted. She saw the midwife next, so she asked her. She said it was fine, right up until the end really, but to try not to squash baby. Like Ari said they never say the baby, just baby. And she told her that the best position during the later stages was lying on the kitchen table. Keeps the bump out of the way."

Julius interrupted, "I can see where this is going," he said.

"Bet you can't," Jon said. "So, we thought we ought to practice that one. I got a quilt and spread it on the table and Ari said, 'I won't be a moment' and went upstairs. Just as I was getting a little impatient, she reappeared. She had tied an enormous cushion around her waist and had a long nightshirt over the top. "I thought we may as well make it as authentic as possible," she said and she was laughing already. Getting her on the table was a feat in itself as she couldn't bend in the middle and the quilt kept slipping. We had to stop as we were laughing so much. At one point Ari nearly slid off the back of the table and I just managed to grab her ankles. That eventually accomplished she lay there like a beached whale still shaking with laughter. 'Come on then,' she said so I did. After a bit she says, 'Are you practising restraint down there Mr Curtis?' That started us off again and I said I couldn't see her properly or hold any part of her that I am accustomed to. I leant forward and she shouted, 'For God's sake don't squash baby.' Enough was enough; we discarded the cushion and the shirt. The end…. But every time I think of her saying, 'Are you practising restraint Mr Curtis,' it makes me laugh."

Julius chuckled. "I must tell Poll," he said. "She will love that."

When he told Poll later that evening it made her laugh too.

"Julius," she then said. "When you retire might we think about moving nearer them. They seem to have such fun. We have nothing to keep us here, have we?" It was a very good thought Julius said, and he did miss Jon.

At the end of their third week Ari went down to Bournemouth. Fred met her at the station.

"Just like old times.," he said giving her a hug. Gwenny had been a joy to have, he said and Sal had enjoyed her company and spoiling her and was going to miss her.

Jon and Tally met at the gallery and supervised the removal of all the paintings to their new homes. Then Jon drove down to Bournemouth and had three days there before bringing 'his girls' home. The first thing he did the next day was to take Gwenny to the animal rescue centre where she chose two grey tabby kittens, sisters, which she named Molly and Dolly. They had time now to settle the cats in, as they wouldn't be going anywhere until the baby was born. Also, Gwenny would be starting at the village nursery school in January and they wanted to make this time special for her.

The local newspaper had produced an article on the exhibition, at the time. Now they wanted a more in-depth interview, as did the colour supplement of the *Telegraph*. Both the reporter and photographer for that one were superb. Jon and Ari were very pleased. There was a two-page article on them with a wonderful photograph. Jon with his arm around a pregnant Ari and Gwenny between them, the two kittens in the background.

Jon had two commissions to fulfil. One was for a private collector, and they were not at all prescriptive but the other was for the atrium of a large London bank and they wanted a landscape that suggested 'bounty'. Shortly after Jon had accepted this commission, the Chairman of the bank invited him to his home to discuss ideas and terms. Mr Adrian Brossard lived mostly in London but had a large country house outside Ludlow, and Jon went there. Mrs Brossard and their daughter Therese were there also. The meeting went well and Jon said he was still in the process of deciding how and what he would paint. He had thought about it for a while. Wiltshire with its rolling fields came to mind, but he said he had decided to look again at North Wales for inspiration. During lunch Therese watched him intently. She was an attractive woman, in her late twenties, and made use of beauty salons constantly. Everything about her was seemingly perfect. She had a string of failed relationships behind her and was now staying with her parents to 'recover' from the last. She was very spoilt and used to getting what she wanted. Over lunch she decided she wanted this intelligent, good-looking artist. After lunch they all went for a walk around the grounds. Therese slipped her arm through Jon's and flirted with him all afternoon. He was too much of a gentleman to object but was glad when the time came for him to leave.

When he got home, he told Ari. "Well," she said. "It could never be just me in this world that thinks you are wonderful, could it? I expect you will get a lot of propositions Jon, as you get more well known." Jon was amazed by her answer. It had never occurred to him, and he had not enjoyed that afternoon with Therese.

He decided to go back to Bala. He remembered his journey up to North Wales, the rivers and streams, ancient mossy woods, the moors and the ever-present magnificent mountains. Even the enormous spoil heaps of slate. There was more than enough to answer that brief here. He set off back to those places that had so impressed him.

The day after he left the phone rang in the house. Ari answered it. It was Mr Brossard's secretary, or so she said. He needed to speak to Mr Curtis urgently. Ari said he was away but gave the details of his hotel in Bala.

That evening when Jon returned to the hotel, Therese was waiting for him in the lounge. He had the dickens of a time getting rid of her, and in the end just told her to go away, he was not interested. He moved on the next day and found a small B&B on the road to Ffestiniog. He hoped that would be the last he saw of her, but of course it was not. She was used to getting what she wanted, by hook or by crook.

Jon came back after a week, relieved to be home with Ari and Gwenny, with a full sketchbook, several rolls of film, heaps of ideas and set to work. The phone continued to ring at odd times. If Ari answered there was no one there. If Jon did it was Therese. Jon stopped answering the phone. Then letters came. He put them in the fire.

In the end he painted an enormous canvas, seven foot tall by six foot wide. In front of a landscape of grey and white scudding clouds and the enormous purple and grey, rain-washed slate heaps of Blaenau Ffestiniog, stood an ancient, gnarled, stunted and wind scoured hawthorn tree. Its twisted leafless branches were black against the sky or etched with grey-green lichen, and it was covered with hundreds of dull-red berries, that even so seemed to glow in the slightly eerie light. At the top of the tree and practically hidden, a solitary blackbird was feasting on the berries. As with all Jon's paintings it was semi abstract but the finding of the bird threw everything into focus.

There was to be a grand unveiling at the Bank and invitations were sent out for the reception, just before Christmas. Mostly family, employees, friends of the bank's board and other influential people. Ari didn't get one. When Jon rang up to inquire why, Mr Brossard's secretary was most apologetic. She remembered writing it and couldn't think where it had gone. She promised to send another but that didn't materialise either, or a third.

The day before the reception, Jon and Ari went down to London. Gwenny stayed with Grace. They went by train as it would be more comfortable for Ari as she had insisted on coming, even though she was now quite large. She would stay in the hotel when Jon went to the reception. At least she would be there for him to come back to.

It was 'black tie' and Jon looked splendid when he left. Ari was lying on the bed, her feet up when he came over to kiss her goodbye. He nuzzled into her neck. She smelled so good. "Be brave Jon, be brave." Ari smiled as she kissed him. When he had left, she got up.

The atrium of the bank was all glass and white marble. Two sweeping staircases led up each side and met at a wide first floor landing. It was between these stairs that Jon's painting was positioned. It would be the first thing people would see when entering the bank. At a board meeting the day before, many board members thought that sheaves of corn, rivers of gold or autumn leaves would most likely feature in Jon's painting. They were very wrong.

The reception went well. Adrian Brossard made a speech and introduced Jon and with some ceremony his painting was unveiled. Therese had attached herself to Jon again. The Chairman and many other board members were speechless when they saw the painting. There was a minute or so of absolute silence, then someone started to clap and everyone joined in. After a few minutes, Adrian Brossard signalled for them to stop. "My wife has just said to me," he said, smiling at Jon. "That that is the most unexpected and downright beautiful painting she has seen in a very long while. It has captured her heart."

There was more clapping and shouts of, "Hear, hear."

Adrian continued, "And I think we all agree with her. Thank you, Jon, for all the exceptional work you have done. We are very gratified to have such a magnificent painting on our wall. We are more than pleased."

Ari had no trouble getting into the reception. She told the concierge she had lost her invitation but was the wife of the artist. He took her shawl and opened the door for her and she immediately saw Jon's remarkable painting on the wall. She was so very proud of him.

There were a lot of people in the room and she couldn't see Jon, so she stood quietly scanning the crowd. An old man got up from a table nearby and came across to her. He introduced himself as Pierre Brossard, head of the family that owned the bank and Ari said who she was and that she was looking for Jon. "Ah yes," he said. "I saw him earlier. I must say his painting is quite spectacular."

"I am a bit wary of plunging into the crowd," Ari said. "I might bowl someone over, being the size I am."

Pierre laughed. "Take my arm, dear lady." He smiled, "We will find him together." And they set off slowly around the room. Many people stopped their conversations to watch Pierre Brossard stroll along with such a beautiful and very pregnant woman on his arm.

A group of men were standing near the side door, discussing stocks and shares. One of them stopped and nudged his neighbour. "Good grief chaps," he said. "Just look at that. Isn't she magnificent." As Pierre and Ari walked by.

One of the others sighed and said, "The Goddess of fertility. Wouldn't you have liked to have been the one who did that to her." Getting a nod from all his companions. Across the room an old man adjusted his monocle and gazed at the young woman longingly.

Champagne was brought around and Therese drank another. She asked Jon if he would like to come to her flat later. He didn't reply.

Everyone was milling around; drinks and canapes being distributed by black-clad waitresses. People were coming up to Jon to congratulate him and a few asked for his business card, which luckily, he had brought with him. Now Jon was talking to the Bank's Head of Design, about typefaces. Therese in close attendance, although she had no idea, or interest, in what they were talking about. She had spent a fortune the day before at the beauty salon. There was not a hair on her body apart from her eyebrows, false eyelashes and her elaborately styled hair. Her dress was new, bright-red and cut with a large slit up her thigh, and she had new red lace underwear. In a minute she would ask Jon again about staying with her tonight. She took another glass of champagne from a passing waitress. There was a strange murmur in the room, conversation had practically stopped. The man he was talking to was not concentrating on their conversation but was looking over Jon's shoulder. Jon looked round to see what the cause was and saw Ari walking towards him on the arm of a distinguished old gentleman who he remembered was Adrian Brossard's father. Ari grinned at him and raised her eyebrows. Her darkbrown hair was twisted and coiled on the top of her head and bound around with dark-green ribbon. It looked very Grecian. She wore a darkgreen chiffon dress, the back and front cut low so that the light caught her smooth creamy shoulders and the tops of her now full breasts. The pleated skirt fell softly and neatly to the floor over her large pregnant stomach. She was very, very beautiful.

Therese drinking yet another glass of champagne said, in a loud, slightly slurred voice, "Who, the fuck, is that?"

Jon detached Therese's hand from his arm.

He laughed. "That," he said. "Is Arianwen. My wife." And he walked across the marble floor of the atrium to her. She just smiled at him and then kissed him and introduced him to her escort. Jon put his arm around her and they walked back to Mr and Mrs Brossard. "My wife, Arianwen," Jon said proudly. Therese had disappeared. Adrian wanted to know why Ari hadn't come sooner, she had missed the unveiling.

"I had to gatecrash," Ari confessed. "Even though Jon asked several times, I didn't get an invitation."

"I wonder why?" Mrs Brossard said.

Ari was not going to hold back. "I would ask your daughter about that," she said.

All the way back to the hotel in the taxi Jon kept kissing her. "You are the most beautiful, wonderful and devious wife anyone could ever want," he laughed. "Thank you, my darling girl. You are the light of my life."

"Well, my lovely man," she said. "I had all that with Tom, didn't I? Never taking no for an answer. Those sorts of people never give up, the more you say no, the more they try. They have to be shown, and I could see it was troubling you. You jumped every time the phone rang and when that car was parked up the lane you thought it was her, didn't you? So, I put on my glad rags and prepared to fight your corner. But she just disappeared when she saw me. I wonder why?" Jon could have told her and most of the men, and the women in that room.

Back at home, in the evening when Gwenny was asleep, Jon would stroke Ari's tummy and perhaps rub some of Belinda's cream into her skin and wonder at the movement of the baby within her. When they had been in Boscombe, Jon had asked Sal if she might come up for the birth. Sal was really pleased he had asked her and agreed at once. She would come at the end of January.

They had a very quiet Christmas, but Lem and Grace invited them for Boxing Day tea and also included David, Shona and Tally. David was much less likely to refuse an invitation now. He had really enjoyed meeting all those people at Jon and Ari's, and he looked forward to seeing some of them again. Ari had finished David's portrait and there was nothing for her to do now, just sit and wait.

The day after Boxing Day, David rang and asked if Ari and Jon could come up to the house. After lunch they walked up, Jon carrying Gwenny on his shoulders. They were surprised to that see Roger, Olive and Shona were there. They went into David's rooms and sat down. It all appeared very formal Ari thought and looked at Jon questioningly. But he had no idea why they were there either.

Roger, in his role as David's solicitor, stood up. He was extremely please, he said, to be able to tell Arianwen about the trust fund that her father had set up for her when she was born, and which had matured on Christmas Day.

Ari was beyond words and it took her sometime to assimilate it all. Stocks, shares, property! She just hugged her most generous father and then burst into tears. Jon thought it was all too much for her and said he would go and get the car and take her home. But Roger volunteered and, on the way, explained there was no rush to sort out anything. He would be there with help and advice when needed. They could leave it all until Secondus was born.

Jon took Ari indoors and settled her on the sofa. He put a blanket over her and in a while she slept. She was overwrought he thought. What with all that stuff with Therese, the going to London and her gate crashing the reception and she was getting tired with only five weeks to go before the baby was due. Olive had said Ari was a completely different shape from her round, compact Gwenny bump, and so it might be a boy. Jon was rather sceptical about that. She was quite round and large now and found it difficult to get comfortable and to sleep. But she was still her lovely self and Jon thought her beautiful when she stood naked in the bedroom and he rubbed her cream onto her tummy.

Jon made the supper and then gave Gwenny a bath. When Ari woke, they were sitting opposite her and Jon was reading Gwenny a story. *Snow White and Rose Red*. Ari smiled, she had loved that as a child. They had supper then and when Gwenny went to bed, Jon and Ari did too. They spent a long time talking about David and all he had done for his precious daughter.

Ari now felt it was about time to check through the things for the baby. There was a large cupboard downstairs in the barn where she had stored most things, so one morning when Gwenny was at nursery, she and Jon went out to see what was there. The dark green pram and the two cots were at the front. Jon asked why two and Ari explained about a cot in her studio for Gwenny. "I didn't paint or draw for some time," she said. "But I had started again when I had Gwenny, so I brought her over here with me. Otherwise, I would have been going back and forth constantly to check on her." Jon realised there were things he had never even thought of about Ari being on her own. He took the cots and the pram out so that he could check them over. Then there was a large suitcase and a big cardboard box. The box contained mainly Gwenny's old toys but the suitcase was a treasure trove. Ari remembered everything, but Jon of course had never seen the beautiful cobwebby baby shawls, knitted by Olive. The little cardigans, hats and bootees, the pram blankets. All wrapped in tissue paper and all knitted with love. Olive had hardly ever put her needles down when she had stayed with Ari. He couldn't get over how small they all were and said so.

"Well, Gwenny was an average weight and size," she said. "Just over seven pounds. But there was a girl in hospital with me, another unmarried mother, who had a premature baby. She took me down to the nursery one day to see him. I think he could have sat in the palm of your hand, and he was all tubes and bandages. I saw her one day in Llandudno, when Gwenny was about one, and he was sitting up in his pram laughing at everyone. It was so lovely." She smiled at the memory.

Jon had not had much to do with babies. His sister had two boys, the eldest born in 1960 but they had lived in Ireland then and Jon hadn't seen much of them. He was sad that he had not held a tiny Gwenny but looked forward to holding his next child.

Then right at the bottom of the suitcase was a slim box, wrapped in an old cot sheet. Ari was sitting on the stairs, having a rest when Jon took it out. "What's this?" he said. She snatched it from him and held it close. She looked so distressed that for a moment Jon didn't know what to do.

He sat down beside her and put his arms around her. "Ari," he said. "Ari?" She gave him the box and inside, beneath layers of tissue paper was his navy jumper. It was folded neatly and a few stalks of dried lavender placed on top. It was very grubby and there was a large streak of blue paint on one sleeve. "Oh! Ari, sweetheart," he said.

"It was all I had of you Jon; until Gwenny came along," she said. "Mam called it that nasty, smelly jumper and was always threatening to wash it. I knew if she did you would be gone. So, I wrapped it up and hid it. I thought it was upstairs in the spare room. I'd forgotten I'd moved it here."

She smoothed her hand over the wool, back and forth. She was silent and Jon could see she was reliving all those awful days. "You know," she said. "That was the only time I can remember Mam ever getting really cross and shouting at me. It must have been early on and I was wandering yet again in a nightie and your jumper." Ari paused and thought for a moment. "'Take that bloody thing off,' she said. 'It won't bring him back, he's gone.' I was so upset. Then when she saw I wasn't going to put it away, she said she would wash it. That's why I hid it." After a moment she carried on, "I know now she was just very worried about me."

He put his arms around her and pulled her close. "I must stop getting upset," Ari said stroking her tummy. "Secondus here is getting agitated." Jon put his hand on the bump. The baby was indeed moving a lot. He kissed his lovely wife.

He took the jumper from her. "We could try to clean it Ari," he said gently. "Then I could wear it again?" She gave him a sad, watery smile. "Could we, do you think?" she said. "I would like that." Jon took it up to his studio. It took him quite a while but he got nearly all the paint off with turps. Then Ari washed it in the sink and they hung it on the airer over the Aga. When it was dry, he put it on. Ari had tears in her eyes but she was smiling. She had always loved him in that jumper.

On the morning of Saturday the 18th of January Ari woke up feeling distinctly not herself. The baby was not due for at least three weeks yet and she had no pain, so she passed it off as just one of those days. After breakfast Jon went across to the barn to finish the last few bits on his painting for the private collector. Gwenny was drawing at the kitchen table and Ari was putting some dishes away. *Children's Favourites* was playing quietly on the radio. *Sparky's Magic Piano*, which Ari never did like. Suddenly Ari's waters broke and gushed all over the kitchen floor, and she had a contraction.

"Gwenny," she said. "Could you go and tell Daddy that Mammy needs him?"

Gwenny looked at the water on the floor and trotted obediently over to the barn.

"Daddy," she called. "Mammy has done a wee all over the floor and she's got a tummy ache. Can you come?"

Jon was there instantly. He phoned Lem in the hopes they could have Gwenny. Lem said he'd be there in a few minutes. Jon dashed upstairs and got a small overnight bag for Gwenny to take, just in case. He sat Ari on a kitchen chair whilst he phoned the midwife. She said no worries, she would be there within the hour. Then Jon explained to Gwenny that she would be going to Grace's house just for a little while. When she came back, she would have a new baby sister or brother. Gwenny was entirely unfazed by that. If Grace was in her pottery studio, she might let her and Skye play with the clay. Lem was as good as his word and came for Gwenny very soon after, then Jon cleaned up the kitchen floor. Ari was by now roaming restlessly around the house. Jon stripped their bed and put the rubber sheet over the mattress and an old linen sheet on top. He found the box the midwife had left for the birth and took out a set of baby clothes from the drawers. As far as he could tell everything was ready.

Ari was now having strong contractions. He had never seen her in pain before and found it most upsetting. However, she just stopped and panted whenever a new wave hit her. The midwife arrived and congratulated Jon on his organisation, then took Ari upstairs to the bedroom so she could examine her. "I've left her up there to rest," she said to Jon. "Shall we have a cup of tea now whilst we wait? Your wife had no problems last time and the second one is usually easier and quicker, so no worries. Baby is fine." Jon smiled at that.

Ari didn't want tea. She just wanted Jon beside her. The midwife said, "Call me Emma," and had helped her undress and now she was sitting up in bed in a cotton nightie, her hair tied back off her face. As the contractions grew more painful and insistent, she held tightly to Jon's hand.

After about two hours Ari said, "I need to push now." But Emma said not yet. In a little while she examined Ari again then turned to Jon.

"Right then," she smiled. "Let's see what this baby is shall we? Off you go Mrs Curtis. Push as hard as you can at the next contraction but stop if I say so."

And Ari pushed and swore about, "That fucking pink dress," and Jon smiled.

Her hair was stuck to her head with sweat and she had discarded the nightie when Emma said, "No pushing now just pant... Mr Curtis, come down this end." and Jon saw the top of the baby's head emerge. A head covered in very dark hair, and then the rest of a perfect little boy. Emma cut the cord and wrapped the baby in a blanket and gave him to Ari. Jon came back and sat beside her. "Ifan," she said. "Welsh for Jon and for your dad as well?" Jon was so proud of her and leant over to kiss her "Don't squash baby," she laughed and Jon kissed her hard.

"Mr Curtis," said Emma. "Could you put your wife down for a minute and take Baby, I need to see to her?"

With which Ari said, "I need to push again." And another little boy slid into the world.

"My God," Emma squeaked. "I didn't see that coming, where was he hiding? Twins and identical too. And just like their father."

"Osian?" said Ari and Jon just nodded. He was rather overwhelmed by it all.

Emma wrote I on the bottom of Ifan's foot and O on Osian's with an indelible pencil and also put a name tape around their ankles. "Just so you don't get them muddled at first," she said. Then she washed them and weighed them, dressed them, wrapped them in shawls like little mummies and having made a sort of nest out of blankets, put them both together in the big cot. "Best keep them together," she said. "Then they will hopefully have the same routine. Now shall we sort you out Mrs Curtis?" But Jon said he would do it. He got a bowl of warm water and Ari's favourite soap and washed her gently all over. Then he brushed her hair and tied it back with a ribbon. That done he wrapped her in a blanket and lifted her out of bed onto a chair. He stripped the bed and remade it with soft linen sheets and lifted Ari back in. "There, darling girl," he said. "Sleep now. I won't be far away."

Emma went then promising to call in the evening. She was going to look at Mrs Curtis' notes too. There was nothing about two babies in them, of that, she was sure.

Downstairs Jon sat on the sofa and couldn't think what to do next. His stomach rumbled and he realised he had missed lunch though it was only just three o'clock. He made himself a sandwich and a cup of coffee then rang Grace and Lem. Grace answered the phone.

"Can we have Gwenny back?" he said. "She needs to meet her brothers."

There was a short silence, and then Grace said, "Did you say brothers Jon?"

"Yes Grace, identical twins."

"Well blow me," laughed Grace. "Can we bring Gwenny after tea. I promised them fish fingers and she is looking forward to that."

"Whenever suits," said Jon. "And thank you Grace."

It was dark when Grace brought Gwenny home. Ari was awake and sitting up and Jon had put the bedside lights on so the room looked warm and cosy. Grace came upstairs but stayed by the bedroom door as Gwenny tiptoed in and went directly to Ari.

"Hello cariad," she said, giving Gwenny a hug. "Did you have a nice time with Skye?"

"Yes, Mammy and I said thank you."

"Good girl," said Ari, giving her a kiss. "And when you were away something special happened here. Can you think what it might be?"

"Did the baby get born?"

"Go and look in the cot Gwenny." And she did. There was a squeak and Gwenny said "Two? Where did you get the other one from, and what sort are they?"

Jon laughed. "Two little boys Gwenny. One was hiding in Mummy's tummy. Ifan and Osian, and you will be their big sister, and help us look after them?"

And Gwenny, bless her, said she would and she always did.

That evening when Jon had put Gwenny to bed, when the boys had been fed and changed, Ari came downstairs. She was slightly wobbly but fine. Jon, drying the dishes was alarmed when he saw her.

"Don't worry my lovely man," she said coming to kiss him. "I'm fine. Not ill or anything. It's nice to walk around. Now I am going to phone David and Shona then Mam, Nan and Marco, and I think you should phone Jen and Julius...and James if you can find him."

Everyone was incredulous that there were two babies. Sal said she would be up the next day to give a hand for a few weeks. That is if they still wanted her to. Well of course they did. Julius whooped with delight. He and Poll were so pleased that everything had worked out so well for Ari and Jon. He asked who the boys looked like and was rewarded with, "Me, so Ari says."

Within a few weeks and with help from Sal they had all settled into a good routine. Jon took Gwenny to nursery in the morning and Ari picked her up at lunchtime. In the afternoon Jon went back to the studio and Ari put Ifan and Osian in their new twin pram, and with Gwenny holding onto the handle they would visit David and Shona if she was there or Lem, Grace and the children, or go to the park. Ari missed her own studio, but she had lots of ideas in her head for when things got easier. Gwenny was marvellous with the boys. They would quieten when she spoke to them and she could often be found hanging over the edge of their cots singing. One day Jon heard her singing *Suo Gân* to them, not the right words he was sure, but a good try for a four-year-old, and his heart turned over with love for his little girl. When the boys got older and more mobile, they would always go off in different directions. This made Jon laugh, he felt like a sheepdog, he said, gathering them up. But if Gwenny was there the boys followed her. The three children were so like Jon that Julius said it was unnerving.

By the summer, when the babies were seven months old, they were sufficiently confident to fly to France, where they hired a car and went to the summer house. Jen was there with her boys and Eric, and they all had the most lovely few weeks. One warm evening, when the children were asleep, Jon and Ari wandered down the garden. It was as beautiful as he had described to Ari several years before. Bats flitted across the darkening sky and there was a heady smell of lavender and ripe peaches in the air. They lay down amongst the long grass and flowers. Jon took Ari in his arms.

"Here we are my darling girl," he said. "At last." He stopped and kissed her, slowly and gently. "I have wanted you here for such a long time," he said. "I love you and always will. Now I am going to make love to you and I will have you know that Mr Curtis will not be exercising any restraint at all."

Ari giggled. "Right my lovely man, I'm all yours," she said and assumed her starfish position.

When they got back Jon insisted they had some help with the children, the boys especially. He was wonderful with them and he and Ari shared most everything, but he could see she missed her time in the studio. They employed a young mother whose children went to the village school. Her name was Carys and her husband, one of Huw's builders. She came every weekday and often got a lift from one of the Curtis' who had taken Gwenny to nursery. Mostly she looked after the babies, did a bit of ironing or hoovering when they were asleep and made lunch for everyone. Someone would have collected Gwenny from nursery and they all had lunch together. Then Carys tidied the kitchen, prepared the vegetables for dinner, played with Gwenny and sorted out the boys. She left at two-thirty to walk to the school for her own children. It was all very relaxed and flexible. She was sure though; she told her husband, that sometimes after lunch Mr Curtis would take his wife up to his studio and shut the door. She had seen her come down about a half hour or so later, plaiting her hair or doing up the buttons of her blouse. But she was not a gossip and really liked both Ari and Jon. She was to stay with them for many years.

It wasn't long before Jon and Ari realised that the house was not going to be big enough. Ifan and Osian were now in their own bedroom, so there was no spare room for visitors. With the money Jon had from the sale of his house and his share of his parents' house, they had Huw build a large two storey extension on the side of the house away from the barn. Three more bedrooms and a bathroom upstairs, and a large bedroom with an en suite bathroom downstairs, which was to be their room. This was behind their living room and had French doors to the garden. Plus, a playroom for the children. Huw laughingly said he considered himself their own private builder.

Ari had not heard from Christina for some time. Letters between the two had been regular, but she had had no reply from her letter telling of Ifan and Osian's birth or in fact a previous one about the wedding. She had phoned Belinda, but she also was worried, having heard nothing from her daughter for months. The last time anyone had heard from Christina was when she was in Manitoba in early 1968, nearly two years ago. Belinda and her husband had started searches for Christina but so far nothing had materialised. They knew only that Christina's ex-husband, who had never accepted the divorce, had flown to Canada in December 1967. Ari was very worried for her friend.

Just before Christmas, when Ari was in the kitchen making mince pies with Gwenny, they heard a car come down the drive. Ari looked out of the window but didn't recognise it. They heard the gate open and a knock on the kitchen door. Gwenny opened it. "Hello," said a voice Ari recognised immediately. "Does Arianwen still live here?"

It was Christina. Ari practically dragged her indoors and gave her a hug. "Oh! Christina, where have you been?" she said.

Over a cup of tea Christina told her. She had had endless trouble from her ex-husband. She had fled from Canada into America and from there to Australia. Everywhere she went, she said, he would turn up and make trouble for her. At work, with her landlord or with friends. When she moved on, she left no forwarding address but he still managed to find her. She had therefore received no letters from either her family or Ari, and she had been afraid to send any in case he somehow intercepted them. In Australia she had sought help from the police but coincidentally he had been jailed for a while for a fraud he had committed. This had given her time to get away and she had come to Wales via Japan, India, Greece, and Denmark. She hadn't gone to her mother, just in case. Could Ari put her up for a while? No question, Ari said yes immediately. Christina was frightened, and exhausted. Gwenny was sent to fetch Jon and he knew exactly who it was as soon as he saw her. Ari told him what had happened, and he, of course agreed with Ari. Christina would be very welcome to stay. They had a very happy evening catching up. Christina had never met Jon and knew nothing of their wedding or the twins. She knew about Gwenny of course and had thought Ari might be pregnant when she had left her in 1964 but wasn't sure.

Thank God for the extra rooms, thought Jon. But it wasn't long before Evan heard that Christina was back and he came to see her. She moved in with him within a few weeks. It was the talking point of the village for some time, but Christina didn't care, and neither did Evan. She was safe, happy and loved.

In January 1970 Gwenny started full-time school and things settled down a bit. Jon had several more commissions and Ari had been contacted by a well-known pop artist to paint his portrait. He lived about an hour and a half's drive away, so it was doable. She visited him several times and he came to her twice under heavy secrecy. Jon laughed. "Roger would like all that," he said.

They went to France again in the summer and it was just as special as it had been the year before. There was evidence that the house had been lived in over the winter and both Jen and Jon suspected their brother James. A little judicious inquiry in the village and they knew he spent most of the year there, moving out only for the summer months. When they all returned home, Jon left him a letter. He and Jen had no problem with James living at the house. Indeed, it was probably a good idea in terms of security and upkeep. But next year they would like him to be there when they came as they hadn't seen him for such a long time. Since their mother's funeral, they thought. Jon also left a photo of Ari with the children and their address and telephone number. He was not optimistic about hearing from his brother but he was very pleased when they had a Christmas card from him.

At the end of September Ari realised she was pregnant again. She had popped into the surgery and now had it confirmed. When she got home Carys was hanging out some washing, the boys playing on the lawn. Ari hadn't been able to give her a lift so just went down the garden to say hello, then she went up to Jon's studio. He was working on another enormous canvas. This time frost laden trees by a semi-frozen lake. Ari stood next to him and he put his arm around her. "That is so very beautiful," she said.

He smiled, "I saw that the day we got together. I had been walking around that bloody lake for hours trying to decide what to do about you."

"You were blue with cold when I saw you. We were both so muddled then, weren't we?" said Ari. "I remember Mr Cooper kept telling me I ought to apply to the RCA, but I just couldn't focus on it. All I could see was you and the end of the year looming when I would have to leave." She stopped and Jon pulled her closer. "I was sort of despairing really. I must have looked awful because Mrs Winter took me out for tea and just kept on asking me what the matter was. She just kept on and on. I very nearly told her who but I knew she would tell you and I didn't want to compromise you."

"All in the past now and look where we are Ari? We are so lucky," Jon said and he kissed her.

"I hope you know who you are kissing," she said and he saw that flash of mischief in her eyes that he so loved.

"Go on then," he laughed. "Tell me who you are?"

"The mother of your fourth child?"

Carys, still down the garden with the boys, heard Jon's whoop of delight.

The next day, in the morning, Ari asked Carys to come into her studio. Carys was there like a shot. She just loved seeing what they were painting. The boys were in the courtyard 'painting' with Jon. Ari made them each a cup of coffee. Carys was standing in front of the painting Ari was working on.

She laughed. "That is so like you all," she said. It was a large canvas and on the left-hand side Jon was leaning on the kitchen cupboard, barefoot and his legs crossed. He was wearing an old white shirt with the sleeves rolled up, his navy trousers were paint-spattered, and he was reading a letter. In front of him stood Gwenny staring directly out of the picture. Barefoot also and her hair in two big bunches. Ifan was walking out of the picture near the right-hand side and Osian was aiming for one of the cats in the foreground. Carys said, "You just expect Mr Curtis to raise his head and speak to you."

"He has always stood like that," Ari said smiling at the memory of him leaning on the bookcases at art school. "And Gwenny does sometimes too." She finished her coffee and putting the cup in the sink, turned to Carys.

"How do you feel about looking after another baby?" said Ari. "I'm expecting in May. Ifan and Osian will only be just over two. Could we manage, do you think?"

Carys said of course they could. That evening she told her husband, Tomos "I'm not at all surprised," she said. "She is so lovely he can't leave her alone."

"Huw had a thing for her at one time. She was on her own then though and he asked her out. Evan was there and he told me it didn't go well," Tomos said.

"Why?"

"Well, he took her to the pub and the rugby boys were in. There were a lot of ribald comments about her and Huw. I don't think he ever asked her again, she was so angry."

"I wonder where Mr Curtis was then. She was on her own for a few years, wasn't she?"

"Yes, strange that. I mean Gwenny is obviously his, but he didn't turn up until she was three. Wherever he was he is back now and she seems to have forgiven Huw. Mind you I think she would only have to crook her little finger and he'd be there."

"Poor Huw," Carys said. "I don't think there is much hope of that with those two as they are, do you? They are lovely people though Tomos and I enjoy working for them," she continued. "A bit unconventional I suppose but arty people are like that aren't they?"

One misty morning in the middle of October, Shona came down the drive with the dogs. It was early and Ari had not yet left to walk Gwenny to school. Shona looked very agitated and white-faced. She asked for Jon. She had gone downstairs that morning only to hear the dogs scratching at David's door. Normally he let them out first thing. She had gone into his room and found him collapsed over his desk. She was afraid he was dead.

"Could Jon come back with her?" Ari put the boys in their pram and set off for school with Gwenny, whilst Jon went back with Shona. The dogs started to howl as soon as they got near the house, so Shona shut them in the stables. As far as Jon could tell, David was indeed dead.

There was no pulse. Jon rang the doctor, who, because it was Mr Rhys Williams, was at the house within twenty minutes. He thought David had had a heart attack, as he had come to visit two weeks previously about pains in Mr Rhys Williams's chest. Mr Rhys Williams had however refused to go to the hospital for tests. He had spent far too much of his life in hospital he had said.

The undertakers then came and took David away. Shona looked very shocked, so Jon suggested she come and stay with them at least for the night. Then they took the dogs to the local kennels, as Shona felt she couldn't deal with them at the moment, and then went back home to Ari, who with Carys was waiting for news. As soon as Ari saw Jon and Shona she began to cry. She had had her father for such a short time. She remembered the delight on his face when she had gone up at the beginning of the month to tell him he was to be a grandfather again. He had been so very pleased, and he had told her that her being in his life had given him so much joy. Now he was gone.

Carys sorted out Ifan and Osian then made lunch for them all. Jon said they must phone Roger who might have specific instructions from David, and later that afternoon that is what he did.

Roger was very upset at the news. He had been a friend of David's practically all his life and had done a lot for him. David, as Shona had suspected, had left complete instructions as to his funeral. No flowers but a donation to a war veterans' charity, cremation and the hymns and music he would like. Shona, Ari and Jon with help from Tally set it all in motion. Roger organised the notices that were placed in the local paper and in the *Times and Guardian*.

The morning of David's funeral was a little dreary but brightened later. Shona had returned home after two nights, and Tally had gone to keep her company and help in any way he could. David's rooms were locked but they opened up two of the large reception rooms downstairs for the after funeral gathering, and Shona got in touch with her very reliable caterers again. Carys came to look after Ifan and Osian and had arranged for her two boys to be brought to her after school. Gwenny, although only five had said she wanted to go to the funeral. Both Ari and Jon were a little dubious about this but she was adamant. She had loved David and wanted to say goodbye. All three walked up the lane, to be with Shona, Tally, Roger and Olive when the hearse arrived. They stood on the terrace as it came slowly up the long drive from the main gate, the funeral director walking in front. Behind two big black cars for them. The hearse stopped in front of the house and the back door was opened. Ari saw the coffin and it was practically swamped by an enormous sheaf of white lilies. It was so large it covered the top of the coffin and hung down the sides. The smell was overpowering. Shona gasped and clutched Tally's arm. Ari looked at Jon. "No flowers?" she whispered. Jon went to see and saw a large card that just said, 'R.I.P David. Lillian'. Shona was very upset. "How dare she?" she sobbed. "How bloody dare she?"

Ari asked the funeral director to take it away; it had no place to be there. He put it in the cavity below the coffin and would dispose of it later.

The crematorium chapel was packed, even upstairs. Local people, dignitaries, tenant farmers, shopkeepers, and many friends and acquaintances from the art world and beyond and a few David had known before the war. And because the vicar had known David in the past the service was lovely and pertinent to him. Roger gave a most wonderful eulogy which was quite heartrending in places. David went to his rest to the music of Ralph Vaughan Williams *Fantasia on a Theme by Thomas Tallis*.

Gwenny was as good as gold but held tightly to Ari's hand. At the end, Jon, Ari, Shona and Tally stood with the vicar, at the door, to thank everyone for coming and to invite them to Cae Coch for refreshments. A woman came up to Ari.

"Hello," said Ari. "I'm Arianwen Curtis, David's daughter." And she held out her hand. Jon had noticed the woman at the back of the chapel previously. She was extremely well dressed in unrelieved black and looked as if she had once been beautiful. She reminded him of the photograph David had shown him a few years ago.

She stopped and looked at Ari for a long moment but did not take the proffered hand. "Yes," she said as if to herself, and then turned away into the crowd. They didn't see her again, though they did look as Ari suspected it was her mother.

The next day a new solicitor came to the house to read David's will. When David had told Ari he was her father he had had another solicitor draw up his will. He did not want any complications regarding any bequest he would give his dear, faithful friend Roger. Everyone was asked to come, even Taliesin. Roger of course understood the reason for this.

David had left the gallery in town, to Shona and Taliesin. Half each, as they had run it together for many years. To Arianwen and Shona the house and grounds and all the little cottages, farms and fields that made up the Cae Coch estate, and also several houses and other property scattered around Wales. To his wonderful, faithful friend Roger, his ancient Rolls Royce and a Georgian town house in Bath. To Jon, his portrait of Arianwen, all his sketchbooks and the motorbike he had used during the war. This was well wrapped up and cared for and was with the Rolls Royce in a garage at the back of the stables. Shona said she had forgotten they were there if she ever knew. Jon was just amazed; he had known David for such a short time. The bike was a Brough Superior. "Just like Lawrence's," he said. Jon became well known in the area for going on his sketching expeditions on the bike. He just loved it, as David had suspected he would. They took a few days to assimilate the bequests, for besides all this there was a great deal of money, shares, antiques and paintings to be sorted out between Ari and Shona. And David hadn't forgotten Olive, Sal and Irene Kendall. Olive and Sal received five thousand pounds each and Irene, utterly amazed that she had been remembered, two thousand pounds.

It was Shona who instigated the conversation about what to do next. She walked down to see Ari one morning and came into her studio. "I can't live in that house on my own," she said. "I'll be rattling around like a dried pea. It is so big and a little scary, and I miss David a lot." She stopped for a moment. "But I love the house Ari, and it's our family home. What to do eh?"

She stayed talking to Ari and they went across to the house for lunch. Ifan and Osian were in their highchairs and Carys had just given them bits of cheese, bread sticks, sliced vegetables and fruit. The twins were quietly working through the lot.

Jon came in and Shona told him the problem. They batted ideas back and forth. Then Carys said, "I know it has nothing to do with me but in my family, we have what we call a table talk if we have a big problem.

Anyone and everyone remotely connected or who could be affected by it comes along and we all sit around the table and we discuss it. Everyone's ideas are listened to. It is surprising the ideas some have that you might never have thought of and it works very well." She stopped and looked at Jon "Sorry Mr Curtis," she said. "I shouldn't have been listening." Jon got up and kissed her on the cheek.

"What a bloody good idea," he said. "Thanks, Carys and no more of this Mr and Mrs Curtis stuff. Jon and Ari, please. You will be in this with us." Carys went quite pink.

They organised a big meeting the following week. They invited Grace and Lem, Huw, Evan and Christina, and Carys and her husband Tomos and of course Taliesin. Roger came too. The only thing they were sure of was that Shona might like to move into one of the Arts and Craft houses at the edge of the grounds, which were in very good condition but had been unused for years. They had been discussing hotels and conference centres for a while but knew these were not the sort of things they wanted. Grace, normally very quiet, put her hand up.

"Some years ago," she said hesitantly. "Lem and I drove up to Scotland to see his parents. We stopped halfway, Yorkshire somewhere. The B&B we stayed in had a leaflet for a house nearby, so we went and had a look."

She looked at Lem and he carried on. "It was a large house, though not as large as Cae Coch," he said. "And they had turned it into a sort of gallery, plus workshops in the stables. They ran courses, life drawing and painting classes, and a Saturday club for children. When we were there about a dozen children were picking herbs and flowers in the grounds to make medicinal posies. It was brilliant."

Grace carried on, "We spoke to the owner and he said they had only been up and running just over a year but it was most successful. They had a weaver, a potter and a leather worker in the stables and they ran courses too." She stopped and looked around. There was silence as everyone thought about what she had said.

Then Shona, with a big smile said, "Bless you, Grace. That's sorted then! Huw, we need a word."

Two weeks later Jon and Tally went up to see the house in Yorkshire. The owner was most helpful. Cae Coch was far enough away from him to be no competition. Jon and Tally came back quite enthused.

Huw, bless him, set to work again, although quite honestly, he was grateful for the work and he liked the people.

They had a lot of trouble with David's dogs, Otho and Nerva though. After the funeral, Shona had taken them out of the boarding kennels. But they would not stay with her. They wanted always to be in David's rooms. If the door was open, they would charge around inside howling occasionally and looking for him. If the door was shut, they would lie across the threshold and snarl at anyone who came near, or scratch at the door. When Shona moved into the cottage, she took them with her but they constantly escaped from her garden. They would race across the lawns towards the house, frightening anyone who might be walking near, and once knocked little Ifan to the ground. They took up residence on the grass beneath the windows of David's room and alternately howled and whined. Not even food would entice them away. Shona took to feeding them there, but they did not eat much. Eventually she consulted the vet. He said they were pining for David. Well, she knew that, and most probably things would not improve. As the poor dogs got thinner and thinner, Shona made the sad decision to have them put down. Lem and Jon dug a deep grave for them near the woods, and Gwenny, who had known them all her life often placed flowers on it.

Huw sorted out a cottage for Shona first and she moved in towards the end of November. The second one was fitted out for rental as a holiday home, and immediately let for Christmas. But what to do with the third?

While they were deciding Huw got on with the house. David's rooms were to be cleared and painted white. A few of his possessions were left, his desk, bookshelves and easel, and two large sofas placed in each room. Then all his paintings were rehung and a large sign 'The David Rhys Williams Gallery' was placed over the door from the hall. All the other rooms were also to be cleared and painted. The attics were bulging with unwanted but very good 'stuff'. They allotted two rooms at the top of the house for life drawing. Rooms for watercolour or oil painting classes. Downstairs a large general-purpose room that they hoped to use for a

Saturday children's club and all other central rooms in the house would be gallery space. Plus, a little room for a shop. Tally had an excellent idea of encouraging artists to bring their work to be assessed and then giving them gallery space for a few weeks if they were suitable. The only stipulation being that they had to prove they were Welsh-born or lived in Wales. The stables were to be reconfigured to provide three large, and two small workshops, with space above for accommodation and or storage. Advertisements were placed in local newspapers and art magazines, for artists or craftspeople to apply to rent them.

Plans for the kitchen involved its extension and a large adjacent room, turned into a dining room, as Ari would like all the family, the staff, students and perhaps the odd visitor, if they had space, to have lunch together every day. Huw and his men worked like Trojans and as their ideas took shape, everyone was very certain they had made the right decision.

That Christmas Jon and Ari invited Julius and Poll. Sal and Fred were going to Maggie and George, who still lived in Tan Y Bryn. They hadn't been back for several years so were quite looking forward to seeing everyone in the street. Queenie and her family now lived next door in Sal and Olive's old house. Olive and Roger had been invited to his brother's to meet Toby and his third wife Sadie and were then going to their new home in Bath with a view to exploring all the city had to offer. And wonder of wonders, Shona and Taliesin were going away for Christmas, together! Ari had high hopes for that one. But before they went Ari and Jon talked to them about the third house. Jon had had an idea.

Poll and Julius drove up two days before Christmas, with a big bag of presents in the back of their car. Ari was taking everything slowly as she got quite tired, and her baby bump was growing. But everything was ready. Jon, Gwenny and the boys had gone to buy the tree and had decorated it. It stood now, touching the ceiling in the living room. Beneath it beautifully wrapped presents for everyone. Ari and Gwenny had made a large wreath for the kitchen door from the trees roundabout. They had even found some mistletoe on an old tree at Cae Coch. Ari laughing had given some to Shona. "You might need that," she said and Shona smiled and blushed.

Poll and Julius were very easy guests and Poll didn't need asking to do things. She had straight away put all their presents beneath the tree and then gone to make tea for them all.

Christmas Eve afternoon and Julius was dozing by the fire. Ari was sitting at the kitchen table with Gwenny and they were decorating the Christmas cake. Two small robins, Father Christmas, several small, stiff Christmas trees and a tube of silver dragées stood ready. Osian and Ifan were playing with bricks on the rug before the fire and Jon was tidying his studio. Poll who always had to be busy said, "Shall I go and help Jon? He won't mind, will he Ari?"

"No," she said. "Just call from the bottom of the stairs." So, Poll did and Jon was pleased to see her. The room smelt strongly of turps as Jon was cleaning his brushes. There would be no painting for the next few days.

It was lovely and warm in the studio and Poll sat down on the sofa by the big window. Jon had nearly finished all he wanted to do.

As usual Poll said, "How is Arianwen, then Jon?" He said he thought she was fine, a little tired perhaps but just as lovely as she had ever been. He said he was fascinated by her, the baby had just started to move and there seemed to be something he could not quite grasp in her demeanour. "She was the same when she was having the boys," he said.

"I think you will find that is contentment, Jon." Poll smiled.

Jon sat down beside her, "Poll," he said. "I am so, so lucky. I love her to distraction, and I think you are probably right about the contentment. She had Gwenny on her own and she told me there were often unkind comments from people, not that she cared, but it must have hurt even so. Some of the nurses in the hospital too. Sal wanted her to wear a wedding ring but she refused."

"She's a girl of principal, your Ari," laughed Poll. "She never would accept second best even as a young child. Look how long she waited for you. And she loves you, Jon. You can see it in everything she does. Including having your babies."

Jon smiled; the making of them had been pretty good too.

Then he asked Poll how Julius was as he was nearing retirement. "I'm a bit concerned about him," she said. "Whatever will he do when he retires? You know he just loves to be around people and he will miss the art school so much. I really don't want him to become like those old men who sit in the library every day and talk to you at length if you let them." Jon smiled to himself. His idea might work.

Christmas day was lovely. The boys got a bit over excited but an afternoon nap sorted that. Julius and Poll has bought Gwenny a Sasha doll. It had dark hair and blue eyes like her and was wearing dungarees, as Gwenny often did. Nan called them 'Sam Pigs' but Ari never knew why. Gwenny loved it immediately and took it everywhere with her. It even went to university with her years later. The boys were given Jukka wooden lorries which they played with all day, making the appropriate noises. What with their presents from F.C, as Jon called him, they did very well and went to bed happily. The grown-ups subsided onto the sofas. Ari as always enclosed by Jon's arm.

"How do you fancy a walk up the lane tomorrow," he asked Julius and Poll. "We could look at the house. I don't think you have ever been inside it have you?"

They both thought that would be an excellent idea.

"I'll come too," said Ari. "And the children. A bit of fresh air and a run round will do them good."

After a special breakfast the next morning, it was Boxing Day, after all, they set off. It was lovely out. Dry, sunny but cold. Ifan and Osian tried to climb the banks helped by Gwenny, or just ran ahead happy to be out and running about. They went in through the wicket in the big gates and saw all the yet uncompleted work on the stables. Jon explained what they hoped to do there. Then they went into the house and Poll and Julius were much impressed by David's gallery and the size and number of the rooms. They went out through the kitchen and walked up towards the three cottages across the wide lawns and empty flower beds. There were people in the last cottage having rented it for Christmas, and the windows glowed orange with Christmas tree lights. Ari pointed out where Shona lived and then the empty cottage.

"We are looking for people for this one," Jon said. "People that can help out, take a life drawing or painting class. Show people around the galleries and know what they are talking about, and generally be one of us." He stopped and looked enquiringly at Julius. "Know anyone who might fit the bill, you two?" he said. Poll got there first; her eyes filled with tears.

"Oh Julius," she said. "That would be just perfect for us. You always said you would like to move nearer Jon and Ari."

Julius when he realised what had been proposed just gave Jon a big hug. "Thanks, old son," he said. "We would like that enormously."

After Christmas things progressed with speed. The house was nearly finished and the stables had tenants, although they hadn't moved in yet. A weaver, a stone mason and a saddler, to begin with, and Grace was going to do some pottery courses from her place. Everyone was very encouraged by the way things were going. They planned to open that summer. It was 1971.

Ari finished her painting of Jon and the children, and Jon, his of the frozen trees and lake. They decided to submit them to the RA summer exhibition. When Shona heard, she wanted David's portrait of Ari included too, and because it was now Jon's he agreed. Tally was going to London, so he supervised the submissions for them. Amazingly all three were accepted, and one very bright spark noticed the family connection. The curator hung all three in a group, on the far wall in Gallery II. Jon's 'What shall I do about her?' Ari's 'All I ever wanted' and David's portrait of Arianwen. There was a lot of interest by the art community and the press in the family connection and in Jon's enigmatic title, but although pressed during many interviews throughout his life, he would not and never did explain.

Ari had had no problems with the pregnancy and now as May approached everything was made ready for the baby. She would have it at home again. Just after midnight on the 7th of May she went into labour. This time it seemed far more painful and was progressing quickly. Emma came and took control and things seemed fine. Just before four o'clock Ari, holding tightly to Jon's hand gave birth to a little girl.

Emma had delivered the placenta and had just finished washing the baby when Jon shot to his feet. "She's bleeding Emma," he called. Emma put the baby in the cot and came over. Ari was white and shivering and a large pool of blood on the bed was growing.

"Mr Curtis," Emma said. "Ring for an ambulance, then phone the doctor. I need someone else here. Tell them it is a post-partum haemorrhage." Jon went. Emma had been in this situation before, so she knew what to do. She began to massage the top of Ari's womb. The doctor came, his trousers over his pyjamas, and gave Ari an injection. He shooed Jon from the room. By the time the ambulance arrived the bleeding was just about under control, but Ari looked dreadful. They took her off to hospital and the baby too. Emma went in the ambulance with her.

"She will be fine now Mr Curtis," she said. "This is just a precaution. As soon as you have someone to see to the children follow us, as I'm sure Mrs Curtis will want you near." So even though it was very early Jon phoned Shona who came immediately and he took off for the hospital just as the sun was rising.

He drove like a madman up the valley and as he approached the main doors of the hospital, he met Emma coming out. She stopped and took him to a bench nearby. "She's much better now Mr Curtis," she said. "But they took her into surgery, in case there was a tear, but nothing needed doing." She stopped and looked at his worried face.

"The baby came a bit too quickly and her uterus did not contract very strongly. Hence the bleeding."

He looked wrecked she thought, poor man.

"Mrs Curtis will probably need a transfusion, as she has lost a lot of blood, but she's in maternity now so I'll take you up to see her." She smiled at Jon then turned back into the building and he followed. The hospital was just waking up and large breakfast trolleys were being pushed along the corridors. People were cleaning the floors and there was a gentle hum of conversation from the wards as they passed.

"It was a bit hairy at one point but these things happen and I promise you, your wife is fine now. Did you get a good look at your daughter?" Emma said. Jon said he had only seen that she had dark hair. Emma smiled, "Well you will be in for a treat then." They got to the ward and Emma showed him where Ari was, in a little room of her own. "I'll just tell Sister you are here then I will be off. My husband is outside and he will take me to pick up my car from your house. I'll go in and tell the children their mammy is fine. Will that be OK?" Jon said it would be perfect and thank you.

Ari was fast asleep and as pale as the sheets on the bed. At the bottom of which was a cot with his daughter, also asleep. He looked in and his heart turned over. She had his dark hair but she was a miniature Ari. The same oval face, straight eyebrows and Ari's beautiful mouth. He stood by her cot for some time just watching her. Ari stirred and opened her eyes. As soon as she saw Jon, she put her arms up for him and he went to her, holding her tight. "I'm so sorry Jon," she said. "I didn't do that very well, did I?"

"All sorted now darling girl," he said. "And you will be back home soon."

"I was frightened for a while," Ari admitted. Jon sat beside her and held her. He too had been frightened. He could not contemplate a world without Arianwen in it.

When he got home Carys was there with the boys and he told her what had happened. She said she had seen Miss Rhys Williams and the boys at the school, taking Gwenny in. Miss Rhys Williams had given her and the boys a lift back and had then gone on to the gallery. He went out into the yard to see Osian and Ifan who were digging with old spoons in the flower beds. They wanted to know when Mammy would be home but otherwise seemed quite happy. Their little world had not been much disrupted. Carys said that she would stay if he wanted to go to see Mrs Curtis in the evening. But Jon had already agreed with Ari that he would not come. They thought it best if he stayed with the children.

He went to their bedroom then and stripped the bed of the bloody sheets and wrapped all the bedding up to dispose of. Then he remade the bed ready for when Ari came home. He would sleep in the spare bed upstairs until she did.

That evening when he had bathed the boys and they were asleep and Gwenny was reading in bed, Jon sat outside on the bench by the kitchen door. He had said his thank you to the sky, that Ari would be well and now just sat quietly. It was lovely out and he could hear the ewes in the field beyond the garden calling their lambs. He remembered Ari telling him that just after she had had Gwenny, that field had been full of ewes and newborn lambs. Come the summer and the farmer had taken all the lambs away. There had been two days of distressed ewes calling for their lambs. Ari had never come across that before and she had found it very upsetting. That made him think again on just how much he missed her. He heard a sound and turned to find Gwenny coming out of the back door. She was in her pyjamas and carried her beloved doll. She climbed onto the bench beside him.

"Are you sad without Mammy, Daddy?" she said.

Jon said, "Just a bit sweetheart."

"Nurse Emma came," Gwenny continued. "And she said Mammy will be home soon and my baby sister. Don't worry, you will be able to love Mammy a lot again soon Daddy."

Jon gave her a hug and Gwenny snuggled against him.

"Shona made me French toast for breakfast," said Gwenny. "The boys were a bit naughty and said they didn't want eggy bread, it was 'yuk', so she told them it was what Zebedee had for breakfast and they ate it all. It was the same really and Shona winked at me. All the way to school the boys were going 'boing, boing'. It made us laugh." She put her arms around Jon's neck and gave him a kiss. "I love you Daddy," she said and Jon remembered that tiny little girl who had asked him if he was her daddy, just a few years ago.

The next day when he went to the hospital Ari was sitting up and looked much better. She had her arm strapped to a board and was having a transfusion. She was now a little pinker, and she was desperate she said for a kiss, so he had to give her a nice long one. Thank goodness she was in her own room he thought.

A nurse came in then and said the doctor would like a word with Mr Curtis. Jon was shown to the doctor's consulting rooms.

Mr Skinner stood up and shook Jon's hand. "I am really pleased to meet you, Mr Curtis," he smiled. "My wife and I are great fans, if that is the right word, of yours and your wife's work. My wife was really upset when we missed your last exhibition. Her friend bought Mrs Curtis' 'Abandoned' and my wife is so envious." He raised his eyebrows.

"Having met you both I can see it was anecdotal." Jon laughed.

"Now," continued Mr Skinner. "Your wife has been very lucky, Mr Curtis. These things are very frightening, and if that particular midwife hadn't been with you, there might have been a very different outcome. She had encountered it before and knew exactly what to do. But everything will be fine now, though your wife might take some time getting back to her old self."

He stopped and folded his fingers together.

"Your wife has had four babies in six years and could go on to have many more if you so wanted. She is still quite young." He stopped for a moment. "This is not really part of my work or my business, but I would say to you, and if she were my wife, no more now, if you want to keep her well." He stopped and looked sympathetically at Jon. The image of 'Abandoned' was before his eyes. "If you want to come to see me, I can point you in the right direction for help with that, but it is your decision." Jon said he would speak to Ari and a few weeks later, when Ari was home and well, he did. There would be no more babies, and Ari's eyes welled up with tears when he told her what they must do.

Ari was home five days later, still a little pale and quiet but so happy to be there. She called Carys in to see the baby.

"We are going to call her Seren," she said.

"She's a beauty," Carys smiled. "Looks like you, Ari."

Ari laughed, "That makes a change then. I was beginning to feel like a little factory turning out clones of Jon. Not that I minded that one bit."

Olive came up to give a hand, and Ari really appreciated the time she had with her Nan, who was gentle and much more even-tempered than Mam.

One warm evening when the children were asleep and Ari had gone to bed early, Olive sat with Jon in the living room. He had just fed Seren and had her over his shoulder gently rubbing her back. She gave a great milky burp and Jon laughed. He cradled her in the crook of his arm. In a while he would take her and settle her in her cot and then get into bed himself beside Ari. Olive said, "I wonder what colour her eyes will be Jon?"

Jon smiled. "What were Ari's like at this age?" he asked.

"Sal didn't look after her until she was seven months, and she came to live with us when she was about ten months old. A nurse had looked after her before that, but when she came to us, she already had her beautiful eyes." She paused a while thinking. "She was a lovely child and very easy to look after, except for the coal shed." She laughed.

"Go on," said Jon, he loved Olive's tales of Ari's childhood.

"Well, you know what Ari is like about smell, texture and things, she is quite sensual isn't she and she was like that even as a young child? She just loved the smell of the coal house. One day we were in the back yard, I think Ari was near two, and I was talking to Maggie over the fence, for quite some time I should add. Somehow Ari got into the coal house and came out with a lump of coal. George had not long whitewashed the yard walls for us. She drew all over the walls and was utterly filthy but very happy. I got a terrible row from Sal when she came home. She was always much stricter with Ari than I was." Jon laughed. Olive was indeed much easier to get on with than Sal. When Sal had come up after the twins were born, she had treated them like two little parcels, but she had them in a good routine pretty quick.

"They daren't do otherwise," Ari had said.

Olive yawned. "Bed for me Jon. Roger will be here tomorrow to take me home." Jon stood up and wrapped the now sleeping Seren in her shawl and came across to give Olive a hug.

"Thank you," he said. "We shall miss you." He had come to love this lady. He could see who had taught Ari to be so generous and forgiving and she had been very trusting and helpful to him. The next day Olive went home, back to Bath as she and Roger had decided to live there.

When the baby was six weeks old Ari had her check-up. Everything was fine. That evening, after the children were in bed and baby Seren had been fed she whispered in Jon's ear. "Coming to bed early tonight Mr Curtis?" And he looked into her smiling eyes. "Yes, my darling girl," he said. "I can't wait."

They opened at Cae Coch at the end of July as planned, although Ari hadn't been able to help with the preparation very much. The long-awaited exhibition of Lem's and Richard's work was set up in their largest gallery, even though Richard wasn't strictly born in Wales. Just over the border in Herefordshire. It was extremely well attended. Richard visited often and one day Jon asked him about Janet. Richard laughed. "She moved on a few months ago," he said. "Inherited a house somewhere, in Wales, I think. She was such a difficult person; there was a great sigh of relief from staff and students when she went." Well Jon could understand that.

The Saturday club took a while to get going as it was the school holidays, but life drawing was oversubscribed. Julius and Poll were now at Cae Coch and Julius took two daytime classes, which were very popular with older ladies and those just retired. Jon was asked by a local art teacher if there could be a life class on a Saturday as he and another art teacher would like to try it again as they had not had much opportunity since leaving art school. This Jon did and he took the class himself, which was boosted by others who worked during the week. One of the art teachers suggested a class just for sixth formers; especially those doing 'A' level art and Jon did that also after school on a Wednesday. The pupils thought he was 'cool' and several girls had a crush on him. Until of course Mrs Curtis dropped in one day at the end of class, accompanied by four children, one a baby.

Ari was well now, but often got tired, so Jon didn't want her doing too much yet. Carys was a great help with all four children and by the end of the year Ari was back to her old self and painting every day. Apart from his teaching Jon was also painting and both Ari and Jon were making quite a name for themselves. They had a joint exhibition to prepare for in the coming year at a large gallery in Cardiff. Things were looking good.

Chapter 6
You to Me are Everything
The Real Thing

1976

The summer of '76 was long and hot. Even in Wales, which usually got the rain first, there had been weeks and weeks of endless sunshine. The town was buzzing with tourists; the car parks full, the quay awash with people strolling around, eating ice creams and watching the boats. A man and a woman plodded slowly up the cobbled street to the gallery. He wore a cowboy hat, jeans and a vest. She had dyed blonde hair with a wide dark parting and wore a long yellow cotton sundress. She carried five or six canvases tied with string, and looked tired, hot and sweaty. They came to the gallery and went in. It was lovely and cool inside and the woman subsided onto a pew near reception. Shona came out from the back office, and the woman struggled to her feet.

"I believe someone will have a look at my paintings with a view to placing some in your gallery?"

Shona felt sorry for her. She looked a little beaten. The man had gone back outside.

"I'm really sorry," Shona said. "But this is the wrong gallery. This is the Rhys Williams Gallery, you want Cae Coch, which is down the valley some way." She stopped. "Would you like a glass of water?"

"No," the woman said abruptly. "Where's this other place then?"

Shona gave her directions to Cae Coch and said there was sure to be someone there to look at her work. The woman left and Shona heard raised voices outside.

The heat hung heavy over Cae Coch. There were several people inside walking around the galleries and in the stable yard there were tapping and chipping noises from the stone mason who had four students just about to finish their week's course. There were other students too. Three, learning spinning with the weaver, and four had driven up for lunch from Grace's pottery on the other side of the village. Five children lay on the bleached grass of the bank below the terrace. They were watching an aeroplane making contrails in the clear blue sky.

There was eleven-year-old Gwenny, barefoot and wearing shorts and a cotton shirt. Her long dark hair in a ponytail on top of her head. Next to her, and never far away, seven-year-old Ifan and Osian, again in shorts and shirts, their dark hair near shoulder length and usually untidy. Then came five-year-old Seren, named for the stars under which she had been conceived, in a wildflower garden in France and with the dark hair of her father and the beautiful grey eyes of her mother. And next to her Michael, just a little younger and with a pale gold skin, crinkly black hair and big brown eyes. Seren's best friend and Christina and Evan's son. They were waiting for lunch.

A battered Dormobile pulled into the car park and a man and the woman who had spoken to Shona got out and went into the house.

The woman was rather surprised to be met by a tall black woman at reception.

"How may I help?" asked Christina.

"I believe I can just bring some of my work and someone here will evaluate it for putting in your gallery for a while?"

"Yes, that's right," smiled Christina. "As long as you can prove you have a Welsh connection."

The woman showed her, her birth certificate. Born in Abergavenny.

"But it is lunchtime now," Christina said. "And we always stop as we have students and guests to feed. You could come back in an hour or stay for lunch yourselves. I believe we have a few spare places, and a pound or so should cover it."

"Will I get a beer?" the man said lighting a cigarette.

"I'm sorry, sir," Christina said. "But no smoking in the house, the paintings you know, and we don't have any alcohol at lunchtime as some of our students use machinery and sharp tools."

Christina looked at the woman. "Would you like lunch?"

"Oh, go on then," she said.

Christina went to the door and called across to the children.

"Gwenny, could you tell the kitchen two more for lunch, sweetheart?"

Gwenny, tiptoed across the hot flags of the terrace and disappeared around the end of the house. "Right ho," she called.

Christina took the paintings and put them behind the reception desk, then showed the man and woman out into the garden where lunch was served. Jon came down from upstairs where he had been supervising the setting up of an eagerly awaited exhibition of the work of a young Welsh painter, which would open at the end of the week.

Christina told him about the woman bringing the paintings. "She is happy to wait until after lunch," she said. "And they are staying for it. I've just taken them outside."

Jon looked out of the back door and was startled and then angry when he saw who was there. He went to look for Ari.

Ari was in David's old rooms, talking to some visitors about his work. When she saw Jon and the expression on his face, she excused herself.

"Jon, whatever is it?" she said.

"Ari, Janet is out there, going to have lunch with us. She's brought some paintings for us to see. Would you like me to ask her to leave?"

For a moment Ari just looked at him, her eyes growing stormy.

"Janet," she said. "What THE Janet?" Jon nodded.

Ari looked at him and smiled. "Oh, no," she said. "This is our place and our people and I'll not run away from her again. I am not going to be afraid of her." They walked down the corridor to the back door. Everyone was beginning to sit down at the tables.

"I'm going to sit next to her," Ari said. "Just give me a minute. I don't want her to see you first and bolt." She kissed him and then went quietly across the grass and slipped into the seat next to Janet.

In the garden there were two long trestle tables set end to end beneath the trees and two young girls, from the village, were placing plates and cutlery on them. Already seated were two elderly ladies who stayed for lunch every Friday after their life drawing class, with 'Dear Mr Winter'. Janet sat down next to them whilst the man wandered off smoking another cigarette. He seemed entirely uninterested in anything. The ladies were soon regaled with tales of life drawing classes at 'proper' art school, and the models they had had like Quentin Crisp. The television programme about him had been on the previous December, so Janet always mentioned her connection, however slim. She then went on to her years as a pottery teacher, not true, and her reasons for changing to painting. The life drawing ladies couldn't get a word in edgeways. Meanwhile the students, the staff, and the family had taken their places. The food was on the table, cheeses, three large salads, two enormous quiches, two very large cold chicken and ham pies, and a big bowl of baked potatoes. Janet felt someone sit beside her but didn't recognise that gentle subtle smell of spice and peaches and carried on talking. She noticed one of the life drawing ladies smile and nod at that person.

A young girl was walking around the table with a large basket of fresh rolls. She stopped by Ari.

"*Heffech chi ychydig o fara,*" she said.

"Diolch Annie," Ari smiled and took a roll.

Janet heard the soft voice and sort of remembered it. Out of the corner of her eye, she saw a slim brown arm reach for a roll. It bore a silver bracelet she had seen many times.

She turned and looked straight into the stormy-grey eyes of Arianwen.

"Hello Janet," said Ari, without a hint of a smile. "This is a very strange and uncalled for meeting."

Janet stood up quickly, her chair falling back.

"Shit!" she said. "Arianwen fucking Morgan, what the hell are you doing here? On a course or something?"

The two ladies tut-tutted their disapproval at the language.

Ari kept eye contact. "Sit down Janet," she said. Janet did.

"No, I'm not on a course," she continued. "What are you doing here?"

"I've brought some paintings that they are going to put in their gallery."

"And have they been looked at yet?"

"No," said Janet. "But I know they will take them if I say I have been to art school." Janet stopped and looked at Ari. "Still got that long hair then," she sneered. "Anyway, what are you here for? Do you work here then?"

Arianwen smiled, "Well I do sort of work here, as it's mine," she said.

"What do you mean 'It's mine'?" Janet mimicked.

Ari made a sweeping gesture with her hand.

"All this, Cae Coch," she said. "My father left it to me and to my aunt. She and her husband run the gallery in town. We do this one."

Gwenny came round the table and stood waiting for her mother to finish speaking. Ari turned to her.

"Charlie has just come Mammy. Can he have some lunch with us?"

"Yes sweetheart, of course," Ari said. "Squeeze him in somewhere." Gwenny skipped off to tell her best friend Charlie, he could stay.

Janet looked sideways at Ari, "That's Mr Curtis' child, isn't it... Looks like him?"

"Yes, she is. She is eleven now. I was pregnant with her when you assaulted me?"

Janet winced slightly at that but carried on. She wasn't going to let Arianwen get the better of her.

"Has it been hard bringing up a child on your own?" she smirked.

Ari smiled and let a few moments go past before she replied.

"Who said I've been on my own Janet? I have three more children. They are sitting at the other end of the table with their father. Just look." And Ari pointed down at the table.

Janet looked and her face blanched. Jon Curtis was sitting at the other end of the table. A little girl who looked like Arianwen on his knee. Beside him twin boys, the image of him, and then the girl who had spoken to Ari, who was helping her friend to some salad. That fucking Arianwen Morgan had got what she wanted anyway. And four children by him.

Janet felt sick with jealousy. She had hated Arianwen Morgan at art school, had forgotten about her for years, and now here she was again with everything she had said, long ago, that she wanted. Janet was speechless.

Ari got up. "Right, I'll just go and tell Julius that you are here and that he is needed to look at your stuff with Jon. Don't worry they will be very fair. Enjoy your lunch."

Janet felt like Daniel in the lions' den. *Was that right?* she wondered. *Should she go or not? Mr Curtis and now Mr Winter.* "Bloody Hell." Janet felt a great surge of regret, mixed with jealousy. She didn't really know how she felt. Her companion, Claude would not be at all interested. But she would stay; they had come all this way. If they took her paintings and they sold that would be good. She needed the money.

Ari walked across to Jon. He looked at her questioningly. "All fine," she said and she bent and kissed him. "Bite your ear later." And Jon watched her as she ran laughing across the lawn to the house where Julius and Poll were just leaving to come for lunch.

Julius now did two life drawing classes in the week and Poll ran the children's Saturday club, a weekly watercolour class and helped out in reception. They absolutely loved their house, the area and most of all being near Jon and Ari. Julius, ever watchful, noticed that the very loving and physical relationship between them was still very evident and he rejoiced in that for Jon, the son he had never had. He also always helped Jon with evaluating any proffered artwork. Like Jon, he knew what he was talking about.

Ari explained to Julius about Janet as they walked back to the house together.

After lunch, Jon and Julius looked at Janet's work then they went to find her. She was still sitting at the table, her companion nowhere to be seen, although a pile of cigarette ends discarded in the grass showed where he had been. Janet reddened when she saw Jon. Their last meeting had been fraught, but Julius spoke to her. "We will take the three landscapes," he said., "But the portraits of the children with tearful eyes do not fit our ethos. We will say no to them.

If you go to reception now, they will tell you what happens next. Leave your address and phone number. We will contact you in six weeks," he added. Jon couldn't bring himself to speak to her, or even acknowledge her. So, Janet left. Her friend was asleep in the Dormobile. The paintings did get sold and they sent her a cheque and an offer of showing more. But they never heard from her again.

Jon and Ari watched the Dormobile lurch down the drive.

Jon turned to go in. "Thank goodness that's over," he said.

"I felt quite sorry for her," Ari said. "She looked forlorn really and her friend didn't seem very interested. They never spoke."

She looked up at her beloved Jon. He had a few grey hairs now above his ears and his reading glasses were perched on his head. She loved him just as much as ever.

"Just think," she mused. "If she hadn't done what she did we wouldn't be here now and have all this. Awful though it was at the time, for both of us, we came out of it still together. I don't think Janet has much hope of love or really knows what it is. That's what is sad. I think life has not turned out for her as she had hoped or expected."

"My darling girl," Jon said as he put his arms around her. "You are always so forgiving."

It was very quiet. The air was hot and still. The children had gone home to Ty Griafolen with Carys and Christina had taken Michael home as he was hot and fractious. Some of the students from the stonemason's course and those finishing the weaving course were leaving and stopped to say goodbye and thank you. Poll was in reception and Julius was somewhere around. They could take an hour for themselves.

Jon turned to Ari. "What about that promise you made?" he smiled raising his eyebrows.

"Come on then," she said and they walked off arms around each other, up to the woods. They passed the grave for the dogs with a bunch of wilted roses beneath the headstone, and a little grave beside it for the cats. Then several wigwams the children had made out of fallen branches. At the top of the woods, they went through a gap in the hedge to the little field beyond. An ancient field that was usually covered in red clover and which, Shona said gave the house its name. There they lay down side by side on the pale dry grass. "Now my darling girl," Jon said, and Ari smiled into his eyes.

The End? Well not really. There is much more to come.